Also by
Davis MacDonald

-The Hill
-The Island
-Newport Bay (due out in the Fall of 2016)

- Recipes and Wisdom - Notes from the
Southern California Wine & Food Society Dinners

Silicon Beach

A Novel

By

Davis MacDonald

"Every day is a journey,…

and the journey itself is home."

— Matsuo Bashō

CHAPTER 1
8:00 PM, Thursday

The Judge walked north along the tideline toward the Santa Monica Pier. The orange ball of flame had just plummeted into the Blue Pacific. A deep blue this evening. The sky behind him was darkening. Out to sea the just disappeared sun faintly reflected on the underbelly of fat floating clouds. Soft pastel pink, lavender, rose and orange.

The beach was quiet. Peaceful. Everyone had left. A hammerhead shark had been spotted off the end of the pier earlier in the day. Eighteen feet. All teeth and violence, the result of warming waters drawing them further north along the California coast. The beach had been closed one and a half miles to either side of the pier for most of the day.

The sand was soft under his shoes, pressing up with moisture as he walked. There was a faint smell of salt and dry seaweed, not unpleasant. A breeze blew in from seaward and whipped froth at the top of the larger rollers gently gliding toward shore.

The wet sand was broken ahead by the gaudy reflection of lights from the circulating Ferris wheel on the Santa Monica Pier a mile up the beach. Bright purples, greens, reds and yellows. Here and there a blue.

The colors spun a reflective pattern, slicing tide in sync with the mighty wheel.

A little like his life mused the Judge. Clipped to the outside of a wheel. Tumbling around and around in a kaleidoscope of flash and color. All noise and risk and derring-do as you strove for the top. Surprise, fear, even panic as you suddenly tumbled over. Crashing down the back side. Your plans set into disarray by events you didn't anticipate and couldn't control.

Picking yourself up at the bottom. Pulling yourself together for another ascent. Perhaps reaching the missed goals you thought you wanted. Only to find their attainment empty. Plunging down again. This time in greater despair.

But always in circles. Pinned at the center to some destiny you couldn't escape. Around and around. All flash and struggle. Ascension and letdown. Yet going nowhere. The young boy, that college kid, the young lawyer, that middle-aged Judge, now the senior attorney. Half a century of flying around in circles. Never straying from your fixed core. He supposed the melancholy of his Welsh roots was showing. He smiled.

Yet in some undefined way a change was brewing. Like the weather. You could sometimes sense a change. You couldn't quite know what. Or why. Just a change.

The beach stretched south to the Palos Verdes Peninsula and north to Malibu. Here it framed the western boundary of Santa Monica, one of several smaller communities adjacent to Los Angeles that spread out across the Southern California plain like rolls of flesh released from a girdle.

Along the beach were strung multi-million dollar homes, high rise condominiums, and lavish apartments, gazing out on the Pacific. People were up there now, sipping their martinis, holding dinner parties, planning their next vacation, untouched by the Great Recession that had swept the country. And discretely ignoring a scattering of poor and homeless down along the beach and on bluffs and streets. Broken people for one reason or another. They flooded in from around the country for the weather, dragging their shopping bags or pushing their purloined shopping carts, receptacles holding their life's possessions. Looking disoriented and beaten.

He thought of the five dollars he'd put in the Styrofoam cup of a young man in disreputable khaki pants and dirty hoody, unshaven and unwashed, sprawled against the low sea wall as he'd walked onto the sand. He wondered about the man's story. Lost his job? Distressed Vet? Emotionally disturbed? Addict? Perhaps just lazy?

The homeless ran the gamut: high living blue collars who'd lost their jobs, homes and everything in the Great Recession; intellectually challenged adults; druggies sliding down the addiction of their choice; ex-cons who couldn't get work; mentally disturbed Vets broken from service in the legions of war. They co-existed in the California sun with worker ants who toiled to create fortunes for someone, building high tech products, services and dreams in the area now called "Silicon Beach".

Silicon Beach spread from its epicenter in Santa Monica and Venice, south through the neighboring beach towns of Marina Del Rey, Playa Vista, El Segundo and Manhattan Beach. It fingered north into Culver City, downtown, and other parts of L.A. Westward it reached into Malibu and over the hill into parts of the Valley.

There was no official boundary for Silicon Beach. It spread and leap-frogged across L.A., propelled by new startups often founded by people barely old enough to shave. A big brawling collection of new ideas, new products, new methods. Competing for space, capital and attention to become the next Apple, Microsoft, Facebook or Tesla. Fortunes were made and lost here as new technology sprouted. Often disruptive to long established industries across the country and even the world.

Silicon Beach boasted a collection of offices, laboratories, plants and warehouses, filled with scientists, social engineers, film companies, entrepreneurs, and venture capitalists. And garages and incubator spaces hidden here and there where the next billion-dollar technology might spawn.

And there were the lawyers, accountants, insurance agents, brokers and staffing people who serviced the companies and their employees. Too many lawyers in the Judge's view. Buzzing like bees among the fresh pots of money pouring in from around the country.

It also had the hangers-on, the charlatans, the want-to-be's and the crooks. This was 21st Century America. All enterprise was encouraged, even implicitly the unethical, the fraudulent and the corrupt. It was a microscopic slice of Coastal America in the early years of this new century.

He'd watched for the green flash as the sun disappeared below the blue horizon, but there'd been none. Or if there had, he'd missed it. Perhaps it was just an urban legend. Still, he thought he'd seen it once when he was younger. When his eyes were strong. He wasn't sure he believed in the green flash anymore. Maybe you had to be young to believe.

The Judge had spent the day in arbitration on a patent case. He was the arbitrator, not a lawyer representing a litigant. It was a good gig, two thousand a day. A former Judge, the work fit nicely with his disposition and temperament. It was easier to judge issues presented by competing parties and their counsel than to sweat it out as a litigator representing one side. But one still got tired. They had been going all week. The Judge was exhausted. And it was only Thursday. One more day and then a well-earned weekend off.

Of course there was no such thing for the Judge. He worked all the time. But he could work from home. It was a more contemplative environment and he wouldn't have to see anyone. Except his new wife and the rascally golden retriever. The two pets for which he was responsible.

The 405 would be a snarl back to Palos Verdes at this hour. As he had been doing each day, the Judge chose instead to wait the traffic out and take a long walk along the beach. Stretching his legs. Enjoying the sunset. Clearing the cobwebs from his mind. Breathing in the fresh air and the salt and spray from the waves tumbling up on to the Santa Monica sand was like a tonic. Refreshing after a long day's slog.

The Judge was a tall man. Broad shouldered and big boned. With a bit of a paunch around the middle, hinting at an appetite for fine wines and good food. He cut an imposing figure in his dark blue Blass jacket, tan slacks, and soft blue shirt open at the collar. He had the ruddy chiseled features of Welsh ancestors, a rather too big nose, large ears, and bushy eyebrows on the way to premature grey.

He had a given name of course, but after he ascended to the Bench some years before people began calling him just "Judge". Even old friends he'd known for years adopted the nickname. He'd been dumped off the bench for almost a year now, replaced in an election by a younger candidate with a large war chest and dubious credentials. But his nickname still stuck.

He smiled. So much better to be out in the real world practicing law. No longer a sitting judge, cooped up in a windowless, breezeless chamber where people bowed and scraped at your pedestal all day.

He sensed movement behind him. A disturbance in the ether more felt than seen. A throwback warning hardwired a million years ago into the human race as it emerged on two feet and hunted the predators that hunted it.

He turned quickly to look back, his eyes ranging down the darkening beach where the soft colors were all but gone. Twenty yards away a young man was coming up the beach. It was the homeless guy he'd contributed a bill to ten minutes before. He was jogging. The Judge had never seen a homeless man jog.

The young man's gait changed now he'd been spotted. He charged toward the Judge at a dead run. The man's unshaven face contorted in a snarl and his blue eyes were wild. A long switchblade appeared in his right hand, fully extended. Held as though he knew how to use it.

The Judge reacted instinctively, whipping off his sport coat and barely wrapping it around his left arm before his assailant was upon him.

As the man attacked, thrusting the knife forward toward the Judge's middle, the Judge turned sideways, thrusting his coat-covered arm up to block the knife. The Judge felt the knife cut through his jacket, sliding into flesh, searing tendons with sickening precision, sending fire up his arm and turning his universe momentarily cloudy.

The Judge pivoted to his left with the thrust of the knife and slammed his right fist into the young man's face, carrying his body through the swing, giving full weight to the punch. The Judge's hand felt like it had smashed into a brick wall, his knuckles collapsing into raw pain which hinted one or more might be broken.

But his blow landed squarely on the side of his assailant's nose, producing a satisfying crunch of cartilage and bone. The young man went down. He twisted around on the wet sand at the Judge's feet, trying to staunch the flow of blood.

The Judge stepped away from him, moving quickly up the beach toward the pier. But his path was blocked. Another young man stood ahead of him, black, also dressed like the homeless. He also held a knife. He was moving forward on the Judge, cautious but determined.

The Judge caught movement on his right, up the slight dunes leading to the bike path and the street. Another young man. Asian. Dressed and armed similarly. He was also moving down on the Judge, carefully, purposefully, a smirk on his face.

The Judge looked behind him again. The man he'd hit was still down. But there was nowhere to retreat. Another young man was moving up the beach on him from behind, stepping around his fallen companion as though he were a pile of seaweed.

The Judge faced the closest man approaching from the front, slowly backing toward the water. Vaguely feeling the cold tide sluice around his feet and into his shoes. Considering his options.

Then he turned and made a quarterback's dash into the surf.

His assailants hesitated for precious seconds, surprised. Then they charged in a rush from three directions to meet at the water's edge.

But the Judge was out sixty feet now, diving under the breakers and swimming straight out from the shore in measured strokes. He jettisoned his shoes.

8

Then kicked off his soggy pants. He made his body relax, falling into the rhythm of the sea with his strokes.

He'd been a swimmer in his youth. He still did the occasional ocean swim between the Manhattan and the Hermosa Piers with a local club. He could do this. He just had to keep his head. He cast an eye back toward the shore. None of his assailants had followed him into the water.

He was out perhaps 200 yards now. He made a slow turn to the right, paralleling the shore. Up ahead, towering now and then above the waves, was the Ferris wheel, its multi-colors sparking the horizon. He aimed for there. For the Santa Monica Pier. For all of its people, and lights and carnival trappings. And particularly for the security guard that would be there. He hoped his assailants wouldn't follow.

He looked back again. They were having an animated discussion on the beach. Likely arguing over who was to blame for his escape and what they should do next. One put his back to the wind and raised his cellphone to his ear.

The Judge had another problem. The knife wound was worse than he'd supposed. It felt like the wound went clear to the bone. He was losing blood in significant quantities, leaving a scent in the water.

He thought about the hammerhead shark loitering off the pier earlier in the day. He didn't want to be dinner. But the immediate problem was blood loss. He was growing weaker. He suspected he was in shock. The cold water wasn't helping. He was turning numb and finding it difficult to think.

9

Nor were the waves friendly. Large swells were alternately lifting him up and casting him down, making it difficult to make headway toward the pier. He was running out of steam. But there was no one to help. He was on his own. Like on the Ferris wheel, sliding off over the top and crashing for the bottom, trying to hang on.

CHAPTER 2
8:45 PM Thursday

He saw the shore only intermittently now. He was too far out. It had gotten very dark. The swells loomed high, periodically lifting him up. Mostly sinking him down, or so it seemed. He used to joke about walking to school as a boy, uphill in the snow in both directions. He smiled at that. Trying to maintain some sense of humor. He maintained focus on the only marker he could see on the crests.

The swirling circle of the Santa Monica Ferris Wheel, each brightly lit spoke revolving in the dark sky, reflecting its ambiance on the tops of the swells. Promising warmth and safety. The seats on its circumference filled with people tearing around in circles. And beneath, and to its sides, the shops and the roller-coaster, spawning gold and yellow light across the water.

He swam mechanically, concentrating only on his strokes. Suddenly the pier loomed up out of the water at him. The current now doing its best to take him cascading into the thicket of supporting beams that held the pier anchored above the tide. With his last ounce of reserve he pivoted toward the shore and with a desperate flurry of strokes catapulted himself back into the curl of a breaking wave, forcing his shoulders and head down as he caught the wave, body surfing the

11

last 50 yards. It took him all the way until his belly slid along the sand.

He lay there a few seconds as the tide receded. Exhausted. Flat on his stomach, sand-caked hair across his face, shoeless, soaked shirt, no pants, scotch plaid polo boxers, and an ugly gash oozing blood down one arm.

He heard a sharp squeal, part surprise, part fear. He moved his head up to see a young couple sitting on the sand twenty feet above the tide line. A blanket spread under them. Wine glasses held suspended as they stared down, distressed now. The young man rising. Preparing to defend. The young lady, blond in a skimpy swimsuit partially hidden by gauzy cover up, clutched at his arm.

"Help me!" croaked the Judge, surprised at his faint voice. "Help me!"

The young man unlatched his companion's death grip. Stood up. Cautiously advanced down the beach.

"I've been attacked," rasped the Judge, doing a bit better with his voice. "Call the police."

"You're bleeding," said the young man.

"Yes."

"An ambulance too then," betraying a slight English accent.

"I guess."

"Hang on old chap, I'm Tony. That's Claire. We'll get help."

"'Kay," said the Judge, rising on to his knees now with considerable effort. Looking back down the beach for his assailants. There was no one visible.

The young man strode purposefully back to his blanket, grabbed the girl's hand, helping her up, and started off, heading for the entrance to the pier. "No cell phone," he called back. "Just tourists. We'll find someone to make the call."

The Judge watched their backs get smaller. He managed to half-stand half-stumble up the beach toward their blanket. Slumping down beside it. Watched them as specks, reaching the edge of the raised parking deck, turning the corner, disappearing. He reached over and poured himself a glass from the bottle of chardonnay. A 2012 Aubert Chardonnay from the Eastside Vineyard. Gulped it down, feeling the liquid bring heat to his throat and then his belly. It was good.

Five minutes later the young couple came around the deck parking structure, stepping onto the sand, followed by an elderly security guard, fitted out plump in a starched grey and blue uniform and a utility belt with everything on it except a gun. The guard walked like his feet hurt.

The Judge was suddenly washed in the stark glare of a light atop an open jeep, flying across the sand hell bent for leather. Its young driver looking like he'd just woken up. The Judge had a sudden vision of tire treads across his back. He hobbled to his feet, picking up and waving the wine bottle in self-defense. It was the beach patrol.

To add to the commotion, a Los Angeles Sheriff's police cruiser sped to a stop at the curb at the sand's edge, red lights flashing but no siren. *It must be a slow night,* thought the Judge. He could feel the adrenaline dissipating now help was close, replaced by a shakiness he couldn't quite control. His arm was pounding.

Blood continued to ooze out and splatter, leaving an encrusted circle of dark brown sand around him.

They reached him about the same time, the young couple standing back, the others huddling close as he slumped back to the sand.

The L.A. Sheriff immediately proclaimed himself in charge, shining his light in the Judge's face and then across his bleeding arm, scrawny white legs, polo shorts, and wet dress shirt covering his protruding tummy.

The sheriff hunched down on the sand closer to the Judge to talk. He was a veteran, early sixties, square jaw, crinkly eyes that had seen it all. He had a large paunch, but looked still able to run the police academy drills with a minimum of fuss. His badge said: Officer Saunders, Los Angeles Sheriff's Department.

"What's your name?"

The Judge offered his given name, adding that mostly he was called the Judge.

Officer Saunders leaned closer, as if to hear better the Judge's words, not so subtly sniffing the Judge's breath.

"Been drinking?"

The Judge now regretted the Chardonnay. But damn it'd been good.

"No… I mean yes… just now. I borrowed a gulp of their wine. But not before."

"Uh huh," said Saunders. "Where's your pants?"

"I took them off in the surf when I got away."

"Uh huh," said Saunders again.

The Judge didn't like his tone.

"See you're bleeding," said Saunders. "Hit the pier in our little swim, did we?"

"I was attacked with a knife."

"Oh… Uh huh. You often swim in your underwear?" asked Saunders. Face blank now, watching. Each pass of his flashlight across the Judge's face was more disorienting.

"Look, Officer Saunders, I was surrounded by a gang. They meant to kill me. One of them attacked me with a knife. There were four of them. Coming at me from three sides. So I dived in the water and swam for it."

"Uh huh."

"And I couldn't swim very well in my shoes and pants, so I shook them off as I headed to deeper water."

"Uh huh. What kind of gang was it?"

"What do you mean?"

"Well, was it a black gang? A Latino gang? Perhaps an Asian gang?"

"The guy I hit was white. There was at least one black. And there was an Asian. And a Latino I think."

"Uh huh…. So you're saying this gang was sort of 'mixed'?"

"I guess."

"Gangs don't come mixed, sir. They're sort of homogenous." Patronizing now.

"And you say you hit somebody?"

"I fended off a knife thrust and hit him in the face."

"Uh huh. That how you got those scrapes on your knuckles?"

15

The Judge looked down at his right hand. Saw for the first time the red patches of serrated skin across three knuckles. Nodded.

"Can I see your ID?"

"It was in my wallet, which is in my pants, which is somewhere out there in the surf." The Judge waved his hand toward the beach.

"Uh huh. You have any arrest record? Maybe for indecent exposure or something?" The cop was using a soothing voice now. Had leaned back a little. Creating distance.

The Judge got mad. He could feel the adrenaline racing. Could feel his face getting red.

"Look officer, I'm bleeding to death here on the sand. You think you can get me some medical attention? We can chat about this later."

Officer Saunders sat back on his heels. The Judge could see he wasn't expecting the tone, or the attitude or the... the... arrogance. Fuck him. The Judge needed medical help. Now.

Wheels were turning behind the officer's eyes. The Judge could see emotions playing out across Saunders' face. He wouldn't be any good at poker. Reassessing everything. Officer Saunders was in over his head.

"Let's get you into my cruiser and we'll run you over to the ER at St John's," Saunders said, gently taking the Judge's good arm now to help him stand. "We don't want you to bleed to death."

But now there were more flashing lights, and a siren, as an ambulance rolled up to the edge of the beach, casting the sand in an second alternating glow of red as its beacon swept.

"You don't look like you need an ambulance," said Officer Saunders. "Come on, I'm glad to give you a ride."

Taking a firmer grip on the Judge's arm. Apparently thinking the Judge might try to escape. Trying to maintain control.

The Judge shook his arm away.

"My arm's throbbing. I've lost a lot of blood. I'm cold. I'm wet. And I'm probably in shock. I'll take the ambulance. Besides, I like sirens."

"Look buddy, you're running around the beach with practically no clothes on. You've got alcohol on your breath. You've got no identification. I'm taking you in." Standing up over the Judge now. Asserting his dominance.

A Santa Monica police cruiser pulled into the parking lot across the sand, lights flashing. Backup.

Officer Saunders looked like he was wanted to grab the Judge by the collar and drag him up and across the sand. He looked at the couple and the lifeguard watching intently, at the paramedics loping across the sand with their equipment boxes, at the backup police arrival. He apparently thought better of it.

The Judge could almost read Saunders' mind by the emotions playing across his face. The Judge had used a certain tone that connoted intelligence and power. Best let someone else play cops and robbers. The Judge might be somebody important. The cop wasn't going to screw up his retirement now he was so close.

"As you wish, sir." he said, rising and putting his light away. "I'll follow behind in case you need any additional help." He handed the Judge his card and stepped back as the two paramedics pounced on the Judge and checked vital signs.

Three minutes later the Judge was prone on a stretcher inside the ambulance. Screeching his way through the Santa Monica traffic for Saint John's Hospital and its emergency room.

The paramedics were trying to staunch the flow of blood out of the Judge's arm, intermittently chatting with the ER over a dedicated frequency, forwarding the Judge's numbers. No one seemed too concerned. The Judge wasn't wearing oxygen. He decided he wasn't going die. Although hospital care being what it was with all the cost cutting and bickering over billing codes, you couldn't be sure. The Judge would just enjoy being in the ambulance and at the center of attention. Life was often unexplainable. Sometimes you had to lay back go with the flow.

If he'd known then where this ride was taking him, he'd have been less sanguine.

CHAPTER 3
9:20 Thursday

The ambulance skidded to a halt at the entrance to Saint John's emergency room and the Judge was trundled out to be assessed.

But "assessed" was a two-step process. First he had to be assessed to see if he could afford to pay the bills he might run up. A pinch-faced nurse demanded an insurance card, a credit card, or cash. He had lost his wallet with his pants. He had neither cash nor a credit card nor an insurance card. The nurse gave him a sour look and seemed disinclined to hear his explanation.

After some reluctant searching on the internet under his direction, she was able to find his insurance company, verify his personal information, and confirm he had insurance coverage. She looked disappointed.

Now he was established as a financially competent patient. She moved on to part two of assessment. The preliminary examination of his injuries. She judged he was indeed injured. He'd lost a lot of blood. But in his current state the injury wasn't life threatening. She shunted him off to the waiting room with a look of satisfaction.

The waiting room was filled with perhaps 60 people, all ages, sizes, shapes, races, and conditions. And all economic levels. This was the great Obama

Care experiment. It gave everybody health care and nobody good service. He'd have to wait his turn. He supposed it was very democratic and fair and all. But he'd just as soon pay the freight and see a doctor now and avoid the four hour wait in less than sterile conditions. That is if he'd had any cash and any identification and car keys for freedom of movement.

He borrowed a phone at the reception desk and called Katy. He didn't like to call for help. It was unmanly. But he had no choice.

Katy was the love of his life. His new bride. And his junior by 20 years. They were continually negotiating over cross-generational expectations and values as they tried to settle into marriage that had only begun the month before. Something of a shotgun wedding, he mused. Katy was two months pregnant. She had subtly given him an ultimatum. He wasn't at all sure he wanted to be a father. But he wanted Katy. It became a package deal.

Katy picked up the phone at once. "Hello!"

"Katy, it's the Judge," he croaked, feeling sorry for himself now he could hear her voice. In need of a little mothering and sympathy, despite her being 29 and he 50.

She caught the distress in his tone. He could feel her standing up, anxiety rising. "What's the matter Judge? Where are you? What's happened?"

"I'm kind of in a jam."

"Tell me."

"I'm in the emergency room of Saint John's. Cooling my heels in the waiting area."

The Judge looked down at his bare feet, protruding out from the blanket they'd given him. He'd discarded the socks. But was still wearing the soggy underwear. Polo. And his wet dress shirt. His feet were cold. His entire body was chilled now. From the swim, from the knife wound, from shock, from... everything. He felt even sorrier for himself.

"Are you hurt?" asked Katy.

"Not seriously."

"Were you in a car accident?"

"No."

"Did you fall down?"

"Not exactly."

"Can you drive? Shall I come get you?"

"Yes, I think you'd better. But I'm not sure they'll let me go."

"The hospital?"

"No... the police."

"Oh honey, I'm coming right now. What's the address?"

The Judge gave her the address; then said, "Can you do me a favor?"

"Anything."

"Can you bring me a pair of pants and some underwear? And some shoes, and a shirt. And a warm coat. Oh, and socks and a hanky." This came out in a rush.

"Jesus, Judge, what happened?"

"It's complicated."

"It sounds almost like you've lost your clothes....?"

The Judge went silent.

"Well, Judge?"

"Well........only my pants."

"Okay Judge, I'm leaving now. When I get there you can explain. And it better be good!"

"Yes, well... Oh, honey?"

"Yes?"

"Better grab my passport, and last year's copy of my state bar card, and last year's medical card, and bring cash. Oh and my second set of car keys."

"I'm on my way."

The Judge pulled the blanket closer around him for warmth and security. It seemed nothing else could go sideways.

He was wrong. As he turned from the phone, barefoot, huddled in the hospital blanket, dried hair askew, a flash went off in his face.

He snarled at the photographer, who was backing away now, suddenly scared. But a firm hand was laid on his shoulder from behind. It was the hand of authority. It felt like the police. But it wasn't the L.A. Sheriff, Saunders. It was a plainclothes detective from the Santa Monica Police Department, shoving credentials into the Judge's face. Too close to read.

The Judge was firmly guided to the farthest corner of the waiting room. The Judge was hoping vainly for some privacy but it didn't exist in this overcrowded facility. He could feel every ear in the room turning. Craning to hear what felony he'd committed.

The cop was much younger than the patrol officer, perhaps early thirties, stocky, with a round face and a pink complexion out of which deep blue eyes studied the Judge suspiciously. His hair was cropped short, orange more than red, matching blotches here and there of sunburn on what was otherwise very fair skin. There was the patina of a college man, only partially hidden by the grey suit with the bulge under one arm and the heavily polished shoes. Black.

He leaned in and introduced himself as Lieutenant Kaminsky, sniffing at the Judge's breath.

Then he asked the same questions the officer had asked. At least the Judge was spared the "Uh huhs." Instead, the Judge's responses were met with a poker face punctuated by narrowed blue eyes. Kaminsky's hand scribbled in a little flip book he carried.

"What were you doing on the beach in the first place, Judge? Late for the beach."

"It wasn't late at all," bristled the Judge. "It was sunset for Christ sakes. What's a beach for? I'm a lawyer. I'd been cooped up in an arbitration all day. I was stretching my legs before a slog back to Palos Verdes on the 405."

"Who were you a lawyer for in the arbitration?" Kaminsky was looking for people who could vouch for the Judge and confirm his story.

"I wasn't lawyering for anybody," snapped the Judge. "I was the arbitrator."

"Okay, okay, so who were the parties, and who was present today?"

"Carl Greene is the defendant. His lawyer, Bruce Williams, was with me all day. And Randel Hicks and his company, 1st Enterprises, are the plaintiffs. Dick was there briefly this morning. And his lawyer, Dick Harper, was with me all day. And my law clerk, Frank Wolin."

"When did your meeting break up?"

"About seven p.m."

Lieutenant Kaminsky's cell phone squawked, then a disembodied voice spouted out a string of number codes from his coat pocket.

"Just a minute, Judge. I've got to take this call. But we're not finished."

He crossed the waiting room and stepped outside, leaving the Judge unattended.

The Judge slumped against the back of the chair in his blanket, exhausted, his mind rolling back through the day.

Arbitration differed greatly from sitting on the bench with the attorneys and parties scraping and carping below you. More informal. This was his first gig as an arbitrator, and he was just getting the hang of it. Strange too that the parties picked him for a patent dispute. He wasn't a retired Federal Judge, or even a patent lawyer. But they'd wanted him, the money was good, and it was binding arbitration. He was the fact finder and decision maker.

He'd hired a law clerk to help him. A nice enough young man, newly minted as a lawyer after passing the bar in the Fall. Frank Wolin was green in assembling the facts and the law for a judge, but then weren't we all… once. Frankie worked hard and was enthusiastic, if perhaps a little misdirected in his scrambling efforts to keep up. The case wasn't all that complicated in the end. But interesting still.

The issue was whether an existing patent was infringed upon by similar technology. Technology that converted natural gas at the well-head into crude. Lots of gas was flared off around the country at oil wells for lack of a gas gathering system. This was lost revenue for the well owner and contributed to the carbons emitted into the atmosphere. There was a need for the technology.

Carl Greene, the inventor of the original technology, was a clever engineer. He'd spent thirty years off and on designing electrical devices for the navy. He knew his stuff. His testimony in the arbitration had been clear and credible. It cinched the case in the Judge's mind.

Randall Hicks, the plaintiff in the case seeking the judicial determination, had out-and-out ripped off of Greene's technology. Hicks may have changed the design of the piping and tanks a little, added a few gauges for window dressing, messed with the ingredients in the catalyst a bit, labeled everything with a different and fancier name, set the protocol for pressures and temperatures to somewhat different scales and parameters, but in the Judge's opinion he'd basically appropriated Carl Greene's patented technology for his own.

But Frankie, the Judge's law clerk, didn't see it that way. Frankie argued passionately for Hicks' position when he and the Judge worked privately together on the case. Frankie believed Hicks had invented something entirely new.

The Judge walked Frankie through his analysis several times, going step by step. Through the testimony. Through evidence produced. Frankie refused to admit any logic to the Judge's position.

His law clerk was cocky. But the Judge let him run, listening patiently while Frankie explained why the Judge was wrong. It was a tradition in the law you listened to and respected opinions from younger lawyers on a case. New eyes often had new ideas and perspectives not considered by old lawyers toiling in the same field for many years.

The fact gathering was now all but complete. Hicks' lawyer had made a demand for production of one more document under the terms for discovery. A confidential report prepared by Carl Greene and handed to the Judge that afternoon. It contained specifications on new technology Greene had created. Not yet patented. Hicks claimed a right to include Greene's new technology within the scope of the dispute. Hicks wanted to review Greene's technology, interrogate Greene, and sought a finding that Hicks' technology did not overlap with the unpatented Greene technology.

The Judge hadn't read the report yet. He was to review it "in chambers", by himself. Determine if this new technology was discoverable in the arbitration. If he concluded it was, the report would be turned over to Hicks and his counsel for review. The Judge's homework for the weekend was to read the report and decide if it was discoverable.

The waiting room doors opened again and Lieutenant Kaminsky darted in. He looked grim. Perhaps that was his nature. But his face was almost florid now. As though having difficulty controlling himself.

He marched up to the Judge with large strides. Towering over the Judge in a way that made the Judge instinctively stand up to face him.

"So the plaintiff in your arbitration was who again?" Kaminsky asked in a tight voice.

"Carl Greene," croaked the Judge, the pit of his stomach starting to turn for reasons he couldn't identify.

"Your Carl Greene was just found in an alley near here," Kaminsky said. Anger flaring across his face now. "Dead. A knife wound in his throat."

CHAPTER 4
10:30 PM Thursday

As the Judge stood there, trying to assimilate what Kaminsky had said, the front door of the ER flew open and Katy came steaming through in a rush, an overnight bag clutched in one hand. Her eyes swept the waiting room and pinned the Judge in the back corner, relief spreading across her face.

Katy was 5'8", slender, all arms and legs. She had long brown hair, twisted together in a pony tail that bobbed when she walked. She had extraordinary eyes, vivid blue like the Caribbean, large and intelligent, with long lashes. Her small features were etched here and there with smile lines. Her nose was a bit long and narrow, but in that it matched her head, also more oblong than round. All very delicate. Her cheeks, rosy already with a newly budding pregnancy that didn't show yet, were even more flushed tonight, making her blue eyes blaze. She was a magnificent creature, thought the Judge, particularly when stirred up. As now.

Lieutenant Kaminsky turned to see who the Judge was staring at over his shoulder, focused on Katy, giving her an appraising glance as she approached. Then showed surprise when Katy made a final dash to throw herself into the Judge's arms, burying her head in his blanket.

The pinched face nurse showed up, motioning the Judge to come into the inner sanctum of the emergency room. As the Judge got up, Lieutenant Kaminsky put his hand on the Judge's good arm, moving his face directly into the Judge's face, three inches from his nose.

"After you finish here I'm taking you to the Santa Monica Police station," he said through gritted teeth. "Depending on what the DA says, I am going to charge and arrest you for Carl's death. Just so you know."

"No," said the Judge, suddenly cold again. "I'm going to leave here and get a good night's rest. Then I'll show up at your station mid-day tomorrow and you can interrogate me all you want."

"That's not the way it works," said Kaminsky.

"We'll see," said the Judge, brushing Kaminski's hand aside and following the impatient nurse into the depths of the ER facility, Katy in tow.

The emergency bandaging wrapped on by the ambulance team, bright red now with blood, was cut away from the Judge's arm, and then the inner bandage was ripped off by the nurse with merciless tugs. The inner bandage took considerable hair and skin with it. It gave the nurse a sort of satisfaction.

Katy gasped as his arm was exposed. A long deep gash ran from just below the elbow, down his forearm almost to his wrist. It was deep. The bleeding hadn't stopped. It would need stitches.

The Judge was left sitting on the bed in a small space in the larger ER bay, created by puke-green curtains on three sides. Katy sat on a chair and watched as the Judge dripped blood into an expanding blotch on the white bed sheets.

The Judge had tossed the blanket and stripped out of his soggy shirt, socks and Polo underwear, now wearing a green hospital gown that matched the curtains. It didn't cover his ass, which was cold. In fact he was all cold. Shock, he supposed

"Did you bring real clothes, Katy?"

Katy reached into her overnight bag and pulled out his old dark blue sweatshirt and sweatpants, saying, "I'm sorry honey, the cleaners didn't make it today and the wash didn't get done. I just grabbed whatever was left in your drawer. I hope these still fit." She looked at him hopefully, still flustered by his strange call in the middle of the night and her rushed trip across town.

He gave her a soft smile. It felt good to have someone concerned about him after being so long a solitary soul. He dumped the puke green gown with relief.

She felt around in the bag and produced a crumpled pair of old underwear she'd found at the bottom of his drawer, handing them over without looking.

The Judge gasped.

The underwear was the most obnoxious pair he owned: a Tulio thong, purchased in West Hollywood, or WeHo as it was affectionately known. Given to him as a joke by an old flame some years before. He should have thrown the pair out long ago. They had the configuration of speedos, tight, elastic, butt hugging in the back, and tightly constricting the male organs in front in

30

a disgustingly small pouch that reminded him of packaged walnuts. They were bright purple with red flames on the sides and a few sparkles glued on for effect.

He held them up to her in horror.

She took a second look. Shock spread across her face. Then her face got pinker and pinker. She tried manfully to stifle a giggle. But all the tension and all the adrenalin had been too much. Her tiny giggle turned into a peal of laughter, forcing her to bend over in her chair and wrap her arms around her sides to contain herself as tears washed down her cheeks. Mostly he suspected in relief that he was more or less in one piece.

The Judge regarded his replacement underwear with distaste. Looked at Katy with mock daggers as she tried to contain herself. Then he shrugged at the obvious lack of alternatives, took a deep breath, and wiggled himself into them. Thankfully he couldn't see them for the overhang of his paunch. He saw no humor in the situation. But if it made her laugh then maybe it was okay.

They waited for about fifteen minutes. Time seemed to slow down and agonizingly drip by, like the droplets onto the sheet.

Finally, a young doctor came in, sandy hair, red freckles, non-committal blue eyes behind frameless glasses. He softly modulated his voice, formally shaking hands and then comradely putting a hand on the Judge's shoulder, saying, "I guess we've had a small accident."

The Judge was sure it was all good patient communication drummed into the young doc in medical school. But his eyes were still aloof behind the glass. Cold, analytical, and what else…? Yes, weary.

The doc quickly examined the Judge's arm, looked at his chart, and concluded the Judge needed no transfusion for loss of blood. He dove efficiently into cleaning the wound. He gave the Judge a shot, expertly slugged in ten stiches to hold the wound together, and slapped on another bandage, this one made with some non-stick-looking material that gave hope it wouldn't take more hide off on its removal.

He turned to the Judge, whispering conspiratorially, "His nibs out there, the flatfoot, wants a blood test for alcohol and drugs. Since you weren't driving as I understand it, I don't think you have to give it to him if you don't want."

"It's alright," sighed the Judge. "What's one more needle at this point? Go ahead."

His respect for the doc increased. He might be tired, but he was sharp. Like a lot of educated young people these days, he didn't automatically roll over for the police, always ready to trample individual rights in their quest for evidence. Maybe there was hope for the country after all.

Because the police often started with a suspect and then worked backward looking for evidence, rather than gathering evidence with an open mind and then working forward toward possible suspects, their process was often flawed. It was a catch twenty-two. They often found only the evidence supporting their theory for the perpetrator of the crime. A self-fulfilling prophecy Combine this with underlying prejudice that still percolated under the fabric of 21st Century America, and you had a at least an arguable hypothesis for why over half of men incarcerated in the U.S. penal system were black or Latino. And why most were poor.

Kaminsky was standing alert by the waiting room door as they came out, hands on his hips, face still pink, clearly intent on hauling the Judge down to his station. The Judge ducked around him and leaned over the reception desk manned by a candy striper with grey hair and helpful-looking eyes peeking out from under steel rim glasses. She was diligently inputting on her computer. He put on his best boyish smile, softened his eyes, and asked her in a hopeful voice if he might borrow her computer for just a minute.

She explained hospital policy didn't permit that.

He smiled again, nodding his comprehension, and asked if she might just take a quick second to access his Google account for him and retrieve an important telephone number from his Google contacts. She looked around worriedly. No one was watching. Then she looked at him again, deciding whether she could trust him. He winked.

That did it. She accessed Google. He gave her his name and password and suddenly his contact list spread across her screen. He asked her to look up the cell number for Martin Handover. Her eyes flew open at the name. Everyone seemed to know Martin right now. He was in a hotly contested run-off to retain his position as the District Attorney for Los Angeles County. The Judge asked her to give him the direct cell number.

The number was retrieved, written on a small slip of re-used paper with some part of a Federal Health Directive on the back, and handed over to the Judge with a matching smile. The Judge borrowed the phone at her desk and dialed Marty. After a short, quiet conversation, the Judge called Kaminsky over and handed him the phone.

Kaminsky held the phone to his ear but didn't seem to do much of the talking. The lines around his mouth turned progressively lower until he was scowling.

He handed the phone back to the candy striper, muttering, "All the animals in the barnyard are equal, it's just some are more equal than others."

The Judge snapped then.

"That's bullshit Kaminsky and you know it. You don't have any probable cause to hold me. I haven't broken the law. You're full of hot air. You like to throw your weight around against small people who don't know their rights and are easily intimated by your police state and your flashy badge. You're the pig on this farm."

CHAPTER 5

11:30 Thursday

The Judge put his arm around Katy, needing more support after his ordeal than he realized, and she helped him limp out, leaving Kaminsky still muttering behind them. The new underwear was tight and binding, almost as uncomfortable as the soggy ones he'd discarded. He just wanted to go home and have a stiff drink.

They got into Katy's car, a vintage Mustang convertible her dad had restored and given her. All candy apple with black upholstery. The Judge always felt silly sitting in the car, like an over-age teenager in an old man's body. But Katy loved to zoom around with the top down. He crawled into the passenger side while she ran the top up.

As they pulled out of the hospital parking lot she turned to the Judge. "What really happened tonight, Judge? What the Hell's going on?"

"I'm not sure, Katy. When I first saw them on the beach, I thought they were mugging me. Hell, they could have had my wallet. I'd have gladly thrown it at them and run the other way."

"But?" asked Katy.

"The first one came at me with a switchblade. He wasn't out for my wallet. He wanted me. He tried to kill me."

Katy gasped.

"Why would anyone want to kill you, Judge?" she finally managed, frightened now.

"I don't know, honey. I'm going to find out. And there's something else."

"Tell me."

"Someone murdered Carl Greene, the plaintiff in my arbitration case."

"Oh my god. What are you going to do, Judge?"

"What do you think I'm going to do, Katy?" The Judge gave her a tight smile.

"I think they made a serious miscalculation, Judge. You're going to follow them to ground and sort them out."

The Judge nodded.

"Be careful, Judge. They're obviously dangerous."

As they proceeded down Cloverfield toward the Santa Monica Freeway, Katy spoke again

"Judge, I think maybe we're being followed."

"What?" The Judge sat bolt upright in his seat.

"I'm not sure Judge, but a beat-up, dirty green SUV was in the parking lot. It pulled out behind us. It's been on our tail ever since."

"Shit! Katy, I don't want you involved in this. Whatever 'this' is."

"Don't worry, Judge. Watch this."

The approaching light was about to change, the cross-walk sign turning to a solid red. Katy slowed way

36

down, almost to a creep, hit the crosswalk on their side at a low speed after it turned yellow, then floored it and ran the yellow. There was a chorus of horns and even a finger from one driver. But Katy timed it well. Just enough of a lead to have her nose past the cross walk and out into the intersection as the light went red. A clear sign she was going through. Despite their bitching everyone waited for her.

The dirty SUV behind wasn't so lucky. It skidded to a stop as a wall of traffic washed into the intersection behind them.

Then Katy hung a quick right, almost on two wheels it seemed to the Judge. A right again at the next block. Then three blocks and she slammed the Mustang left. Katy took the corners like a race driver, ignoring the stop signs as they flew by. As they turned on to the third darkened residential street no one was behind them. She turned to the Judge with a glint in her eye.

"No more car chases until you learn to put on your seatbelt."

The Judge looked down. She was right. No wonder he'd flown all over his side of the car, bouncing his sore arm against the damn center console. He hated seatbelts. But now his wound was throbbing again. He was so tired.

"Perhaps we should settle somewhere else for the night and think this through, Judge."

"Where?"

"Let's go to your boat. We can snuggle in the master's cabin… Master." Katy smiled at him, saluting with her free hand. Relieving the tension.

The boat was a 50-foot motor yacht and the Judge's favorite toy. That is if you excluded his young wife and his golden retriever. It was close too. Just a couple of miles to the south in Marina Del Rey.

Katy swung the Mustang in a tight arc around the next corner, still in race driver mode, and headed toward the Marina.

The Judge's boat was kept on an end tie in an anchorage part of a major condominium complex. It had manned guard stations and cross gates at its two entrances. And security guards roaming the property on rounds through the night. It felt safer than their Malaga Cove villa to the south in Palos Verdes. It was closer too, allowing the Judge to crash. He was exhausted. The pain pills from the ER were wearing off, leaving him with a mounting pain shooting up his arm to his shoulder.

Katy displayed their sticker at the complex entrance, then whipped the Mustang into the underground parking reserved for slip holders.

The Judge's boat was a Chris Craft Motor Yacht, 43 feet long, named *The Papillon*. A joke of sorts since it meant in French both the butterfly and also the hinged double-panned iron omelet maker used in French cooking. There was a lot of iron in the two 650-horse Detroit diesels under the floor, propelling the boat through the water up to 30 knots an hour and consuming an enormity of fuel. Quickly making one a poor man.

The yacht was all white with deep blue stripes at the waterline. It had a raised aft deck flush across the stern, and a ladder at the back going down to a wide swim step. The engines were laid amidships under the floor of a generous salon three steps down and forward of the aft deck. The interior was done up in blond wood paneling, light blue carpet, and beige leather upholstered settee and chairs. A collection of small antique oils, all of boats on one sea or another, most dating back a century, were displayed in carved gold frames, providing a rich contrast to the sleek blond interior. Two steps down again and forward was a galley to port and a dining settee to starboard, with a second guest bedroom and head in the bow.

Next to the steps down from the aft deck, a second set of short steps reversed, leading aft and down under the aft deck. The master's cabin was replete with a picture window in the stern, a queen bed with blue silk embroidered spread, a flat screen TV, and to starboard, a separate head with its own shower into which the Judge barely fit.

Because the bed was rounded at its bottom corners to fit the space, the Judge had to sleep at an angle so his feet didn't stick out. But he didn't mind. It was a good excuse to stay close to Katy.

It was a wonderful toy. Almost as much fun as Katy. He couldn't say that of course. Katy would take offense at being compared to toy. But there was still that boyish imp in him that made him smile at the thought.

The Judge poured himself a stiff scotch, a 15-year-old Tobermory, and followed Katy to the Captain's Cabin aft. He stripped off his outer clothes.

"Boy, Judge, you look really racy in that ball-clutching thong," said Katy, a twinkle in her eye. "If there's reincarnation… maybe I'll come back as your thong."

The Judge looked down, but couldn't quite see the underwear beneath his damn protruding paunch.

"Maybe you could do a little dance, Judge. Like Tom Cruise in *Risky Business*." All we need's a little Bob Seger music. She giggled.

The Judge turned to look at her.

"You weren't even born then, Katy. And you're still too young to watch a movie like that," said the Judge, sounding pettish even to himself.

"That's why I've got you to teach me dear," Katy said, sliding under the covers without a stitch and patting the bed next to her.

The Judge crawled his way under the covers like some giant old bear, suddenly cold. Recurring chills made him shake. Perhaps he was still riding out the shock.. He clung to her with a desperate need for her warmth.

He vaguely thought about sex, but discarded the idea. He was way too beat up now. Besides, although all the books and the doctor said sex was okay in the early months of a pregnancy, he wasn't at all sure. It felt very odd to share one of his favorite places, inside Katy's body, with another budding creature. Very odd.

The last thing he remembered was Katy curling her body around him, trying to warm him up. Hold back his shivering. Her body temperature ran a few degrees higher than his. It felt very nice. Very... mothering. He wasn't certain he'd like sharing her with some new brat who'd want all her attention. They'd only just found each other. It seemed way too soon.

The sunlight streaming in through the transom window snapped him out of sleep. He'd been dreaming about wet sand. Wet with blood, his blood. And someone squirming around with him in the dark sticky sand, trying to stab him in the stomach.

40

They'd forgotten to pull the curtain closed. Damn!

They'd also forgotten about the dog. The one-year-old golden retriever was the bane of his existence. Annie would have been wandering around the house all night, alone, and distraught that no one had returned. He could only guess at the mischief she'd have gotten into. He loved that dog. But she was a holy terror.

The Judge had a spare dress shirt, slacks and sport coat in the cabin's locker closet. And thank God, other underwear. He shaved and dressed quickly, skipping a shower. There wasn't time, and besides he would need a plastic bag for his heavily bandaged arm to avoid soaking the dressing.

Katy appeared in the doorway of the tiny head, wearing nothing but her belly button, which sprouted a small sparkly diamond pin piercing, as was the custom with young women these days. It was hard to believe an old fart like him had actually married this beautiful creature, with her fancy degree in Psychology and her diamond-studded belly.

She made no bones about what she wanted now, giving him a lusty look that raised the heat in his loins. In seconds they were joined again on the bed, rolling, laughing, coupling and gasping.

Afterward she made him buy her coffee at Killer Shrimp. He knew she wanted him just to stay on the boat with her for the day. Not go to his office. She was worried about his wound, about his general condition, about his safety. She embarked on a stalling strategy, initiating a discussion of his patent case, knowing full well he'd be unable to refrain from expounding. She was clever. And all female.

CHAPTER 6
8:30 AM Friday

"Okay, Judge. Tell me about your case. But keep it simple. I'm a simple lady."

"Well, Katy, let's suppose you developed something," said the Judge. "Say a... a new hamburger flipper. Maybe it helps cook the meat more evenly, or drains the fat away, or has some other special feature."

"Oh, I like this Judge. I can flip you off with my new flipper!"

"Katy..."

"Sorry, honey. Even though I'm... we're newly pregnant, I still can't get enough of you. After you explain about your flipper, you're going to have to demonstrate." Katy giggled.

"Well anyway Katy, this new hamburger flipper is your original idea. Its novel and never been used before. So you file with the U.S. Patent Office and get a patent."

"Whoopee, I have a flipping patent."

"Yes, well, anyway, let's suppose some rival lady who lives with some other ex-Judge on a boat in L.A. Harbor develops a flipper which *might* be similar. She patents it after you but beats you to market. She starts selling her flipper."

"In violation of my patent? I'll flip her off too."

"Or you might bring a law suit in Federal District Court for infringement. Seek damages and an order putting the rival lady out of business."

"So that's what this Carl Greene did? He had his patent and he sued this other guy?"

"Eh, no. One would have thought he'd do that, but in this case he didn't."

"Wait, Judge. You promised 'not complicated'. Why didn't he sue?"

"He likely lacked the money."

"Oh, poor Carl. So what happened?"

"Well suppose, like Carl, you don't have lots of funds around to pursue a patent infringement case."

"On my flipper?"

"Right. But the rival lady is making lots of money selling her flipper."

"I bet she is. The bitch."

"So the rival lady sues you."

"Me?'

"Yes, you."

"But I'm the injured party. She can't sue me, Judge. That's not right."

"Well she can. For the cost of the filing fee in this country anyone can sue anyone for anything. The claim might get thrown out. But it's open season on filing claims."

"You lawyers. You guys have everything rigged as an attorneys' full employment act. So how can she sue me?"

The Judge took a big breath, preparing to explain. He knew Katy wasn't terribly interested in this stuff. It was boring. Nothing like the movies or *Law & Order* stuff she liked to binge on Netflix. But she knew he relished talking about it. It was what he did. The job defined the man.

She let him ramble on because she loved him. And he appreciated that. But she also was trying to mother him. Using every trick in the book to discourage him from going to his office today. That wasn't going to work. But she didn't know that yet.

"The rival lady says her flipper embodies novel technology," the Judge continued. "That your patent isn't valid to preclude her from selling her flipper. That her product isn't really a flipper at all. It's a scraper. She wants a court order saying her flipper doesn't infringe on your patent. That she's free to market it and sell it and license it. And you can't ever complain because her flipper is so different in design from yours."

"But you said her flipper infringed on my patent, Judge."

"No. I said the technology 'might' be similar."

"Okay, so what happens?"

"A judge has to make a decision: is the design different enough that the rival lady can legally market her flipper?"

"So there's a lawsuit? We love lawsuits Judge. It pays the rent."

"Yes. And now you're dragged into litigation that you wanted no part of because you have limited funds. You have to defend. You are the defendant. You don't want a judge to issue the order your rival lady seeks. You believe her technology is an out-and-out copy of yours."

"Okay Judge, so I hire my lawyer. I'd always hire you darling. Cause I wouldn't have to pay. You could take it out in trade. Me and my flipper."

"Yes. Well here's where it gets a little tricky."

"We like 'Tricky', Judge. But we only want to be 'Tricky' with you."

Katy giggled. The Judge pushed on, determined to set out some sort of coherent explanation and then make a break for his office.

"Your lawyer suggests you make an offer to waive all infringement claims against the rival lady and she would waive all claims against you. Just to make the law suit go away. So the rival lady can continue selling her flipper without paying you anything. And you can sell your flipper without paying her. You two share the flipper market."

"I have to do that?"

"Well if you don't have the money to defend, what can you do?"

"Damn."

"But here's what's strange."

"Okay, what?" Katy leaned forward, feigning intense interest, determined to hold him beside her as long as she could.

"Your rival lady turns you down. She doesn't want to settle her suit and go away. She wants a full legal judgment that she has the patent rights on her flipper, and her flipper doesn't infringe on your flipper patent."

"But she's got practically everything she wants with the settlement, Judge. She's stolen my technology. Wouldn't that be enough for her?"

"One might think so."

"Why doesn't she go along and settle, Judge?"

"It's a good question. I'm not sure. There might be another agenda here."

"So what happens?"

"The case goes forward. You start shelling out for legal fees to defend. You have no choice. Otherwise you might lose rights to your technology. You'll certainly lose the right to stop her from stealing your technology and ruining your market."

"Damn."

"Next, the rival lady suggests binding arbitration instead of trying the case in front of a patent judge in Federal District Court."

"And I agree because I want to save money, right Judge?"

"Yes. You agree."

"And why does this rival lady suggest arbitration?"

"Well it's cheaper for her too. And she gets it before an arbitrator who maybe isn't a patent lawyer."

"Like you, Judge. The crotchety old judge with the all seeing eye."

"I'm not crotchety, and I'm not old."

"Crotchety only sometimes, Judge. And old is a relative term." Katy gave the Judge her big smile with all the teeth, taking the sting out of her words.

"Maybe the rival lady thinks it will be easier to convince a non-patent lawyer acting as the arbitrator that her flipper doesn't infringe your patent. And maybe, just maybe, the rival lady thinks she may be able to get away with broad discovery."

"Just like you, Judge."

"Me?"

"Yeah. You have broad discovery of me. I'm the broad. And you had your discovery. And a broad discovery it was. Course you took your rights a little far I must say. You've left me in a delicate way." Katy batted her eyelashes.

"I haven't left, Katy. I never will. Until I kick off. You're stuck with me."

She reached over to hold his hand.

"Okay, Judge, so far so good. Then what happens?"

"The rival lady originally sought an order declaring that her flipper doesn't violate your patent."

"Okay."

"But now she's heard you might have developed an even better way to flip."

"Nobody flips like I do, Judge. I'm a natural born flipper, at least with you."

"But the rival lady's afraid you'll claim someday that your new way to flip is entitled to its own new patent that takes priority over your original patent. And you'll claim the flipper the rival lady is selling now infringes on your 'new' patented way to flip."

"And I have a patent on this new way to flip, Judge?"

"No. Not yet. You haven't disclosed it to anyone. You haven't filed for a patent yet. It's your proprietary confidential information."

"I'm hot shit aren't I, Judge. Well I really am anyway, but go on. So the rival lady can't be sure what I've got, Judge. It's confidential."

"That's right. But she wants you to tell her."

"She can suck air, Judge. I'm not telling her a thing. How'd she hear about it anyway?"

"I don't know. Another good question."

"So what's next, Judge?"

"She asks the Judge for an order to force you to disclose your new technology in the arbitration."

"She can't do that."

"She argues she's entitled to an order that your new method of flipping, to the extent it takes priority over your existing patent, doesn't preclude her from selling her flipper. She makes a motion to the arbitrator for a discovery order. An order requiring you to disclose to her your new technology for flipping."

"That doesn't sound right Judge."

"Well, it depends on how close your new flipping ideas are related to your existing patent, and to our rival lady's flipper technology. Have you created something brand new, or is your new flipping idea perhaps a follow-on, or even a supplemental part of your original patent? She may have a point."

"The only point she has is the money to hire fancy lawyers, Judge. How can the rival lady open up a claim against my new and secret flipper design?"

"Courts favor handling all the legal issues in a case at once, Katy. So the case doesn't have to come back to the court again. The court, or the arbitrator, will at least listen to this sort of argument and consider whether it's a valid request for discovery."

"So the arbitrator's going to make me disclose my new secret flipper technology to the rival lady. Everyone can argue about it and then the arbitrator can decide?"

"Not quite. The arbitrator is not convinced that discovery in the lawsuit should include your new flipper technology. He's not sure whether it's closely related to your existing patent, or something brand new."

"So?"

"So he orders the information on your new flipper technology to be produced in Chambers."

"For your eyes only, Judge? Just like me."

"Right. You give the information just to me first. I'll have a look and see if it's so entwined with your original patent that I should deal with both claims at once."

"Okay, so you as arbitrator have a first look-see. And if you decide my patented flipper and my new confidential flipper technology are closely entwined, what do you do, Judge?"

"I'll order the rival lady to sign a confidentiality agreement."

"Good luck on that, Judge. The bitch will be stealing my ideas and manufacturing my stuff in China in a heartbeat, regardless of what she signs!"

"Eh, well, anyway, then your new flipper design will be disclosed to the rival lady. Both sides will make their arguments about whether the rival lady's flipper infringes your existing patent. Then the arbitrator will decide. If there is no infringement, then the arbitrator decides if the rival lady's flipper will infringe on your new confidential technology that, once patented, will take priority over your earlier patent."

"What happens if I win, Judge?"

"Then the arbitrator will find the rival lady's flipper violates your patent. The rival lady will have to either stop her production of flippers or make a deal with you to pay a royalty."

"And if I lose?"

"Then the arbitrator will find that the rival lady can sell her flipper. He might also find your new confidential flipper technology can't be used because it violates her filed patent."

"So she's free to go on with her business?"

"Yes."

"And she might stop me cold from commercializing my new flipper technology?"

"Yes."

"She must be doing a lot of flipping to spend all that money on lawyers. She's probably got a gang of pretty flippers on every street corner, stirring up traffic."

"It would seem."

"You said my rival lady might have another agenda, Judge?"

"Well, the way my case has played out so far, it almost seems like Hicks, the plaintiff in my case, is more interested in the disclosure of Carl Greene's new confidential technology than he is in winning his case."

"But your case isn't about flipping hamburgers, is it Judge? This is Silicon Beach. It must be about some fancy software or gizmo."

"You would think. But actually it's more about basic chemistry. And an old substance we all take for granted."

"What's that, Judge?"

"Oil..!"

CHAPTER 7
9:45 AM Friday

The Judge left Katy there, staring after him over another sip of coffee. When her delaying tactics stopped working she'd tried to bully him into staying. But he'd have none of it. He was too old to be mothered. Well… for very long, anyway. He wanted to get to his office. He wondered who would show up. The plaintiff, Carl Greene, was dead. But would his attorney come? Would he know the circumstances? Would the defendant, Randall Hicks, come? And his attorney? What did they know about last night's events?

He had Katy's spare key to his car so he could retrieve his wheels, and had borrowed folding cash and one of her credit cards. He looked back at her from the Killer Shrimp Café parking lot, perched on her deck chair, nose buried in the morning's newspaper. Her annoyance at his departure had evidently been short-lived. She was laughing uproariously at something in the paper, her gold ponytail bobbing with mirth.

He called Uber from the pay phone on the dock and told them he needed a ride. He'd never actually used Uber before, but what the hell, he figured he be modern and give it a try. They laughed at him on the phone.

"Look Sir." There was that damn 'Sir' again. Jesus he hated he was old. Could they tell even over the phone?

"You can only get an Uber from your cell. You have to go online on your cell, and then find the App, and then download it to your cell, and then figure out how to work it to talk to one of our drivers. Why don't you ask your son?"

"Patronizing son of a bitch," muttered the Judge. He called a yellow cab.

He directed the taxi driver, who was willing to chat with him, and smelled good, and since he was from Bangladesh had interesting things to say, to take him to Santa Monica where his arbitration office was located. His car was still parked in the garage beneath the office.

The Judge got out of the taxi feeling woozy. His arm was throbbing. The pain pill had worn off. But it was nothing to the shock he got as he glanced inside the newsstand box outside his office.

The front page of the Los Angeles Times bore a nasty headline, blaring at him through the plastic box: LOCAL EX-JUDGE LOSES PANTS IN NOCTURNAL SWIM.

"Son of a bitch," the Judge muttered under his breath, feeling his face go crimson.

And there was his picture, hair matted, wrapped in the blanket, looking half-crazed. He'd been in shock, and it showed. The photo was credited to Lou Garo. Someone would pay for this. He would ferret out the people behind the attack, and he was damn well going to see their collective ass was fried.

The Judge had the corner office of a floor operated as an executive suite in a building at the intersection of Main Street and Marine Avenue, two blocks from the Santa Monica Beach.

It was 9:50. The Judge was a little early. In the reception area, an open bay with well-worn purple sofas, faded black carpet and somewhat battered end tables stacked with stale magazines, sat Bruce Williams, the lawyer for defendant Carl Greene, playing with his cell. Across the small space Dick Harper, the lawyer for plaintiff Randall Hicks and his company, sat on the edge of his seat, watching for the Judge to step out of the elevator. Both lawyers leaped to their feet. It might not be as majestic as his old court room, thought the Judge, but he still had a measure of power.

Dick Harper reached the Judge first, sputtering with ill-concealed glee, "Carl Greene is deceased, Your Honor. There is no defendant. We are entitled to our judgment and an order for discovery of Greene's new technology so we can establish that it does not impact our technology."

"Not so fast, Dick." Bruce Williams waded in behind. "I now represent the Estate of Carl Greene. His estate wishes to proceed with our defense."

The Judge held up his hands. "Gentlemen, gentlemen. Let's move to my office and hash this out there."

They both clamped their mouths shut in mid-sentence, conditioned to strict compliance with the order of a judge, and fell in line behind him.

He marched them down a long hallway, narrower than current building codes would allow, covered with a fresh coat of soft yellow to make the space seem larger and less dated.

His corner office was a medium sized room, perhaps fifteen by twenty, containing a long narrow conference table surrounded by leather chairs of uncertain vintage. In the corner, shoved against the windows on one side, sat a roll-top desk with its cover down and locked. A clock and old photos of Santa Monica in chipped Mexican frames hung on the walls, and to the left of the door sat a small bureau with locked drawers. A coffee pot, kettle, cups, bottled water and canned soda were neatly stacked on top.

In a nod to modern technology, a smart TV hung on one wall, available to Skype and to play video. An octopus-like box sat in the middle of the table to facilitate joint conference calls.

This had been the Judge's home for some weeks now, though in truth most documents were in the cloud and the Judge's laptop. He could work from anywhere.

As they settled in and helped themselves to coffee and water, Frank Wolin, the Judge's new law clerk, slipped into the room, five minutes late, and slid into a chair, trying to look like he'd been there forever. Frankie had just recently passed his bar exams, and was helping the Judge under a temporary arrangement until he found a full time lawyering job. Medium height, pudgy in the middle, with a sandy complexion and sharp brown eyes, he'd proved himself reasonably smart, quietly aggressive, and a little stubborn.

Frankie seemed convinced Hicks' technology did not infringe on Carl Greene's patented technology. A view the Judge had discredited as he'd listened to and then sifted through the evidence. Frankie jumped to judgement a bit too quickly.

Dick Harper, Hicks' lawyer, went right into argument mode again.

"There's hardly been time to open a probate estate with the Probate Court for Mr. Greene, have an executor appointed, and give the executor authority to hire counsel and pursue the estate's defense in this arbitration. How can defendant possibly go forward?"

Bruce Williams, Greene's lawyer, came right back, smug now.

"There is no need for a probate. All of Carl Greene's technology is in an *inter vivos* trust and I am now the temporary successor trustee. I am charged with continuing the defense of the Trust in this arbitration and preserving the assets for the trust beneficiaries. Our position continues to be that Hicks' technology blatantly infringes on Greene's patent, that Hicks must cease and desist using the technology, and that Hicks has no right to see or review new technology developed by Greene and now owned by the Greene Trust."

Harper sat still and tried to hide the grinding of his teeth as Bruce Williams produced for the Judge, with a flourish, a copy of Carl Greene's Trust document and his Will.

"Gentlemen," the Judge said, looking up after skimming the document title pages and signature pages, "these documents look to be in order, although there may be challenges in probate court. I rule that the arbitration proceeding may continue with the Carl A. Greene Family Trust standing in the place of the deceased Carl Greene as defendant. If counsel for the plaintiff has objections with this finding he can take them up with the Federal District Court, but meanwhile this proceeding will continue. Now, to business. Late yesterday, Bruce, you produced discovery materials, actually a report, from defendant Greene which you said was responsive to plaintiff Hicks' demand for material on Greene's new technology."

"That's right, Your Honor," said Williams. "We believe you'll rule Greene's new technology is not relevant to this case and is not discoverable by Hicks."

"And you personally reviewed this report, Bruce?"

"No, Your Honor. I was instructed not to look at the report. Just to place it before you in this proceeding."

"That's a little unusual," said the Judge. "Did Plaintiff say why you couldn't look at the report?"

"No, Judge, but his instructions were quite specific. I assumed it was because I was not the original attorney he consulted in preparing the contents."

"Who was the original attorney?"

"I don't know. Mr. Greene didn't tell me."

"Alright gentlemen, I have the report and I'm going to review it."

Frank Wolin, the Judge's law clerk, suddenly stood up, looking distressed.

"I'm sorry Judge... Gentlemen," he said. "I've entirely forgotten a dental appointment I need to keep. Please excuse my early departure. Judge, I'll be in on Saturday to do that legal research we discussed."

"That's fine Frankie. I'll be in too and we can discuss it."

Frankie scurried for the door and disappeared.

"As I was saying gentlemen," continued the Judge, "I am going to review this report over the weekend and make a determination. Let's plan on meeting here next Friday morning to wind up the discovery phase. The proceeding is adjourned until then."

The attorneys packed up their briefcases and scooted out the door after Frank. Off to bill other clients for other services. The Judge thought about starting his read of the report, glancing at the locked bureau drawer where he'd secured it. But his eyes were tired. His arm throbbed. His head hurt even worse, a consequence of too many pain pills. He decided to leave it until tomorrow when he and Frankie could puzzle over it together. He needed the results of Frankie's legal research as well. Hopefully tomorrow his head would be clear.

He considered going back to the boat and lying down. But it was early, only noon. And he'd promised to appear at the Santa Monica Police Station and allow himself to be grilled about last night. He supposed he should get it over with.

He called Lieutenant Kaminsky from the number on his card. Kaminsky's voice got low and flat after the Judge identified himself. The Judge said he could come to the Santa Monica Police Station in about an hour to give his statement and the good Lieutenant could compete his paper work. Paperwork was everything to a cop.

Kaminsky said, "Swell."

The Judge could hear lingering anger in Kaminsky's voice. The Judge's instinct told him something else was going on.

CHAPTER 8
12:15 PM Friday

The Judge locked his office and walked over to the *Groundwork Coffee Company*. A hole in the wall joint, it was still the coffee place of choice for the denizens at the southern end of Santa Monica. The place was popular at all hours, but right now attracted a collection of younger people, mostly in jeans, a few in skirts, all glued to their cell phones, oblivious to the people around them strolling in and out.

The Judge snagged one of the few tables when someone got up suddenly. Like many lawyers and like Wild Bill Hickok, he preferred his back against a wall. It felt more... defensible. He liked to people-watch the room and the passing traffic outside. Times had changed since 1886 when Hickok had been shot in the head from behind, the one time he didn't sit with his back to the wall. But there was still a cautious caveman mentality somewhere deep in the Judge. Particularly after last night's attack.

He sipped his brew, letting the aroma of the coffee waft up his nose, and considered what he knew.

Yesterday he'd been attacked on the beach by a gang that seemed intent on disposing of him for good. Apparently somewhat earlier Carl Greene had been attacked and killed. Were the two events related? It was an awfully strange coincidence if they weren't. The murder of Carl and his violent attack had to be related. But how? Where to start?

He finished his coffee and drifted out and down Main Street, back to his office building's underground parking garage.

He retrieved Katy's key from his pocket, threw his briefcase in the back of the car, and roared up the underground ramp and out on to Main Street.

A half hour later the Judge was staring into Kaminsky's cold blue eyes across a metal table in a small interview room at the Santa Monica Police Station. Kaminsky looked tired. There were dark circles around his eyes. It must have been a rough night.

The Judge finished a complete re-narration of the attack of the night before, a first time, then a second time, and finally a third. Kaminsky looked just as skeptical this morning as he had the previous evening. Perhaps his universal look for all occasions.

"How well did you know Carl Greene?" asked Kaminsky.

"I met him in the arbitration. But I didn't know him. I mean he wasn't a friend or anything. I didn't know him socially."

"How many times did he show at your arbitration?"

"Three times. Once at the beginning. That's where we were first introduced. Once when Randall Hicks, the plaintiff in the case, gave his testimony, and once when Carl himself gave testimony."

"So you never had coffee with him? Met him for lunch, or anything?"

"No."

"Ever give him your card?"

"No."

"That's curious, Judge. See your business card was found in his pocket at the murder scene."

"It's not curious at all. There's a card stand at reception in my lobby where anyone can help themselves to my card. And a similar card stand on my desk in my office. And his attorney, Bruce Williams, no doubt had my card since I was arbitrating Greene's case. He could have picked it up anywhere."

"When's the last time you saw Mr. Greene?"

"Like I said, when he came and gave his testimony in the arbitration."

"And when was that?"

"About ten days ago."

"So why do you think he was still carrying your card in his pocket Thursday night when he hadn't been in your office for ten days?"

"He had a crush on me? He collects lawyer cards for a hobby? He wanted a memento of his testimony? How the Hell do I know?"

Kaminsky looked daggers at the Judge, then scribbled a note in his little flip notebook. The Judge decided Kaminsky was trying to be intimidating. It was water off a duck to the Judge.

"Ever meet Mr. Greene's ex-wife?" Kaminsky consulted his notebook. "A Yana Greene? Lives in Santa Monica?"

"No."

"So no social connection between you and Mr. Greene at all?"

"Not as far as I know."

"What about a business connection?"

"Just the arbitration."

"No other connection? No reason you might be angry at Greene about something? Might want to get even?"

"No. Where's this going, Kaminsky? Am I a suspect in Greene's murder? A person of interest or something?"

"I think you're the bastard that killed Carl." Kaminsky blurted out. Then clamped his mouth shut.

So Kaminsky wanted to tag him for Carl's murder. Damn.

"Where were you before your little nocturnal swim, Judge?"

Kaminsky had picked up the words from the newspaper headline. Damn, damn, and more damns. He would hear about his 'nocturnal swim' now for the rest of his career.

"As I explained, I was at my office all day. We had sandwiches sent in. I worked on the case for about an hour and a half after the attorneys left. Looked at a motion for discovery. Looked at the law a bit on the scope of discovery in patent matters."

"Your law clerk, Frank Wolen, was with you?

"Yes. For a while. Then he left. He said he had a hot date with his girlfriend. An anniversary or something."

"So you were alone for an hour or so in your office?"

"Yes. Then I walked down to the beach and out to the tideline. Started what was going to be a brief walk along the beach toward the Santa Monica Pier, and then back."

"You ever been arrested for any deviant behavior, Judge?"

"I resent that question. And no. I'm sure you've checked my record."

"Sometimes things like that get expunged. Particularly if the perp has friends in high places. Are you gay, Judge?"

"I don't think that's a question you can ask legally, Kaminsky. But I'll answer it anyway. No. I'm not gay."

"Never had a boyfriend?"

"No."

"Never had a little experimental fling with Carl Greene?"

"No."

"How'd you walk from your office to the beach?"

"Down Ocean Park, across Nielson Way, across Beach Park to the sand, and directly out to the surf."

"About what time again?"

"About 7:30."

"Which side of the street?"

"The north side."

"So you were walking down Ocean Park Boulevard about the time Carl Greene was being attacked and killed. Killed in an adjacent alley running parallel to your street. Just on the other side of the buildings from the alley. With easy access down the side yards of most of the buildings to that alley. And you didn't hear a thing?"

"That's what I said. I didn't realize he was killed so close to my route."

"And you just happen to have a relationship with the deceased. The only one we can find in the area at that time who knew Greene."

"It wasn't a relationship. I'd met him professionally is all."

"Doesn't that seem like an enormous coincidence?"

"Yes it does. It seems to me the attack on me and the murder of Greene are connected somehow."

"How?"

"I don't know."

"You don't seem to know much."

"No. But I'm going to find out more."

Kaminsky opened a large brown envelope he'd brought into the interview room with him, and shook out its contents on to the table in front of the Judge. It was a clear plastic evidence bag. Inside was a wallet. The wallet looked familiar.

"This your wallet?" asked Kaminsky.

"Looks to be," the Judge said.

Kaminsky took the wallet out of the envelope and slid it across to the Judge. The Judge opened it. His smiling face was on the laminated license staring up at him. The credit cards were all there. Eight one hundred dollar bills were neatly stacked in the cash compartment. The ink on his business cards kept in one compartment had run a little. The cards looked like they'd gotten soaked and then dried out.

"How'd you find it in the surf?"

"We didn't," said Kaminsky. "We found it next to Carl Greene's body."

Oh shit. They were the only words that came to the Judge's mind.

"We found something else," said Kaminsky.

The Judge braced himself.

Kaminsky opened a large bag leaning against the wall behind him in the room. He dumped out another clear plastic evidence bag. It contained the slacks he'd worn yesterday. The ones he'd jettisoned in the surf.

"And you know the most interesting thing, Judge? Beside the fact that your credit cards and cash are all still in your wallet?"

"What?" croaked the Judge.

"When the officers arrived on the murder scene and found your pants and wallet, which you claim to have lost in the ocean, both items were quite dry."

CHAPTER 9
2:00 PM Friday

The Judge knew Kaminsky had to let him go. He could see the Lieutenant wanted to hold him. But Kaminsky didn't have quite enough to sell the case to the DA. The Judge admitted to being close by at the time of the murder. The wallet and pants allegedly placed the Judge at the scene. And the Judge admitted knowing the victim. But Kaminsky had no motive. And he wouldn't have gotten lab results back yet that he'd hope would produce physical evidence on the body linking the Judge to the crime.

"Can I have my license back at least, Kaminsky?" asked the Judge

Kaminsky gave the Judge a sour smile, not bothering to answer a stupid question. He reluctantly walked the Judge out of the interrogation room, through the office, and out the front door of the police station.

"I'll want to talk again soon, Judge," Kaminsky said, not shaking hands, a not-so-veiled threat in his eyes.

The Judge spent the afternoon waiting in line at the DMV for a temporary replacement license, cashing a check at his bank using his passport, picking up a new wallet and cell phone, and making multiple calls to credit card companies to cancel his existing cards and order replacements. It was one big pain in the ass.

He and Katy were in periodic contact once he had his new cell. No one had appeared around the boat. She'd swung by their house in Malaga Cove after work to confirm all was undisturbed. They agreed to hang out at the boat for the weekend at least. Perhaps longer even. Until things blew over.

He made an early dinner date with her at *Via Veneto*, one of his favorite restaurants in Venice, silently promising himself a fine bottle of Italian wine. It had been a rough week. Perhaps an Avignonesi 1995 Occhio di Pernice Prugnolo Gentile would suit, $400 on the hoof. Katy couldn't drink of course. He'd just have to man up and have it all himself. He pulled up to the restaurant right at six, dropping the car with the front door valet just as the place opened, commandeering his favorite spot, a small two-person table set in the restaurant's windowed façade. Katy came tearing up five minutes later, screeching to a stop in her vintage Mustang at the last minute like the race driver she was, giving the small Latino valet a fright. And the Judge as well.

He awkwardly stood up, hoisting his large bulk behind the small table, as she bounced in. She leaned over to give him a solid kiss on the lips. She was nothing if not affectionate. A year ago he'd have been appalled to see such a public display by some couple at a restaurant, particularly if it was some old codger and a younger woman.

But now he found he immensely enjoyed this attention lavished on him. If the waiters and the three or four other early patrons in the place disapproved, tough. Besides, Katy and he were now married. He'd somehow captured this golden young woman, much to his utter amazement.

They traded stories of their day over freshly made pumpkin ravioli, and a chilled bottle of Colterenzio Sauvignon "Lafoa" (Alto Adige) for the Judge. They didn't have the other bottle he'd wanted. He made do just fine.

They moved on to larger dishes, a chop for him and branzino for her. Since they were married now and enjoying intimacy most every night, his appetite had gone through the roof. He washed the meal down with the Lafoa. It was everything he'd anticipated and more. Katy had Pellegrino.

"So Judge," Katy said, turning serious. "You really think they were trying to kill you last night?" A certain flatness in her voice belied the nonchalant way she asked the question.

"I don't know what else to think, honey. They found my pants planted with Greene's body. My wallet was in my pants. My cash and credit cards all there. Robbery wasn't a motive. Even more bizarre, they must have tossed my pants into a dryer first. Kaminsky says they were dry."

"Somebody wants to frame you for Carl Greene's murder, Judge. But why? It relates to your arbitration, doesn't it?"

"It must. They killed the plaintiff. They attacked me."

"Did you see the paper this morning, honey?" Katie asked softy, changing the subject, putting her hand across the table on top of his.

The Judge reached for his wine and took a large gulp, his eyes narrowing, anger etched across his face.

"I did. And the bastards are going to pay for that. Big time. Whoever painted me into this corner is going to regret it. They're going to find my very large foot imprinted up their ass."

The Judge took another large swig of wine for emphasis. He could feel himself turning pink.

Katy quickly changed the subject, launching into a narrative about a troubled youth she had counseled that afternoon. Katy worked as a high school counselor at Palos Verdes High School. It was more than a job for her, it was a calling. She also privately counseled teenagers on the side, which meant she wasn't entirely idle during summer vacation. By the time she finished, carefully soliciting the Judge's advice as she told her story, he'd forgotten the morning's headlines. She had an amazing ability to calm him.

"Don't forget, Judge, dinner with my parents Sunday night."

The Judge shifted uncomfortably in his chair. He couldn't help himself. He wasn't looking forward to this dinner. Really a post marital interview, though Katy's parents didn't know that. This would also be his first time meeting her father, as if there wasn't already reason enough to be nervous.

"Are you sure this is really the best time to tell them we're married?" asked the Judge.

"Yes. We can't wait any longer. We'll tell them how we eloped. Then a week later we'll surprise them with our news of the baby. I'm going to be showing soon."

The Judge sighed. "How about you just take your mother to lunch and tell her. Then she can go home and yell at your dad. Wouldn't that be easier on everybody?"

"No, Judge. You can't chicken out. I'm counting on you to back my play. Crowded restaurant. My dad there with my mother. You at my side at the table. It'll all work. My mother won't make a scene."

They parted after dinner, Katy returning to the boat, and the Judge back to his office to finish up a little work, and to retrieve Carl Greene's report on his new technology. He'd read it tonight on the boat, then meet with Frankie tomorrow to sort out the law and make a determination. Working on Saturdays came with the turf practicing law. It was a collaborative affair and often chewed up weekends and holidays. It would be useful to hear Frankie's view.

It was eight p.m. when the Judge pulled into the underground parking under his office. The lot was empty, as was the lobby, the elevator, and the common reception area to his office. It was after all Friday night. The security guard was missing from the downstairs desk, likely making his rounds. The Judge wondered if it was wise to waltz into his office alone at night, particularly after the attack on the beach. He set the thought aside. He'd be damned if he'd live his life in fear.

He made his way down the narrow corridor to his office and opened it with a replacement set of keys the suite manager had given him earlier. He walked over to the bureau, retrieved the bureau key from his new key set, and opened its drawer.

The   report   was   gone!

CHAPTER 10
8:15 PM Friday

The Judge squatted down and examined the bureau lock. There were small marks around the keyhole on the face of the drawer, and on the edge of the drawer at the top, right above the latch, as if someone had used a small screwdriver on it, scratching the wood in the process. It wouldn't have taken much force with a small flat head with a long handle to force the lock.

The Judge locked up and went down to the lobby to find the security guard on duty. He turned out to be relaxing in a small room off a utility hall running behind the elevators, engrossed in a baseball game on TV. The Giants were getting trounced. The man looked about the Judge's age. He had a larger paunch and apparently sore feet, judging by the way his shoes were off and his feet elevated. The odor of used socks permeated the room. The Judge asked if he'd seen anything unusual. If anyone had asked for the Judge. If anyone had come in late over Thursday night or early Friday morning. The guard had seen nothing unusual. The Judge wasn't sure he would have, even if there was something to see.

The Judge rode down a floor to retrieve his car and headed back to the marina and his beloved boat. His arm was throbbing and he needed more meds. He didn't know what he would do about the missing report.

70

He parked in the boat owners' parking area and hoofed his way to the water and the docks. As his dock gate closed behind him and he started down the steeply angled ramp to his boat there was a sudden commotion aboard *The Papillon*. A blond shape came hurdling off the boat down the boarding steps, tumbling in an excited crash of legs at the bottom before regaining balance.

It was Annie, his year-old golden retriever. She'd escaped to meet him. Katy must have stopped by their house in Malaga Cove and picked Annie up. She came tearing down the dock at him like a runaway projectile, her paws going in mismatched comic relief, her tail spinning about like a prop. She almost knocked him over when she collided with him, causing them both to recoil from the impact. She immediately jumped up and demanded to have her muzzle rubbed, her ears stroked, and other attention lavished as was her right. She was irrepressible. All caramel fur, soft brown eyes and flagman tail.

Katy appeared on the aft deck as the Judge and the dog walked down the dock, also glad to see him, and relieved.

The Judge followed Katy down the steps to the main cabin, where she turned and threw her arms around him. She'd changed from her traditional grey slacks and blouse she wore as a counselor, to pale blue silk house pajamas, soft and inviting, complementing her blond hair and picking out the blue in her eyes. She noted the pain and weariness behind his eyes and prescribed a stiff gin and tonic, Bombay. The drink seemed to magically materialize in her hand.

He went further below, aft, to the captain's cabin, and unwrapped the dressing on his arm. In the midst of his rewrap, his cell phone, left up in the salon, went off with the stirring notes of the USC fight song. A small vanity he allowed himself as a reminder of his days there years before.

"Can you grab that for me, honey?" he yelled up the stairwell to the salon. He heard a "sure", and then muffled conversation on the phone he couldn't make out.

Suddenly Katy appeared in the stairwell, his cell phone in hand. A glint in her eyes didn't bode well. Then she gave the Judge a 'stinky fish' look and handed his phone down to him with two fingers, keeping her arm outstretched and away from her body in mock disgust.

The Judge, puzzled, took the phone and said, "Hello."

"Oh thank God I've got you Judge," a very distressed female voice squeaked over the phone. "I had to search everywhere until I found your private number." The voice sounded vaguely familiar and very upset.

"It's Barbara."

The only words that came to the Judge's mind were *Oh shit*.

Barbara was a tall brunette, beautiful, divorced now, and on the prowl for her next husband. She and the Judge had been an item of sorts a year or so before he'd met Katy. Item, hell, they'd had a passionate affair behind her then husband's back. Images of wild nights on a fur rug fireside in Vail, and a tangle of legs and twisted clothes in the back seat at the Seattle Airport parking lot, flashed though the Judge's mind. Like daguerreotypes lifted up to the light from an old box in a dusty attic.

The affair had ended when the Judge insisted Barbara either fish or cut bait. Leave her husband and run away with him, or mend fences at home and end their liaison. Barbara decided economic issues outweighed love. She couldn't leave quite yet. So the Judge had.

Unfortunately for the Judge, he seemed destined to run into Barbara frequently. Most recently on Catalina Island. And always it seemed Katy was just around the corner, invariably catching him talking to Barbara, guided by some internal intuition he didn't understand. Katy took a dim view of Barbara. Was it because Barbara was beautiful? Or perhaps because she was oversexed? Barbara exuded a certain feminine sensuality that hung like musk in the air when she entered a room.

Perhaps it was because Barbara was single now and on the prowl for a new attachment. Or because Barbara was still infatuated with the Judge. That was obvious, he thought smugly. Perhaps because the Judge was the one Barbara let slip away.

He brought himself back to the present, trying to understand what Barbara was wailing about on the phone, looking up to see Katy staring down from above on the steps, arms crossed in disapproval.

"Barbara, Barbara, calm down," he said over the wail. "Take a big breath and then tell me slowly."

There was a brief silence on the line. Then Barbara began again.

"He's dead Judge. The bastards killed him. Snuffed him out like you'd step on a snail. Then dumped him like a piece of trash. He's gone." She started to wail again.

"Okay, Barbara, I understand. Slow down again and tell me more."

"We were about to be engaged. Talking about marriage. I had it all planned out. He loved me. I know he did. It would have worked this time. Do you know how hard it is to find an eligible man in this town, Judge? Particularly when you're 29."

The Judge knew damn well Barbara was pushing 40. It didn't seem the time to correct her.

"They've killed him, Judge. And they've destroyed my life. You've got to do something. Find them. Make them pay. The bastards must pay big."

"Okay, Barbara. I understand. What was your boyfriend's name?" The Judge forced himself to ask the question. Against his better judgment. Katy would not approve of his involvement.

"His name is… was Carl. Carl Greene," said Barbara, lapsing into a wail again."

The Judge went silent. Christ! It seemed he was destined to stumble into these damn situations. How many times had he turned a corner, only to walk smack into himself coming back around from the other side? He took in a big breath to steady himself.

"Okay, Barbara. Okay. I am definitely going to help, but we can't do much tonight. Can you meet me in Santa Monica for coffee tomorrow, maybe about nine a.m.?"

The Judge could feel weight shifting on the stairs above him, almost hear the teeth clinching together, the eyebrows furrowing, eyes turning a colder blue. Well shit, Katy shouldn't be eavesdropping on his phone conversations.

The Judge ended the call, and then spent the better part of an hour smoothing ruffled feathers. He got himself another gin and tonic, then started by telling Katy how much he liked her new pajamas.

"It's a jump suit," she icily corrected.

He commented on how slim she looked. "No bump showing yet." That was the wrong thing to say as well. Apparently one didn't call it a bump. Her feathers went up several degrees. He joked them back down, talking soothingly, directing conversation to their upcoming dinner where he'd meet her dad. How she'd go about announcing their marriage. How she planned to smooth things over with mom by trotting out budding plans for a grand reception for family and friends at the California Club. And there was the pregnancy to consider. Still a well-kept secret to be released at a subsequent dinner.

It had indeed been a whirlwind courtship and marriage. His head was still spinning from it all. And Katy's must be too.

As the Judge finished his second drink, Katy leaned way over their small boat table to clink her orange juice glass with his glass, the front of her jacket spilling open to reveal small perky breasts. Intentionally, suspected the Judge. Females were tricky.

He openly admired them. Then looked up to see her watching him, anticipation in her face. He reached across the table for her then, walking around the table and into his arms. They made a beeline for the aft cabin and the partially circular queen bed.

"Are you sure this is all right?" asked the Judge. "It won't hurt your baby?"

"Our baby, Judge, and he'll be fine with it."

"How do you know it's a 'he?'" asked the Judge.

"I don't for sure," Katy said. "Just female intuition. The only thing I know for certain is it's ours, and it's going to be wonderful."

The Judge gave her his best reassuring smile, hiding his doubts.

She grabbed him then, pulling him to her and grappling with his belt. Sixty seconds later they were joined, the Judge on top, crushing her into the mattress, beginning their ritual of love.

He always worried he would crush her, or break a bone, or maybe just smother her. But females were apparently far hardier then they looked. Of course he'd had no experience with a pregnant one. This whole pregnancy thing was a little unnerving, frightening even. He was sharing her body with another entity that was in the process of taking over. And he suspected the 'taking over' didn't end with birth. In fact that was likely just the beginning. He was very unsure what he'd gotten himself into.

CHAPTER 11

9:00 AM Saturday

The Judge met Barbara at the *Crepe Café* in Santa Monica, at the beginning of the 3rd Street Promenade. The Promenade lodged a popular smorgasbord of shopping and dining, garnished by the antics of street performers along its three block stretch. Musicians, hip hop dancers, magicians, folk singers, clowns; you never knew what would show up. It was his favorite spot for people watching on late summer afternoons when the law business was slow.

The *Crepe Café* was a small French-inspired place. Black and white checkered floor with a long food bar with stainless stools. Sort of Champs-Elysees in Santa Monica. Plentiful outdoor seating made it useful for a discreet chat.

Barbara was early. Holding down an outside table. She was all yellow chiffon, wrapped by a huge collar creating a plunging neckline. In the Judge's view it displayed a tad more than was proper. The dress was tight across her small waist and flowed out over long tan legs that seemed to go on forever.

The Judge knew her voluptuous breasts were new equipment, recently enhanced, and about which Barbara was most proud. He was a small breast man himself. Disfavoring artificial enhancements that distorted the female body, and which, as far as he could tell, never felt quite right.

But he kept this opinion to himself, dutifully glancing at her exposed chest with his best expression of awe and admiration. It was expected. He and Barbara went back a long way.

Today she had small blotches under her eyes, unevenly covered by dabs of makeup. She hadn't gotten much sleep. He suspected she was still in shock over the death of her.... Lover? Boyfriend? Fiancé? Whatever he'd been. With Barbara you could never be sure.

The Judge had only observed Carl in the arbitration, giving his testimony or sitting quietly with his legal counsel while the business of sorting out the facts was carried out by opposing counsel. Early fifties, blue eyes, medium height, a little chubby inside a conservative suit likely dictated by his counsel. A large head with what was left of blond hair on a receding hairline, a round English face, punctuated by an aquiline nose, prominent, and pointed in the direction he spoke. At people, at exhibits, at the Judge. Not a handsome man by any means, but with an air of underlying confidence and authority that would attract many women.

Carl looked quite capable of creating the invention at the heart of the controversy. And he was supposed to have lots of money. Or so Frank, the Judge's law clerk, had foolishly whispered, earning him a stiff rebuke. The law was supposed to be blind to such matters. But then again Carl Greene would have to have money to attract Barbara. She was anything but blind.

"Oh Judge," Barbara launched in, "it was to be my... our... new future together. We'd planned it all. I was setting up our fancy engagement party. He was going to buy me a townhome we'd share for six months. Then a big wedding. We'd be happy forever. Now it's all gone. Poof. Ended in some damn back ally in Santa Monica. Life really sucks." Barbara was close to tears again.

"It sounds like it was a very quick romance, Barbara."

"Oh, it was, Judge. It was wonderful. We'd be married now, but of course we had to wait."

"For what?" asked the Judge.

"Well, you know, stuff, and of course the divorce."

"So Carl was still married during all this?" asked the Judge, sitting back in his chair a little to absorb this.

"Well yes, but it had been a miserable marriage, Judge. They hadn't slept together in years. And then she filed for divorce and has been trying to steal his money and grab all his inventions. He was going wind it all up right away so we could be married. File new papers and all. You know. All the formalities."

Yes, thought the Judge. All the formalities. Often a slip between cup and lip when it came to those formalities.

"How long were you seeing each other, Barbara?"

"We met just after that horrid weekend in Catalina when we were together."

"Barbara, we weren't 'together'. We were on the Island at the same time."

"Oh, I know, I know, Judge. You were with that young child, Cathy or something. Way too young for you dear."

"Katy. I was with Katy. And we're married now," said the Judge, finding it difficult to hide his satisfaction.

All Barbara could say was "Oh," doing her best to hide her malice for all 'younger' woman in general and this one in particular.

"How did you meet Carl?" asked the Judge.

"Well, that's a little sensitive, Judge."

"Anything you tell me is privileged, Barbara. You know that."

"We met at a club."

"Nothing unusual about that."

"Yes, well, you see, it was kind of a different club."

"How so?"

"Barbara looked around to be sure their conversation was private, then leaned closer over the table, batted her pretty brown eyes with the extended eyelashes at him and murmured, "S & M club."

"A what?" asked the Judge, fully astonished now, thinking at first he must have misheard. Sitting back even further in his chair.

"You know, sadomasochism. Where they tie people up and stuff. It's called The Grotto. Its right here, near LAX. It's all very hush hush. But loads of fun."

The Judge was taken aback.

He'd never associated Barbara with kinky sex. Their coupling had always been forthright, lusty, and passionate. And she'd been a bit of an exhibitionist. She got excited attacking him in places where they might get caught or seen, often to his puritan discomfort. But never anything strange or off the track. Had he been a satisfactory lover? Or had he only known the tip of the iceberg so to speak. He forcibly put the thought aside.

"How'd you end up in a place like that, Barbara?"

"My girlfriend's boyfriend is a member. He took us. It was slave auction night. It was so cool. It made you feel really free…"

"And you met Carl there?"

"Yes, he was a member in the club. I met the Grotto Mistress, Shadow. She's a famous dominatrix. She introduced me to Carl."

"Did you go back there with Carl?"

"Oh, many, many times Judge. You should go. You'd learn how to get out of your skin."

The Judge considered his skin was just fine as it was, even if there was a bit too much of it across his belly. But he was more interested in Carl's skin right now.

"But then it all changed, Judge." Barbara continued.

"How so?"

"About two weeks ago Carl told me he wasn't going back to The Grotto again. He said someone there wanted him to do something. And when he said no, they'd threatened him. He said they were powerful people. But that he wouldn't be bullied."

"Do you know what they wanted him to do?"

"No, he wouldn't tell me. Said it was better if I didn't know. Said he shouldn't have told me anything."

"Do you know what they threatened?"

"No."

"Any inkling of who they were?"

"He just said powerful people. Do you think they had something to do with what happened to Carl in the ally?"

"I don't know, Barbara. When did you last talk to Carl?"

"Thursday afternoon. Briefly." Barbara was tearing up again.

"What did you talk about?"

"Oh, you know. The date for our engagement announcement. An engagement party at the Johns' Beach Club. Stuff. He said he was going back to The Grotto that evening. He had to put a business matter to rest."

"Did he elaborate about the business matter or who he was meeting?

"No."

"Did Carl have close friends in the club?"

"You mean besides me? We were in a mad affair you know. It was so magical. And you can't image the kinky stuff we did. It was all so... delicious."

The Judge definitely didn't want to imagine. He deliberately pictured an elephant sitting at their table and then he tried not to think of the beast. That sometimes worked.

"There was one guy, a big importer or something, that Carl had a longtime bond with. I don't remember his name. But he's almost always at the club Saturday nights."

"Perhaps we could attend... if that's the right word... the club. And you could introduce me."

"Oh Judge," Barbara considerably brightened now. "You're asking me to go to The Grotto with you? What a sweetie. Of course I'll go."

Barbara's lashes batted up and down again. Like window shades.

"Barbara, you called me because you wanted me to find out who killed Carl. And it so happens I'm already trying to figure that out. I need to know what was going on at that club with Carl, and who was threatening him."

"Oh," said Barbara. "So it's not really a date?" Barbara was pulling up one of her pouty looks. "Can we at least pretend?"

"Barbara, Barbara, come on now," said the Judge. "We go back years. You know full well I'm newly married. Let's work together and see if we can find who did this to Carl."

Barbara's pout disappeared in a heartbeat, replaced by a soft smile.

"Kay, Judge, I understand. You can't blame a girl for trying. Perhaps there'll be another day when you're not so married. Life's like that you know. One big circle."

Like a Ferris wheel, thought the Judge. Turning, but never really moving.

"Shall we go tonight?" Barbara continued.

"Let's," said the Judge. "What time shall I pick you up?"

"Ten p.m., Judge. Here's my new address. The Grotto's just 15 minutes away, on the north side of LAX."

The Judge ordered Barbara another café latte, paid the check, and left. He glanced back to see Barbara staring after him with a mixture of fondness and sadness in her face.

Katy would not be happy about this, mused the

Judge.   Perhaps he wouldn't mention his... er... appointment, to his new wife.

CHAPTER 12
11:00 AM Saturday

The Judge stopped by his office, but decided to work from the boat over the weekend. It would be more comfortable with his arm. He collected some files to take and left a note for Frankie, his law clerk who'd be in later, giving some guidance on where to research the law on the scope of arbitration discovery, then left. Returning to the boat, he found Katy in a lather.

He'd bounded up the stern ladder to come face to face with her standing in front of the hatch. She stood with her hands on her slender hips, her chin tilted up at a thirty degree angle.

"You said you were going to be about an hour, Judge. It's been two and a half."

He could see she wanted to stamp her foot, but was manfully controlling herself. He knew something about females, always tricky to understand, but not much. His intuition told him this was not about being late. It was about Barbara. He'd definitely keep his old flame's name out of the conversation.

"The traffic was bad. I stopped at the office to pick up some files." He held up his file folder like it was exhibit A in a court room drama. "And I stopped for a Starbucks. I was desperate. Don't favor the coffee at *Crepe Cafe*. Not enough caffeine in it." He gave her his best cheerful smile.

Katy didn't buy it.

"Judge, we're having a baby together. And we're married now," as if it were an afterthought. "You can't go cotton-tailing around with old lovers on my time. Particularly not that woman." This last was said with a venom that made the Judge want to step back. "It's not right."

"Now Katy, this was strictly business."

"Bullshit, Judge. Tell me you didn't enjoy your secret little tete a tete with that floosy. Didn't admire her fake boobs. Didn't enjoy the walk down memory lane."

Katy was turning very pink now, her blood pressure no doubt near froth level.

"Look honey, why don't I take you out for a nice lunch and we'll put this all aside."

"You mean forget it. Give you a pass. You don't understand, do you Judge? Men! You don't understand at all."

"I'm trying to, Katy. Explain for me."

A tear eased down one cheek now. She was now feeling very sorry for herself. The Judge was damned if he could figure out why.

"It's like this Judge. You made me pregnant. Now I've got this little person growing in me. It's getting bigger and bigger. It's going to make me very fat. It's going to give me stretch marks. It's going to make my boobs unseemly big. It's going to suck away all my energy. It's going to give me tidal hormone swings and mood shifts that'll rock my psyche. When it finally comes out, things will be worse. I'll get no sleep. Be exhausted all the time.

We're supposed to be in this together. You're supposed to want me and love me even though I'm turning into this ghastly creature. Supposed to love my 'bump' as you've called it, making fun of me. You're supposed to support me emotionally, and be here for me. How do you think I feel when you disappear for hours for brunch with your ex-floosy?"

"I thought you wanted the kid, Katy."

It was the wrong thing to say. He knew it. But the words just came out unbidden. There was no way to take them back.

She spun on her heel and headed for the master stateroom, slamming the door behind her. He heard the distinct click of the lock.

Annie the dog roused herself out of a sound snooze to saunter over and plant herself in front of the closed door, giving the Judge an accusatory look.

The Judge stood there, not sure what do. Then he walked over to the door. He heard soft sobbing inside. He felt like a heel. He tried to get closer to the door to talk through it, but Annie wouldn't budge. The only way he was getting closer was to step on her. Annie just looked up at him, daring him to compound his sin with his foot.

Finally he shouted over the animal. "Katy, let me in. Let's talk about this. I'm really on your side. This Barbara meeting was just business."

This produced a small wail on the other side of the door.

He gave up then. Turned his back on the females, wife and dog, and stomped aft, up the steps, across the deck, and off the boat. Women were such annoying creatures. Emotionally unsteady. He had important things to do on his case. This whole discussion must wait. He fled for the sanctuary of his office.

CHAPTER 13
7:30 PM Saturday

The Judge returned to the boat as the sun disappeared into the horizon, having buried himself in a bundle of work piled up during the arbitration. Frankie never showed up to do the legal research as he'd promised to do. But the Judge was just as glad, valuing the solitary time to work on other clients. Delving into his work allowed him to forget about the upset with Katy. He wasn't so good at focusing on more than one thing at a time. And the work took pure concentration. Now as he lumbered aboard the swim step and up across the aft deck, he hoped this morning's unhappiness had just gone away.

The hatch was closed. It was getting dark and it was time to put lights on. But there were no lights aboard. This didn't bode well. He wished he'd thought to bring flowers. But it was too late now.

He opened the hatch and stepped down the stairs, softly calling, "Katy." There was no answer. He peeked around the main salon, then in the master's cabin. No Katy. No Annie the dog. No anyone.

He could feel old abandonment issues pressing in. Memories from his childhood he'd never quite got rid of. Had she left? Had he been that insensitive this morning? Was she okay? Perhaps someone had grabbed her as a way to get to him. He took his cell phone out and hurriedly dialed.

It rang twice and then went to voicemail. This wasn't good. He called again. It rang and rang again, unanswered. But this time he heard a companion cell ringing on the dock. Her cell phone. He recognized the special ring she'd set up for calls from him. Music from *The Phantom of the Opera.*

He got scared then.

He rushed up to the aft deck and peered down the dock in the deepening gloom.

There was Katy, walking down the dock. Her arms were loaded with two bags of groceries. Annie's leash wrapped around one wrist, the dog obediently in tow beside her.

The Judge gave a sigh of relief and lunged to the boat steps and down on to the dock. He took the groceries from her and set them down. Then he wrapped his arms around her and just held her. He could feel her melt into him, as though they were a single being. That's when he knew it'd be okay.

They didn't speak about the morning's disturbance for a while. She busied herself setting up a formal table cloth, candles, and flowers she bought, peonies, on the dining settee opposite the galley.

She handed him a vanilla vodka martini as he walked into the tiny galley space, and then turned to throw her arms around his neck, snuggling her body against him again. She cooked steaks in the small galley, smothered in burnt onions and a wine sauce. There was also a wedge salad with Russian dressing and steamed asparagus. It was delicious.

After the steaks and fixings were consumed, he reached across the table to put his hands on top of hers.

90

"About this morning, Katy."

She smiled at him then. That smile. Starting with her lips and rising into her aqua eyes, dancing with affection.

"It was an incredibly stupid thing to say, Judge. But I know you didn't mean to hurt me. You just blurted it out without thinking, as you do sometimes, dear."

He nodded, relieved, not wanting to risk words.

"The fact is I was having sort of a hormone attack. I couldn't control my emotions. This being pregnant with 'your' son is playing hell with my hormones. Sometimes I lose all rationality. I kind of go nuts over things which normally wouldn't bother me. I know you love me, Judge. I know I can trust you not to cheat. I know that burned-out wreck, Barbara, is no threat. But knowing it rationally is one thing. Dealing with it emotionally is different. Particularly with all the hormonal changes that sweep over me like a tide. It'll probably happen again, more than once, before we're through this. But next time, Judge, just come and hold me…. And keep your mouth shut." She smiled again, to take the sting out of her words.

The Judge nodded he understood.

"How'd your day go, dear? Did you make any progress on your case?"

He could see memories of the night before flooding into the back of her eyes as she spoke. His emergency call from the ER. His wound. The attack. The murder of Carl Greene. The possibility they were being followed.

She reached over and put her small hand on his arm again.

"Judge," she said, "you have to be careful. I don't want to lose you. And there are two of us counting on you now."

He flinched as she played her "two of us" card. He supposed this card would be in play now for a long, long time. Females were great, and needed and all. But damn, they were such compulsive nesters.

"How are your preparations going for this new arrival?" asked the Judge.

The Judge took a heavy swallow of his second martini and settled back to listen as Katy waded into a discussion of doctors, hospitals, and nursery needs. The Judge was tired, but tried to remain attentive and to insert pithy comments here and there to prove he was paying attention.

Somewhere along the way he worked in he had to go out again in a little bit to work on the case. He'd likely be back late. This got a brief pout, instantly replaced by a stiff upper lip expression worthy of the London Blitz. She was a hundred percent behind whatever he needed to do.

He followed up quickly with a question on baby car seat technology in an effort to distract her from asking for details. Where? Who? It worked. She immediately delved into a technical discussion of the latest designs of infant car seats and the pros, cons and statistics of each. She'd done her homework. She spent a good fifteen minutes educating him, cramming in more information than he'd ever want to know. Was it really significant which seat was more fire retardant? But he was attentive. It was important to her. So it was important to him that he listen.

His conscience was bothering him a little for being evasive and tricky about his 'appointment' later in the evening with Barbara. He wondered if he should just tell Katy. He'd feel better he knew. But then she'd be upset, perhaps wait up for him. Maybe jump down his throat again on his late return to the boat. He was undecided what to do.

"So, Katy, we're married now."

"We are."

"And we're sharing a life together."

"For all time."

"So we need to be honest with each other."

"We do, Judge."

"I mean honest about our feelings and stuff in the relationship."

"Absolutely."

"Open communication."

"Yes."

"Free from judgement."

"Well, I don't know about that, Judge. I mean if you're just wrong about something, dear, I'll tell you. Course since I'm rarely wrong it won't be an issue for you." Katy gave him a smirk.

"Hah." Said the Judge.

"So Katy, suppose there's information one of us has outside our relationship. Doesn't affect our relationship. Could be hurtful, or cause stress to the other. Should we be open and share that information, or be more protective of the other. Be discreet. Not share upsetting information that has no relevance to us?"

"That's an interesting question, Judge. I guess it depends. Can you give me an example?"

"Well, suppose I found out I had terminal cancer. That it would be quick. I'd die suddenly. But I didn't have long. I'd have an agenda I'd want to pursue. And you'd be at the center of it. But if I told you, you would be stressed, sad, panicky. So maybe that's something I wouldn't tell you. So we could enjoy our last times together just naturally."

"Christ, I'd want to know about that Judge, absolutely. But that's a bad example isn't it?"

"Perhaps."

"Why don't I short-circuit the issue for you Judge?"

"Okay," said the Judge, feeling like a spider entrapping a fly.

"If you're going out to meet that hussy, Barbara, tonight, I definitely don't want to hear about it."

The Judge opened his mouth to reply but found he had no words. So he just shut it again. This female was a god damn mind reader. He would have his hands full now they were married.

He left the boat about 10:00 p.m., leaving her to clean up and do the dishes. She didn't seem to mind domestic chores. In some ways females were so domesticated, and in other ways still so wild. He liked Katy's wild ways in bed. This thought made him smile as he briskly strolled off the dock and headed for his car.

Barbara lived in an older but established house in Playa Del Rey, part of her treasure trove from a generous settlement with her ex-husband. High on the edge of the bluff, it looked north out over the Playa Vista Wetlands, the Marina Del Rey Boat Harbor, and on to the Santa Monica Bay, curving along the City of

Santa Monica, Pacific Palisades, Topanga Beach, and all the way to Malibu.

Barbara opened the door on the first ring, as though she'd been standing behind it, waiting to spring. She was dressed in a red designer gown, full length, with engineered structural support to expose a plunging décolletage that seemed to go to her navel. It altered the geometry of her breasts so they looked twice as big as they really were. The Judge knew this "first hand", so to speak, because of Barbara's advances to him in Avalon some months before.

"Judge, how nice of you to pick me up," she cooed, as though his presence hadn't been pre-arranged. "Come in and let me make you a martini. I bought some of that special vodka you like."

"Now Barbara," he said, sounding even to himself like a prudish schoolmarm, "I think we should just go. This isn't a date. This is business. And touchy business at that. This is about murder."

She blinked at his bluntness, gave a soft sigh, and reached back inside for her coat and her purse. "All right, Judge. But you're missing a lot of fun we could have. You know you can lose your pants in my pad anytime you like." This was said with a smile that had just a hint of malice.

The Judge blushed slightly, but ignored her allusion to yesterday's headlines.

"Maybe next time," Barbara whispered, putting her hand on his arm and softening her barb.

The Judge just smiled. Barbara was incorrigible.

They drove out of Playa Del Rey to adjacent LAX. The Judge turned left, parallel to the airport, and later turned again, on to one of the main streets crossing the northern edge of the airport, following Barbara's directions. Planes settled low over them on final approaches, all roar and dark bulk, lit here and there with flashing strobes. The distant sky was alight with more planes coming in for landing in sequence, like fireflies strung out over the Los Angeles plain.

Barbara directed the Judge to park on the side of the road, next to an older warehouse complex, small, two story, with office space built out in front. A typical incubator space from the eighties. There was a low porch light on in front, barely illuminating small steps and an adjacent ramp for handicapped access, but no signage. Industrial blinds were closed across the small office windows and only a faint light showed through here and there. It didn't look like anything at all. Certainly not any type of club. The Judge looked over at Barbara, questions in his eyes.

Suddenly headlights pulled up beside them, and then the car parked along the curb in front. It was a new Cadillac Escalade sporting metallic blue paint so popular with the young generation. In the Judge's opinion it was a color hard to see on the road at night and in need of constant wash.

A man jumped out of the car, mid-thirties, animated, and walked to the rear lift-up door in back. Dressed in black slacks, black polo shirt and black sport coat, he was as dark as his car. Like a shadow. The rear hatch light went on, displaying a small overnight bag, black, and a red blanket thrown over some items arranged on the floor of the back compartment.

The man surreptitiously looked around, not noticing the Judge and Barbara in their darkened car sitting twelve feet away and watching through their front windshield. The man lifted the red blanket. He picked up a set of silver handcuffs, unlocked them, pocketed the key, and carefully put them in his bag. Then he picked up a long whip, all green and red woven leather. *Christmas colors,* thought the Judge. He carefully coiled it, almost caressing it as he did so, and deposited it in his bag. He held up a pair of leather thongs, briefly admiring them before depositing them in the bag. He picked up a yellow ball, with straps dangling from it. It reminded the Judge of the balls he'd seen lodged in people's mouths. This also was almost caressed before being deposited in the bag.

In a rush now, the man grabbed what looked like two rubber straps, a box of Kleenex, a folded towel, hand sanitizer in a pump dispenser, and a box of Trojans, tossing them all into his bag. He grabbed his bag and closed the hatch.

"Toys!" whispered Barbara with an impish giggle.

The Judge suddenly felt very uncomfortable. Even a tad queasy. Perhaps this wasn't such a good idea.

The man marched up the steps with his bag and rang a doorbell at the side, then turned and presented his face to a small video camera mounted just under the porch light. After 30 seconds there was a whirring and a buzz, and the front door apparently unlocked itself because the man pushed the door open and disappeared inside.

"Alright then," said the Judge, finally starting to breathe again, "Shall we go in?"

CHAPTER 14
11:00 PM Saturday

The Judge and Barbara followed in the footsteps of the man with the bag of toys. Barbara stuck her face up in front of the camera and they were buzzed in. They walked into a small office area, staffed by a chubby young lady behind a small nondescript wooden desk that had seen better days. The Judge could have been in any small manufacturing company's front office, except it was in the middle of the night and the young lady had enormous boobs covered only by a thin, almost see-through silk camisole. She wore stonewashed jeans and heavy violet eyeliner running up her lids and into her eyebrows. She smiled at Barbara, apparently a known patron of the establishment.

"Hi Leslie," said Barbara with a conspirator's smile.

"Hi Barbara. Who's your handsome escort?"

"This is my special friend for the night." Barbara sounded almost coy. "He goes by the name, 'Judge.'"

Leslie extended a hand laden with three rings and violet nail polish, softly shaking the Judge's paw. The Judge felt himself being assessed by skilled eyes, as if by a merchant in the bazaar.

The Judge produced his most benign smile, playing his role as uninitiated newbie, which of course he was.

Leslie pressed a button under her desk and a separate door unlatched behind her, allowing the noises of a large party in progress to drift in.

"Have fun, kids," said Leslie. "Don't do anything I wouldn't do." The look that passed between the two women raised the hair on the back of the Judge's neck.

Barbara swept through the door into the inner sanctum, territorially leading the Judge by the hand around a modesty wall that shielded a view of the bigger space from the open office door. The room was cavernous. Black walls supported a high black ceiling from which black air ducts and track lighting were suspended. A small stage rose at the other end of the room, surrounded by a semi-circle of sofas, small café tables and chairs, and a few benches.

The room was packed with people yelling at each other to be heard over the din, all the seats taken, with a large crowd left standing.. There might have been 250 people. It was hard to tell. Many wore outrageous costumes, or semi costumes. It was a kaleidoscope of color and movement and… sexuality. You could cut the pheromones in the air with a knife.

There was an auction of some sort going on atop the stage.

"It's the Saturday slave auction," giggled Barbara.

The Judge edged closer to her for security. Feeling very uncertain…

A small pink man, mid-forties, with a shaved head, was being introduced on stage by the auctioneer, a middle-aged lady of amazing girth with tousled blond hair and blue eyes peering out from puffy lids and pink cheeks. She wore a pink flapper's dress, pink pearls, and a pink boa wrapped around her neck, matching her cheeks. She was reading off a list of dos and don'ts. Mostly don'ts. Things the man apparently would not do.

"No water sports."

"No bloodletting."

"No drugs."

"No bareback."

"No needles."

"No piercings."

"No penetrations except with prior consent."

Satisfied, she folded the form she was reading, apparently filled out by the soon to be slave, and gestured for a round of applause which was fairly given.

The small pink man stepped out to the edge of the stage, waved at the crowd, and proceeded to disrobe. There was a titter from the audience, mostly from females but also from a few males, as the slave took off the skimpiest tightest leather briefs the Judge had ever seen, to display very modest plumbing, made smaller no doubt by the attention. He looked very shy. The Judge felt himself shriveling in sympathy.

The auctioneer lady reminded everyone they needed to have auction dollars to bid. They were to deposit canned goods stage left as part of a food drive for the homeless, in exchange for auction dollars. The Judge saw a large stack of canned and dry goods, packages of spaghetti, rice and such, and a small line of people with boxes and cans in hand, waiting their turn to make contributions in exchange for auction dollars. It was a macabre scene. Stacked food on one end of a stage, and the small pink man, nude, swirling his leather briefs over his head on the other.

The man made a bow, slowly turned to face the rear of the stage, and did another low bow, exposing what little had previously been left to imagination. This brought another round of enthusiastic applause and a few wolf whistles.

Then the auction began. And spirited it was. After early bids had washed out, the auction settled down to a price duel between two bidders. A tall thin man in the back corner of the room, late thirties, white, crewcut, small mean eyes and a tight smile that was almost a smirk. And a buxom blonde at the front, mid-fifties, pleasant features, but with leathery skin suggesting too much sun. The blonde won.

She bounced over to the corner of the stage where a brief sidebar was held between the new slave, the auctioneer and the blonde, after which the slave retrieved his briefs and put them on. The Judge sighed in relief. A paper was produced, filled in and signed, perhaps a contract.

The slave kneeled down on all fours. The blonde produced a shiny silver collar from her purse with a dog leash attached. With great tenderness she affixed the collar around the slave's neck. He was walked off by the leash, crawling on all fours, down the stage steps and off to the side. Toward private rooms at the back, Barbara informed him gleefully.

Another round of applause went up as he was led off. It was a lusty audience.

A very well-endowed blonde, female, mid-thirties, squeezed into a too tight bikini that looked like it might explode across the top, ascended the stage next and waved at the crowd. Another roar of appreciation. She was the next slave to be auctioned.

The Judge leaned over to Barbara and whispered, "Do you see Carl's friend in the audience?"

"No, Judge, but he might be in one of the back rooms behind the stage. Let's take a little tour."

They squeezed through the crowd and down the side of the stage, stepping around the pink man in his leather briefs and silver collar, still on all fours, still at the side of the stage, being asked to sit on his haunches and allow the crowd to pet his head.

There were a series of small rooms behind the stage, outfitted with various fixtures and furnishings. The first room had a king size bed with mirrors on all four walls and the ceiling. Barbara whispered that couples could stay the night here if they reserved it in advance, then gave the Judge a stage wink.

The next room held a large wheel with a polished wooden rim and iron spokes running from its center hub to the rim, big enough to tie someone onto it spread-eagle. Barbara pointed out the large array of iron spokes, explaining that arms could be tied at almost any angle, from high over your head, to perpendicular or straight down, and your legs could also be tied at various angles.

"Why is that important?" asked the Judge.

"Some club members are older and find it difficult to be tied on at a position with arms bound perpendicular, Judge. So this allows a 60 degree angle, or a 40 degree, or even a 20 degree."

"And what happens after you're tied on?"

"Judge! You're so cute. This is where your partner flogs you with a soft whip."

"Oh," was all the Judge could manage. His stomach was starting to churn again. He was regretting the heavy steak and the two martinis earlier.

The next room seemed to be a dress wardrobe room. Racks ran around three sides holding expensive gowns and dresses. The outfits all seemed unusually large.

"Are all the women Amazons?" he asked, pointing at the dresses and spreading his hands to show how large and long many were.

"Oh no, dear," said Barbara. "These outfits are for you, Judge, and other big men who enjoy cross dressing."

"I don't enjoy cross dressing," muttered the Judge.

"How do you know if you've never tried, Judge?" asked Barbara. "I'll bet you'd find it very liberating to be in a sequin dress and no underwear. You might want to skip the heels though, Judge. They're tricky."

"Good God," was all the Judge could manage. He seemed to have run out of vocabulary this evening.

The next room was the toy room. The shelves and bins running around its three walls were loaded with all manner of paraphernalia. Whips, chains, vibrators, rope, rubber ball gags, masks, gloves, hoods without eyeholes, paddles, handcuffs, floggers, hog ties, ticklers, and various other restraints and toys beckoned from the shelves.

"You can check out whatever you want here, Judge," explained Barbara. "It's like a lending library of toys."

The Judge quickly shoved his hands into his pockets, not wanting to touch anything. Barbara moved from bin to bin, picking up various implements and caressing each one gently. Explaining to the Judge which ones were the most fun.

The Judge suggested they move on, suddenly focusing on the possibility someone here at the party might know him.

Another room held a couch and a small bed. There was glass partition mounted floor-to-ceiling on one side, behind which sat an expensive looking TV camera on a mechanical pedestal.

"The club rents this space out to people who have porn websites. They can perform right here and blast it out across the net, just like a movie studio."

Further along there was a room with a large spa bubbling away. Awaiting frolicking bodies later in the evening.

There were two other rooms with beds, couches, and mirrors, one with a dining tables but no chairs, the other with two sets of head stocks right out witchcraft New England in the 1700s.

The Judge didn't ask about them. He didn't want to think about it.

Beyond the 'private' rooms, at the back of the warehouse, was a larger room, perhaps a third of the size of the front hall, with its own small stage decked out in ropes, rope swing, and hammock suspended from the ceiling. A bar ran down one side, with two busy bartenders, and a crowd clamoring for drinks.

Barbara pointed to a medium-size man, with powerful arms and shoulders encased in a beautifully cut sport jacket. Grey slacks offset a starched white dress shirt with French cuffs, open at the collar with several buttons undone, exposing the beginnings of a forest of hair.

He head had dark hair tightly cropped in military fashion, slightly receding, and a beard running down the sides of his jaw and ending in a modest goatee. His swarthy complexion and features suggested Southern Italian descent. Lively light brown eyes peered out from under bushy eyebrows, intelligent and warm.

Barbara tucked her arm in the Judge's and swanned them over to the end of the bar line in which the man was standing, leaning her head slightly on the Judge's shoulder.

The Judge wondered if there would be damning powder or make up on his coat. This little soiree could get him in a lot of trouble if he weren't careful. Unfortunately, it was a bit late for such concerns.

The man appraised the Judge keenly as they approached, then smiled as he recognized Barbara.

"Hello, Barbara," he said. "And who's this distinguished guest on your arm? My name's Allan Clark." His hand shot out to give a firm handshake.

Barbara introduced the Judge.

"Well, well," said Allan. "So you're the famous 'Judge'. I've heard about your exploits. Wasn't it Palos Verdes? And then in Avalon?"

"You get around," said the Judge.

"I hear things." said Allan. "What brings you to our club? Are you in the play?"

"He will be," interjected Barbara. "He's just never experimented before. But I'm going to help him along. He has the makings of a real player. I'm certain."

"No. No," protested the Judge. "I'm just a tourist here tonight. It's all very interesting. But not quite my cup of tea." He gave Barbara a soft nudge with his elbow.

"Oh, Judge," giggled Barbara. "See Allan, there's a part of him that really wants to play."

It was the final straw. The Judge wanted to keep to the business at hand. And then get out of this... this... club..

"Actually, Allan, I 'm now looking into the death of Carl Greene, a member of your club. Barbara tells me Carl was a friend."

Allan looked startled, poker face sliding down to replace the smile.

"Well, you're direct, Judge. I'll give you that."

"Perhaps we could have a private chat for a minute." Said the Judge. "I'd very much welcome any information you might have about Carl." Deliberately softening his tone and trotting out his best smile.

Allan's posture unstiffened a little, and warmth came flowing back to his eyes.

"Of course, Judge. If I can help in any way, I'll be glad to. I was horrified to hear about Carl."

The Judge stuffed a 100 dollar bill into Barbara's hand and asked her to buy drinks for the three of them. Barbara was miffed to be excluded, but couldn't think quickly enough to get around it, so she took over Allan's place in line, sticking her tongue out over Allan's back at the Judge as she did so.

Allan discreetly steered the Judge away from the drink line and over to an unoccupied corner at the side of the stage, making small talk as they walked. He produced a gold embossed card that declared him a customs broker, giving it to the Judge with a flourish. He was a charming bastard.

Leaning with Allan against the stage, the Judge said, "I understand you sponsored Carl for membership in the club."

"Yes. The club's not for everyone. But Carl and I had great fun exploring its unique character."

The Judge didn't want to imagine what this meant. Where was his elephant?

"When's the last time you saw Carl?"

"About two weeks ago. He said he was resigning his membership. It was an odd conversation. He said he didn't feel safe here. That he needed to avoid certain people in the club."

"Did he say why?"

"He implied there was some business offer he had turned down. The other side was not happy with the rejection. They were taking it personal, he said."

"Do you know what the business proposal was about?"

"No, not really. Something to do with technology Carl had invented was my impression."

"Did they threaten Carl?"

"I don't know."

"Do you know who it was in the club Carl was referring to?"

"Carl didn't say. But I saw him a couple of times in heated argument with one of our members. The woman wouldn't leave him alone. Kept pestering him about something. It got so every time he saw her he'd turn and head the other way. It may have been her. Course I can't say for sure. She didn't look like she'd be much of a threat. But perhaps she has friends."

"Is she here tonight?"

"Over in the bar line, next one up to order a drink."

Allan pointed to a woman in a black sequined dress, black shiny hair, mid-twenties. She looked to be an Asian Caucasian mix, probably part Chinese. She had the short frame of Asian ancestors and looked to be all well-toned muscle. Generous breasts were well displayed through the bra-less dress. High cheek bones framed her pale face and offset dark piercing eyes.

"Who is she?" asked the Judge.

"Cindy Kwan. A real estate broker and general fixer for deals on the Westside. Well known. Travels with lots of politicians. State, Federal and local. Represents a lot of big public companies, I understand. A go-to person to get things done in government, if you've got the budget. But dark rumors sometimes swirl about her."

"Like what?"

"Just gossip really. Nothing solid. Whispers of political payoffs, mob connections, international liaisons with rich offshore people, wild parties, and such. Don't take any of it serious myself. She's always been pleasant to me."

"How did Carl play in this club, Allan?"

"What do you mean, Judge?"

"Was he gay? Was he a switch hitter? Did he cross dress or go in for dominance or submission?"

Alan smiled now.

"Carl was a bit of a voyeur, like me. But it's all innocent fun. We like to watch. Occasionally we'll join in. But we're both really just dabblers. Not hard core like some of the members here. Just a bit of experimentation now and then. Keeps life interesting. I think Carl was mostly straight. But he was fascinated by some of the crazy antics that go on here. I think he was sad to leave the club."

"What about his wife?"

"You mean his ex-wife. Yana and Carl unofficially ended some years ago. Carl was in the process of trying to negotiate a property settlement in the split-up. He claimed it would cost him an arm and a leg. Trying to weasel out of sharing a portion of the community property. New technology stuff."

"Other than this disturbance with Ms. Kwan, did Carl have any other enemies, or perhaps difficulties with anyone?"

"No. Not as far as I know."

"Can you introduce me to Cindy?"

"Of course, Judge, follow me."

Allan sauntered over to Cindy with the Judge in tow as she pulled away from the bar.

"Hi gorgeous, meet my special friend. We all call him the Judge. He's been quite smitten by you from across the room."

Allan gave a wink and departed to help Barbara ferry drinks.

"So you're the Judge," said Cindy.

"That's what they call me."

He felt himself being scanned head to toe by a pair of large Asian eyes, so dark he couldn't see pupils.

Limpid damp pools filled with emotion. He could see interest there, curiosity, and then something else flared. What was it?

"I'll bet we could be an item, Judge," she said, putting her hand on his arm.

It was lust. He could feel it, like a white heat, reaching out to engulf him. He wanted to step back, but he held his ground.

"I see you're wearing pants tonight," she smirked. "But I understand they come off easily… for nocturnal swims…. My panties do too. Want to swim with me sometime? We could see how we fit together? Lots of things could swim between us."

Her eyes were full of excitement now. He had the feeling she wanted to get closer and perhaps bite him on the neck. He restrained an urge to flee.

Clearing his throat in his best judgelike manner, hoping to bring the conversation back to civil talk, he stood taller and said, "I'm investigating Carl Greene's murder."

This stopped her cold. Her hand left his arm like it had been scalded. She took a half step back, reappraising him now.

"Surely you don't think I had anything to do with that."

"Did you?"

"No."

"I heard you and Carl were not on the best of terms." Said the Judge. "That there were arguments. You made threats. He became frightened. He abandoned his membership here to get away from you. You wanted his technology is what I heard. Trying to bully him into a deal to sell it."

"You heard wrong, Mr. Judge." Her voice was ice. "Mr. Greene was unreasonable in his approach to business. He didn't understand the complexities of taking technology like his to market. He had childish ambitions to do it all himself. He would have failed. Business deals get proposed and rejected all the time. It's a common occurrence."

"So you didn't threaten Carl?"

"Never. And I'm not having a two bit-lawyer who pretends to be a judge slandering me or the interests I represent. You could get sued. You could find yourself with a restraining order. You could find yourself with thousands of dollars in legal defense bills in a heartbeat."

She held his eyes with hers now. Unblinking pools of pure malice. "You could go swimming again without your pants."

And then in a low hissing voice: "Perhaps even without your balls."

The Judge had to step back now. An involuntary reaction to the force of her venom.

"It looks like I touched a nerve," said the Judge. "Exactly who are these interests?"

Cindy spun on her heel and stalked away, leaving the Judge staring at her back. She did have a nice ass.

Barbara snagged him then, handing him a vanilla martini, and steering him back toward the main hall where another slave was being auctioned for the evening.

"You have to meet Shadow. She's so cool. She's the Mistress Dominatrix for The Grotto."

They waded through the crowd back to the office door, stopping short just past a second bar. A tall thin woman was there, chatting to guests. Perhaps six foot two, dressed in a white sequined gown, long spindly legs and arms, and an oblong face punctuated by an aquiline nose. She focused old wise eyes on the Judge, soft, brown, direct. She was much older than the Judge expected, perhaps early sixties.

But there was an aura about her of another time and place. Perhaps a salon in Paris two hundred years ago, or even much farther back, a crowded ceremonial tent somewhere in India with Alexander the Great.

The Judge extended his hand to grasp a frail birdlike hand with long delicate fingers made to play the piano. They made the Judge's large Welsh paw, designed to dig coal in the southern British Isles, look coarse and blunt.

"My name is Shadow," she said. "I heard you might come. It's an honor to meet you, Judge."

The Judge found himself bowing slightly in acknowledgement, showing old world manners he didn't know he had. "You have quite an establishment here," he said, trying to be non-committal, and hopefully sounding non-judgmental.

"There are vibrant communities of interest like this all over the country, Judge. All over the world. We try to establish rules here for safety, mutual respect and informed consent, prior to our play. I do hope you find your visit interesting tonight. And perhaps adopt a perspective for viewing our activities which is unfettered for a little by society's popular mores."

The Judge didn't know what to say. He smiled, bowed slightly again, and allowed himself to be led off to the bar by Barbara.

CHAPTER 15
2:00 AM Sunday

The Judge didn't get back to the boat until late. He crept aboard, hoping Katy would be asleep. But although the aft blackout curtains were pulled closed, she was stretched out in his white terry cloth robe two sizes too big on the master's cabin bed, reading a mystery novel.

She jumped up to give the Judge a hug, then pushed herself back from him, leaving air between his outstretched arms, her azure eyes narrowing as she inspected him.

"You smell like that woman," she said softly. Too softly for his liking.

"Who?" he said, momentarily disconcerted.

"You know fine well who. Barbara! You're wearing Barbara's dodgy signature scent all over you like a cheap suit. I acquiesced in you meeting her tonight, Judge, but I didn't expect you to crawl all over her."

Damn, damn, damn, thought the Judge. Katie was a Goddamn bloodhound.

He explained about The Grotto, and Carl's abandoned membership, and meeting Cindy and... and... Oh yes. It was Barbara that had been dating Carl, and so it was Barbara who had helped him get into The Grotto.

114

Katy listened with a poker face that was hard to read. Her arms were tightly crossed in front of her chest. When he'd finished, there was a lengthy silence that the Judge found intimidating.

Finally Katy smiled. One of her smiles that started in her lips and reached way up into her aqua eyes. It was like the rising sun. The Judge always smiled in return. He could feel the tension leaving her body. And for that matter, his as well.

"We're married now, Judge. You legally belong to me. Forever. And I'm carrying your child. We are bound to each other for life. I don't like that floozy. But I trust you. You do whatever you need to do to solve this case…. Within bounds of course."

There was that magnificent smile again. God he loved this woman. He took her in his arms and the two of them fell together across the queen bed in the captain's cabin. She hurriedly unbutton his shirt and undid his belt. She stood, took off his shoes and socks with a flourish, then grabbed his pants, underwear and all, tugging them off in one pull, leaving him nude on the bed. She dropped her terry cloth robe to the floor and lay down beside him, stroking his body in the places he liked most, using her hands and then her lips.

Soon he was over her, almost in a missionary position, but supporting his full weight with his hands, doing a plank.

"Come on," she whispered, "join with me. Come inside. I want to feel your weight. I want to hold you with my body."

He blushed, a rarity for the Judge.

"I don't want to squish the baby," he said.

She giggled then. "You won't squish him dear. It's very small right now. The size of a kidney bean. Come into me. I want you so."

And so he did.

Katy and the Judge awoke early the next morning. They walked over to the *Killer Shrimp Café*, a few steps from the boat, and settled in at one of the tables on its sun-washed deck for breakfast. The Marina was all blue water and light blue sky, calm and still.

Katie ate an enormous breakfast. She wolfed it down like she was starving. Perhaps she was. She was eating for two now. The Judge just had coffee and spread open his Wall Street Journal. He could feel her looking at him curiously over the coffee cup she was holding. Then she poked him under the table with her foot. She was like a pet, thought the Judge. She wanted attention, and she wanted it now. He folded up his newspaper and looked at her, his irritation evaporating.

"Okay, Judge. Tell me something exciting," she said.

"Like what?"

"You said once our patent system was broken. Start there."

"Oh, well, yes," said the Judge, brightening up at the prospect of expounding on U.S. patent law. He knew she was toying with him, but he couldn't help but snatch the bait. She played him like a fiddle sometimes. And he loved it, every damn time.

"Our U.S. patent system is encumbered by out-of-date procedures, limited resources, and obsolete guidelines, Katy. One result is the commonplace granting of overly-broad patents. Another result is an explosion of unjustified lawsuits by speculativ e patent

116

holders against large and small companies alike. The enormous legal costs to defend in such litigation, and even the mere threat of such litigation, is stifling the very technological innovation the patent system was supposed to secure and protect."

"Is that where the trolls live, Judge? They sound like they live under bridges and come out at night to make trouble."

Yes, patent speculators, or so called 'trolls', claim overly-broad patents for technologies that they do not intend to develop. Then they aggressively enforce their patents against anyone they can find and endeavor to negotiate outrageous licensing fees. If the licensing arrangements are declined, they have a war chest assembled to litigate their claims. Their suits are often brought against smaller companies which lack the resources to adequately defend themselves. They are also notorious for filing their suits in certain district courts around the country that are known to favor plaintiffs in patent lawsuits.

The current patent law and regulations encourage such lawsuits, fostering huge court costs and expenditures paid to lawyers by those who have to defend. Capital is wasted that would have been used to create jobs, invest in further research and development, increase product value, and increase shareholder value. Our patent system is threatening the core competitiveness of the U.S. as our companies jostle for business with competitors across the globe."

"What's the fix, Judge? Shoot all the attorneys? That's a common solution I hear. But what would I do without you?"

"The U.S. Patent and Trademark Office needs to be revamped, Katy. New procedures and better trained staff so that overly broad patents are not granted in the first instance. It needs to tighten its standards and deny new applications that are too obvious or not novel. Software patents have been issued for rounded corners and bouncing lists. Trivial patents that have little value and only spawn litigation. There's easily a quarter of a million such bad patents out there.

A post-patent grant procedure must be added, whereby third parties and companies can examine, independently evaluate, and challenge the patent grant, at the Patent and Trademark Office itself in a fair, public and expedited proceeding, outside the traditional courts system and before litigation can be initiated.

Damage awards in successful patent litigation must be limited to the proportional value of the component challenged, not the value of the entire product. Punitive damages should never be awarded automatically, but only where egregious willful conduct is proven. Forum shopping should be discouraged by requiring a reasonable connection between the jurisdiction and the underlying claim. Companies should not be held liable in U.S. courts for worldwide damages where acts of infringement are claimed to have occurred in other countries. And we should make the losers in patent lawsuits pay their opponents' legal fees."

"Wow, Judge, don't hold back on your opinions."

The Judge smiled, realizing he'd been on a rant.

"Okay, Katy, you tell me something exciting."

"I think we should paint the nursery a robin's-egg blue."

"Suppose it's a girl, Katy?"

"I'm certain it's a boy, Judge. I've known from the beginning when I felt that jolt inside when a part of you found my egg."

"You actually felt that?"

"I did. I didn't know what it was, then. But it was almost like a soft electric shock. Something I'd never felt before. Some part of me connected with some part of you and I could feel it. It was very exciting. Course now I know exactly what happened."

She smiled at him. All blue eyes, wide smile, and flush colors of a mother to be. They sat there for a while in silence, just enjoying the presence of the other, the quiet companionship, as lovers do.

Then Katy reached over to take his hands in hers and said softly, "Remember, dear, we have our big announcement to make tonight. I'm sure my parents will be thrilled to know you've made an honest woman out of me."

The Judge flinched. He'd put the blasted dinner with Katy's parents entirely out of his mind. Had forgotten it. Like an appointment with the dentist and his drill. You put it out of your mind until your calendar screams at you at the last minute that it's time.

She must have expected his reluctance. That's why she had both her hands clutching his. There appeared to be no escape.

Damn, Damn, Damn.

CHAPTER 16
10:00 AM Sunday

The Judge decided he'd go to his office Sunday morning to catch up on work. Perhaps Frankie would be there. But as the Judge pulled out of the Marina he thought of Friday and the unpleasant interview with Kaminsky. Kaminsky believed the Judge had a hand in Carl's death. He didn't like the Judge. He'd made that clear. It behooved the Judge to put a close on this Carl Greene case quickly and take Kaminisky off his back.

Barbara said she talked to Carl Thursday afternoon before his death. Carl had said he would return to the club that night. The night he was murdered. Things seemed to center on that club. The Judge decided to defer the office work and pay a visit to the club now, in the daylight. See if he could find out more about Carl's relationships there. The Judge swung his car around and headed for the northern side of LAX.

The front of The Grotto in the day was even drabber looking than at night. One more nondescript structure in a line of industrial buildings across from the landing apron for the airport. Windowed office in front, two story warehouse in back. There was no sign advertising The Grotto. You either knew about it or you didn't.

It was Sunday morning. He assumed the prior night's party was over, but expected there'd be cleanup after the fun. He parked in front and marched up the ramp to the office's glass door, which was unlocked, and pushed his way in.

Leslie was there behind her desk, now in modest clerical attire, large circles under her eyes. She'd no doubt stayed on late. She was working up art on her computer for some future event. She remembered the Judge at once and gave him a big smile, making him feel good.

"Hi, Leslie," said the Judge, "How're things?"

"Things is good, Judge. Could be better, but it don't help t' complain."

"Perhaps you can help me, Leslie. You know Carl Greene? A member here. Suddenly quit his membership a couple of weeks ago? Died in an alley Thursday night."

"Oh my God. I just heard 'bout it last night. Terrible."

"You know him?"

"Sure. Knew Carl real well. From the ground up you might say. Nice guy. Well endowed."

"Yes, well… was he here at the club last Thursday night, Leslie?"

"Didn't see him Judge. But I'm always 'coming and going' in the evenings. In and out like." She gave the Judge a tawdry wink. "I don't see everybody."

"Had Carl been around much lately at the parties?"

"Not lately. No. Not maybe the last two weeks."

"Did Carl have any enemies? Or people who disliked him?"

"I heard he and Cindy had a catfight a couple a weeks ago."

"Cindy Kwan?"

"Yeah."

"Anybody else?"

"Not that I know."

"Did he have any special relationships?"

"Y'mean other'n me?"

"Yes."

"Well, now ya mention it, think there was a guy he liked."

"On an intimate basis?" asked the Judge.

"Yeah. Carl was a switch hitter. Liked variety. Think he got in a little 'too deep' with this guy."

Another wink.

"Carl actually had a relationship with a gay guy?" the Judge asked.

"So I heard. A torrid affair. But over quick. Carl just dropped him. Crashed him on the rocks's what I heard. There was hurt feelings, anger. Ya know how gays are. They get emotional. Its cause their drives are strong. They're always out there."

The Judge didn't know. Didn't want to know.

"Do you know who the guy was, Leslie?"

"No. Was just a rumor. And some things Carl said."

"When did it end?"

"Not too long ago."

"Know anyone who might want to do harm to Carl?"

"God no, Judge. He was polite, clean. Followed the rules. A perfect member. I don't know anyone who'd wanna hurt him."

"What about his friend, Barbara?" asked the Judge. "How was that going?"

"Oh, poor Barbara. She must be crushed. Looked like she was tryin' awful hard to mousetrap Carl. Get him to put a ring on it. She's a hot mess. Running out of money and all. Poor dear."

"Did Carl make a commitment to her?"

Leslie sat back in her chair, looked at the Judge for a few seconds with knowing eyes, then showed a soft smile.

"Carl liked to make promises in the heat of passion, Judge. Don't we all? We all wanna please, maybe pretend it's about more than just getting off. But in the end, after you get off, reality always comes back."

"What are you saying, Leslie?"

"Carl was a player. I think he was no more gonna settle down with Barbara than he was with me, or anyone else. Carl was having too much fun."

"Do you think Shadow might know some things about Carl?"

"You can ask. She's here. Lemme just see if she has time."

Leslie lifted her bulk up from her desk and disappeared through the door into the warehouse.

A minute later Leslie was back, nodding to the Judge that Shadow could talk now.

"You should come back and have serious fun this evening, Judge," said Leslie. "I could give you a private tour. It'd be a lot more intimate than the one Barbara gave you. Promise. I get busy, but I think we could find a place to squeeze you in." A bat of the eyelashes.

"No, no Leslie, I'm married. Recently married." For some reason the Judge was starting to sweat.

"That don't bother me Judge. Come back when the honeymoon's over. And bring your gavel."

The Judge was buzzed into the door behind Leslie and told to walk to the back of the cavernous space, which he did, eager to put distance between himself and the front desk. These people were so direct they were scary.

The club looked different in the daytime. Without its dark shadows, purple and fluorescent lights and its eclectic crowd mingling about in strange attire, it looked tired and tawdry.

The stage was still there of course, a rope hanging from its ceiling, as were the velvet purple sofas, the individual rooms with their various equipment, and the makeshift bar, now empty of help. The Judge noticed there was no liquor license posted. No posting of room capacity. No lighted exit signs at the doors. No fire extinguishers hanging in handy places. The club was truly an underground establishment. Unpermitted. Unlicensed. Uninspected by the Department of Health and Safety. Why wasn't he surprised?

The Judge found Shadow at the bar at the very back, taking inventory of the booze. The Dominatrix looked different in the morning light too. Gone was the wild up do hair and the tight spandex jumpsuit that emphasized every line and muscle. Replaced by ragged looking jeans and a sweatshirt that didn't quite hide small breasts swinging around underneath. She looked tired without her makeup. Dark circles under her eyes. A pallor to her skin that implied exhaustion. It must be tough to run a club like this, thought the Judge. And she was no spring chicken.

She extended a slender hand, completely ringed across each knuckle, for a limp handshake.

"Have you heard about Carl Greene's death, Shadow?"

"I read about it in the paper yesterday. Shocking. Poor Carl. He didn't deserve to go like that."

"Like how?"

"The article said it was a knife fight."

"That's what I understand too," said the Judge. "Did you know Carl well?"

"He was a member for several years, Judge. Got to know him pretty well. But dominatrix services weren't his style. We were never intimate. I understand he had liaisons with several of our members."

"What was he like?"

"Carl was a lovely guy, Judge. Did you know he was on the streets once? Part of the homeless here in L.A., in Santa Monica I think. He was the one got the club to start its food drive for the homeless. You saw the fruits of that last night. Carl had empathy for people."

"Did he have any special friends?"

"Allan Clark. Cindy Kwan for a while. Leslie out front. And of course Barbara. He resigned his membership a few weeks ago you know."

"Yes, do you know why?"

"I don't really. I heard there was something of a continuing altercation with one of our female members."

"Cindy Kwan?"

"Yes."

"You know what it was about?"

"Judge, you might not understand, but I'm like a mother figure here. People confide in me. Tell me things they wouldn't tell anyone else. Seek my opinion and my advice. Trust I won't repeat things they disclose. Like a priest in a church. If I knew what the spat was about, I couldn't tell you. It'd be confidential."

"Even in the face of murder?"

Shadow sighed. "Yes".

"I understand Carl had a brief fling with a guy?"

"Yes."

"Who was the guy?"

"Again, Judge, what I know was told to me in confidence. Particularly in this instance. If the story got out it might destroy somebody's career."

"The gay guy?"

"Yes."

"Because he's closet gay?"

"Yes."

"And might have killed Carl in a blaze of anger over being dumped?"

"I doubt that. But it doesn't matter. I won't speak of the things told to me in confidence as the Mistress of this club."

"Carl told you about it?"

"Yes. He sought my advice. The man was a little intimidating."

The Judge could see Shadow would not bend.

"How'd you get started in this business, Shadow?"

Shadow's face broke into a smile.

"That's a long story, Judge. Got about three weeks?"

"Got a short version?"

"Born in New York. The Bronx. A very long time ago. Dad was from Germany. Mom from what's now Pakistan. Poor family. I was the oldest. Always interested in music. Someone gave me a broken down old accordion when I was nine. It was as big as I was. Later I saved and got an electric guitar out of a pawn shop. I loved that old guitar."

"How'd you get out of the Bronx?"

"As a teenager I became a groupie for a rock band. Abandoned home and moved into their tour bus. It was the acid scene back then. Free love. Open relationships. Art and music were sacred callings. I became assistant manager of the band. Then when the manager tripped out, I became manager. We traveled all over the U.S., Europe, the Far East. In my thirties I started organizing local rock concerts, first on the East Coast, then across the country. Raves were a new idea, so I moved into that space. That brought me to Los Angeles. This city's more open to alternate life styles than most. Better weather than San Francisco."

"And then?"

"Fell in love with an older man when I turned 40. We were together for 15 years. Best years of my life. Rented a place up in the Hollywood Hills. He was a lawyer like you, Judge. A kind man. I started a small S&M practice to keep busy. We had a wonderful life together. We all need love, Judge. We all seek that one person to connect with, trust, drop all our defenses with, share our small victories, and lament our periodic defeats. Curl up with and just touch. The human race is

127

so diverse in its sexual interests and responses, but at the bottom we're all the same. Small, furless, lost little creatures who think too much. Yearning for that warmth we lost when we departed the womb."

"What happened to the relationship, Shadow?"

"He died." Her eyes were wet now. Remembering. "So that was the end of the Hollywood Hills. I turned more to the S&M practice, partly for money, mostly because I needed to throw myself into something. Became a full-fledged Dominatrix. I'm good at it. Started a small club in the Valley. Reached out to my old friends from the rock band days in London, Frankfurt, Tokyo, as well as across the U.S. Did some traveling, lecturing, public performances. Built something of an international rep. Later I moved here with some longtime loyal employees and created The Grotto. That's my story, Judge. Kind of a checkered landscape. Sometimes that's our karma."

"What was your original name, Shadow, all the way back there in the Bronx?"

Shadow softly smiled.

"Bernard Schwartz."

CHAPTER 17
11:00 AM Sunday

The Judge thanked Shadow for her time and left, retracing his way through the warehouse, the small front office, and out into the bright California sun. Leaving behind a nest of shadows that couldn't follow.

He pulled the business card Allan Clark had given him out of his shirt pocket as he walked to his car. Clark's card said 'Customs Broker and International Importer'. The Judge wondered what he imported. He made a quick call for an appointment as he drove back toward Marina Del Rey.

He considered stopping by the boat to see if Katy wanted to come, but rejected the idea. Things were moving too fast. And he seemed to be in the middle of it, or perhaps falling through it. Like a fall guy. He needed to find out who killed Greene and quickly. He didn't want Katy associated with the case and getting hurt.

Clark had an expensive apartment beside the Marina Del Rey breakwater, practically hanging over its rocks. It was a picturesque site, blue water and boats, bright sails steaming seaward out the channel. Folks taking a weekend sail, or perhaps a sojourn to Catalina, the only inhabited island Southern California could boast along its shore. Not like Miami, a boater's paradise. Even so, he wouldn't trade all the Florida

Islands for the California weather. Even in late June.
No, particularly not in late June.

Clark's apartment building was one of several
attached units. All cedar shingles in varying shades of
fading walnut with matching dark trim. It felt like the
structure had washed up from the sea, somehow re-
assembling itself on the breakwater.

Clark opened the door on the first ring. Unlike
Shadow, he looked none the worse for wear. He
presented the same charming smile and elaborate
gestures that made him look so polished the night
before. He wore a white linen shirt with epaulettes on
the shoulders and double buttoned pockets right out of
the Philippines, the sleeves rolled up to display powerful
arms. His unruly chest hair was still on display below
his neck, the shirt unbuttoned one too many buttons.
The Judge wondered idly if he combed it at night.

"So nice to see you again, Judge. And so soon.
What a surprise. Sit down, sit down. What can I get
you? Perhaps a Dos Equis?"

The Judge settled into an overstuffed sofa
covered in a heavy rose brocade and looked around.
On three sides white walls supported dark beams and
displayed a large collection of landscapes, big and small,
all from the Far East, some brightly colored, others
horizon less images in muted colors. The fourth wall,
opposite the door was sliding glass, opening to a patio
and the Marina Del Rey channel beyond. He could see
the tops of sails gliding by. The magnificent view was
partly broken by the full size rickshaw to one side of
the patio, painted in bright orange and red with green
trim. A six foot porcelain Buddha sat to the other, all

bright yellow enamel with gold earrings and turquoise markings.

"You look to be a world traveler," said the Judge.

"I travel a lot in my business, Judge. Particularly the Far East. I import all sorts of fabulous things. It's great fun. And it pays the rent."

"I've always admired the vivid colors of the Orient," said the Judge. "Particularly when juxtaposed with the washed out drawings of the Zen artists."

"Oh, let me show you, Judge." Clark jumped to his feet and marched the Judge around the living room, explaining the providence and intent of each piece in a whirlwind tour.

"You have a marvelous collection, Allan, and obviously a good eye."

"You're so kind, Judge. I've been collecting for many years and this is just the tip of the iceberg. Perhaps when you have more time we can visit my warehouse."

"I'd like that. The reason for my visit was to get a little more background on Carl Greene. What were his habits? Who were his friends? And his lovers?"

"I'll help all I can, of course, Judge. Carl was a complex man."

"I understand you sponsored him into the club."

"Yes. Carl and I go way back. Practically grew up together. Best friends for years. I went to Shadow and arranged for Carl to join the club after he moved out on his wife. Shadow, Carl and I met for drinks. It turned into dinner, then some clubbing. Then we closed down a couple of my favorite bars in WeHo."

"West Hollywood?"

"Yes. Carl and Shadow hit it off immediately."

"What was Carl like?"

"He was very smart. A brilliant inventor. His training was electrical engineering. He was warm, friendly, very accepting. As you likely guessed, all sorts of lifestyles are represented in our club. Carl was very open to differing realities. Very relaxed."

"Did he participate in some of these differing realities?" asked the Judge.

"Oh yes. Carl liked to dabble."

"What sort of things was he into?"

"Well, you know. Different stuff. Dominance games. Ropes and knots. Role Playing. Obedience. I think he even did a little cross dressing."

"You introduced Barbara to Carl I understand?"

"Yes. Barbara's a one-off. Very clever. Very inventive in her play. Carl was attracted immediately."

The Judge didn't remember Barbara like that. He wondered how much she'd changed in the two years since they'd split. He'd have to ask. She what she'd say.

"Did he have liaisons with people other than Shadow and Barbara?"

"Of course. But very discretely. I don't think Barbara knew."

"Men as well as women?"

Allan blinked. He hadn't been prepared for the question. But he recovered smoothly.

"Gosh, I don't know Judge. I never saw him with a guy."

"I'd heard he had a male friend and it had been a fairly tempestuous relationship."

"Really. Well I don't know."

"Were any of his female relationships serious?"

"I don't think so. I don't think there was anyone special except Barbara."

"What about in his business, Allan. Did Carl have any business partners?"

"Funny you should ask that. I had the impression at one point there was a silent partner helping Carl with his new research."

"What made you think that?"

"It was something Carl said. How you could never trust partners. 'A partner was only as good as their money', or something like that."

"Do you know who it was?"

"No.

"Did Carl say this recently?"

"No. It was some time ago. Carl sounded bitter about it. Perhaps there'd been a falling out."

"I understand Carl was married."

"Trying to finalize a divorce and screw his ex." The statement just popped out of Allan's mouth and lay there. His face turned pink as he struggled to regain composure.

"Well," continued Allan, "what I mean is the divorce had been going on for a long time and I guess they were both sick of it. Carl and his attorney kept trying to force through a property division. Carve out his new technology as his separate property and so on. But Yana wasn't having any of it. Or so I understand."

"You seem to understand a lot, Allan. Carl told you this?"

"Yes. Well more or less."

"But you know the ex-wife?"

"Eh, no, I don't. Just what Carl told me and I heard around. You know how people gossip." Allan look uncomfortable.

"But you know her name is 'Yana'?"

"From Carl."

"And you knew about Carl's new technology?"

"Well, yes. I mean, no. Not really. Just tangentially. I mean Carl would refer to it sometimes. But never in specifics."

"How did you spend Thursday night, Allan?" the Judge asked.

Allan blinked again. His friendly cheerful face was dissolving now, like a wax mask left in the sun.

"I was in WeHo, staying over with friends."

Said just a little too quickly and a lot too defensively, thought the Judge.

"Look Judge, you think I had something to do with Carl's death? That'd be crazy."

"Would it?"

"We were old friends. Confidants. We shared wild times. I'm hardly a candidate for engineering his demise."

"Let's cut the bullshit, Allan. You do know Yana, don't you?"

The Judge was bluffing about what he knew. This time it worked.

"Ahhh, I guess maybe I do, now I think about it. I misspoke."

"You've met her more than once is what I understand."

The look of an animal caught in a trap flashed across Allan's face.

"Okay, so I've met her a couple of times. What's wrong with that? She's unattached. Free, white and over twenty-one."

"Is she pretty?

"Very."

"Why the breakup with Carl?"

"I think Carl just regressed. Forgot how to maintain a permanent relationship with a woman. A female is like a plant. She has to be watered, tended to, nurtured, made to feel safe, special, treasured. She needs to be spoken to, listened to, and taken care of. For females it's all about the relationship."

The Judge wondered what Katy would do if he came back to the boat and watered her. He bet he'd get slugged.

"And Carl couldn't provide those things for Yana?"

"Not anymore."

"Why?"

"I'm not sure. He was growing older. Feeling trapped I think. Feeling he was missing opportunities to have extraordinary experiences and do crazy things. Soon he'd be too old, then dead. He was running out of time. I guess we all feel that sometimes."

"When did you meet Yana?"

"Right after Carl joined the club. She called me. Worried about Carl. She said she wanted advice about Carl and the club. I think she had the wrong idea about the club."

"And you gave her advice?"

"I gave her the best advice I could. And she wanted to talk some more, so we met again for dinner."

"More than once?"

"I don't remember."

"Oh come on, Allan. That's not the sort of thing you'd forget. How many times did you and Yana meet up?"

Allan hung his head now, muttering, "Perhaps five or six"

"You mean a dozen."

"Yes."

"What's Yana like?"

"She's young for her age. Beautiful girl. Trusting. A little lost in this country. Russian. Very naïve about business and money. But sweet. Wants to do the right thing. Wants the divorce settlement to be fair. I tried to help her a little is all."

"So you discussed Yana's pending divorce with her? The property settlement? Who got financial rights in the new technology?"

"Yes." Another mutter.

"Did you give advice to Carl as well? About the divorce? About the property settlement? And the new technology?"

"I might have."

"Did you try to pressure Carl to include his new technology in the divorce settlement as community property? Help Yana get her fair share?"

"What if I did?" Allan showed anger now. "The bastard was sitting on that technology like it was his god damn turd. Wouldn't license the rights and convert it to cash. A lot of cash. Fighting tooth and nail to squeeze Yana out of any right to share in the proceeds. Was going to leave Yana out without a penny. She was going to end up on the street. Part of the homeless. Carl was an ugly, bitter old man underneath. He deserved what he got."

"Were you and Yana lovers, Allan?"

Allan opened his mouth but no sound came out. He looked like he was going to be apoplectic.

"Look, I don't think I have to answer that, Judge. You're not the police. You can't ask me personal questions like that and expect an answer."

"I think you just gave me the answer, Allan. Did Carl know?"

"No.... I mean there was nothing to know."

"Still seeing Yana?"

"We have dinner occasionally. So what?"

"Who owns the technology now that Carl's dead?" asked the Judge.

"I'm not sure. I guess perhaps Yana. Carl had no other relatives."

"So if the new technology works out, Yana could be very, very rich."

"She could."

"With Carl dead I can see you and Yana galloping off into the sunset with a lot of money to fund an extraordinary life. Doesn't that sound like a motive for murder?"

Allan's jaw clamped shut. Then he muttered, "I'm not answering any more questions, Judge."

The Judge stood up, extending his hand as a peace offering between gentlemen.

Allan shook it with relief, then sped ahead of the Judge to show him out the door, closing it quickly after him.

CHAPTER 18
4:00 PM Sunday

The Judge returned to *The Papillon* from his office, his arm reminding him it was time for another pill. And perhaps a nap. He and Katy were to have dinner with his new in-laws tonight. They didn't even know they were in-laws. They were about to find out. He'd have to be in top form.

Katy was gone, but Annie the dog was there, sprawled in the middle of the aft deck like a fur rug, refusing to move. The Judge had to step around her. She perked up as he headed into the galley. She knew full well where the food was stored. The Judge was usually good for a tidbit or two if he was eating. He knew he shouldn't feed her people food. But she was irresistible and she knew it. She played him like a fiddle.

His foot crunched down on the remains of a box of soda crackers. Left too close to the edge of the counter, they'd been fair game for the quadruped. Now there was nothing left but chewed cardboard and a lot of crumbs. No wonder her water dish was empty. She much have been very thirsty. He replenished her water and then cleaned up the mess on the floor. With the dog there was always something.

He washed his pain pill down with a beer. He knew he wasn't supposed to but Annie didn't object and Katy wasn't there. Then collapsed on the semi-circular bed in the master's cabin, the dog at his feet. The next thing he knew it was two hours later. Katy was climbing aboard, rocking the boat slightly.

"Hi sailor," she yelled down from the salon. "Any interest in taking advantage of a poor farm girl? A female bedazzled by sailors?" She giggled.

Prone on the bed, he stretched his arms out wide, and she came flying down the three steps in a rush, leaping over the ball of fur on the floor and throwing herself onto him. He held her like that for a long time, feeling her heart beat through her breast, listening to her breath, smelling the scent of her hair and her body. Gradually she made soft purring noises. She was asleep.

Later they made long passionate love, melding their bodies together the way lovers do. Unable to get enough of each other. He left her there spread eagle on her back, drifting off to sleep. He showered, shaved again for good luck, than settled on the settee in the salon to do some legal work before what promised to be a confrontational dinner.

Sometime later he was immersed in the elements of discovery law when he was jolted out of his online treatise by a screech.

"Eeee-yikes, Judge, we're way late," shouted Katy, hopping up the three stairs from the aft cabin, one heel on, one in hand. "You should have woke me. Oh my God. We're really late. Mom will be standing outside the restaurant pounding her foot."

Ten minutes later the Judge watched scenery fly by like a superfast slide show as Katy drove madly though the small and angling streets of South Venice in her Mustang, running yellows and scattering pedestrians, a determined look on her face. The Judge wondered if he ought to store a crash helmet on her back seat for next time he was a passenger.

He thought about the checkered history of this small beach community as it slid by. Founded in 1905 as the "Venice of America". Greedily snapped up in 1926 by the octopus city of Los Angeles. The teens and twenties saw it replete with amusement pier, miniature steam railroad, and Venetian style canals with arched bridges, imported gondolas and gondoliers. The depression hit hard, as did a succession of fires and floods, but Venice recovered in the early sixties with the 'Beats' who brought their Bohemian art, poetry and new-jazz to its coffee houses.

The hippies came next, and then the flower children. The 1984 Summer Olympics brought more tourists. Artists, vendors, musicians, body builders, palm readers, sidewalk artists, and all the rest followed, setting up shop on the Venice boardwalks. More recently Google, Snapchat, JibJab Bros. Studios, and a host of other high tech and film companies arrived. Part of the migration to the new 'Silicon Beach'.

And with the traffic came the homeless, swelling into a river of light occupation as the Great Recession of the early twenty-first century unfolded, then lingered. Venice now had some of the most expensive beachfront homes in Los Angeles. Yet certain streets were so poor and dangerous you didn't dare walk them at night. And the homeless were everywhere if you opened your eyes to look. Camped out on boardwalks. In the parks. On the streets.

"We're getting close," Katy shouted, interrupting the Judge's musings, gunning the Mustang down the final stretch toward the finish line.

The Judge wondered if little girls grew up fantasizing about bringing 'the one' home to dinner to be introduced. Like a proud fisherman, hauling home an enormous carp over his shoulder. The Judge was actually feeling a bit like a fish out of water. Awkward, and queasy. It was a dinner the Judge was not looking forward to. He'd not met Katy's father. But her mother, Florence Thorne, or 'Flo', was a pistol. And she didn't approve of their relationship. Then again, would he were their situations reversed?

You have a baby daughter. You nurture her into childhood, spend your life and your money bringing her through adolescence and high school. Fund college. Advise her as she chooses a career, seeks her first job. You hope for a good life for her. A good marriage to a good man. And perhaps if you're lucky, some grandchildren.

Then your child goes out and falls in love with somebody 20 years older. Hell, when he was born Florence was only seven. He could understand Florence's perspective. He could empathize with her angst. Her doubts. Could a relationship like that last? The dimming prospects of grandchildren. The certainty Katy was throwing half her life away on the Judge. The best half.

And who knew. Maybe Florence was right. Half of marriages seemed to end in divorce these days. And that was before you factored in their large age difference. A whole generation.

It didn't help his standing when Katy announced that she and the Judge had moved in together. It would be worse when Flo heard he and Katy were married, having eloped to Vegas a couple of weeks before. Depriving Florence of even the satisfaction of a big wedding where she could swan around amongst her fancy friends, showing off her daughter, if not the aged son-in-law.

Florence would hardly want to show off the Judge. A worn out and broken down old lawyer who'd somehow captivated her daughter. Beguiled Katy into an April-December marriage doomed from the start. No, his stock was not high with Katy's mother. There wasn't much he could do about it.

Tonight was the first part of Katy's plan. First the announcement they'd married. In a couple of weeks a second announcement that Katy was pregnant. The Judge was all for Katy simply taking her mother to lunch and breaking all the news, leaving him out of it. Katy called his plan for what it was. The Judge was just 'chicken'. And perhaps Katy's plan was best. She knew her parents. He was going to have to get along with his in-laws for a very long time.

Katy said it would be better to make the marriage announcement over a public dinner. Much like the ploy to tell your lover it was over. In a public place there'd be less tears, fewer angry words, and if you were lucky a plate wouldn't be thrown at you. Or so the theory went. But then again with Florence you never knew. The Judge was prepared to duck.

He gave a sigh. Katy's small hand immediately shot out to touch his thigh, giving it a reassuring pat. She was trying to buck him up. Well, he needed it.

142

Katy screeched to a stop almost in front of the restaurant at 7 p.m. sharp, then fidgeted nervously in her seat, waiting for the car ahead to be valeted away by a tired old valet.

Chinois On Main was a small satellite restaurant operated by the famous chef, Wolfgang Puck. He showed up from time to time to mingle with guests, dressed in his ceremonial starched white uniform with the button across the chest flap. The Judge had met him twice. A good showman.

Chinois had gaudy pink and turquoise neon lights spoking out around its front window. Like the Ferris wheel. All floating light and sparkle. Not going anywhere. The joint was tethered to this mixed block on Main Street with its tattoo parlor to one side, and its incense shop to the other.

Like the Ferris wheel, the Judge wasn't going anywhere either. Katy was his now, and her old bat mother could like it or lump it. He got out of the car, shoving his hands into his pockets, steeling himself for battle.

A homeless man was staked out on the pavement a discrete couple of feet from the restaurant door, positioned so you couldn't miss him as you entered. Unless you really tried.

The Judge reached into his pocket and dumped a twenty into the small wooden salad bowl beside the man. For luck. The man muttered some sort of blessing under his breath, saluting the Judge with two fingers to his forehead.

Or maybe it was a spell uttered against the approaching devil. A strident voice rang out behind him. "Hi darling… and, ah… Judge." Florence had arrived.

The restaurant was a long narrow retail shop space, converted with a bar down one side. At the far back was an open kitchen where a plethora of white-dressed cooks bustled around sizzling pans and flickering flames. Back to back ovens and stoves anchored the kitchen middle space. Chopping boards and food containers spread around its outer circumference. The cooks worked in the middle on both sides of twin ovens, alternatingly chopping, mixing and cooking. At the front of the kitchen sat a patron bar with high stools towering over the space as an overlook.

The space running from the patron bar forward to the large glass window in front was squeezed with too many tables filled with too many noisy patrons, their voices echoing off the open ceiling and exposed ducting. The concrete floor added to the din.

The patrons huddled together in line to announce themselves to a young hostess, dressed in sort of hippy cowboy leather, black chaps and vest over a short sleeve cream blouse, one arm covered with creeping tattoos. She sported a silver nose stud. The Judge was baffled by the markings and punctures affected by young people. More proof he was growing old.

After giving her daughter a big hug, Florence formally offered her hand to the Judge.

The Judge was always surprised by her strong handshake, that of a rancher or a farmer. Florence's blue eyes, similar to Katy's but a bit paler with age, pinned his with her usual sharp intensity. A line from

Don Quixote drifted across his mind: "still strong in tooth and claw."

Florence was all that.

She had just turned her odometer over past 60, but she carried herself well and kept herself up. Her reasonably slender figure and elegant carriage gave her a more youthful appearance. She was dressed tonight in a blue satin cocktail dress that deepened the blue in her eyes, and matching high heeled pumps. A gauzy pale blue scarf hid her leathery neck, covering wrinkles and age spots. A product of too much sun in Palm Desert. Her addiction of choice.

Their table wasn't quite ready yet, which was just as well as Daddy Thorne hadn't arrived. They threated through the crowed tables to the back of the restaurant, electing to wait on the tall stools overlooking the kitchen. They watched the dish preparation frenzy, turning now and then to view the lusty crowd chowing down at their backs. The kitchen was a ballet of pots, pans, multi-colored food stuffs and flame. The staff was all Latino. Scents of fragrant spices drifted up from the sizzling pans and mixing bowls, lending an exotic aura to the jumbled activity and the general din.

Katy discreetly sat between her mother and the Judge, giving him some buffer. The Judge didn't want to sit too close to Florence. He harbored an irrational fear he might be bitten.

Apparently Katy's dad, Ralph Thorne, was in route from a downtown meeting and running late. It would be a schlepp this time of night.

They watched as a cook pulled a large lobster from a cage. He held it up so it could shake its claws at them. Then plopped it down on his cutting board and

145

with one quick chop, cleaved the creature in half lengthwise. Both sides continued to move in contortions on the cutting board, apparently uncertain what had happened. Thinking it was still alive. It was a sad little dance, interrupted when the cook plunked the two halves into a large hot sauté pan, which immediately went onto a roaring fire on the range top. The halves hissed for a while, a high keening little noise that made the Judge ill. Then the halves went silent, giving up the ghost.

Florence looked over at the Judge to see what he thought of the show. Why did he feel those light blue eyes were measuring him for similar treatment?

Thankfully just then Katy's dad arrived.

He'd been away until just recently on a five-month assignment for the Navy, fine tuning the radar guidance systems on Navy ships carrying nuclear armed missiles. He was an engineer and an inventor, retired from one of the largest aerospace companies. He now spent his time as a contracted consultant for the Navy. Katy had said his work was so secret and his security clearance so high there were many countries he was not allowed to travel to, even on holiday. Surprisingly, they included the U.K., France and Germany.

The Judge watched him, awkwardly but with good nature, winding his way among the crowded tables to reach their position. He was perhaps six feet, but scrawny. Early sixties. With the lean face of a Yankee Farmer, punctuated by a large mouth that immediately broke into a generous smile upon seeing the Judge, standing off his bar stool to be introduced. A large bony hand shot out to shake the Judge's. Soft brown eyes looked directly into the Judge's with good humor. The Judge liked him immediately.

Instead of the traditional sport coat sans tie, or the flamboyant casual street attire of Venice, he wore an expensive looking but well used leather jacket over an engineer's blue checked shirt, and designer jeans that did little to hide a scrawny butt. He looked like he'd just arrived on his motorcycle. A Howard Hughes sort of character suddenly thrust into the twenty-first century, comfortable with his personal style and oblivious to what others thought.

The waiter arrived to report their table was ready. They abandoned their bar stools and headed toward the front of the restaurant, the Judge casting one last look at the poor halved creature sizzling in the sauté pan, vowing to avoid the lobster.

They were shown to a table set against the glass window which fronted the sidewalk and the street. Katy took over seat assignment, asserting her authority as the hosting party. The two women sat together, as did the men. The Judge was given the seat with his back to the side wall where he could watch the room and still look out the window, secure no one could sneak up from behind. Katy knew him well.

The perpetual string of pedestrians wandering by eyed them with interest. Particularly Katy. The Judge felt like he was sitting in a fish bowl. If he raised from the table a little he could see the shaggy head of the homeless man sitting outside under their window sill.

Katy was to his left, her back to the crowded restaurant, and her dad, Ralph was to his left, his back to the window. Florence sat opposite, where she could watch the cranking heads outside as people passed by and had a look at her daughter, and still view the tables to her left where split lobsters and other delicacies were being consumed.

Florence turned to the Judge with small smile, then said, "I understand you have trouble keeping your pants on, Judge." Referring to Friday's newspaper story with an underlying relish that verged on mean.

"I do," said the Judge, "Particularly around your daughter."

A light blush rose across Florence's cheek bones. The Judge grunted as he felt Katy's elbow shoved into his ribs with a vengeance. He didn't give a damn. If this was how it was going to be, by God it'd be shot for shot.

Katy's dad immediately waded in, giving Florence a "hold your damn tongue" look.

"Katy told us about the attack on you Friday night at the beach. We were appalled. How is your arm?"

"It's going to be okay. An inch to the right and I'd have a severed tendon." Assuming the role of victim now. Hoping for cover, and perhaps a little sympathy.

"Tell us what happened?" asked Ralph. Encouraging him to carry forward the wooden leg role.

The Judge launched into a colorful description of his Thursday evening on the Santa Monica Beach, the attack, diving into the water, jettisoning his pants, the swim, the Ferris Wheel, the fear of the hammerhead shark, coming back ashore, the LA Sheriff, the ambulance ride, and the pinch-faced nurse. As he described it, he had the feeling he was overlooking something. There was something out of place. But he couldn't quite put his finger on it. It was there though, locked in his self-conscious. What was he missing?

The waiter came as the Judge finished, and wine was ordered, a Shiraz by Farr, 2010, from Geelong in Victoria, Australia.

Katy accepted her glass of wine and pretended to sip from the glass, but the Judge noted the level of the wine never went down. Tricky.

Florence turned to the Judge and nodded at the top of the head of the person sitting on the sidewalk just outside their window. The one the Judge had given the money to as they'd walked in.

"You shouldn't encourage the homeless, Judge," Florence said. "They need to find jobs and stop mooching on other people's good will."

The Judge looked across the table at Florence. He knew she was baiting him. It was her nature. She couldn't help herself. Did he want to make a scene? It was going to be an arduous evening however it was played. He rationalized a poke or two might be justified without too much blowback from Katy.

Besides, Flo was technically his mother-in-law although she didn't know it. He was her son-in-law. A very old son-in-law indeed. But full-fledged just the same. Both parties had to envision a continuing relationship, for Katy's sake, and for the small peanut she was carrying.

It was good to establish some ground rules early on about how the relationship would be. That was done by the give and take in early contacts like this. He was a little handicapped of course. He had to tread more delicately since he knew they were now in-laws and she didn't. Still…..

"So, why do you think we have homeless, Florence?" He softened his blue eyes as he asked the question and tried to look innocent. Not like the steel trap jurist he was.

"They mostly have a screw loose, Judge. Some part of the population is always in that condition at any point in time. Of course we have more people now, so there are more of them. I'm all for live and let live. If they want to live in squalor and avoid working, let them."

She sat back in her chair, waiting to see what the Judge would say.

"Do you feel threatened by them?"

"Threatened? No. Well if I were in Watts or something I suppose. But not here in Santa Monica. I don't make eye contact. You make eye contact, you encourage them. They're all over you. Wanting money. There was some a lady in line to get on the freeway in front of me yesterday, Judge. She offered this guy standing at the on ramp with his cardboard sign a Carl's Whopper. After all, his sign said he had no money for food. 'No thanks', he shakes his head. He opens one palm and taps it with his finger, bellowing 'I need money for my rent, got any spare ones?' She rolled her window up and kept moving."

"So you don't think we should try to help them, Florence?"

"You can't really help these people, Judge. They're on the street because they want to be. So let them be. There have always been people like that.

Even in the thirties, and before. People too lazy to work."

"So I'm not sure what you're saying, Flo. Do they mostly have a screw lose, or are they mostly lazy?"

"Some are one, some are the other. Lots of them are both. We just have to ignore them and hope they'll go somewhere else."

"What sort of categories of people become homeless, do you think?"

"Like you said, Judge, looneys and lazies."

"There are some others I think , Florence. There are the vets, who fought for our country in the Middle East and Afghanistan. They have posttraumatic stress disorder, and find it difficult to cope. They often end up on the street. Should we ignore our vets?"

"Well… no. Course not. They served on the behalf of all of us. Those people need to be guided back into VA programs and such. We have a moral obligation to help them."

"I agree," said Ralph. "We have to stand by our vets."

"What about families, Florence? Dad lost his job. Jobs are tough to get in this recession. He does what he can. Part time jobs flipping hamburgers, serving as a night watchman. Little jobs. Not enough to save the house. Two small kids. A wife that also tries to get part-time employment. They're living in their car right now. Trying to save up the deposit so they can rent. Spending time during the days in parks. Struggling to feed everybody and keep the kids in school. Terribly embarrassed about their situation. They try to hide their poverty and pretend they are still okay. Their extended family may not even know they're living in their car. Do you help them?"

"Food stamps, day care after school, that sort of thing. Sure."

"How about temporary shelter? Until they get on their feet financially. Free job counseling and tech training to develop new skills in areas where jobs exist?"

"Okay, I'll buy into that."

"Who pays for it?"

"We all do I guess. Taxes."

"Okay, Florence, how about the alcoholics? People who had jobs and families and lives, but go down a long spiral through alcohol addiction. Now they've lost everything. They live only to feed their addiction. Do we help them?"

"How?"

"Shelter first. Rehab programs, counseling, ten-steps, job training. Dry them out. Get them qualified, then occupied. Try to fix their inside issues afterward."

"I suppose we should."

"What if it's a drug addiction?"

"I'm not for helping druggies."

"Is it any different than alcohol?"

"It's illegal."

"Does that make the wretch who's caught in the addiction any less worthy of help?"

"They have it coming. They should have known better."

"You can say the same of the alcoholics. Yet you're willing to help him."

"Well....."

"What about the people who are mentally ill? Perhaps schizophrenia or bipolar disorder. Do we take them off the streets and put them in some level of help facility? Night shelter, congregate care, a secure facility so they don't wonder off. Away from help. What have they done wrong to deserve a wretched life on the street?"

"That might get expensive"

"We're the richest country on the planet. We send thirty billion every year to assist the rest of the world's needy. Perhaps a lot of those dollars are better spent at home on 'our' homeless."

"Perhaps." A grudging admission.

Flow was turning visibly pinker as the Judge painted her into a corner. Katy jumped in, giving the Judge a sharp kick under the table.

"I'm going to have the branzino," she announced. "How about you, Judge?"

"Oh, sorry Katy, haven't looked," said the Judge, turning back to Flo.

"So another significant category of homeless are ex-cons, Florence. The people who for whatever reason got caught up in our antiquated criminal justice system. They are spit out the other side with felony records. They don't have a prayer of getting a job in this recession unless they luck into a handful of programs or have family connections. What do we do about them?"

"They're the dangerous ones," Flo said. "Surely you don't want to spend money on them."

"That's why I do want to spend money. They're the ones most likely to go back to their old life of crime if there's no other way to get by. If you or I had a family to support and no way to feed ourselves or them, wouldn't we steal?

We either spend to provide temporary shelter, job training and a reasonable method to expunge criminal records once they've done their time so they have no felony record, or we accept the existence of a whole underclass of desperate criminals on the streets of our cities."

Florence went silent, frustrated but unable to think of a reply.

"I think we're on the verge of solving the homeless problem here, Florence." The Judge couldn't resist the small taunt. Katy gave him a glare that would peel skin.

Ralph came to Flo's rescue, suggesting it was certainly time to put the dinner order in.

After the dinner order the party settled into polite conversation. The girls talked about new fashions and the escalating price of food. The Judge, reverting to his basic shy nature, peppered Ralph with questions, learning about his career and the many places he'd traveled. Avoiding disclosure about himself. The Judge peeked occasionally at Florence, who seemed to be going along with the flow, not chewing her lip as much. Maybe she was mellowing.

After the wine was poured, Ralph raised his glass and proposed a toast.

"To our new friend."

Katy raised her wine glass in the toast, but again the level of the wine didn't go down with the toast as she pretended to sip. Then Katy raised her glass again, saying, "I'll do you one better, Dad. We have an announcement." All heads turned.

"The Judge and I are no longer living in sin. We eloped three weeks ago. We're married!"

Florence's jaw dropped almost to the table, her eyes blank in shock. A huge smile spread across Ralph's face. He immediately extended a large hand over to the Judge, his eyes dancing with pleasure. This was no doubt where Katy got her wonderful smile.

"Welcome to the family, Judge," said Ralph, pumping the Judge's hand. Then he stood up and leaned over to give his daughter a big hug.

Florence took a huge slug of her wine. Then pasted something of a smile on her face, dutifully congratulating the Judge and her daughter, demonstrating a good sport attitude the Judge had to admire.

Katy was then peppered with questions about how they eloped, when and where, and asked to recite an elaborate description of all that happened.

"My daughter seems very happy," Florence said, turning to the Judge. He hoped this might by a symbolic olive branch.

"We are both very happy, Florence," said the Judge.

"I am a bit sad she didn't have a formal wedding. But people in Katy's generation don't seem to worry so much about the old traditions these days," said Florence.

Was this an indirect dig, wondered the Judge? Old Traditions. Katy's generation. Or was he just overly sensitive?

Katy immediately waded in to make another surprise announcement.

"We've decided to have a big reception, Mom. The Judge has reserved the California Club downtown for a Saturday Brunch. In twelve weeks. In the Lady's Dining Room. We'll need your and Dad's guest list right away so we can send the invitations out. Feel free to invite whoever you like. And I'm going to need your help planning the invitation, the menus, the table design, the flowers and just everything. Of course we'll have go shopping for new gowns to wear.

We'll have to take lunch at the California Club and check it all out." This was all said in a rush that left Katy quite breathless.

The Judge could see Flo's face visibly brighten. He'd won some points back here. This was good.

The girls went into planning mode now, Katy soliciting preliminary advice about menus, wines, flower arrangements, and music. Florence followed up with questions about what she should wear, what would Katy wear, who should be invited, and so on. Katy produced a proof of an invitation which was scrutinized by two bobbing heads. Ralph and the Judge were ignored.

Ralph had questions for the Judge. Where he went to school, where he grew up, why'd he become a lawyer, how come he was no longer a judge, was he enjoying his fresh start rebuilding a law practice, what sort of cases did he handle?

The questions were politely introduced in the natural ebb and flow of conversation, slowly drawing the Judge out of his shell. In the space of 15 minutes the Judge was surprised how much he'd told his new father-in-law. But it felt okay. Ralph had a real interest. He wanted to know the Judge better. And his questions were soft and perceptive, interwoven with sharing similar information about himself, his past and his future aspirations.

The Judge sensed a very soft but shrewd man. Relaxed with himself. Curious about the world around him and the people in it. Open to accepting the Judge into his family and creating a lasting friendship. The Judge found himself drawn to the man. Liking him more then he'd expected. The man was a gentleman of the old school.

The food arrived. By agreement, shared family style. There was Szechuan beef, Chinese chicken salad, tempura ahi sashimi with uni sauce, a whole sizzling catfish with ponzu dipping sauce, crispy spinach and duck fried rice. Shanghai lobster also showed up, mostly for Flo. Neither the Judge nor Katy could bring themselves to eat the poor creature. An Australian bottle of Hill of Grace Shiraz washed it down, leaving everybody but Katy a little lightheaded.

Between the wine and the warmth of Katy's dad, the Judge was feeling quite festive by the time the plates were cleared and desert menus arrived. Even Florence seemed more relaxed, small splotches of color appearing on her cheeks from the wine.

For the two females at the table planning the wedding reception was a blood sport.

CHAPTER 19
10:00 AM Monday

The Judge got a late start off the boat, and then sat awhile in his car, considering his options. Instinct told him he'd best set his other clients aside for now and get to the bottom of the Carl Greene case. This Ferris wheel ride would take him over the top and slam him down if he wasn't careful.

He pulled out his laptop, and searched for a Yana Greene in Santa Monica. She lived in a penthouse condo on Alta Avenue and Ocean. The high rent district.

The Judge dialed her number. When she answered he explained he was investigating Carl's death. He implied he was acting in an official capacity without saying so. Asked if he could speak to her for perhaps 20 minutes.

"Yes Mr. Judge. Come over," Yana said. She sounded a little sloshed.

The desk man in the lobby, a dapper young college student, called Yana to announce the Judge, then buzzed the elevator down for him. He was whisked to the 10th floor and deposited onto a flamboyant purple and grey carpet in a hallway paneled in mahogany and framed with expensive Andy Warhol and Roy Lichtenstein prints, all signed. A door opened at the far end and an attractive lady in bright purple booty shorts and black top beckoned him down the hall.

Yana wasn't at all what he'd expected. Younger than Carl, perhaps 34, but definitely not a mere girl as Allan Clark had said. And a looker all right, but more in an exotic kind of way. Short cropped black hair framed large blue green eyes with the slight hint of Mongolian lineage in their shape. She wore full on makeup, giving her a face a uniform color, except for the blush expertly applied along high cheek bones. She was tall, perhaps five foot nine, athletic and graceful. All strong muscular calves and thighs supporting a tight bottom, small waist and flat stomach. She had small breasts, barely covered by her soft top a size too small.

She didn't look the part of the grieving widow.

She said, "Good Morning," betraying a Russian accent and the scent of vodka. She invited the Judge in, leading him to a breakfast nook off a stainless steel kitchen that looked brand new and equipped to serve meals for the Ritz.

The Judge settled in with her over coffee and admired the view from his ten story perch. The hustle of traffic along Ocean Avenue, the greens of Palisades Park across the Street, and the blues of the endless Pacific Ocean stretching out to the horizon.

He could also see small drab shapes here and there on the Park lawn. Homeless souls sprawled out in the shade, their few possessions in shopping bags close beside. He wondered how the cliff dwellers in this building felt about the tragic stories working themselves out below. Did they even notice?

"I'm so sorry about your loss, Mrs. Greene."

Yana smiled a radiant smile.

"It is Miss. I filed for divorce from Carl. But please, call me Yana."

"Alright, Yana. I'm looking into Carl's murder. I'd like to ask you a few questions about you and Carl. Is that ok?"

"Do I have to answer?"

"I'd think you'd want to help catch Carl's murder, Yana. I'm sure the police have talked to you already. But we could call them back if you prefer. Make it more official."

"It is okay. Go ahead. Ask."

"I understand you were in the middle of a divorce?"

"Not middle. We are almost done. And then Carl gets himself killed. Screws everything up. Just my luck."

"Was it a friendly divorce?" asked the Judge.

Yana snorted.

"Don't be naive Mr. Judge. There is nothing friendly about divorce. It is about money. There is nothing friendly when it comes to money. Who gives what? Who keeps what? Who pays what? Who gets screwed? That is divorce. My ex-husband, Carl, was very angry. And he wanted to be cheap. But I have good lawyer.

That is joke, Judge. There are no 'good' lawyers. Only 'mean' lawyers. My lawyer is very expensive. Very mean. And Carl has to pay for him." Yana smirked with satisfaction.

"So it wasn't friendly?"

"It was fight. I get this place, Mercedes. I let Carl keep stupid dog. We still fight over whether I get interest in Carl's new technology."

"How did you and Carl get together?"

"I came over on student visa. To find a man. In Moscow we call it hunting visa. You hunt down American husband. Then you get green card. Then you are set. You don't marry Russian men. They drink too much. Cheat too much. Never home. Expect you to work, make money for them. And you still have to keep their house. You are allowed no opinions. No rights. Your job is to fuck in bed, have boy children, and keep your mouth shut. Some even beat you for sport. American men are soft, simple creatures. Much easier to get along with, to steer. Are you married, Judge?"

The green eyes narrowed, suddenly focused on the Judge. It made the hair on the back of his neck prickle. Like being watched from the jungle by a large cat. Assessing.

"Yes," said the Judge, perhaps a shade too quickly.

"A shame. You have nice eyes."

"How long were you married, Yana?"

"Eight years. It would have been better for me if it were over ten. But I could not take it anymore."

"How'd you meet?"

"I was having coffee, studying. Starbucks near Santa Monica City College. Carl comes in one afternoon, picks me up."

"Carl was older?"

"Yes, fifteen years. And has money. At least back then. There is nothing not to like."

"So you started dating."

"We date two years before I get him to propose. He is hard to corner. He is… was, slippery. But I

161

maneuver. We get married two years later. I was twenty-five. Carl, forty."

"Were you two happy for a while?"

"We were. It was my dream. Then trouble began."

"Trouble?"

"We had been married two years almost. One night I come home from classes, he is not home. A day. Then another. A week. No Carl.

I call all his friends, talk to business associates. No one has seen him. His mother and father died years before. He was only child. No family. There was an uncle back East somewhere but not close. I track down phone number and call the uncle. No Carl.

In middle of the second week I go to police. They could not find him either. Useless, just like in my country. So I am in foreign country. Married but no husband. I cannot even find someone else. The money stops of course. Carl had saved little. It was total crap place to be.

Four months later I literally stumble over Carl. In Palisades Park. Down there."

She nodded out the window at the park below. "I was running. Every morning. In park. Maybe that is why he's there. Maybe he wants to be found."

"What happened?" asked the Judge.

"It was early morning. No classes so I run. I was jogging along path. Tourists are out walking, other runners. It was sunny day. We're all having good time. But homeless are there too. Here. There. You step around. Don't make eye contact. They are mostly harmless. Sleep on grass with their stuff. Smell of urine and body odor. Thank God there is full time maintenance crew. Keeping things tolerable, yes?"

"It's not much different today, Yana. Except there's more of them."

"You're right. Anyway, homeless person has lined up two garbage bags filled with soiled blankets and clothes on patch of sidewalk. Their bed for the night. Blocks my path. I start to jog around. The man pops head up, looks at me. Recognition in his face. I stop. Bend down for closer look, he seems familiar. I almost fall over. Beneath wool cap, dirt and bruising, whiskers, it is Carl.

"In the park?"

"Yes, part of homeless. He was much disoriented, undernourished, and sick. Says he is conducting 'long term socioeconomic study', some bullshit, yes? Claims FBI stole his identity."

"What'd you do?"

"I took him to restaurant for soup. We turn heads walking in. Me and homeless man. But I have cash. They have to serve us. I persuade him to come home with me. That afternoon I get him cleaned up. Out to see a shrink doctor."

"What happened?"

"Carl was diagnosed with bipolar disorder and severe depression, yes? They put him on medication. Put him into counseling. The program works. Brings Carl back. We live together again. All fixed."

"So you were back together, Yana. That was good. So why the divorce? What happened?"

"Four more years. I am only twenty-three when we first meet. People grow up Mr. Judge, change. Get old. Grow apart. It is huge age difference, fifteen

163

years. We are different generations. It was unreasonable to expect to last, yes?"

The Judge shifted uncomfortably in his chair.

"Things slowly died. Like long dance where music gradually slows down, slower and slower. You find yourself barely dragging across floor. Slowed steps you take more out of habit than desire.

It is not all Carl's fault. It is not all mine. It just is. He comes home later and later. All the time he is moody and depressed. Bitching about his work. Like it is my fault.

I stop looking forward to him coming home. I widen my circle of friends. Younger, my age. Many single. Or married and bored. Like me, yes? I am going out at night sometimes with friends. I am making my own social life since there is none at home. Carl barely talks to me anymore.

In the end, he is not interested in coming home at all. And I am no longer caring.

Then I hear Carl is chasing other women. One fantastic Russian woman is not enough for him. It is awful. When he is does come home at night, he is smelling of cheap perfume, sweat, sex. This is final straw. I kick Carl out of my bed. Out of here. He seems happy to go."

"Where'd Carl go?"

"His condo. He sets up shop in Playa Del Rey with stupid dog. Good riddance."

"And that's how it ended, Yana?"

"No. Then! Then! Carl almost wrecks my citizenship. I was still on green card. I have decided earlier when things are starting to fall apart I should better become citizen. Protect myself, yes? To get citizenship you must go in with husband and talk to government twits in separate rooms. Talk about tooth paste. What side of bed you sleep. What you are liking to cook. Sex life. What kind condoms you use. Hah! All this domestic crap.

But Carl is not living with me. He has moved out. So he knows nothing. I am having to drag him back. Make reconciliation. Work on him to cooperate. Pound information in so he will remember. Dragging him downtown. Make him go through interview. For a clever engineer he is incredibly dense."

"But the reconciliation didn't last?"

"No. We have developed separate lives by then. I am very young when we married. Maybe I just grew up. Maybe Carl just grew old."

"What made you finally file for a divorce?"

"After we split again, was only thing that made sense. I got citizenship. Then I file. It was obvious what needs to happen. I thought we could be friends. Have friendly divorce. I was being naïve."

"Carl was angry about the divorce?" asked the Judge.

"He is livid. Male pride. Then when it became clear there will be property settlement, that he is to give me half his property, he squeals like stuck pig."

"And the divorce drug on?"

"Almost two years. I have to wait and wait and wait. Carl won't agree to nothing. In Moscow we don't wait like this. It's very clear. Your ex signs the papers, period, or someone comes along and breaks leg. You Americans are very inefficient."

"And did you see Carl occasionally?"

"Not at first. This last spring Carl wants to try reconciliation again even though we're living separate. Carl found out how much the divorce was going to cost him. So we started talking. Meeting for coffee. No booze. But there was nothing there anymore. He let slip about his new technology at one of our coffees. That's how I found out about it."

"Do you know who Carl's current friends are?"

"I am thinking they are mostly from that awful sex club he joins. The Cave, or The Cavern, something."

"The Grotto?"

"That is it. Awful place. I also heard Carl's taken himself guy lover. A gay….Men!"

"Did he have any close female friends?"

"Just that woman."

"What woman?"

"Some older woman he picks up at Grotto."

"Older than Carl?"

"No one is older than Carl. Carl is born old. This was some local female. A retread. Married before. Looking for new guy to latch on to. Barbs or something."

"Barbara?"

"That is her. Nice enough I guess if you like American woman. I meet her once. Fake boobs. Body starting to sag little. Trolling desperately for new nest."

"You don't think much of American women?"

"They are okay if you like that sort of thing. Soft. Spoilt. Entitled. Opinionated. Boring in bed. Don't really understand how to hold a male once they have one. That is why I like it here. Russian women have advantage."

"Did Carl have any enemies? Someone who might have threatened him, or had a reason to dislike him?"

"Besides me? I want to kill bastard myself. Holding me hostage in divorce crap two years. You will probably be hearing about this. Last time we met outside courtroom, after another dumb hearing, he tells me he will keep this crap going ten years, just to watch me squirm. I get mad. Tell him he is dead man. I would have some Russian friends pay him visit."

"How'd he respond?"

"He just laughs. That's when I claw his face. My attorney has to pull me off him. I would have strangled him right there."

"Besides you, was anyone else angry with him?"

"No idea."

"I heard you were angry that Carl wouldn't give you a half interest in his new technology. As part of the divorce settlement."

"My lawyer still fights on that. He is saying we have difficult case, but will try. That is big jackpot. Carl's new tech stuff. Carl's pretty much broke except for that. Poured all his money into it last two years."

"Do you know what the new technology does?"

"No. He is careful not to let me know anything about it. Did not want to share information or admit I had stake in it. But I heard he had offer to sell it. That's what needs to happen. He needs to sell and give me my half. Carl is stubborn and unrealistic. Thinks he can commercialize it himself. No way in hell. He has no smarts, no experience, no capital. My lawyer will try to force sale through divorce court if we can prove it is part of our assets. Our community stuff."

"Ever run into an Allan Clark?"

"Don't know the name."

"That's strange, he says he knows you. In fact, he implied he knew you intimately."

"Hah!" Color now appeared in Yana's cheeks. "I am Russian girl. We don't keep track of men we screw. It is natural thing, like scratching your back. Nothing more. We don't have your silly Puritan attitudes."

"So you remember Allan now?"

"I am not married anymore. I do as I please."

"But Allan was an old friend and confidant of Carl's."

"So?"

"So did you use Allan to find out what was going on with Carl's new technology? Maybe encourage Allan to persuade Carl he should sell out and split the cash fifty-fifty in your property settlement?"

"Carl was being pig as usual. There was legitimate offer to pay quarter of billion dollars for rights to his new stuff." Yana's eyes got big and round. "Carl needed to take offer and split cash with me. He knew it. I knew it. We all knew it. It is fair. So maybe Allan and I did work together to encourage what is fair."

"And you paid Allan with intimacy, Yana?" The Judge couldn't help himself from asking the question. He was being petty and he knew it. She was a Russian woman, if not a girl. He couldn't fault her for ignoring the perspective her adopted country placed on such transactions.

"Of course. I give him wonderful romance. Secret dinners, rendezvous at boutique hotels, hidden emails. All very dramatic. American men love their drama. Allan enjoyed every inch of it." She smirked. "I guess it is over now Carl is dead. Shame. Perhaps I will continue, but just for fun this time. Have to see."

"Who was the buyer for the technology, Yana?"

Yana's head snapped up. Fear flickered in her eyes.

"I have nothing to say about that. Nothing. Powerful people with money."

"So you wanted the technology sold. Carl wouldn't sell. You enlisted Allan Clark to persuade Carl to sell. That didn't work. It was the only source of significant cash for you out of the divorce. Did I get that all right?"

"Pretty much."

"So might you have considered getting rid of Carl as a solution to the problem? You said in Russia you break legs. Do you also lose people when they become troublesome?"

"You think I killed Carl? I go into alley with carving knife and stab him in the gut?" Yana's chin came up. She was angry now.

"Perhaps you used Allan Clark. Or some homeless gang of ruffians you knew. Or perhaps your powerful buyers for the technology arranged it?"

"You son of bitch. How dare you accuse me? Get out of my kitchen now. You know nothing about me, or Carl, or relationship. I'm not talking anymore."

Tears welled up in Yana's eyes.

"You still have feelings for Carl," said the Judge.

"I loved the *gavnoyed* you idiot. In spite everything."

Yana turned her head away, one hand over her mouth, holding back a sob, pointing back with the other toward the door. Motioning for the Judge to leave.

"I'm sorry I upset you Yana. But certain questions needed to be asked. I'm going to find out who did this to Carl. And I'm going to put them away. Here's my card in case you think of anything else."

He got up then, laying his card on the table. Leaving the condo. Leaving Yana there, head turned, staring out at the blue Pacific, her narrow shoulders shaking with grief.

CHAPTER 20
11:00 AM Monday

The Judge checked his watch. He pulled one of his arbitration files from the back seat, the one with the name and addresses of the parties and their lawyers, and flipped through to Carl's contact information. Only his home was listed.

He thought a minute and then reached for his cell, dialing Barbara. She answered at once.

"Hello, Judge. What's you up to?"

"Hi Barbara. I may need your help again. You said you and Carl were engaged. Were you part time living with him?"

"Absolutely, Judge. I spent more time in Playa Del Rey than I did in my own apartment."

"Do you still have a key? Perhaps personal things still there?"

"Yes and yes, Judge. Some clothes and some of my jewelry. And my favorite necklace. The one with the little jade stones you bought me in Nassau. Remember our get-away? You were so strong, Judge. God that was a trip. When we came back to L.A. I walked bow-legged for a week."

The Judge could hear a titter at the other end. Jesus, Barbara had a memory like an elephant.

"That was a long time ago, Barbara. But I'm glad you have good memories." It sounded lame but it was all he could think of. "Why don't I pick you up

171

right now and we'll drive down to Playa Del Rey Beach and get your stuff. I'd like to see inside Carl's apartment."

"You mean like another date? Oh Judge, I'd love to. What a great idea. Pick me up in fifteen. You can count on me. I'll be special ready for you."

The line clicked dead before the Judge could protest. It was useless discussing things with Barbara anyway. You just had to keep a strong wall.

The Judge called Barbara again on the cell as he pulled up in front of her bluff home. She came tearing out of the front door in a blue polka-dotted dress barely legal in length and cut, clearly unencumbered by bra. When she turned to lock her door, he admired her back, bare skin exposed in a deep V cut. Jesus, she still looked good.

She piled herself into the car, hiking her skirt up further. Leaving it at the high water mark, perhaps anticipating a flood. The Judge endured Barbara's endless chatter, mostly about the old days and how perfect they'd been together, while he plowed through traffic, winding his way down the bluff to the beach, and then to the North end of Playa Del Rey where it cozied up to the Marina Del Rey breakwater.

He cut across Culver Boulevard and into the warren of narrow streets and small overbuilt lots that was Play Del Rey at the beach.

Carl's condo was part of a small development on Vista del Mar, facing the sand. There was no security gate. The six units were each one story. Each with its own small porch entrance. Barbara jumped out of the car and marched up to the one on the right with an attitude of possession. There would be no questions from neighbors the Judge was sure.

She opened the door a crack with her key and called softly, "Wheezy, Wheezy, here Wheezy."

"Who's Wheezy, Barbara?"

"Carl's pit bull. Someone must have taken him to the kennel. He's not here."

Just as well, thought the Judge.

He stepped into a small entry hall with a guest half bath to the left. There was a fair-sized living room, blond wood floor, light beige walls, two expensive oriental carpets dividing the space. A seating area around a fireplace in the back wall and a second seating area to the Judge's right directed toward windows that looked out on the beach. Across the living room a small hall led to what looked to be two bedrooms on one side, and a master bedroom and bath on the other. A small dining area to the left was adjoined to a small kitchen, divided by a bar and bar stools.

It would have been a nice place to settle into if it hadn't been completely tossed. A professional had gone through. In the living room the furniture was all overturned so the underneath and bottoms could be examined. Firewood had been dragged out of the fireplace and scattered. Pictures had been removed from the walls, inspected and then dumped on the floor. The two carpets were upside down in two large lumps. The kitchen cabinets had been ransacked, their contents strewn on counters and the floor.

Barbara gasped as she came in behind the Judge. Then she sank onto one of the bar stools and began cry.

The Judge wanted to console her. But experience whispered not to get too close. Barbara was emotional. But she was also tricky, territorial and very sticky. You got too close, you could get stuck. It was then hard to get unstuck. She'd love to restart their old affair. Any weakness on his part would be interpreted as encouragement.

He carefully walked around the dishes strewn across the floor of the kitchen and peered into the open cabinets. They were mostly empty. He moved to the refrigerator, which was closed. Things inside were re-arranged, some things on their side. The ice cube trays were all upside down in the freezer, and frozen waffles and cookie dough had been pushed together to one corner along with ice cream and frozen hamburger.

The Judge walked down the hall and peeked into the master bedroom and then the bath. It was the same story.

Carl was an engineer. If he'd hidden something important here, where would he hide it? He walked into a second bedroom. It had been converted to an office. A table desk lay tipped over on its side, a desktop computer, smashed and dumped on the floor beside a now broken desk lamp. An upside down office chair, its upholstery ripped open from the bottom. Miscellaneous papers were strewn here and there, apparently from the desk top, its two small drawers, and the overturned file cabinet in the middle of the room.

The Judge turned to Barbara, who had come into the bedroom behind him, eyes wide.

"Did Carl have any secret hiding place in the condo? A place the people searching here might not have found."

Barbara thought a minute.

"In the living room." She said. "I saw him once sliding a brick underneath the fireplace mantel. He got quite agitated when I caught him. Snapped at me to stop sneaking up on him."

"Show me."

Barbara took him back to the living room. The fireplace was built atop a platform of brick which was perhaps six inches off the floor. The brick served as a low seat in front. The brick top had a lip extending over the brick wall beneath that supported it. Barbara pointed underneath the lip, at the left corner.

The Judge got down on all fours with his head on the floor and had a peek. Then he reached in and tried to dislodge any loose bricks.

"Get me a knife or something from the kitchen, would you Barbs?"

Barbara came back with a steak knife and handed it down. The Judge shoved it under and pried out the corner brick. The brick was hollowed out, as was the one behind it, leaving a small pocket. The Judge reached in and came out with a jump drive, pleased at his success.

"Is it something important?" asked Barbara.

"Perhaps, Barbara. We'll have to see. Where are your things?"

Barbara led the way back down the hall to the third bedroom. The closet here was where Barbara kept her stuff. Like many women, Barbara had a shoe fetish. There were over 20 pairs. The shoes no doubt had been neatly stacked in built-in shoe shelves made for them, but someone had yanked them all out, dumping them in a pile on the carpet.

Barbara made a small animal noise and slumped to her knees on to the carpet, reaching out with her arms to sweep the shoes in close, as though they were small pets that had been violated. The Judge saw tears of anger as she carefully examined each one, matched it with its partner, and stood the pairs up in a semi-circle around her.

He found trash bags in the kitchen and helped Barbara pack up her clothes, shoes and jewelry, carting it out to his car, filling up first the trunk and then the backseat. It took several trips. Particularly for the shoes. Barbara's ancestors couldn't have been camp followers. They'd never have found enough bodies to move their stuff from their first camp.

Barbara was morose and silent on the ride back to her house. Not at all her bubbly self. She finally muttered as they hefted the last two loads of stuff into her living room, "You get 'em Judge. You find out who killed poor Carl and you fry their ass."

CHAPTER 21
2:30 PM Monday

The Judge headed to his office, perplexed. There seemed to be several people upset with Carl, and plenty who'd benefit from his death. Over fifty percent of homicides in the United States were committed by someone the victim knew. Those odds would suggest Carl knew his killer. But the Judge believed the person who stuck the knife in Carl's neck was someone Carl didn't know.

The Judge didn't know the gang member who attacked him on the beach. That could have been a one-off attack of opportunity on a solitary beach walker at night. Or the gang was out to get the Judge and it was a contract job. The Judge believed the latter. And that the two events were tied together. The Judge's assailants were going to use knives. Carl was killed with a knife. Both attacks happened about the same time and in the same geographical area. The same gang that attacked the Judge had killed Carl in the ally. He was certain of it.

The question became who hired the gang? Who put out the contract on Carl? And maybe the Judge? And why?

There was Carl's ex-wife, Yana, aligned with her paramour, Allan Clark. She, and perhaps Clark if he wasn't merely being used, stood to gain big time if Carl's new technology ended up in Yana's lap.

There were the mysterious 'powerful' interests that wanted to buy the technology. Frustrated by Carl's refusal to sell. Perhaps they engineered his demise in the hope the technology would settle into more reasonable hands. Hands willing to deal.

There was Cindy Kwan from The Grotto, with whom Carl had had some sort of altercation.

There was the mysterious gay man who Carl may have jilted, perhaps throwing him into a jealous rage. Allan Clark had said Carl might have had a silent partner in the technology and perhaps there'd been a falling out.

There was Shadow, who seemed likable enough. But who knew what went on in her head. She claimed she never played S & M games with Carl. The Judge wondered if that were true.

Even Barbara might have a motive if she thought Carl had no intention of becoming engaged, particularly after stringing her along for months. But the Judge couldn't picture it. It took quickness to get close enough to kill someone with a knife. Unless of course you already knew them. Barbara was a lover and often a whiner, but not a killer.

If strangers were killing under a contract, it was unlikely a crime of passion.

More likely a motive relating to business. And money. This was Silicon Beach. People would do lots of things for money here. Money was security. It was power. It was self-esteem. It was everything to the denizens of the Southern California Plain.

The money and business motive made more sense. The Judge and Carl were tied together by the patent case. And the patent case was all about money, as most civil suits were. Since the attack on the Judge and the murder of Carl were connected, the motive would relate to Carl's current patent, or Carl's new technology, or something similar.

Carl's existing patented technology was interesting. The ability to convert flare off gas at the wellheads around the country back into oil. Many wells were primarily oil wells. They had no gathering or distribution system to capture the gas, which was just burned off at the wellhead. Carl's patented invention solved that. It might increase the output of such an oil well anywhere from five to ten percent. It was very valuable technology no doubt. But it wasn't disruptive technology. Hardly worth a murder in the Judge's opinion. He wished he'd read the missing report on Carl's new technology. That report could bring clarity to this mess.

As he stepped out of the garage elevator and into the building lobby, still lost in thought, a solid hand was laid on his shoulder from behind, bringing him up short. He swung around to protest and came face to face with Kaminsky. The Lieutenant released his hand but still stood close, his face in the Judge's.

"We need to go over to my office and talk. Now, Judge. There've been more developments in the Greene case."

There was a certain satisfaction in Kaminsky's voice that the Judge didn't like.

The Judge shook himself to full alert, clamped his mouth shut, and vowed to say little. Only listen. Perhaps he'd need his own attorney soon. Maybe now.

They walked out to Kaminsky's car, parked illegally in front of the building, and climbed in. Kaminsky drove them over to the Santa Monica police station. A 15-minute trip. At least he was allowed to ride in front instead of shackled in the rear. But instinct told him things weren't good.

"Are you a native Angeleno, Judge?" Kaminisky asked conversationally. Switching gears into his nice cop mode.

"I am, Kaminsky. Grew up on the Palos Verdes Peninsula."

"How'd you get in the law business, Judge?"

What Kaminsky wanted to ask was how he knew the DA so well, the Judge thought. He was just working up to it.

"Was your father an attorney?"

"No, an accountant," said the Judge, deciding he would play this game back. "He worked all his life for a large accounting firm down on Spring Street back in the day. Lybrand, Ross Brothers and Montgomery. Through a succession of mergers they got bigger and bigger. Now they're Price Waterhouse Cooper. How about you, Kaminsky? Is that a Boston accent?"

"Yes. Grew up there, started in the Boston Police Department."

"Was your dad a union man?" asked the Judge.

Startled, Kaminsky looked at the Judge.

"How'd you know that?"

"A guess."

"Blue collar meets ivy league, huh Judge? My dad drove a small pickup truck all his life. Raised three kids and put me through school on a nothing salary. Then when he wanted to retire, his trucking union tried to ax his pension. Cut it by two thirds. Said 'cause he only drove a pickup, he wasn't really full time. Wasn't entitled to all the credits he'd earned under their pension plan."

"Did you help fix it?"

"I did. Sometimes people and organizations aren't so fair. Like that union and its plan administrator. They weren't so fair with my dad. They needed a little help to see the right thing to do."

"So what'd you do, Kaminsky?"

"I was already out here then. Working for the Santa Monica Department. But I called a couple of my old buddies from the Boston Police. A pair of them went down and talked to the union's pension plan administrator. Explained how it was going to be. It got all worked out for my dad. Real quick. Bastards!"

Kaminsky turned to the Judge again. "So growing up in Palos Verdes must have been pretty pleasant, Judge. Don't some people call it the PV Bubble on account of the air's so rarefied?"

"They call it that because there's only four main roads on to The Hill. At the best of times it's a minimum twenty minutes from any freeway. People from the greater L.A. area don't wander into Palos Verdes much. Except for the bike clubs, mostly it's only the residents that come and go. Growing up there you're not much exposed to the people who co-exist on the flats."

"You mean the poor," Kaminsky said. A touch of bitterness at the back of his voice.

"Yes," said the Judge. "We're all products of the place we grow up. Can't help it. How about you, Kaminsky? Where'd you grow up in Boston? Codman Square? Perhaps Four Corners?"

"Guess it shows doesn't it?" said Kaminsky. "Yeah. Four Corners. Irish neighborhood. Bunch of pricks. Gangs, violence, shootings, stabbings, muggings, depression, despair. We had it all. Wasn't no bubble there. As a Polish boy I learned how to take care of myself early." His eyes narrowed, old memories flashing through his mind.

"So are you jealous I grew up in a bubble and you grew up in a tough neighborhood in Boston?" asked the Judge. "You don't seem to like me very much, Kaminsky."

Kaminsky turned full in the driver's seat then. Leveling his cold blue eyes at the Judge. The Judge could almost taste the venom there. Could see the angry color spreading up Kaminski's cheek.

"I'm not jealous, Judge. I just don't like silver spoon assholes who receive special privilege. Use high powered friends to get around police procedure. Call up the chicken-shit DA and suddenly I have to wait twenty-four hours to get your statement. That gave you time to figure out what your story was. You probably talked to your lawyer. Accumulated all the verifiable facts and moved your story around to match. Even rehearse the story a little 'til you got it down pat."

"So you think I need a defense lawyer, Kaminsky?"

Kaminsky let the question lay there unanswered, allowing the tension to build, as he escorted the Judge from the car into the station and back to the mean little interrogation room where they'd talked before. This time the lieutenant didn't offer coffee or water. Kaminsky was trying to be more intimidating.

But settling into the chair on his side of the table, Kaminsky switched again to his conversational voice.

"Look at it this way, Judge. I got a murder victim. He didn't jab that knife into his own neck. I have your wallet with your license and your social security card and your insurance card, and even your California Bar card. Found next to the victim in that alley. You were clearly there with Carl Greene.

There was $800 in cash in your wallet. That tells me this was no robbery.

I've got your pants beside the victim. This is no OJ case where the shrunken glove doesn't fit. You've admitted they're your pants. Suggests to me this was maybe a crime of passion. People don't usually take their pants off for just anyone.

I've got you wandering around the Santa Monica Beach, disheveled, booze on your breath, wearing no pants. And you've got a knife wound on your arm, suggesting you were in a struggle.

I got you admitting to walking along the street parallel to the alley where the murder occurred, about the time of the murder.

So what do you think, Judge? Do you need a lawyer?"

The Judge stayed silent.

"The only thing I'm missing is a motive. Why would a fancy Judge like you want to kill old Carl Greene? Were you lovers perhaps? Was this a tryst between two mature guys gone wrong? I couldn't figure the motive out."

"Carl did have a gay lover," said the Judge.

"How do you know that?"

The Judge related what Shadow had said about Greene's gay affair.

"Do you know who it was?" asked Kaminsky.

"Not yet."

"Well I do. We know how to do our job here too, Judge. We talked to Greene's gay friend at length. He checks out. Has an iron clad alibi for the time the murder was committed."

"Who is he?" asked the Judge.

"That information's part of this investigation. It's not for public consumption. If we need him to testify for some reason then it'll all come out. Otherwise, we have no need to embarrass the guy."

"But you have no problem embarrassing me. Picking me up in my own lobby and dragging me down here for this little chat," said the Judge. "This feels almost like a vendetta, Kaminsky."

"I admit I don't like you much, Judge. I don't like your fancy yacht and your fancy house high on the hill in Palos Verdes. I don't like your arrogant smarter than everybody attitude that comes with your bullshit law degree. I don't like you've got a wife that's young enough to be your daughter. I don't like you had rich parents, raised you in the PV bubble, sent you to finishing schools and set you up as a lawyer. I don't like you got enough money so you really don't have to work.

I don't like you get 550 an hour or more, and I hobble along on 80 an hour and try to make do with my family in this expensive town. You swan around and play this debutante detective. Meanwhile, the rest of us have to do the work.

Oh, yes, and I don't like you as a judge. I was in your court once. I was on the stand as a witness. We had this two bit drug dealer dead to rights, sitting on his drug stash in his garage. You let the defense attorney bury me. No due process, no reasonable cause to search, no warrant, no hot pursuit. All this crap.

You threw the evidence out. Just like that. Poof! No case. The creep walked. Two months later two little girls, 15 , died in his garage from an overdose.

That was your doing, Judge. You're responsible for their deaths. So yeah, you could say I don't like you."

"That feel better? Get that all off your chest?" asked the Judge.

"Not really. But you asked me. I'm telling you how it is. You want to repeat it to anybody up the line, I'll deny it. I just thought us girls should have a frank discussion. So here are the rules, Judge. I'm going to be in your face. You make a mistake with your little games, you lie to me again, I'm going right up your ass." Kaminsky smiled, displaying white teeth firmly clenched.

The Judge smiled back.

It was the final straw.

"I think I'm going to have your ass for this Carl Greene killing," Kaminsky snarled. "All I need to find is one little mistake. I'm going to nail you solid."

"Why would I do such a thing?" asked the Judge, determined to ask questions but make no statements.

"That stumped me for a while too, Judge. Particularly when you said you had no relationship to the victim outside of his brief appearance twice in your patent arbitration. I couldn't find a motive."

"Because I don't have one."

"So you said, Judge. But you lied to me. You out and out lied."

"How's that?"

"You had a very personal motive for wanting Carl Greene dead."

"What are you talking about, Kaminsky?"

"I know about your mistress."

"My mistress?"

"Being newly married to that child bride and all I can see how you'd want to keep it quiet. But the facts invariably come out Judge."

"What facts?" asked the Judge. A sickening suspicion of where this was going settled in his stomach.

"Carl Greene took your lover away from you, Judge. He wasn't as successful as you. At least not yet. But he was apparently a better lover. Must have stung. Hurt your pride. Particularly after all the time, money and attention you lavished on the relationship. For years. And the risks you took sneaking around behind your new wife's back. You must have been very angry."

"What are you talking about, Kaminsky?"

"You couldn't let her go. Certainly couldn't lose her to someone like Carl. You had to put a stop to it. And so you did. You killed Carl Greene in a jealous rage after you discovered he was screwing your mistress behind your back!"

"And who would that be?" asked the Judge.

"Miss Barbara Thompson."

CHAPTER 22
3:30 PM Monday

The Judge took a deep breath, steadied himself, and smiled at Kaminsky.

"You don't have a case and you know it Kaminsky. I haven't had a relationship with Barbara in four years. We're just casual friends. Ask her yourself. I have no motive for killing Carl Greene."

"I have talked to Miss Thompson. She says you're very close, despite your recent marriage." Kaminsky had his forefinger up now, pointing accusingly at the Judge, trying to bait him.

"Did she say we've had a current affair? ... No." The Judge answered his own question. "Did she say we'd been physically intimate at any time in the last four years? ... No. Did she say I knew about her relationship to Carl prior to his murder? ... No. Aside from a brief contact in Avalon this spring, did she say I've had any contact with her at all in the last four years? No. Even the idea I could be involved is ludicrous. You'd want the DA to present a case where a man kills another man with a knife, somehow badly cuts himself as well with the same knife, leaves his pants with his wallet and ID at the scene, and then decides to call attention to himself by taking a pants-less swim at night next to the Santa Monica Pier? Good luck on that."

"Stranger things have happened," said Kaminsky, but his voice cracked a little. The Judge knew he had the upper hand for the moment.

"Kaminsky, I've got other things to do. I'm walking out of here. I've got nothing more to add to my account of what happened Thursday night. If you want to charge me, go ahead. My lawyer will have the charge thrown out on arraignment. That assumes the DA will go along and file a criminal complaint, which I doubt. You need to go fish some other stream."

The Judge rose, turned and walked to the door. Kaminsky didn't move. The Judge could feel Kaminsky's eyes boring into his back. The Judge opened the door and walked out, letting it close behind him, leaving Kaminsky fuming in his nasty little room.

The Judge emerged into a bright Santa Monica afternoon from the dark police station, squinting, a little disoriented by the light. And by what he'd just been through. Damn. How'd he get himself pinned to the middle of the target on this one?

He walked across the street to a coffee shop and settled into a quiet corner where he couldn't be overheard. He dialed Barbara. She answered on the first ring. She must have been nesting her cell phone.

"Hi, Judgie. Want to meet for a drink?"

"No. Barbara, did you talk to the police about Carl?"

"Of course, Judge. They were the ones who came to my door and told me." There was a catch in Barbara's voice.

"Did you talk to them again? More recently?"

"Funny you should ask, Judge. When I got back from our date, that nice lieutenant, Minsky or something, called."

"Kaminsky," said the Judge.

"Yes, that's him."

"What did he ask you?"

"Who Carl's friends were. Who knew we were engaged. Stuff like that."

"Did he ask about me?" asked the Judge.

"He did, Judge. Such a nice man."

"What did you tell him about me?"

"Well, you know, Judge. I was discrete of course. Told him how we had this mad passionate affair while I was still married. How you couldn't bear to think of me in my then husband's arms so you had to break it off. How heartbroken we both were."

"What else, Barbara?"

"Well, gosh, I don't know. I guess I told him how you had this child bride now, but you still had strong feelings for me. How'd we been on a couple of dates already. Explained how a more experienced woman knows so much better how to please a man. You know what they say, Judge. 'You don't teach a grandmother how to suck eggs!'"

Barbara lapsed into a peel of giggles.

"Not that I'm a grandmother by any means." More giggles.

"Did you tell Kaminsky you'd told me about Carl and your planned engagement?"

"Oh yes. I explained how you didn't take it well. I mean, let's face it Judge. You did sound a mite jealous when you found out."

"But Carl was already dead when you called me and told me about your engagement. Remember?"

"Well… I guess that's true. But you were probably jealous thinking about the past. All the fun you missed because Carl took your place."

"Did you tell Kaminsky I didn't find out about your engagement to Carl until after he was dead?"

"Uh… no. Guess I didn't think about that, Judge. Did I do something wrong?"

The Judge unclenched his teeth with difficulty.

"Barbara, Barbara… Barbara. You're incorrigible."

"I'm sorry if I screwed up somewhere, Judge. A girl's got to keep plugging until she finds someone who appreciates her. I'd prefer you always, dear. But if it can't be you I have to share myself with someone. At least until you tire of Cathy."

Words failed the Judge. He muttered a "Goodbye" and hung up, taking a large slug of his coffee. He got up and treated himself to an old fashioned donut, hoping the combination of coffee, fat and sugar would calm him. It didn't.

He called a taxi and rode to his office. Everything was there as he'd left it Saturday morning, undisturbed. Including his note he'd left for Frankie about the discovery research needing done. There was no research memo. Frankie hadn't been in. Well, it had been the weekend. He supposed young attorneys had better things to do on the weekends these days than slave over research in a law office. Times were different when he'd started practicing law. But Frankie should have been in this morning to do the work. He was usually more reliable.

The Judge settled in at his desk and opened his laptop. He fished in his pocket and produced the jump drive he'd found in Carl's apartment, plugged it in, and scanned the list of files. There were document files and picture files. He pulled up the picture files first.

Pictures of Carl, Carl and Barbara, Carl and Yana, Carl and Allan, Carl and Leslie, Carl and a dog, a pit bull. They flew by in a kaleidoscope of color and activities. Sailing, surfing, camping, sports events, parties. Even Monte Carlo, Paris, and London. But some pictures were more telling.

There were pictures of the front of Carl's warehouse, giving away its address: Compton. On Santa Fe Avenue. Definitely beyond the boundaries of Silicon Beach. The Judge decided he would pay a visit across town this afternoon.

There were selfies of Carl and Barbara in compromising positions. If the Judge tried some of those he'd be limping around with a crimp in his neck for a week. He'd probably have a crimp somewhere else as well. Carl had been a horny old goat.

Barbara's new boobs were as abundant as one would expect. She looked like she might blow over in any sort of tail wind.

Another file contained pictures of Carl cavorting with Yana, likely when they were married. In her younger days she showed well. Well, she still showed well for that matter. All soft and girl next door cuddly on the outside. Tough as nails on the in. The pictures were mostly X-rated. He supposed he was becoming a bit of a voyeur. It was a disturbing thought. He shut that file quickly and moved on.

The next file held more pictures of a pit bull. As a puppy, a year old, and then perhaps three. The dog looked relaxed around Carl. But one picture showed it baring sharp teeth at another dog. What did Barbara say its name was? Sneezy? Wheezy? Something like that.

There were pictures of Carl and Allan Clark on a fishing trip, likely in Mexico by the look of the boat. Smiling, each with an arm around the other's shoulder, holding bottles of Dos Equis. Best buds. And earlier pictures of dinners together with Yana and another guy who sat close to Clark. Travel pictures of Carl and Clark in the Philippines and in Thailand with young native girls. More X-rated stuff the Judge closed quickly.

The next file had pictures of Carl in a jock strap, tied to the big circular rack at The Grotto. Shadow was standing over him, one of the mock whips in her hands, pretending to flay him. She wore a skimpy black bodice embroidered with lace and bearing a Nazi symbol across its chest. She looked ridiculous.

Shadow had lied. She had been into games with Carl. Why did she cover it up? Did she have something to hide?

The next file contained pictures of Carl and another man in various steamy situations. Carl's gay lover. The man wore a ball cap and kept his face away from the camera so it didn't show. He was very shy. You couldn't say that for Carl. Greene had been an experimental old fart. It made the Judge's occasional dalliances over the years look tame.

Perhaps Carl's murder had been over a lovers quarrel after all? Jealously? Rage? Revenge for being jilted or replaced? Or perhaps unrequited love? The human animal was capable of intense emotions, particularly in sexual relationships. Emotion overwhelmed reason. Heinous acts could be committed by even the most buttoned down people.

But somehow a switchblade in an alley didn't conjure up images of an agitated lover. No, the Judge was pretty sure Carl's death was about his work, and the technology. But how did Carl get into the alley in the first place? What was he doing there? Had someone asked him to meet?

The Judge turned his attention to the document files. The first file contained emails, apparently carefully selected and preserved here, but with no consistency in their times, senders, dates, or subject lines. The Judge whipped through them quickly, giving each a cursorily scan unless something looked relevant.

There was an email from Barbara, desperately pressing for a firm date for announcement of their engagement. Apparently things weren't quite as sealed up as Barbara had said. As though saying it could make it so. Some people never change, mused the Judge.

There was an email from someone named Roberts, no first name, threatening foreclosure on a loan unless the payments were brought current immediately.

A second email from Roberts gave a tally of what was due. About $48,000 in delinquent interest payments on the loan. Roberts said he was going to foreclose on Carl's technology. The tone was angry. Roberts was an angry man. A new name, thought the Judge. Who was Roberts? What sort of relationship did he have with Carl? Important enough apparently to go on to Carl's secret jump drive. The Judge jotted the name down in the small notebook he carried, and Robert's email address.

Another file had a copy of an award. *"Award to Carl Greene, Benefactor of the Year, Southern California Homeless Coalition."* It was presented last year. Apparently Carl had heavily supported the homeless cause in L.A. It made sense given his own battle to recover from the streets.

There was an email from Cindy Kwan, dated four weeks earlier, stating she had an offer in hand to purchase Carl's new technology and the purchase price by wire transfer would be in the middle eight digits. She wanted to present it in person. Suggested a meeting in Santa Monica, near the Judge's office, at a local coffee shop.

Someone wanted Carl's new technology bad.

A subsequent email said the exact price offered for exclusive world-wide rights was $40,000,000, with $10,000,000 paid up front and the balance paid on an earn-out basis as the technology was commercialized and produced revenues.

A later email from Cindy was curt, suggesting Carl was a fool for turning down her group's offer. Stating Carl's counter offer of $800,000,000 was ridiculous.

A follow-up email from Cindy the next day read:

"Carl, you know you can lose a lot more than money here if you're not careful. My group is not accustomed to taking no for an answer. You'd better reconsider, and quick. Why don't you counter at $44,000,000?"

And there was Carl's email response:

"Cindy, tell your group to fuck off."

Another email from Cindy Kwan:

"Either sell or expect to lose your technology in the ensuing legal fight."

And a final Cindy Kwan email:

"There are things one can lose more important than money. Mobility for instance. Health. Even Existence."

It sounded like Cindy and her friends were prepared to play rough.

The Judge moved on to the next email. The same day as Cindy's last email, but later. Allan Clark had emailed Carl:

"Carl, Cindy has told me of her group's offer and your correspondence. She is hoping I can persuade you to accept. We've been best friends for years. I have often acted as your confident and financial advisor. Being purely objective on your behalf, which I am, I think we should make a counter offer of $48,000,000 and make this deal happen."

It was signed: *"Your best friend and the one watching your back... Allan."*

Carl's reply back to Allan was terse:

"Glad to hear how you have no conflict Allan. Only my best interests at heart. Is that why you're sleeping with my ex-wife? As to having my back.... You're more likely watching the back of her ass."

There was a week-long break in the emails saved. The last was from Allan Clark to Carl Thursday afternoon. The day Carl was murdered.

"Carl, Yana and I want to make peace. Why don't you come meet me and Yana at Chaya Venice for a drink tonight? We can work this out. There is more than enough money for everyone. Yana isn't greedy. She just wants to maintain a reasonable lifestyle. Please, can we three meet and talk this

evening? Later you and I can go to the club and have some fun. Just like old times. My treat."

The Judge re-read the email. *Chaya Venice* was a well-known restaurant frequented by locals and tourists alike. One thoroughfare over from where the Judge had walked to the beach on Thursday evening.

It was just around the corner from Marine Court, the alley where Carl's body was found.

There wasn't much else on the jump drive. No plans or specs on new technology. No copy of the missing report. Just personal information and pictures about the man that once had been.

Life was so fleeting. And could end so suddenly. A last pass over the Ferris wheel and poof! Ride over.

CHAPTER 23
4:30 PM Monday

Carl's warehouse was on a small triangular piece of ground sandwiched against an active railroad track and a residential street, cut off at the tip by a major boulevard.

It was in a rough part of Compton. Broken down homes and apartments leered at the Judge through barred windows from across the dusty street. Tarted up here and there with flamboyant graffiti. There was no one on the street this afternoon. But the Judge could feel eyes peering out from behind shaded windows as he got out of his car and walked up to the ten-foot corrugated fence surrounding the property. A roll of barbwire strung along the top further discouraged intruders. The Judge hadn't the faintest idea how he would get in. Unless someone was there actively working.

He walked fifty feet along the fence from where he'd parked his car and came to a gate, built out of the same corrugated metal but mounted on wheels so it could roll, permitting vehicle entry. It had a thick steel cord linking the frame of the gate to the fence post, with a heavy padlock on it. A small hole had been cut in the fence metal so you could reach in if you had the key and unlock the lock from the street side.

The Judge reached in out of curiosity and tried the padlock. Its top slid open on well-oiled pins. The padlock had been twisted around to look closed, but had not been pressed down to lock. He undid the steel cord and tried to slide the gate open. It hardly budged. He brought his weight against it and it opened a tad, exposing sharp wire to either side. He sucked in his damn stomach as much as he could and was just able to squeeze through.

He was immediately struck by the smell of gas, oil, and old rubber. The place stunk like a toxic dump. Inside was a yard sufficient for a large truck to turn around, and, across the yard, a small warehouse with two large bays covered by sliding metal doors. The parking area was empty of vehicles. But one sliding door of the warehouse was open about eighteen inches, displaying a strip of dark cool within.

He walked softly across the parking area, crunching on gravel spread over disintegrating asphalt, trying to be quiet. He wasn't sure why.

He reached the partially open bay door and pushed to open it further. But it was stuck like the front gate, or locked or blocked. Turning sideways again, he pushed and wiggled his way through, cursing the paunch once more. With age it had become more and more impossible to jettison.

It was dark inside. The only light came from two large skylights, clouded with dirt and grime. He stood still, letting his eyes grow accustomed to the gloom. Shapes emerged. Two old boilers, large, reaching almost to the roof two and a half stories above. And strung around them four small, newer boilers, each about the size of Volkswagen Bug. New metal, fresh piping and wiring bristled around the smaller tanks, ornamented with measuring gauges and sensors. They looked like electronic snowmen, in from the cold.

At the other end of the building was a small office built into the space, windows dark, door closed. He stepped toward it. Then froze.

Coming slowly toward him, almost staggering, was a pit bull.

Wheezy!

But Wheezy wasn't wheezing. His eyes were bloodshot and dilated. His jaw hung open, displaying a great deal of salivation, foam like, around the needle sharp teeth. He was shaking a little as he walked, whether in rage or sickness, it was unclear. His hind legs were dragging a little, suggesting some paralysis. He was focused on the Judge. A low nasty growl rumbled from deep in his chest.

The Judge was in trouble and he knew it. He might turn and reach the bay door before the animal was upon him, but there was no way to close it. He'd never make it across the yard.

It was likely rabies. Even if he could fight the dog off, he wouldn't escape without a bite or a scratch. A course of shots for rabies wasn't something he wanted. The dog would go for his throat. There was no assurance he would even survive an attack. He needed a solution and he needed it quick.

He gave his best low bestial growl from deep in his chest, and charged at the animal. Startled, it stopped in mid-step, then tried to make its rear feet perform to move back a little.

At the last second the Judge veered to the left, scrambling atop one of the smaller boilers. They eyed each other for a while. The Judge from his perch and the dog from a squatting position, still trying to get better control of its hind legs. Then the dog gave one further nasty growl and dragged itself back, out of sight, into the dark shadows of the big boiler behind the Judge. Between the Judge and the warehouse bay door he entered by.

The Judge waited five minutes. Then slid quietly down from the boiler, picked up a large monkey wrench lying on a nearby bench for defense, and strode purposefully, but without running, toward the end of the building. Hoping for safety inside the office. If only the door were unlocked. He could hear the animal scrambling out of the shadows behind him. Now beginning a staggering pursuit. Breathing heavily.

The Judge reached the office door and turned the knob. Thank God the door opened. He stepped through and closed the door firmly into the face of Wheezy, who was gearing up for a final lunge, eyes aflame.

There was a solid thud as the dog hit the other side of the door, followed by a second and third thud, and then angry scratching. The Judge leaned against the inside wall of the office, trying to get his breath, stilling his heart beat.

He flipped the light switch by the door, and overhead lights flooded the office with white light. It had been thoroughly searched. File drawers hung open at one end, their contents scattered around the floor. At the other end an old fashioned roll desk stood in disarray, roll top up, drawers open, papers from the desk scattered about.

He picked up a metal chair on its side on the floor and propped it against the door. He rubbed a clear spot in the dirty shop window and looked out into the warehouse, craning his neck to see down close to the door. The animal was there, hunched down, breathing heavily, focused with angry eyes on the door. Shit!

He looked again around the office. He doubted there would be anything useful here. Someone had gone through its contents with a fine tooth comb. If there'd been a copy of the missing report here, it'd be long gone now.

Then he spotted something of interest, tucked partly under the desk where it had been kicked in the effort to search the office. It was an old fashioned rolodex. The kind with two metal rods wrapped around a metal base with 3x5 cards notched to attach and slide around. He went right to the Rs, segregated by a separate card tab. There was only one Roberts, and it was a George Roberts. A dentist with an office in Santa Monica. He copied the contact information into his notebook, then snapped all the used cards off their rings and slid them into his pockets. Hoping they wouldn't impede his running ability.

As he stepped away from the desk he heard a crunch as his foot came down on something hard. He'd stepped on a small vial on the floor, smashing it. It created a tiny yellow green puddle on the beige linoleum. A hypodermic needle lay nearby.

He squatted down and used his pen to turn a portion of the glass over, displaying a small label neatly hand printed in Spanish: *virus de la rabia*. He sprang up immediately, away from the oozing substance, dropping his pen on the floor, leaving it, putting distance between himself and the puddled material.

Christ, poor Wheezy. Someone had created a trap for the next sucker to walk into the warehouse. Someone had infected Wheezy with rabies and left him here.

The Judge got out his cell, went on the internet, and located the number for DACC, the Los Angeles Department of Animal Care and Control. He dialed them up and explained the situation, discreetly declining to give his name. Only his location. He explained about the vial he'd accidentally stepped on. They said they'd have someone there in thirty minutes. He was to leave the premises immediately and wait for them out on the street. Good luck with that.

He went back to the shop window and peeked into the warehouse. Wheezy was still there, laying down now, tiring, but still focused on the office door. Fortunately there was another door at the other end of the office. The Judge opened it to find himself outside, on the far side of the warehouse.

Walking slowly and as silently as he could over the gravel, ninja like, he picked his way around the warehouse and back to the front gate. He sucked his air in again and with a rush tried to squeeze his way through the gate and out to the street. As he did so he head a soft tearing sound and realized he was stuck. The open wire on one side had snagged his pants, ripping a sizable hole on his fanny in the process. The pants remained stuck on the wire.

That's when he heard rushing paws crossing the gravel. He gave one panicked yank and the pants came free, leaving a large panel of material on the wire. With newfound strength he heaved on the gate, forcing it closed. Wheezy hit the gate a split second later, throwing his whole body against it with a low growl. But the gate held.

No rabies shots for him after all. Back up the Ferris wheel for one more circle.

He wasn't sure what Katy would say about his pants, but he knew he'd be laughed at. Hopefully there'd be no photographers around.

This would become a part of the rollicking story to trot out periodically along with his nocturnal swim, and enjoyed by all. Damn, damn, damn. It seemed to be his karma.

Perhaps he should have been a dentist. Like this Doctor George Roberts.

He drove to his office. He was disappointed to find that Frankie, his law clerk, wasn't in and researching the law on discovery as he'd assigned on Friday. He looked around his desk in vain, hoping for a memo perhaps prepared on Saturday and left for him. But there was none. What was up with Frankie? It appeared he hadn't been in all day. Perhaps it wasn't that urgent now the report was missing and Carl was dead. Carl's estate would have to produce another copy of the confidential report for his review. Still, Frankie should have been more on the ball. He called Frankie's number and left a message, trying to give a firm reminder while keeping the annoyance he felt out of his voice.

CHAPTER 24
7:00 PM Monday

The Judge headed back to the Marina and his boat. He was heartened to see Katy's car in the parking lot. He needed a little R and R. He was feeling old and tired.

Katy greeted him with all the enthusiasm only a young lover can have. Throwing her arms around his neck and giving him a long sensual kiss. But as he turned around in the salon, he caught her trying to hide a smile. She'd spotted the missing panel in the seat of his pants.

He'd forgotten about it on the drive home. And unfortunately he was wearing bright red polo underwear which no doubt showed in a large swath across his butt. He couldn't really see but he must have looked like a flagman from the stern.

"What's with you and your pants these days, Judge?" she asked. "You're either losing them or ripping them up."

"Don't ask," said the Judge. "I'm going to start wearing overalls. Next time you see me I'm going to look like a plumber."

"Great idea. Come over here, Judge. I've got some plumbing needs some attention."

They embraced for a long time. Then, still holding each other, maneuvered down the three steps to the Master's Cabin where Katy discreetly pulled the curtains closed.

The Judge slept in the next morning, Katy having left early for some meeting at her high school. She'd maliciously opened the aft curtains again, perhaps for air, and eventually the sun shifted around so golden honey rays spilt in over the Judge's face, making it difficult to sleep. Giving himself a long stretch on the bed like some large cat with a paunch, he roused himself to shower and shave in the tiny head.

He had legal work to do later, but he decided he'd first pay a visit to George Roberts, Carl's dentist, and perhaps the financier for Carl's new technology.

George Roberts practiced his craft out of a dental office with several assistants in the Water Garden Office Complex at Cloverfield and Colorado in Santa Monica. It was a new swank office. The dental chair bays, defined by high modern cubical separators with sculpted sides, looked out on a large lily pond, dry now because of a California drought. Mauve carpet and upholstered furniture contrasted with stark white walls hung with posters of smiling teeth and pink gums. It was a very odd feeling to walk in and be surrounded by teeth. Almost like in a shark tank.

The Judge explained to the young girl manning the front desk, all whited up in uniform with a small white cap and looking about fourteen, that he was a friend of Carl Greene's, who was a friend of George Roberts, and he needed to speak to Dr. Roberts briefly.

The girl looked doubtful. Until the Judge switched to his gravelly judicial voice and bullied a little. She buckled quickly, scurrying off to find the good dentist.

The man that came out to shake his hand, also all whited up, was not what the Judge expected in this fancy dental office on the flats below Brentwood. He was tall, perhaps 60, slender and sinewy, with white hair, bristly white mustache, and narrow tanned face and features. He could have been an old cowboy poking along on a broken down horse across some pass in Montana. He had the look.

His large pale blue eyes now examined the Judge minutely, but not in an unfriendly way. They were intelligent and calculating. The Judge suspected Dr. Roberts missed little.

The Judge explained he was investigating the death of Carl Greene. The pale blue eyes didn't blink. Just watched the Judge.

"You knew Carl I understand," said the Judge.

"Who says that?" Roberts asked.

"Your name keeps cropping up. I heard Carl might have owed you money," said the Judge.

For a second suspicion and perhaps a touch of anger flashed across Roberts' face. But gone in an instant as his poker face returned. Looking relaxed again, comfortable, and smiley.

"Are you working with the police?" asked Roberts. "You're not a policeman yourself since you showed no badge. Do you have any legal authority to be asking me these questions? Any right to compel me to answer?"

"I understood you and Carl were friends," said the Judge. "I thought you'd want to help find his killer."

"Mr. Greene and I weren't exactly friends, Judge. In fact our relationship, such as it was, had soured of late. I don't feel any compulsion to help catch his killer, if that's truly what this is about."

"What else could it be about, Doctor?" asked the Judge.

"Perhaps a scam of some sort."

Roberts flashed a scowl that was again quickly covered.

"Can you explain your relation with Greene.?" asked the Judge.

The pale blue eyes just stared at the Judge for a while. Considering. Assessing. When Roberts spoke it was with finality.

"No, Judge. I won't explain anything. Come back with a police officer in tow if you like, and give me a chance to arrange for my lawyer to be here too, but I doubt I'll have much more to say even than Now, if you'll excuse me, I have a chaired patient waiting nervously for my return with a shot."

Roberts turned his back and walked away, not bothering to shake the Judge's extended hand. The Judge stood for a moment looking after him. Puzzled. Both by Roberts' attitude and by the hostility in his eyes at the mention of Carl's debt. Something was off here. The Judge couldn't figure what. But he was damn well going to get to the bottom of it.

The Judge left the Water Garden and drove back to his office. He was expecting to find Frankie there, working up the legal research. But his office was locked. Empty. Where was Frankie? He hadn't made it in on Saturday as he'd committed to do. He'd missed Monday without a call or an email. Hadn't returned the Judge's call. And it seemed he was a no-show today as well. It wasn't like him. Had he gotten pissed off and quit? The Judge knew he wasn't the easiest boss to work for. He supposed he might have to find a new law clerk. What a headache.

CHAPTER 25
1:45 PM Tuesday

As the Judge settled into a hamburger over his desk, he glanced at the bureau in his office. Something had troubled him about the bureau but he couldn't quite put his finger on it. Now he had it.

On Saturday, he'd opened his locked bureau drawer, and Carl Greene's confidential report was gone. But the drawer had been locked. He'd had to use his key to unlock it. Sure, there were significant scratches around the drawer at the top near the latch. As though the drawer had been forced. But if the drawer had been forced open, why did he have to unlock it? The lock wasn't broken. And it wasn't a spring lock that would snap back into place if the drawer were closed. You needed a key to relock it, once the drawer was opened. Only two people had a key. The Judge. And his law clerk, Frank Wolen.

The more the Judge thought about it, the more troubled he became. He decided to pay a surprise visit to Frankie at home. Immediately.

The Judge finished his lunch, used a wet towel in the men's room to wipe a spill of Russian dressing off his pants where a piece of lettuce had squirted out, and returned to his office to put his work away. Ten minutes later he was maneuvering through early afternoon traffic down Main Street, over to Lincoln, and out past Play del Rey

Frankie lived in a walkup apartment in Playa Vista, the yuppie wet-lands beside Playa Del Rey, transformed into new luxury condos, apartments and commercial buildings. The cavernous Howard Hughes Airfield hangar remained from the old days, but that was about all. And it was now occupied by Google.

These large new modern spaces gave L.A. the edge in competing with Santa Monica for the young entrepreneurs of Silicon Beach and their smart new companies. Big outfits like Yahoo and Facebook moved in too, abandoning the garret-like spaces squeezed into old Santa Monica and Venice for the wide open space of Playa Vista buildings.

Frank's condo was in a Neo-Italianate structure with some 50 apartments built into five floors, all balconies and railings, earthy pastel plaster and dry blue green landscaping reminiscent of Italy.

The Judge parked in guest parking, caught the security locked entrance door on the fly as someone left, and elevatored up to the third floor. Frank was renting 307. As the Judge approached down a long corridor to its end, something didn't feel right. It was Frank's front door. It was slightly ajar. The Judge knocked and the door just swung open.

He called, "Frank, Frank… it's the Judge. Can I come in?"

No answer.

The Judge pushed the door all the way open and stepped into a small flat with white washed walls and soft caramel carpet in a berber pattern. Prints of seascapes decorated the walls. Beige upholstered furniture clustered around a small space that served as the living room, opening on to a tiny balcony. White

211

blinds were firmly shut, but light bled in around the edges, softly illuminating the space. A small bookcase to the left supported a few law books, the California Civil Code, Code of Civil Procedure, Corporations Code, and a directory of graduates from Southeastern University Law School.

To the right was a porter's kitchen, separated by a dining bar, with dirty dishes in the sink looking to have been there awhile. Spaghetti, the Judge guessed. The meal of choice for a young man on a budget. Beside the kitchen a small hall led off with a closed door at the end, likely the bathroom. A door midway down on the right would be the bedroom.

The Judge called again. "Frankie? Frankie, are you here?"

He felt a little uncomfortable invading Frank's privacy. On the other hand he was concerned. What was it? Why was the hair raising on the back of his neck? Everything looked in order, if a little untidy. The door had been left unlatched, but that could easily happen. Dashing to meet a friend or whatever.

Why was the Judge's alarm going off? There. There it was again. The slight whiff of something. Something you never forgot once you'd had it in your nostrils.

The Judge strode quickly down the hallway and looked in the bedroom through the open door. The covers on the bed were askew, suggesting a toss and turn night. But that was all. The bedroom was empty.

The Judge turned to the bathroom and tried its door. The door was firmly locked from the inside. But the smell was stronger now. This wasn't right.

The Judge called, "Frankie, Frankie" again, pounding on the door now. No response.

The Judge pulled his cell phone and dialed 911. He thought about crashing the door open with his foot. But his nose told him whatever was in there was long past help. Besides, it looked like a strong door. It might look easy to kick in a door in the movies, but the Judge wasn't going to break his foot trying.

Fifteen minutes later the paramedics arrived. He'd reported there was a locked door. They'd brought an ax. Thirty seconds later a large hole was axed in the center of the door. A paramedic reached in and unlocked the door from the inside. The smell poured out now, wrapping the three of them in a stench that was the stuff of nightmares.

Frankie was there. Slumped in the bathtub. Fully clothed. Brown slacks and white dress shirt open at the neck. Brown loafers, no socks. Just as the Judge had seem him on Friday afternoon. But his body was cold and stiff. His face, hands and neck a mottled grey-blue.

A small caliber handgun lay beside his hand. The hole in his temple hadn't bled much. And the bullet hadn't exited the other side. There were no blood and brains blasted about. But all Frank's bodily fluids had drained into the bathtub. Unfortunately for all concerned the stopper was down so the tub hadn't drained.

"Jesus," muttered one of the paramedics. "Another damn suicide. A young guy too. What a waste."

"I'll radio the police," said the other. "Not much we can do here."

The Judge sadly wandered back to the living room, knowing he would have to wait and explain his presence in the apartment. He looked around. There wasn't much in the little unit that was Frank. It looked to be a package of rented furniture and decor, matching and dull.

He idly wandered into the kitchen, looked in the kitchen cupboards, then under the sink, pulling out a small trash can. There were paper towels from what looked like a spaghetti spill on top.

The Judge lifted them to reveal a torn dark brown envelope beneath. One with a label: "Additional discovery materials in the case of Hicks vs Greene, delivered subject to Attorney Client Privilege." The empty envelope had contained the missing discovery report. Damn. What the hell had Frankie done?

He surveyed the rest of the apartment. Shuffling through Frankie's desk in his bedroom, peeking into his small closet and the night stand drawers, examining the books shelved in the living room. He even got down and peaked under the queen bed. There was no missing report. There were no other legal or research documents either.

The courier style brief case Frankie was so proud of, all leather with a bronze emblem, given to him by his girlfriend, was missing. As was Frankie's laptop.

As the Judge finished his brief search and moved back to the living room, a Los Angeles Sheriff's officer rushed in. Christ, it was Officer Saunders, the flatfoot from the beach Friday night. Damn. The Judge figured his presence at Frankie's death scene would be relayed back to Lieutenant Kaminsky in about a minute and a half. This was not good.

Saunders recognized him immediately. "The nocturnal judge with the missing pants," he said, a twinkle in his eyes. He handed the Judge another of his cards which the Judge shoved in his pocket. Then he stepped around the Judge and walked down the hall to the bathroom to have a look, the two paramedics standing aside. His face changed immediately. Hardened.

He turned back to the Judge, who had followed him, and said in a low voice:

"You'd better have a good explanation for what you're doing here, Judge. The detective is going to want to hear it. And it better be good. Sit down over there and think it through carefully. I know you're a judge and all, but if you need a criminal lawyer I've got a good one I can refer you. You might want to sit tight until you got a lawyer present. Good luck."

As officer Saunders finished, another officer came in. He turned out to be a sergeant, LAPD. A big beefy guy in his mid-forties with pale brown eyes and thinning blond hair, long and combed over to hide his pate. He'd left his cap in the car.

He nodded at Saunders, surveyed the scene in 15 quick steps from room to room, ending in the bathroom, then motioned the Judge to sit down on the sofa in the living room and wait.

Two other LAPD arrived behind him, setting up tape at the front door of the unit, dealing with the small crowd of neighbors and a distraught property manager gathered in the hall. Then a plainclothes detective showed up, did a similar walk through and sat down beside the Judge to take his statement. He flipped open his badge carrier, identifying himself as Lieutenant Carter.

The Judge explained that he was Frankie's employer. That he was a lawyer in the middle of an arbitration. That Frankie was his law clerk. That Frankie had not been in the office since Friday as far as he knew. That Frankie had missed scheduled appointments to work with the Judge on Saturday, Monday and now today. Had left no call-in message of being sick or unable to work. That the Judge had become worried and dropped by to see if Frankie were okay. That the apartment's door had been unlocked and slightly ajar. But not the bathroom. It had been locked from the inside.

That the odor in the apartment told the Judge something was wrong. That he'd called 911.

Carter took it all down.

"Looks to me like a straight up suicide, Judge. Way the pistol's positioned. The locked bathroom door and all. No note of course. But they often don't leave notes."

The Judge nodded noncommittally. He knew studies suggested only about 37 percent of suicides left notes. The rest just happen. But few people die by suicide without letting others know how they are feeling, either directly or indirectly. They give clues which are often cries for help.

The Judge thought back to the class he'd taken and some of the verbal statements sometimes clues of suicidal intent:

I can't go on anymore.
I wish I was never born.

I wish I were dead.
I won't need this anymore.
Everyone would be better off if I were dead.
Life sucks. Nobody cares if I live or die.
They're so cruel to me. They'll be sorry someday.
Nothing will ever change, will it?'

He could recall no such clues from Frankie. His clerk seemed very happy with himself and his life. The Judge told the lieutenant as much.

The Judge left the apartment a half hour later in deep thought, moving mechanically as he punched the button in the elevator for the ground floor. As he stepped out of the elevator into the lobby he nearly collided with someone sprightly stepping in. He stepped back to apologize, looking down into the face of Dick Harper, Randal Hicks' lawyer in the arbitration.

Recognition shown in both their faces at the same time, Dick looking first stunned, then guarded, then all smiles as his features settled into his public face.

"Just dropping off some files for one of paralegals working at home today," said Dick, perhaps a tad too quickly. "Has the flu." He hefted a small brief case he was carrying up in front of him as though it were a prop to emphasis his purpose.

There was the faintest sound of sucking in breath. Often a telltale sign of tension. The Judge wondered why Dick felt the need to explain his presence and mission to the Judge. Was it a coincidence this was the same building where Frankie resided? Dick's explanation was also a little thin. What firm sends a $750 an hour partner to drop off work for a paralegal out with the flu?

But Dick was all smiles now, shaking the Judge's hand and commenting on what a beautiful day it was in Playa Vista. The Judge exchanged pleasantries for thirty seconds, then walked on across the lobby and out into the afternoon. After 30 yards he turned to look back toward the building. Dick was still standing at the elevator entrance, perplexed, wringing his hands, looking at the paramedic truck, the two LAPD police cruisers, and the L.A. Coroner's truck just pulling up. He seemed to have second thoughts about delivering his documents to his sick paralegal.

As the Judge drove away, he recalled that some years before Dick Harper had been in some trouble with the California State Bar. He'd very nearly lost his license. The detective he'd been working with had gone to jail. It had involved Hollywood personalities in civil litigation. There'd been allegations of illegal phone tapping and bugging of the other side's law offices. It had cast a cloud over Dick's professional ethics which still lingered. Did Dick Harper have anything to do with the murder of Carl Greene and now the mysterious death of Frankie. Maybe a suicide. Maybe not.

The Judge drove back to his office on automatic, not seeing the road, trying to get his head around Frankie's death.

He settled at the long table in his office, a note pad in front of him. He drew circles and boxes and lines and arrows, trying to piece things together. But he didn't have enough facts. He was smack in the middle of what was going on, but its outlines were still shrouded.

Had Frank really committed suicide? Had someone ended his existence? And if so why? What was the envelope that had contained Carl Greene's secret report doing in Frankie's trash? Frankie must have taken it. But why? And why scratch up the bureau drawer to make it look like the lock had been forced? So he could deny he'd taken it? And where was that damned report now?

CHAPTER 26
4:00 PM Tuesday

The afternoon lingered as the Judge soldiered on, doing legal research online for a client. Not his favorite task. After a while he put the work aside and took a break, closing his eyes for a moment, settling back in his large overstuffed chair in his small office. A half hour later the Judge's cell phone rang, startling him out of a comfortable nap. It seemed he needed a power nap more and more these days when his schedule could accommodate one. Some said as you got older you got tired more quickly, but it was okay because when you worked you worked smarter.

The Judge suspected you just got older.

He was old and a little beat up. As he reached for the phone, flashes of pain shot up his arm, reminding him of just how deep the knife had struck. The doctor said he'd been lucky. What sort of luck put you in a knife fight with an unknown assailant? He needed no more luck like that.

"Judge, we need to talk." The gravelly voice on the other end was vaguely familiar. It suggested smoke damage, too much booze, and late nights partying until you'd exhausted everyone you could party with and were alone. Who the hell was it?

The voice answered the unspoken question in low growls. "This is Randall Hicks."

It was the Plaintiff in the patent case! The Judge immediately started to protest the call, but was cut off.

"Look, I know all the attorney bullshit about not talking to the judge, and I waive all that. And that little squirt, Carl Greene is dead, so I know he doesn't care. And I don't want to talk about the case anyway. At least not the part you're arbitrating."

"This is against all judicial procedure and ethics," sputtered the Judge.

"Just hear me out, Judge. Just be quiet a minute and listen."

"Go ahead."

"I think I'm in deep doo-doo, Judge. I just heard about your law clerk, Wolin. Murdered! I think I might be next."

"The police don't know yet whether it was a suicide or what," said the Judge. "You're jumping to conclusions."

"Oh I know, Judge. And so do you. You're no fool. This thing has gone way far beyond what was intended. First Greene gets killed. Now your clerk. And I'm being shadowed. I think I've been set up. I may be next to have a sudden accident. I want to talk to you now Judge, private, close by, and quick. There's more involved than you know."

Against his better judgment, the Judge assented. "Meet me around the corner at *Chaya Venice* in a half hour Mr. Hicks, and bring your attorney along. I don't want to talk to you alone. I'll see you there."

"I'll be there," said Hicks.

The Judge finished the legal point he'd been researching when the nap struck, saved his work, grabbed his keys and headed for the door.

He'd met Randall Hicks when he'd appeared at the start of the case, and twice more, once when he testified, and once when he sat in to listen to Carl Greene's testimony. A tall lean cowboy, late forties, with a quick smile and a line of bullshit that wouldn't quit. As though enough words thrown at something could make it true. Shifty eyes always looking for advantage. And of course the gravelly voice. A sign of hard living.

The Judge had met the type before. Los Angeles was full of them. In his experience they couldn't be trusted. Smarter than a used car salesman but with the same lack of ethics.

Chaya Venice was trendy, on the border between Santa Monica and Venice. Only a block from the Judge's office. The restaurant was known for its crowded bar of young people playing dress-up and trying to appear important, arrogant, and condescending to one another. Tonight was no exception. The bar was packed. All the tables and stools occupied and people standing around between. *Chaya's* claim to fame was its happy hour menu, which started at five p.m. and lasted all night, but only in the bar and the adjacent sushi bar. Hence the raucous crowd squeezed into the tight confines.

The Judge elbowed his way to the bar with difficulty, getting no respect for his senior status, and ordered a pineapple infused martini. One of his favorites. As he paid he felt a tap on his shoulder and turned to find Randall Hicks at his elbow.

Hicks shouted over the din, "I've got us a quiet table at the back."

Hicks led him to a small table . The other tables in the dining area were mostly vacant. A little too early for the dinner crowd. Hicks' attorney was nowhere in evidence. The Judge settled in a seat with his back to the wall and a view of the room.

When Randall Hicks had given testimony, he'd been very confident, his answers crisp and well-rehearsed. As you'd expect with Dick Harper as your counsel. Dick would have spent hours asking the questions he'd ask Hicks in front of the Judge, and the questions he'd anticipate the other side would ask. Getting the answers down pat. With just the right inflection and earnestness. Clear, concise, open answers, with no handles for the other side to grab.

As a lawyer you never asked your witness a question you didn't already know the answer to. But a skilled attorney did so much more. So many ways to tell the same facts. So many shades of accusation or guilt, competence or innocence, surprise or malice. You could project whatever shading you wanted into the facts, just by word choice.

The English language was a magnificent creation, lending itself to ambiguity and artifice, innuendo and pathos, passion and horror. The facts were the facts and truth was truth in the mind of the listener. But only based on what he took away from the testimony, giving advocates free play around the edges to manipulate the story to be told. Speech was an imperfect tool for getting at the truth. But then again at the bottom, each man's truth was different.

Hicks settled into a seat across from the Judge. He didn't look confident and well-rehearsed with all the answers this evening. He looked haggard. Continual tension and a lack of sleep showed. He nervously scanned the restaurant as they sat, then nursed his drink for a minute. Finally he lowered his head, projecting his gravel voice softly off the table so the Judge could just make him out.

"Thanks for coming, Judge. I need some advice."

"Look, Mr. Hicks. I'm not your lawyer. So I can't give you any legal advice. And I'm the sitting judge-arbitrator on a case in which you're a party. Talking to you and your lawyer outside chambers is highly irregular. And speaking to you without your lawyer present is forbidden."

"Don't speak then, Judge. Just listen. You came because this whole case is irregular. Someone snuffed old Carl out. They tried to kill you too. And now your law clerk's dead. I'm scared I'll be next."

"Okay," barked the Judge, not happy. "I'm listening."

"Here's how it started, Judge. Early last year I was desperate for cash. My public company, 1st Enterprises, had gone bust. Our new technology for purifying water held promise. Unfortunately, we'd run through the investor capital we'd raised privately to fund the company. The investors who'd put up that money had their lawyers sharpening their knives."

"Where'd the money go?" asked the Judge. "Did it all go for development or did a large chunk go for salaries and overhead?"

Hicks blinked.

"Like anyone else I had to live, Judge," he wheedled. "My executive salaries might have been a tad high, but we were worth it. We needed prestigious offices in order to persuade people to invest. And courting those damn investors wasn't cheap. There were lots of airplane rides and hotel rooms and expensive dinners and functions. Some wanted secret rebates to invest. The brokers who placed shares got full boat commissions and often a little extra under the table. And when the initial pool of investors dried up, I had to hire a sales room to make cold calls around the country. We had some great closers. But it all takes money."

"So how much did you raise in this so called 'private' offering?"

"About five million."

"And how much went for actual product development?" asked the Judge.

"Maybe half that. Like I said, there was a lot of overhead. Anyway, Judge, that's not the point."

"Okay. What's the point, Mr. Hicks?"

"We needed another five million minimum to keep going. Carry on the development. Cover overhead."

"So what'd you do?"

"We went public."

"Of course you did," said the Judge, a touch of sarcasm in his voice.

"We hired an IR. group. That stands for investor relations."

"I know," said the Judge.

"And we heavily promoted the stock. News releases. Direct mail. Multiple web sites. The cold call room. You know."

"Unfortunately I do, Mr. Hicks. And how did generating interest and I assume sales volume in your public stock help your company raise the missing capital?"

"Oh, that was easy. My brother was selling shares into the excite market and loaning the money back to the company, and presto, we had another three million pretty quickly."

"So that enabled you to complete development of your water purification system?" asked the Judge.

"That was the next problem, Judge. The system didn't work out. We got it up and running okay. But it was too expensive for the Third World and not needed here. We just couldn't get the price point down anywhere close to what it needed to be to be marketable. I guess we'd been a little too optimistic about our prospects for success. Maybe after we'd issued so many bullish press releases; so many optimistic projections on the website and stuff, we just started to believe our own shit. Anyway, we just did the usual things you do to make a stock run. My inside partners all took the opportunity to sell their shares. But as CEO I couldn't sell. When we ran out of money and the stock crashed, I hadn't sold any of my stock. I was stuck."

"And your brother?"

"He'd sold all his 'aged' shares, Judge. He didn't have any more to sell. And he'd loaned the proceeds all back to the company and we'd spent it."

"And let me guess what happened next," said the Judge. "The SEC came in and charged it was a pump and dump."

"How'd you know?"

"You've just explained how you violated several Federal and State securities laws, including the Securities Act of 1933, and the Securities Exchange Act of 1934."

"Okay, well that's not the point either."

"What's the point, Mr. Hicks?"

"So there I was last January, with no assets of value and no cash left in the till. A lot of angry shareholders. Lawsuits threatened. The SEC starting an investigation. My partners all disappeared offshore to who knows where. Just me. My ass hanging out. I needed a new gig in a hurry to take some of the heat off."

"Go on."

"So my attorney, Dick Harper, comes to me, Says he has this group will transfer new technology into my company because they like me and they like 1st Enterprises. Says I have to give up control but I can still be President. Says they'll cover my two hundred thousand a year salary as CEO and my expense account. All's I have to do is accept the transfer of the technology into my company for a handful of shares, start to commercialize it and make some sales. Oh, and incidentally, start this patent infringement action against this rival guy who had patented competing technology. They'd cover Dick's cost for all that."

"The rival guy was Carl Greene."

"Yes. I signed whatever Dick told me to sign and geared up my I.R. guys to spread the word about the new direction for 1st Enterprises. The stock price soared. The shareholders stopped rattling sabers. The SEC got less interested in the company as its price climbed back up. It was a Godsend. Put me back in the game."

"And the technology?"

"It was the technology in our arbitration. Convert the flare off gas at the wellhead to oil. They assigned it into the company. Then Dick had me file against Carl for patent infringement."

"For an order declaring there was no patent infringement," said the Judge.

"I guess. Whatever, Judge. Anyway, they wanted to get Carl's new technology. They were more interested in his new technology than in the patents they'd assigned to me. I didn't care. They paid my bills."

"So it looked like you'd lucked out and your problems were solved, Mr. Hicks."

"I thought so. Until people started dying around me."

"You mean Carl?"

"And your law clerk. And the attack on you. Everyone who's seen the report on Carl's new technology seems to be in harm's way."

"Have you seen the report, Mr. Hicks?"

"Me? Oh no. I haven't seen anything."

Hicks looked away as it said it, unconsciously brushing his mouth with his hand, perhaps to push away a lie.

"But I'm sure I'm being followed. Watched very carefully. I could be next."

"Next?"

"Dead, Judge, dead."

Hicks looked scared now.

"Why come to me now?"

"It was Frank. I just today found out he's dead."

"You knew Frank? My law clerk?"

"No."

"But you said Frank had seen the report. How'd you know that?"

"Frank called me. Reminded me who he was. Said he'd got the report I wanted. Was going to put the original one back. But had made me the copy."

"When was this?"

"Thursday evening, around 8 p.m. Said he wanted his check. Told me to call off my uniform. Said he would meet me at the Coffee Bean across from Concert Park in Playa Vista at 10 p.m. We'd trade. I was to bring his payment. $500,000 in cash. He'd bring the copy of the report. Said from now on he'd only deal with me. Wasn't going to be strong-armed or threatened anymore."

"What'd you say?"

"Said I hadn't a clue what he was talking about. He got really angry then. Called me a lying son of a bitch. Then he hung up."

The Judge sat back in his chair. What the hell was Frankie doing?

"Anyway, Judge. I don't trust anyone now. I don't trust the people sending me my check. I don't trust the police. Hell, I don't trust my own attorney, Dick Harper. I guess the only one I trust is you. They tried to kill you. So I figure you're not involved."

"You should go to the police with your suspicions, Mr. Hicks."

"I've been warned not to do that. That there could be immediate adverse consequences for me."

"By who?"

"By those who have been paying my salary. Some conglomerate in Hong Kong. Never met them. Just a name. 'Wang'. All by email and wired funds."

"You seemed to have painted yourself into a corner," said the Judge. "But I don't see how I can help."

"I want to stop the arbitration. Just stop everything. I don't want more discovery. I don't want the missing report re-submitted. I don't want to know anything about Carl's new technology. I'll just sell my products and take my chances someday his estate may claim I'm infringing. I just want out of all of this."

The Judge sat back in his chair. He hadn't expected this.

"Have you talked to your attorney about it?"

"I tried. He said the patent suit couldn't be terminated right now. Too many things going on. Too many moving parts, or some bullshit. Legal procedure mumbo jumbo. I don't know. He wouldn't look at me when he said it. And he got real fidgety. I know when I'm being lied to. So I called you."

"I'm not sure what's going on, Hicks, and no I'm not involved. But I'm going to be. I'm going to get to the bottom of what's going on here."

"I hope you do, Judge. But right now I just want out. Life's too short. I'll find some other way to make my nut. Screw their salary. I want to abandon this patent law suit now."

"I'll talk to Dick Harper, Mr. Hicks. See what he says. I don't see why you couldn't elect to withdraw your complaint. If Dick won't do it, if he's compromised in some way and unable to give you impartial advice, you may want to hire another attorney."

"Will you do that, Judge? Talk to Dick? I want out. I don't want to end up on a slab at the morgue. I just want out."

He stood then. Offered the Judge his hand. Turned and stalked out. He looked eager to be away from the Judge. Hicks was a bit slimy, but he was no fool.

It reminded the Judge of the old proverb about rats leaving a sinking ship, or, as Pliny the Elder said in

77 AD, 'When a building is about to fall, all the mice desert it.'

If Hicks was a mouse, there could be a large exit of rats behind him. The Judge intended to accelerate the exodus.

CHAPTER 27
6:30 PM Tuesday

The Judge pulled in to the marina and parked. Every bone in his body was tired. He slowly made his way on to the boat. Katy was in the galley chopping vegetables for dinner. She gave the Judge that bright smile that made him melt. Every time.

"You're looking very domesticated in the galley Katy," the Judge smiled.

Katy shot the Judge a look of bemusement.

"How about we go to a movie after dinner, Judge?"

"Baby I'm beat. I'd like to stay home. Have a strong drink. Dinner with you. And go to bed early."

"How long have we been living together, Judge?"

"Six months."

"How long have we been secretly married?"

"Almost a month."

"Did you have an idea about how it would be, Judge? I mean having a permanent domestic relationship with a woman?"

"Well, I was married before, Katy. So I guess I kinda knew what to expect."

"That's right. You're my second hand hubby."

"Ouch."

"So were all your hopes and dreams knocked out of you years ago. Judge?"

"We all have fantasies about how things are going to be, honey. To hope and dream is human."

"I know, I know. But it's just as a young woman and not used to living with a man, there are… surprises. Things you expect that are different. Things you didn't expect. Had no idea about."

"For instance, Katy?"

"Well, I never envisioned my husband would snore."

"I don't snore."

"The whole house shakes!"

"Well, maybe a little when I'm congested," admitted the Judge. "I have allergies."

"Judge…. You snore!"

The Judge shrugged his shoulders. He supposed all men snored some. "Is that all, Katy," he asked hopefully.

"I thought my husband would know how to work the dishwasher, and the washing machine, and the dryer. All skills you claim to lack. I thought I'd live in a house with empty closets in every room for my stuff. The idea of a house seemed so big. I didn't know I'd be moving in to a house with my husband's years of accumulated stuff already jammed in."

"I've given you half the closets, Katy. We're clearly fifty-fifty on closets. A fair split."

"Yes, but I think you kept the better located ones. Anyway, there never seems to be enough storage. Oh, and I thought I'd marry a man who appreciated exquisite artistic work."

"Artistic work? Like what?"

"Like my shoe collection."

"Oh," said the Judge. Sniggering now. "I've never understood about your shoes. You can only wear one pair at a time. Some of your shoes don't even fit."

"Doesn't matter." Katy's chin ratchetted up a degree. "Those ones were very expensive. I have fond memories associated with them. And it's a collection."

"Kind of like a shell collection?" asked the Judge.

"No, NOT a shell collection, Judge." Katy had her hands on her hips now, aggravated.

"Besides, you have collections too, Judge."

"Me? No honey. I have the one pair of brown shoes I wear, one pair of tennis shoes for exercise, one pair of slippers for cold nights before I had you, and one pair of black shoes for funerals."

"Ah, that's another thing. You have cold feet. But seriously Judge, you do have collections too. You collect boats."

"Boats?"

"Yes. You have this yacht, and the little Zodiac that sits on its roof, and the little Century at the back for running around the harbor, and the SeaRay in Avalon for playing around the island, and the Boston Whaler for your dock in Lake Arrowhead, and the Canoe on the dock... and... I've missed one."

"Oh, but Katy..."

"I've got it. The 1932 Chris Craft Woody you keep in that garage. If that's not a collection I don't know what is. Don't tell me you drive all those boats at once."

"But that's different, Katy. Those are each separate pieces of naval engineering. They're expensive.

"Just like my shoes," said Katy. Giving the Judge a *gotcha* look.

The Judge threw his hands high in the air in mock surrender.

"I accept your implied apology, Judge." Katy said. "But back to my point. As a girl growing into a woman you do have fantasies about how life will be with your future husband. I assumed my man would love to eat the same things I love to eat, and we'd dine out a lot, enjoying wonderful meals together."

"And we do."

"We do go out. But you like burnt red meat. Heavy potatoes. Greasy Mexican food. Spicy Thai. Even Hamburgers. Yuck."

"Gourmet hamburgers," the Judge corrected.

"Indeed. An oxymoron if ever there were. I assumed we'd continue to do the things together I liked to do before we met, Judge. Things that have fallen off my calendar now we're married."

"Like?"

"Like movies, honey. I love to go to the movies. I used to go once a week before we became involved. Now we never go. You consider them a waste of time."

"You knew I wasn't a big movie fan, Katy. It's synthetic experience. Not real. Someone else's fiction and fantasy. I'd rather walk along the beach, take a drive, and go off on a trip, even just out to dinner. Live my own experience for real, not someone else's pretend reality projected on a two dimensional screen with phony surround sound, nestled in the middle of a zombie audience."

"I got it, Judge. I understand. I like movies. You don't. What happened to old fashion compromise when we have competing interests?"

"Okay, okay. I'll take you to a movie, Katy. This weekend. I promise. What else?"

"Health food restaurants. You'll go with me to keep me company but you won't eat the food. Dance clubs. We hardly ever go out clubbing anymore."

The Judge smiled, a twinkle in his eye. She'd teased him too far.

"As my dad used say, Katy, 'You don't chase the bus after you're aboard.'"

"Grrrrr." Katy made claws out of her hands and spread them threateningly out toward the Judge. Annie the dog, asleep in the corner, leaped up, sure she was under attack.

"Besides, Katy," the Judge added, "you can't drink right now. There'd be no point to go clubbing."

"You don't drink at movies, Judge!"

The Judge got another *gotcha* look.

"And I didn't envision I would inherit this dog, more puppy than dog that came along with my new husband."

Annie the dog, fully awake now and listening intently to the shaded inflections in their voices, caught the word "dog" and began to thump her tail on the floor. She was now included in the conversation. Any attention was better than none.

"I don't mind picking up your dirty socks you leave in a pile on the floor Judge. But Annie grabs them and hides them all over the house. She even buries them in the yard. Somewhere, somehow, you've given Annie a sock fetish. And I'm always cleaning up

Annie's mess. I've never seen a dog that could get in so much trouble. Yesterday she got the butter dish and spread butter all over the boat carpet. This afternoon she snuck her snout up here on the counter and snagged my loaf of garlic bread for dinner. She's going to be pooping garlic farts all night."

Annie licked her chops, as though on cue.

"I brush her. I feed her. I walk her. I take her to the vet. I arrange for her home sitter when we're off to the Island. It's like being responsible for a small child."

Annie got up and wandered over to thrust her muzzle affectionately against Katy's thigh, seeking love and attention. Katy reached down and ruffled the dog's ears.

"Good practice for having a child," said the Judge. This earned him another mock glare.

"And it's kind of weird having to account for my time, Judge."

"How so?"

"We're expected to coordinate what we're doing. To tell each other when we're leaving the house. What we're about. We're each suddenly accountable to the other for our schedules. It's just polite I know. And it helps keep our busy schedules in sync, but it's weird. It's like we're one person instead of two. I've lost my identity. And chores, Judge. I fantasized my husband would share in domestic chores. Taking out the trash. Paying bills. Shopping for toilet paper. Picking up the cleaning. That falls solely to me now, Judge. I think you were looking to marry a housekeeper."

"Well, errr… I am awfully busy, Katy. But you are the keeper of our cave." Trying to make it sound a prestigious title.

"I am indeed, Judge. I guess my fantasy husband wasn't a workaholic. I didn't anticipate the time I'd spend folding clothes. I hate folding clothes. Matching socks. And making the bed. How is it you never learned to properly make a bed, Judge?"

"I do make the bed sometimes," said the Judge.

"Hah! Not to any sort of standard you don't."

"You have very high bed-making standards, Katy. You make the bed ever so much better than I do. You're the best bed-maker on the entire planet. Of course when we're together in the bedroom, Katy, I'm very good at messing the bed back up. It's sort of my specialty. And rocking it too. I'm a great rocker. It's all because you're so irresistible."

Katy crossed her arms and sighed in exasperation, trying to hide the smile creeping into her eyes.

"And I don't see my old single friends so much anymore, Judge. That's not your fault, but it's different. Something I hadn't anticipated. I don't have much in common with them anymore. We used to share our rollicking experiences hunting for men. Current sightings. Blow by blow descriptions of skirmishes and huddled plans for future trappings. What we wore. How we met. Who said what. Whether he called. Should I call? Where'd we recommend to meet guys. To go on a date. It was all very intense. But I'm not included in those war powwows anymore. I've got nothing to contribute now I'm married."

"I hope not honey," said the Judge. "You've hunted me down. You don't need to look anymore. But you'll make new friends. Married friends who'll have more in common. When the kid arrives you'll make a whole other set friends. Ones with young kids."

"I guess. And the finances, Judge. You control the finances. We've pooled our incomes. I get an allowance and budgeted amounts for household and so on. And I'm not complaining. You do a much better job at managing our finances than I ever would. It just wasn't in my picture of what marriage would be like. It feels funny giving up my economic independence. Having to come to you if I want to make a purchase of any size."

"We make joint decisions, Katy. We have to plan financially for a grand old age for you, with your children, and your grandchildren. It all takes money, which means careful planning. Remember I'm 20 years older. And women live on average five years longer than men. I'm budgeting for twenty-five years sometime in the future without me, dear. I want to make sure you're covered financially and can afford a respectable toy boy for fun and frolic in your old age."

"Judge… stop it. I don't want to joke about that."

"What else, Katy?" asked the Judge.

"I guess I get a little sad sometimes when I think about how we eloped for a quickie marriage in Las Vegas. No formal wedding. None of the excitement of shopping for a wedding dress. No showers with friends. No showing off my trophy catch. No bachelorette party. No ceremony in a church. All the stuff that a young girl's fantasies are made of."

"I'm sorry about that Katy. But you wanted to move quickly for obvious reasons. I could have waited."

"No, no, it was the right thing to do. We're bringing this little guy into the world. I didn't want him to look back at pictures of his mom in her wedding dress with... with... with a... bump."

"There's stuff I didn't plan for either you know Katy. I suppose I had my own fantasies about what it would be like if I ever got married again."

"Like what?"

"Well... like the baby for instance."

There was complete silence. Katy didn't move. Just looked at the Judge. Stricken.

"I didn't mean that the way it sounded, Katy," the Judge said quickly. "It just came out. But you know we don't have to do this if you don't want."

"Do what?"

"Have the baby."

"What are you saying?" she asked softly.

"I'm just saying there are options in the first trimester."

"Go on."

"Well, we never actually talked about having a kid. You just told me the situation and we decided to get married. And I love you dearly. I'd marry you again in a heartbeat. Under any circumstances."

"And?"

"Do you ever wish there were more time for just us two, exploring each other, building memories together, before a kid arrives?"

He could see the shock at the back of her eyes. Her arms swung across her belly, protecting it. She looked very… closed.

"Don't get me wrong, honey. I'm excited about the baby."

"Our baby, Judge."

"Yes. Our baby."

"It's just. Just…. I'm just worried I'm not going to be much of a dad. I'm already 53. I'll be 54 when the kid arrives. Pretty old for a new dad. When the kid's 8 and wants to play soccer, I'll be 62. Too old to coach. When it starts high school, I'll be 68 and collecting social security. When it starts college I'll be 72. By the time the kid hits 21, I'll be 75. Ready for a retirement home. And how am I going to relate to a kid when there's such an age difference? We'll have nothing in common. Any ideas I have will sound old and tired. I'll be two generations ahead of him. Old enough to be his grandfather. And then there's the money issues," continued the Judge. Plowing ahead despite the drop in temperature.

"Go on."

"At 72, when the kid starts college, I'm likely going to be too old to work. Where will the money come from to put it through USC?"

"You don't want our baby, Judge?" She asked in a tiny voice, a small tear escaping from one eye. Looking scared.

"Well… no. No, Katy. Of course I want the baby. It's just… just. You're going to have to help me a lot on being a dad. I'm going to lean heavily on you for advice. And you and the kid will have to appreciate there will be certain things I can't do. Certain things I won't understand. Certain things you'll have to talk me through."

She took a deep breath and pulled herself together, standing unnaturally tall behind the galley bar.

"You love me don't you Judge?"

"Of course."

"You're glad we're married?"

"Of course."

"You don't want to re-think that?"

"Never."

"I know this baby wasn't planned, Judge. We didn't discuss it ad nauseum and intellectualize it all out. It just sort of happened. But I have to believe it was meant to be. I know you're a planner, Judge, you're very intellectual. You're very good at organizing things. It's the way you run your life, your clients, Annie the dog, and now me. All very intellectual and carefully planned. And that's all good, to a degree. But sometimes surprises like this come along that are just wonderful. They change your life. You have to let go of your organization and planning. You just have to take a chance. Jump in and make an emotional commitment. Like you did when you proposed to me. Our baby is going to be a wonderful thing for us both. I know it."

"You really think so? You really think I can hold up my end? Be a good dad?"

"Of course. And there are lots of things still to discuss about our child."

"Like what?"

"Like boys names for instance. And which room he's going to have in that dusty old house of yours. And shall we have a baby shower? Which kind of crib? What color are you going to paint his room for me? Can we afford help for a few days when I bring him home? What will Annie the dog think?"

"You're certain it's going to be a boy?"

"Yes, Judge. And here's another question. Will you be there in your scrubs? In the room. When he's born?"

The Judge gulped. He hadn't considered being in the room when it was born. He wasn't at all sure he wanted that.

"Besides, I know you Judge," Katy went on. "You could never terminate our baby. You couldn't bring yourself to do it. It'd be saddest thing to do in the world."

"You sound like you've had experience, Katy."

"Some. I went with my best friend in college, Judge. With her and her boyfriend. To a dingy place in the valley one evening. She terminated her pregnancy there. They decided together to do it. They were very much in love. But they weren't through school yet. There was no money. It just wasn't practical. So they made what they thought was the right decision. For all the right reasons. And she asked me to come along."

"And…?"

"She was very brave. He felt very guilty. He seemed smaller, shrunk into himself, sitting on that couch in the waiting room. She marched right in behind the closed doors, head held high, confident she'd made the right decision."

"Well there you go," said the Judge.

"It wasn't like that 45 minutes later when they helped her out through those same swinging doors. She was sobbing. She couldn't even look at her boyfriend. I think it wounded her soul. She wouldn't ride home with him. I drove her home. They broke up the next week. Never saw each other again. And she was sad for a long time after that. It changed her somehow. In ways she hadn't anticipated and couldn't explain."

"Oh," was all the Judge could manage.

"But that's not us, Judge. We're having our baby and he's going to be wonderful. Healthy and happy. And he's going to look just like you. A damn Welshman. He's going to be so much fun."

Katy put her chopping knife down and came around the galley counter to give the Judge a big hug.

She said, "I love you so much. Ignore the things I said earlier about missing my old life. And my foolish young girl fantasies about marriage. All I care about is to be with you and make you happy."

They stood there for a long time. Holding each other tight. Until Annie the dog felt compelled to intercede, poking her muzzle between them, demanding a share of the affection.

CHAPTER 28
Noon Wednesday

The Judge had busied himself in his office with client work all morning. Then he decided to skip lunch and to use the time for a stroll along the Venice Boardwalk. A good place to people watch, particularly in summer. He took his car, allowed himself to be waved into a parking lot on Pacific Avenue near Mildred by a flag man chumming in vehicles, and walked the block and a half along 18th Avenue to the Boardwalk and its summer throng.

He strolled north for a while, then reversed, walking south past 18th Avenue, watching the bikers, skaters, surfers, joggers, tourists, and homeless drifting by. It was a human stream meandering over concrete and sand in both directions. Everyone going some-where. No one in a hurry. It was too hot.

The Judge took a break, leaning against the fence surrounding the outdoor weightlifting area at the south end of Venice's Gym on the Boardwalk. Hard bodies and spectators crowded around at this end of the Venice Beach Recreation Center called "Muscle Beach", watching the active pumping iron in the Cali-fornia sun. The name was now generic for the numer-ous gyms and fitness studios in the area, including the original Gold's Gym, where Arnold Schwarzenegger and other legendary bodybuilders pumped iron in the

1970s. The Judge looked up at the giant concrete bar-bell atop the roof of the Center and wondered how long it had stood. Had it ever fallen in one of the great L.A. earthquakes?

As he watched, a more organized knot of people approached along the boardwalk. It was a "Right to Go Topless" demonstration. More parade then demonstration. Eight ladies in bikini bottoms, topless, mostly middle aged with boobs of assorted sizes, shapes and lift, and one looker, early twenties, pristine, marched down the Boardwalk with signs proclaiming their right to go topless like men. They were surrounded by a cadre of enthusiastic men, mostly younger, some also holding signs. A crowd of tourists following behind. Here and there piranha-like junior paparazzi darted around, snapping pictures.

The Judge watched a stout lady take hold of her husband's arm, wanting him by the ear, and steer him 180 degrees around in the opposite direction while he tried to crane his head back for another look. It was Venice in late June.

The Judge stepped back under the shadow of an adjacent awning to be out of camera range. All he needed was his picture in the paper ogling boobs at the bare-breast parade.

As he stood admiring the fauna, he felt a hand touch his arm. He looked around to see a young boy standing there. Perhaps twelve. Thin, oily black hair, deep tan, faded jeans, threadbare T-shirt from too many washings, disreputable Nikes. A faint slant to large brown eyes, suggesting Chicano lineage somewhere, but mixed.

247

He seemed part of the homeless that were everywhere these days. But he looked awfully young. Desperate people with young families usually got priority access to the limited shelter and counseling services. Their children were plucked from the streets and put in school.

"Hi," said the Judge.

"Hi, mister. I seen you on the beach last week. You swim pretty good for an old guy."

The Judge swung around, the parade forgotten.

"You saw me on the beach?"

"Yeah."

"You saw those guys come after me?"

"Yeah."

"Did you call the police?"

"Not my business, mister. I stay away from the police."

"What's your name?"

"Marty."

"Hi Marty, people call me Judge."

"That's a funny name. You go around judging stuff? Like surfing maybe? Or boobs?" Marty nodded at the parade disappearing down the Boardwalk.

"No Marty. I'm a lawyer. I used to be a Judge on the Superior Court. Now I just practice law."

Marty imperceptibly moved back several inches, putting distance, regretting he'd opened his mouth.

"I'm not going to call the police, Marty. Or the school people. Or whoever you're worried about. I figure live and let live. You want to be out here watching a boob parade 'stead of school. Why not. I might make a similar choice. In fact I have. I should be working, but I'm here."

Marty relaxed. Inched back a little closer.

"You know a good place for ice cream around here?" the Judge asked. "It's hot. I think I need ice cream."

It was the right button. Marty puffed right up. Pointed down the Boardwalk.

"Just down there. The next corner. *Monkee's Burgers*. They got the best stuff."

"I could buy you one too."

Marty looked suspicious. Measuring the Judge. Then shrugged his shoulders.

"Sure. Follow me."

Marty turned his back on the parade and sauntered along the Boardwalk, the Judge in tow. *Monkee's Burgers* turned out to be a small store in the middle of the Boardwalk shaded by a bright red awning, with garish pictures of the fast food it offered posted across its exterior, and large plastic soft-serve ice cream cones hanging from each corner of its awning. The pictures of the food made the Judge want to reach for his Tums. But Marty seemed happy with his joint.

The Judge had an extra thick caramel shake, trying to ignore the small voice inside berating him for the breach of his diet. The young man had a triple scoop with three toppings and lots of gummy bears. It looked like a dentist's dream.

They found a bench to sit down and ate quickly, racing the sun trying to turn the ice cream to slush.

"So can you tell me a little about what you saw on the beach, Marty?"

"Why? I ain't telling the police or no one. I could get hurt."

"I've got a fifty dollar bill in my wallet. It's yours if you'll tell me all that you saw."

Marty's eyes narrowed. The avarice there was clear. Fifty dollars would go a long way on the streets.

"No one will know I talked to you? No one. No police?"

"No police."

"Let's see the fifty."

The Judge brought the bill out of his wallet and laid it between them, putting his empty shake container on top to emphasize his position.

Marty sent a sticky hand across the table for it, but the Judge nodded no. Waiting.

"It was pretty dark. Didn't see much. There was four of them I think. Two coming up behind you, one coming from the land side, and one ahead. I saw one of them earlier, watching you from up the street behind you. On his cell phone. Looked to be following you. You walked past another one when you walked onto the sand."

"Then what happened?"

"They kinda spread out around you. Then ran at you."

"And then?"

"Shit, you punched one of them. Broke his nose. Then you dived in the water. Pretty smart."

"How far away were you?"

"I was hanging out in the lifeguard stand. Smoking. I could see okay."

"Then what happened?"

"They huddled there for a minute on the sand where you went in. One was on his cell phone, looking up the beach toward the pier. One took his shoes off and waded into the surf up to his waist. Pulled out your pants.

"How do you know the guy's nose was broken?"

"Uh… I just heard. You know. You just hear things."

"I don't know Marty. Who were these guys who attacked me?"

"How would I know? Just some guys on the beach."

"Then how do you know the one guy's nose was broken?"

"Well, maybe I don't. Just guessed maybe."

The Judge looked at the fifty under his plastic cup. Pressed the cup down harder on to the bill. Marty watched, licked his lips. The bill was important. Almost within grasp.

"Who were they, Marty?"

Marty looked around the bench, up and down the boardwalk. Lots of tourists. No one was close. No one was paying them any attention.

"There's this gang. Hang out with the homeless people. But not really homeless. Or maybe homeless but not really poor. Don't know. Anyway, they hire out to do stuff."

"Like what?"

"I hear they collect money. Beat people up. Steal stuff. Rob houses, jack cars. They can snuff somebody. You pay, they'll do anything you want."

"These guys are the ones attacked me?"

"I think so."

"What're their names?"

Marty leaned low across the table to whisper.

"The black one's called Juno. The white guy whose nose you broke, he's Arty. I don't know the other two."

"What do they look like?"

"Like I said, Arty's a white guy. Juno's black. There's a Latino, like me, and an Asian. I think the Asian's the leader. They're all old guys. Old enough to drink. But they don't surf very well."

The Judge thought how relative age was, depending on which end of the barrel you looked through. 'Old' to Marty was 'kids' to him. He supposed he was way too old to surf well.

"How do you know about Arty's broken nose?"

"People talk on the street. I just heard somewhere."

"How do you know these guys have money?"

"You kidding? People pay them for stuff all the time. They dress up like they're poor, but I've seen them on the beach, drinking Jack, smoking joints, roasting marshmallows, throwing out bills to girls. They all got fancy cell phones. Seen them pile into their own SUV and roar away. They hang out during the day with the street people. Dress down. But they go somewhere fancy to sleep."

"You know where?"

"No."

"Where can I find them during the day?"

Marty looked worried again. He had said more than he'd intended.

"This fifty will go aways, Marty. It's yours. And a second fifty later if you help me. No one will know. Can you ask around and find out where they hang?"

The Judge lifted his plastic cup and a grubby hand shot forward to retrieve the bill, retracting at once into a worn pocket.

"I got to be going now, Judge. But I'll see what I can find."

Marty slid from the bench out on to the Boardwalk, disappearing into the throng like a pebble into a stream.

CHAPTER 29
2:00 PM Wednesday

The Judge had an afternoon meeting with a possible new client who had called out of the blue. You never knew when the next gig was coming, or from where. But after practicing law for a number of years and doing the best you could for clients, you built a reputation and clients just seemed to come.

The meeting was at *Gelila* on Abbot Kinney. Located several blocks from Venice Beach, Abbot Kinney Blvd. was a collection of boutiques, salons and other establishments, just a tad off the beaten track. In the 80s it'd been little more than old cottages and empty industrial buildings. But activists and property owners undertook an extensive cleanup and campaigned to bring in new shops, restaurants and galleries. The resulting eclectic mix offered everything under the sun in just a few blocks. The foot traffic attracted some of the best restaurants in L.A., several bars of note, some intimate, some rough, and of course the homeless, all but invisible to the tony shoppers plying Abbot Kinney's sidewalks.

Personally the Judge found it a little too jumbled to be cool and a little too city to be pretty. But what'd he know?

Gelila's rustic courtyard was patronized by beautiful people, fashionably disheveled and looking to be casually cool. It was quiet this afternoon with only half a dozen tables occupied, providing a quiet place for confidential discussion.

He entered the courtyard and started to retrieve his cell phone to call Mr. William Strong, the potential client. But a bearded gentlemen across the court set his coffee down and stuck his hand in the air, waving vigorously. Apparently the client.

The Judge threaded his way through the tables to the other side, already assessing the 40ish man beckoning him. He wore a dark grey suit, wool, and a club tie of reds and grey. His beard was clipped into a goatee around his chin and attached to wide sideburns which snaked to his ears. The drama was heighten by contrast. He was totally clean shaven on top, apparently preferring a Star Trek Picard to a Friar Tuck. Dark eyes regarded the Judge as he approached with a sharpness which belied the broad smile on his face and his articulating hands motioning the Judge to sit.

The Judge sat and ordered a cafe latte.

After some brief preliminaries about the weather, where the man was from (Detroit), where he was staying (the Ritz Carlton in Marina del Rey), how he had found the Judge (the internet), and his profession (public accountant), Mr. Strong got down to business. He had a slight accent the Judge couldn't place.

"I represent a certain conglomerate, Judge. It has unlimited money and would like to buy your knowledge and expertise."

"I'm flattered," said the Judge. "Exactly how do they need my help?"

Strong opened the briefcase at his side and took out a sealed white envelope which he slid across the table to the Judge.

The Judge took the envelope and opened it. A single piece of paper was inside. A cashier's check drawn on Chase Manhattan Bank, made out to the Judge, for $500,000. The Judge blinked at the number.

"That's a rather large retainer. What do I have to do for it, Mr. Strong?"

"You have a particular document. My employer would like you to discreetly make a copy for him."

"What document would that be?" asked the Judge, getting a sinking feeling in his stomach.

"It's a report that was prepared by Carl Greene and given to you pursuant to a request for discovery."

The Judge sat back in his chair. Every time he turned around he ran into this damn case. Was it never going to let him go?

"Exactly who is this conglomerate you represent?" asked the Judge.

"That's of no importance. They're offshore. I assure you their money is good."

"If I had that report, and I'm not saying I do, do you think this money would be considered a bribe?" asked the Judge.

"I wouldn't call it a bribe. We'd expect you to do some light legal work around the edges to justify its payment." Strong was all smiles now, ready to cut a deal with an interested recipient.

"I couldn't consider such a proposal when I don't even know who it's from," said the Judge carefully. He wondered if he was being recorded.

"Let's say there's a certain Russian conglomerate then. Nothing sinister. Just industrial interests in Russia and Eastern Europe."

"Are there National Defense overtones here?" asked the Judge.

"No, of course not. You've seen the report. Understand the significance of the technology. But there's no secret military weapon here. You know that."

"Sometimes weapons can be economic."

"Judge, let's not... how do you say it, beat the bush. You would like the money. We would like the report. Mr. Greene is dead. It's a simple exchange. No one gets hurt. No damage is done. No one ever knows."

Again the broad smile.

"I'm afraid you've picked the wrong man, Mr. Strong. As a lawyer I'm an officer of the Federal Court, and in this case, also the appointed arbitrator by the litigants. I don't take my oath lightly."

The smile cracked and fell from Strong's face. Leaving him looking cold, angry, and dangerous. There was now only malice in the dark eyes. He said nothing more. He simply snatched the envelope with the check back from the Judge, put it in his briefcase, rose, and strode out of the courtyard, not looking back.

The server brought over the Judge's latte, and a check for two lattes. Damn, stuck with the check. That seemed his Karma these days. He sipped the steamy foam off his drink and considered their brief conversation. Everything that had happened seemed tied somehow to that damn report. He wished to hell he'd read though it when he'd had it in his hands. Damn Frankie. Damn, Damn, Damn.

He drove back to his office and settled at the long table in an uncomfortable side chair, a pad in front of him. He drew circles and boxes and lines and arrows, trying again to piece things together.

How did Strong know about the technology? And more particularly, about the report? Did Frankie offer it on the internet or something? Would he have been so foolish?

Everybody seemed to know about it. As though everything that happened in the arbitration was common knowledge. How could that be? Were people watching the arbitration? Following it step by step?

He stood up and began a close examination of his office, starting with his desk phone. He examined it carefully, unscrewing the earpiece end, then the mic end. Nothing looked out of order, though he wasn't sure he'd know. He examined the base, then put the phone down and looked around the office. It was sparse. There was the long table, chairs, bureau with coffee and drinks on top, an old fashioned clock on one wall, and an inexpensive reproduction of a seascape on the other. He scanned the frame around the seascape. It seemed normal.

He walked over and stood on tip toes to be eyeball to eyeball with the clock. It was mounted on a flat circular piece of wood, a metal frame projecting outward encasing the clock face. Just below the metal rim, in the wood, was a small glass bead. He looked closely. It looked back at him. It didn't light up or blink. But somehow he didn't think it belonged.

He lifted the clock, back plate and all, off the wall. Turned it over on the table. A hole had been drilled all the way through the wood. The glass bead was mounted in front and two fine wires came out the back and ran into the mechanism box. He pried off the metal back of the clock mechanism box. The wires ran into a small box lodged inside, about the size of a thimble. Out the other end of the box projected a small antenna. A third wire ran to a battery, hearing aid size, glued to the inside of the box. It all looked professional.

Son of a bitch, thought the Judge. It was a bug. But who? The little he knew about over the air transmitters left him with the impression their broadcast range wasn't far. Was there someone else in this executive suite watching even now as he fiddled with the damn clock?

Someone had been watching his confidential discussions held separately with each side in the arbitration and his private discussions of the case with Frankie. Someone who perhaps saw him flip through the confidential report, then put it back in the brown envelope and lock it in his bureau.

They probably watched him take his naps in the afternoon. Listened in on his calls to Katy. The Judge felt like he'd been violated. Like he'd been stupid to ever trust the security of this place. He hung the damn clock back on the wall.

He strolled out of his office and went door to door to the other offices in the executive suite. It was late in the afternoon and most everyone was gone. Many doors were locked, some were open. There was only one that was vacant and for lease. It was the office second over from his, a small card posted on its door: "For short term lease." On the off chance it was unlocked, he pushed at the door. It swung open.

259

The office was furnished exactly like his office, down to the same seascape print on the wall and the same bureau at the other end under the window. There was even the same wall clock. He hoped at least the bureau keys were different.

He walked to the window and tried the bureau drawer. Unlocked and empty. He bent down and opened one side cupboard in the cabinet. Also unlocked and empty. He opened the other side cupboard. It wasn't empty. It had a small DVD player/recorder sitting on the shelf, happily running, its little green light blinking at him. A small box sat on top with an antenna. Here was the dump for the video being recorded in his office. He was sure.

He punched a button on the little recorder and a DVD player dish smoothly slid out, displaying a twirling disk. He plucked it out and slipped it into his coat pocket. He strolled back to his office, brought out his laptop, and inserted the DVD.

It started to play at the beginning of the disc. It was his office. He and Frankie were there discussing plaintiff's motion for production of Carl Greene's new technology. Frankie was making an impassioned argument that plaintiff Hicks was entitled to see Greene's new technology. And to seek a declaration that Hicks' technology didn't infringe. Frankie argued that Carl Greene's report be turned over to Hicks' legal counsel immediately. The Judge wasn't so sure, pointing out that the new technology might be totally unrelated to what Hicks was doing. It sounded like a fishing expedition to the Judge.

The Judge fast forwarded through several minutes of conversation. Then Frankie left for the day.

He said he had a hot date. The Judge held up the brown envelope that Greene's attorney had produced at Thursday's meeting. The one containing the secret report on the new technology.

The Judge was alone. Or so he'd thought. He'd hadn't known a video camera watched over his shoulder. The Judge opened the brown envelope just as he remembered. He watched himself page through it. He'd been too tired to read it and his reading glasses weren't handy. There'd been a summary about how much money the new technology was worth at the beginning. Lots apparently. He'd gotten no farther than that.

But the camera didn't register what he'd read, only that he'd studied the report for perhaps five minutes. He'd then put the report back in its brown envelope and locked it in his bureau drawer, foolishly thinking it was secure. He'd turned off the office lights and left his office. The video went off. It was apparently activated by movement.

The Judge watched the next clip. It was dark in the office now, but the camera had a dark light feature that picked up much of the detail. The door had opened, the motion triggering recording. This must have been Thursday night after he'd left.

Christ, it was Frankie. He'd turned on the lights and went right to the bureau. He brought out a screw driver and pried away at the drawer lock a little to leave marks. Then unlocked the drawer with his key. He pulled a white plastic trash bag from his pocket and shoved the brown envelope into it. Then hurriedly locked the drawer again and left.

The recording started again with the return of the Judge and the two attorneys on Friday morning. A few minutes later Frankie slid in, looking tired and anxious. The entire hearing was there on video. Frankie looked scared when the Judge started discussing the report. He jumped up and excused himself, fleeing the room.

The Judge fast forwarded to the end. The last entry showed the Judge a half hour ago, opening the door and going to his desk to make notes. No one had recovered the DVD and put a new one in since the middle of the day on Thursday morning.

Damn, thought the Judge. Frankie must have been sweating bullets that the Judge would open the bureau drawer and find the Carl Greene Report missing during the Friday hearing. It explained why Frankie had left so quickly. Randall Hicks hadn't lied. Frankie had taken the report, presumably to sell a copy to somebody. And Frankie had been hired to sway the Judge into giving Hicks access to the report.

But who had bugged his office, recording everything that happened, including his confidential discussions of the case with his law clerk? He backed up the DVD player file on his computer. Then he looked at the disk properties. The screen indicated that the video took up about 95 percent of the space on the DVD. He popped the DVD out and put it in his coat pocket. He pulled a blank DVD he had in his supply cabinet out of its sleeve, walked back to the empty office, and inserted the blank disc into the DVD recorder. He wondered who would retrieve it. Whether they'd notice it was a different brand.

CHAPTER 30
3:00 PM Wednesday

The Judge returned to his office and stared at the DISC he'd taken for a while. Wondering who he could turn to for help. There was one person who immediately came to mind.

Manny Leibowitz operated a small computer repair shop in a dilapidated little place in Playa Del Rey Village. Manny had helped the Judge before, setting up his computer and bailing him out when it'd caught a virus.

The Judge headed for the elevator and the parking garage. It was worth a 15-minute drive over to Play Del Rey Village to see if Manny could find anything else on the DVD.

Manny had a small shop on Culver behind the flower shop, with a sign in the window touting computer repair. He gave the Judge a big smile as he walked in. A small, rotund little man, in his 70s now, with long hair and a full beard that had been red once but now was mostly grey. He shook the Judge's hand vigorously, bowing slightly as he did so. Then asked the Judge what he needed, crinkly dark eyes assessing the Judge with good humor.

The Judge produced the DVD. Was there anything else Manny could tell the Judge about the DVD's origin or use?

Manny took the DVD and put his reading glasses on.

"It's a common brand of read write DVD," he said. "Available in any of the larger computer stores."

Manny popped the DVD into the laptop on his counter and lighted it up.

"It's almost full," he said. "I'm guessing that's your video."

The Judge nodded.

"Sometimes people make a mistake and re-use a disc. Wipe it and re-use it. They save two dollars that way. Let's see."

Manny opened software on his computer designed to retrieve inadvertently deleted files. He fiddled with settings. The machine hummed and swished for a while as the DVD spun. Eventually a read out of lost files appeared. There was only one. A Word file. Manny printed it out and handed the sheet over to the Judge. It was a memo from Dick Harper to his Accounting Department. It listed a string of his billing hours on some client matter for the Law Offices of Jordan, Biggs and Stolewater, Dick's law firm. Dick had been spying on him. Damn the slippery bastard..

Manny retrieved the DVD and handed it back to the Judge. "That's all I can tell you Judge."

"What do I owe you?"

"It's on the house. But don't be a stranger."

The Judge thanked him and walked back to his car. He recalled again Dick Harper's troubles in California over allegations of illegal phone tapping and bugging of the other side's law offices. Dick was reverting to his old tricks.

The Judge returned to his office. He deleted the video which showed him discovering the clock camera, and swapped the original DVD back into the hidden recording machine in exchange for the blank he'd inserted.

CHAPTER 31
7:00 PM Wednesday

The Judge parked in his usual spot in the marina and walked to the dock gate. He was looking forward to seeing Katy. Settling into his bed aboard *The Papillon* with a vanilla martini in one hand and Katy snuggled in the other. Maybe there'd be an old movie to watch on Netflix for a while. He'd take one of the Vicodin the doctor had given him and just drift off. He wanted to sleep forever. He paused for a minute, admiring his boat at the other end of the dock on the side tie. She was a beauty. It was a long dock with 30 and 40 foot boats, power and sail, nosed in to slips to either side. There were lights on aboard his new neighbor to the left. A beautiful Beneteau Oceanis3 55, fresh from the dealer, its outline just recognizable in the shadow of his boat as the afterglow disappeared from the sky. But he was too tired for introductions now. Perhaps in the morning they'd have a chance to meet. He'd love a tour of the new boat, or even a sail sometime if it were offered.

Back in the day he'd raced a Newport 30, a sleek and fast sailor in its time. And with some limited success. But he'd been younger then. He'd gotten busy building his law practice. It had been difficult keeping a racing crew together. And somehow that part of his life faded away. Now he was old. He was a stink-potter, and happy to be one. Queen size beds, showers, forced air heating, electric blankets, TV, fully equipped galleys, spacious salons with comfortable furniture, and most of all quick speed in broaching the channel to Catalina. This was his new norm.

But some days he still missed the rattle of the sails in the wind. The singing in the rigging on a tight reach to windward. And the heel of a boat driven through the water with a silent power so strong it left a huge wake on top of the surrounding white caps.

He clambered up the fiberglass steps and aboard amidships. Katy and Annie the dog rushed him at the same time, Katy elbowing the dog out of the way to throw her arms around him and press her tummy with its still very small bump against his. Transferring heat and sexual energy that warmed and excited, making tensions and frustrations of the day fall away forgotten. It was good to be home. And home was now wherever Katy was.

They had an early dinner aboard. Katy produced special steaks from Bristol Farms and microwaved baked potatoes from the small galley. He did the salad, whipping together his home made Caesar Dressing with raw eggs and assorted ingredients, sautéing self-cut croutons in butter on the stove top. Annie the dog contributed moral support, her eyes never far from the steaks lest one might be dropped and need retrieval.

Candlelight, and a 2010 Cakebread Cellars Reserve Chardonnay for the Judge, which Katy watched him drink with envy, was the final touch to a special evening for the three of them. Annie dined on steak scraps with the gusto of her golden retriever breed, more or less swallowing them whole.

The Judge took Vicodin, ignoring Katy's protest that wine and drugs don't mix, and the two settled into the queen bed in the Captain's Cabin. The Judge lying slightly at an angle to fit. Katy wrapped around him. The dog settled on the floor at the end of the bed. The lights were turned off and the boat did its gentle rock as the tide receded. They drifted asleep.

An hour later Annie suddenly jumped up and gave her best oversized growl. The Judge softly called to her to be quiet. It was the new Beneteau neighbor in the next slip, coming back to his boat late. The Judge heard the sail boat's generator start, then settle into a low putt putt barely noticeable above the tide and slight rocking of *The Papillon*. It was the last thing the Judge remembered as he drifted off.

It seemed like the Judge had just closed his eyes, but it must have been an hour later. He half awoke, vaguely feeling a sticky wet tongue lapping about his face, alternating with high urgent whimpers. Annie was very upset. She tried to pull his covers back with her paw. She was quite desperate to get him up. Damn. She likely needed to use the artificial turf pad laid out for her on the aft deck. Damn and double damn. She rarely had this problem.

He struggled through weariness and pills to fully wake up. He didn't want Annie peeing on the carpet. But making his brain work was difficult. His vision seemed blurred and he felt dizzy as he sat up. It was difficult to breath for some reason. Katy had been right about wine and the pills. His stomach was churning and he thought he might vomit.

With enormous effort he stood up. Katy was asleep beside him, not moving. Annie was still stirred up. She jumped up on the bed, imploring him with her glistening brown eyes and soft whimpers.

Something was wrong. He could dimly feel it. What was it? Damn, why wouldn't his brain work? He shook his head. That was a mistake. Fireworks went off behind his eyes.

It seemed stuffy. Some primitive instinct told him he needed air. The picture window behind him in the stern was closed, locked down with toggle latches against the cold night air. Willing himself to move, he twisted around and fumbled with the toggle locks. Why were they so difficult?

Finally he managed them, pushing the window out and open, sending a cold gust of air into the small cabin. It helped. But is head still wasn't working right. An intense headache had settled in.

Shit. It was fumes. The entire master's cabin was filled with fumes. Likely from the damn boat generator next door. He could smell them now.

He grabbed Katy and shook her. Her head rolled to one side and she seemed barely responsive.

He grabbed her by the waist and half carried her, half dragged her out of the bed and up the three steps to the main salon. Annie followed, barking now. He laid Katy on the settee and sprang to the windows, opening them all, letting the cold moist air flow in with a rush.

Katie started to wake up. Panicked. He could see it in her face. He slung her arm over his shoulder and they stumbled together up the last three steps and out on to the aft deck.

They slumped there on the steps leading up to the bridge for what seemed the longest time. Shivering in the cold, but taking in large gulps of the moist ocean air. Finally the Judge stood up, tousled the dog's mane in a special show of thanks, then moved forward amidships and carefully shifted to the boarding steps and descended to the dock.

The lights were still on in the Beneteau, and its generator still chugged along in quiet rhythm. It was one in the morning. It didn't make sense. He moved closer to the sail boat.

He could see now it wasn't the boat's inboard generator going at all. Instead, someone had set up a small portable gas driven generator in the cockpit of the boat. This was what was running. There was a hose attached to the exhaust on the little generator. It ran off the boat and on to the dock.

The Judge got closer and followed the hose in the dark. The hose ran across the dock and was duct taped to his boat, to the grey water drain just above the water line for the sink in their small head just off the captain's cabin. Someone was pumping the fumes and carbon monoxide from the small generator into his master stateroom.

He climbed aboard the Beneteau and opened the half doors over the hatch leading below. He leaned down and looked in. Only one light was on below. No one was aboard.

He fumbled with the switch on the portable generator and turned it off. Then he returned to his boat. Holding his breath, he descended through the salon and down into the Captain's Cabin. He entered the small head and kneeling, slid open one of the louvered doors to the compartment under the little sink.

The hose attached to the sink drain had been cut in two. Leaving a clear path from the outside drain to the inside of the cabinet. The fumes had been fed in here, then found their way through the openings in the louvered cabinet doors out into the Master's Cabin. The carbon monoxide, settling low to the floor, had slowly built up to fill their sleeping compartment.

Someone had tried to kill them. Someone very likely watching from a distance even now. Ready to come pick up the hose and portable generator once it had done its work. All the police would find would be two adults and a dog, dead from carbon monoxide poisoning. To all appearances a freak accident.

The Judge grabbed his cell phone next to bed and bolted back up the stairs. Out to the aft deck and fresh air.

He called 911.

CHAPTER 32
1:00 AM Thursday

The police arrived about fifteen minutes later in the form of Officer Saunders, Los Angeles Sheriff's Department's finest. The same officer who'd helped after the Judge had crawled out of the surf the Friday before. As he walked down the dock, another police cruiser pulled up behind him, followed by a lab truck. All their lights were flashing, sending reflections off the water around the dock, turning it a deep red. And lights were going on in the circular tower of condos above the dock as people got out of bed to see what was going on.

"You must be very unpopular, Judge, to have all these people gunning for you," said Saunders. Smiling. "What'd you do to deserve all this attention?"

"I'm not sure, officer. But you're right. I'm getting a lot of attention."

"Perhaps you should take a vacation. Get out of town until we catch these people. Or ask the department for assigned protection or something. I know I would. I'd go trout fishing." Saunders' lined face broke into a happy smile at the thought.

He turned then, noting the vehicles that had just pulled up.

"The Lieutenant is coming now," said Saunders, pointing to a thin young man cautiously making his way down the ramp, slippery with the night dew. The lieutenant didn't look like a sailor and he clearly didn't like water. He was slowly inching down the gangplank and on to the dock.

Saunders turned and huffed back up the ramp, still walking like his feet hurt, past the lieutenant and toward the lab people unpacking gear off their truck and looking for direction.

The next hour was consumed with telling their story to young lieutenant Cochran, then telling it again, and finally a third time, while a techie ran around the Beneteau, the small generator, the hose, and *The Pappilon's* master's cabin and head, taking pictures, dusting for fingerprints, and looking for physical evidence. The owner of the Beneteau was called but knew nothing about the matter, being out of town and not having been on the boat in a week.

The dock master for the marina had been called and felt compelled to roust herself from bed and troop over to her marina, looking as sleepy and as disheveled as the Judge felt. She promised new codes on the automatic lock for the gate to the dock first thing in the morning.

The lieutenant asked if *The Papillon* had been locked during the day.

"No, the dog was aboard, so we left the main hatch open so she could go back and forth. Have access to the artificial turf pad on the aft deck to pee," said the Judge.

"How come the dog didn't bark, or attack the intruder?"

"She's a golden retriever," said the Judge.

"Oh... of course."

Finally, a little after two in the morning, everyone packed up and left. And the Judge, Katy and Annie settled back in the master's cabin and prepared to go to sleep. They'd opened all the windows, and a soft sea breeze had aired the master's cabin out, leaving only the scent of the sea. The drain hose for the sink had been taped off at both ends and the boat's door and forward hatch locked securely. They'd discussed going to a hotel, but what would they do with Annie, who was now officially a hero? Besides, the Judge was damned if he would be scared off his own boat. He unlocked the secret compartment under their half circle bed in the master's cabin, and brought out his Pietro Beretta 360 automatic, 9 caliber, short barrel, 13 shots including the one in the chamber, placing it on the built in night stand beside the bed. If someone wanted more trouble, they'd jolly well find it here.

Katy snuggled against the Judge, calmer now than she had been, but clearly very worried.

"We're okay, Katy," said the Judge. "Whoever did this would be foolish to come back, and I'm prepared if he does."

"That's not what I'm worried about, Judge."

"What then?"

"I breathed a lot of that carbon monoxide. Do you think it did permanent damage?"

"You're okay now, Katy. You're breathing fine."

"Not me, Judge. Our baby…!"

CHAPTER 33
10:00 AM Thursday

The Judge left the dock for his car in the parking garage and checked his messages. He was surprised by the third call in.

"Hello Judge. This is your new acquaintance, Cindy Kwan. Can you meet me for lunch today? I'd like to clear the air between us."

The Judge returned the call and agreed to lunch at noon at *James' Beach*. Then headed for his office, wondering what Cindy Kwan wanted.

As the Judge got out of his car in front of *James' Beach* two hours later, Cindy Kwan pulled up behind in a cherry red Mercedes SLK, with its top down. A sports car the Judge was too old and too fat to fit in.

She wore a white dress which flew up as she threw her legs up and out of the car first with a flourish, then propelled the rest of her body out, deliberately displaying beautifully toned calves, slim thighs and a brief glimpse of cherry red panties.

The parking attendant stumbled over the curve, more intent on the view than his job, nearly knocking into the Judge. It was well staged.

Cindy immediately extended a small slender hand as she approached, her dark eyes pools of intensity that drew the Judge in despite himself. She was beautiful, charming and dangerous, all at once.

From some other world, crashed here to wreak havoc on the male population. A part of the Judge wanted to be havocked.

He took the small slender hand in his, felt the surge of energy that radiated from it, and gave it a delicate, almost wimpy shake. He felt it might break if he wasn't careful.

Her eyes flashed to his from under long eyelashes. He saw, or felt, the same attraction, the same lust, he'd felt before when they'd been introduced. He could see its counterpart in her eyes. He felt his loins stir.

Some part of him wondered if it was like this for her with all men. Or just with him? He wanted to think it was just him. But experience suggested different. He now understood the meaning of the word "Siren". No wonder Carl had become so caught up in her.

James' Beach the quintessential Venice 'beachy' bar and restaurant was in the middle of a narrow street, a handful of doors from the boardwalk and the beach. It was known for its three separate bars, its Mahi Mahi fish tacos, its indoor palm trees, and the swim trunks hanging from its ceiling lights. The crowd was always animated and the bars tended to be jam packed on the weekends all the way into the wee hours of the morning.

They sat down at a table in the patio covered by stiff canvas. Cindy modestly folding the white chiffon around her now most everything had been displayed. She'd established her credentials.

"I'm glad you called, Miss Kwan," said the Judge.

"Don't be formal, Judge. You're not stuffy underneath. I know. We've been lovers before."

"We have?" The Judge was startled.

"In a former life, dear. In several. I recognized you as soon as we met. We shouldn't have allowed ourselves to be distracted by business." A flash of perfect ivory teeth. "Just call me Cindy, and perhaps later just Honey."

The Judge felt distinctly out of his depth.

"Tell me about Carl."

"Right to business. No foreplay with you Judge. But you were always that way. Quick. To the point. Knowing exactly what you wanted… and how you wanted it."

"Yes… err, well, let's stick with Carl for the moment."

"Okay, Judge, the bottom line first. For you. I didn't kill Carl. I didn't kill your law clerk, Freddie or Frankie, or something, and I don't know who did. Carl and I were lovers. I'm a sensual woman. I have needs. For a time Carl satisfied some of them."

"How long were you together?"

"Together is the wrong word, Judge. We had our intimate moments. They were fun. But life's a smorgasbord. You don't fill up on one dish."

There were the teeth again. The hairs on the back of the Judge's neck stood up. He knew she wanted to sink her teeth into the soft intersection of his neck and his shoulder and nibble. But how the hell did he know that? There was a lot of non-verbal communication going on he couldn't control. It made him uncomfortable.

He was starting to sweat. And she knew it. He could see the hint of satisfaction in the dark pools that were her eyes. There was a certain flat quality to her eyes now, though. Like a snake. Watching intently as its next meal approached.

"What happened between you and Carl to disturb the smorgasbord?" asked the Judge.

"I haven't changed much either, Judge. Around and around we go, through the cycles of life and death and rebirth. But we don't really change."

"Like a Ferris wheel?"

"What?"

"Nothing. Never mind. So what happened?"

"I'm Chinese... Mandarin. If you thought about our past before, you'd know why if broke it off with Carl."

"Business before pleasure," murmured the Judge. It just came out. He didn't know from where.

"You remembered. More teeth. Because of my intimate acquaintance with Carl I was approached to present to him an offer to buy his technology."

"The one that is the subject of a patent suit?"

"Catch up, Judge. The technology Carl hadn't filed for yet."

"What does the technology do?"

More teeth inside a big smile.

"You already know that, Judge. And if by some quirk you don't, I'm not at liberty to enlighten."

"And Carl was not receptive to your offer?"

"No. He wouldn't even talk about it. Stuck a hand, palm out, in my face. It made me furious. And apparently he didn't even fully own the technology. He let slip at one of our shouting matches that he had a

278

silent partner who would never go for the deal. The group kept piling on financial incentives for me if I could persuade Carl to sell. And they kept sweetening the pot for Carl too. And his secret partner. The pile of money and points offered grew quite large. And so did Carl's recalcitrance to even discuss it. My last intimate meeting with Carl, in his room in the Marina Ritz Carlton ended in a screaming match."

"When was that?"

"About six weeks ago. Our communication at the club and elsewhere has been stilted since then. The old fool. There was no way he was going to develop that technology. He had no capital. No investor prospects. In me he had a realistic opportunity to complete development, market and sell it. We would have made mega fortunes together."

"Did your group threaten Carl?"

"I don't know."

"Come on Cindy."

"Perhaps a tad. I told Carl these were both determined and dangerous people. He should wise up and cut a deal. They wouldn't give up. They'd make lots of trouble."

"How'd Carl respond?"

"He laughed in my face. Told me he'd been threatened before. Wasn't going to be intimidated by a bunch of Vodkalkies."

"So your group is Russian?"

Cindy's chin came up and her dark eyes flashed. "I didn't say that."

"Was this an offshore Russian backed group?"

"You've already seen how dangerous this amateur probing can be, Judge. You should leave this investigation to the police. Walk away. Move from the center of the target. It's not your fight."

"People have dragged me into the middle of it, Cindy. Now I'm going to find out what's going on."

"You've always been stubborn, Judge. In your last life, and the ones before. It's cut things short for you more than once. Let it go this time around. There are dangerous interests in play here."

"So there is more than one party involved?"

"That's enough business, Judge. Let's talk about us in *this* life."

"I'm an old, fat, displaced Judge, Cindy, with a new wife and a baby on the way. I don't think there's room for an 'us'. At least in this 'go around.'"

Cindy's eyes held the Judge's for a while, measuring his resolve.

"That's a shame, Judge. But let's give it a year or three and we'll see. Wait until this baby arrives and she's spending all her time and attention on it. She'll forget about you. All she'll want to talk about is the kid. You'll get tired of that. She'll put on weight. Won't want to go out much. She'll be tired all the time. You won't want to take her out. There'll be nothing to show off anymore.

You'll compensate. Dive deeper into your work. Become less communicative. There'll be squabbles about money. The kid needs this, the kid needs that. The kid needs a college fund. She'll complain you don't spend enough time with the kid. Or with her. She'll have left her job for the kid and won't have much to say over dinner. Once she exhausts stories about nursery school or later how the kid's in the school play, there'll be long silences. Your interests will broaden with your legal practice. Hers will narrow with the kid.

You'll find more satisfaction in working late at the office, or a drink out with the boys. More interesting than going home to endless kid stories in minute detail about how it moved this finger, or that toe, or had this thought or that dispute at school. She'll find more satisfaction in social interaction with other moms, sharing each nuisance of development of the blessed offspring.

She'll grow weary of pretending to understand and be interested in your complicated stories of law practice and your small victories and defeats at the hands of clever opponents. The dinner silences will grow longer. And so will the inertia that keeps you later at the office and more often out with the boys.

I'll give it four years, Judge. I'll be 30. You'll be who you are. Who you've always been. Mine to take. I'll look you up."

She showed the Judge more teeth. Stood up. Extended the graceful hand for another small shake. And gracefully floated away toward valet and her car. A small young thing in white Chiffon.

She left the Judge sitting there. Silent. Thoughtful. And …. Apprehensive?

CHAPTER 34
2:00 PM Thursday

The Judge was back in his office, trying to catch up on other client work. Both sides in the Greene arbitration were arguing in probate court now over the right of the Greene Estate to proceed in the arbitration case in the stead of Carl. The Judge had made his ruling the Friday before, the day after his nocturnal swim, and it had been promptly appealed by Hicks' attorney, seeking a court order on who now actually owned rights to the technology and patent. It was out of the Judge's hands for the moment, and just as well. He had lots else to do.

Katy had packed up and headed back to their hillside villa in Palos Verdes with Annie the dog. It appeared no less safe than the boat now and it was a hell of a lot more comfortable.

His cell phone rang and he answered, hoping it might be a new client in need.

"Judge?" He recognized the gruff Boston accent. It was Kaminsky. Crap, what'd he want now?

"Yes?"

"Where are you right now?"

"At my office, working."

"Anyone with you?"

"Don't tell me I need another alibi?" the Judge said, half in jest.

"This isn't a joke, Judge. Anyone with you?"

"No."

"Anyone been with you this morning?"

"No. Yes. A lunch from 1 to 2."

"Where'd you spend the night last night?"

"In the Marina, with my wife, on my boat. Where all hell broke loose. Someone tried to kill us last night with carbon monoxide."

"I thought as much." Said Kaminsky. "What time did you get up on the boat this morning?"

"About 9:30 am."

"What time did you leave the boat?"

"About 10:00 am."

"For your office?"

"Yes. Then my lunch meeting at noon. I came back to my office from lunch about 1:15."

"Where's your wife?"

"After an unfortunate experience on the boat last night, we've decided to go back to our home in Palos Verdes. She left with the dog right before I left. 10:00."

"Where's your wife now?"

"No doubt in Palos Verdes. What's this about?"

"I'm on your dock in the Marina. Get your ass over here, and I mean now. You've got fifteen minutes. Then I'm sending a black and white."

The phone went dead before the Judge could respond.

He retrieved his car from the garage and headed to the Marina, calling Katy on the fly to be sure she was okay. She was at her high school in Lunada Bay, doing some consulting. The dog was relaxing at home.

His dock was crowded. There were two cruisers and a County Morgue Van parked long the bulkhead, along with a nondescript dark blue four-door the Judge guessed to be Kaminski's. A Fire Rescue truck was just leaving. A Harbor Patrol boat was slowly tooling around the docks, two Harbor Patrol leaning over the side and scanning the murky water. There were two officers and two morgue people on his dock.

And of course Kaminski, strutting around like the popinjay he was, with the young Los Angeles County detective from last night, Lieutenant Cochran, in tow. Apparently this was a joint investigation of some sort by the Los Angeles County Sheriff's Department and the Santa Monica Police Department, although Marina Del Rey was clearly L.A. County territory.

There was also a stretcher, with what looked like a body covered by a white plastic sheet. Water was oozing out from under the edges of the sheet, staining the dock. A small crowd had gathered at the dock gate to watch. His pretty dock master (or was she his dock mistress? That sounded so much better), was back, restraining the crowd from coming down the ramp or blocking the gate. She looked tired. Not surprising. She'd also been out here at 1:00 a.m. If this thing continued she might kick him out of the Marina docks.

She stepped aside as the Judge approached, allowing him through the gate and down the ramp. Kaminsky made a grandiose movement with his index finger, pointing at his feet on the dock where he expected the Judge to come. As though the Judge were a small boy.

The Judge ignored it, choosing instead to walk over to the body where a morgue attendant obligingly raised a corner of the sheet.

Christ! Randall Hicks stared up at the Judge, pale blue eyes unfocused, void of expression, his mouth open in a kind of gasp. Water was still leeching out from his clothes onto dry dock. They must have just pulled him out.

There was a smattering of blood still matted in the hair at the side of his head. He'd smashed it badly on something in his fall into the water. Or someone had smashed it for him and pushed him in.

Kaminski strutted over, notebook in hand.

"Well, well, it's the good Judge. Come to visit his dock, see what's going on. Death seems to follow you around like a bad smell, Judge. Every time I turn a corner there's a body. And there you are, connected somehow to the victim. You know the deceased?"

"Randall Hicks."

"You're right, Judge. Got it first try. Had his wallet on him. Had your business card in it. Question is, what the fuck's he doing in the water beside your dock?"

The Judge spread his hands and shrugged his shoulders.

"How do you know him this time, Judge?"

"He's the president of 1st Enterprises, Inc., a public company."

"And? Come on, don't leave us hanging."

Lieutenant Cochran had carefully walked over to listen. He looked as uncomfortable on the floating dock as he had before.

"He was the Plaintiff in this patent dispute case where I'm the arbitrator."

"The case Carl Greene was involved in?'

"Yes".

"Well, well. And this patent case is the same patent case your law clerk, Frank Wolin was involved in?"

"Yes."

"And these folks are all dead?"

"Yes."

"Don't that make you a little nervous, Judge? Make you want to take some life insurance out or something?"

"Was this an accident?" asked the Judge, ignoring Kaminsky's barb.

"What do you think, Judge?"

"I don't know. That's why I'm asking."

"Well it's your dock, Judge. You knew the guy. It's your case people are dying over. Where you been all day?"

"As I told you, Lieutenant, we got up late, I went to my office, then had a lunch meeting.."

"And that young wife of yours?"

"We got up together. She and the dog left for Palos Verdes before 10."

"And you saw nothing unusual when you walked off the dock this morning."

"No, nothing unusual."

"See anyone else on the dock?"

"Like who?"

"Anyone?"

"No."

"There must have been a hell of a splash, Mr. Hicks is a big fellow. You sure you didn't hear a big splash sometime last night after the police left?"

"I'm sure."

"Didn't hear any altercation? Or perhaps a struggle, before you say you left?"

"No."

"Mr. hear no evil, see no evil, say no evil, huh?"

"You got it Kaminsky."

"When's the last time you saw Mr. Hicks?"

"On Tuesday, about 4:30 p.m."

"In your arbitration hearing?"

"No. We met privately at *Chaya Venice*."

"Isn't that illegal?"

"What?"

"To meet someone you're judging outside the case proceeding? Was his attorney present?"

"No."

"No, Hicks' attorney wasn't present? Or no, it's not illegal?"

"Hicks' attorney wasn't present. And no it's not illegal, but it can be a violation of the Canon of Ethics. It's never a good idea."

"So why'd you do it?"

"Hicks said it was an urgent matter. Not involving the arbitration case. He needed to meet immediately. In person. I told him to bring his attorney. But he showed up alone. He waived having his attorney present and all that. I explained it wasn't a good idea. He promised it wasn't about the arbitration case. Said he was desperate to talk. Said I should just listen. I considered all that was going on. The attack on me. Your bodies, Kaminsky. So I sat down and listened."

"And what'd he have to say?"

"Hicks said he was in a mess. Said he sold control of his company to some shadowy Hong Kong group who instructed him to start the patent suit. But what they wanted was Carl Greene's new technology. The technology he hadn't disclosed to anyone or filed a patent for."

"Was that new technology part of the arbitration?"

"Plaintiffs were trying to make it so. I ordered an in-chambers report on the technology. What it was about. How it worked. What would be in a patent application once filed? All confidential. For my eyes only."

"Did you get this report?"

"Yes."

"Where is it now?"

"I don't know. Someone stole the report before I had a chance to review it."

"Who took it?"

"I suspect it was Frank Wolin."

"Your dead law clerk?"

"Yes."

"Now we're finally getting somewhere, Judge. What else did Hicks say?"

"He said Frank was promised money for the report. Frank thought it was Hicks' money. That Hicks was behind it. Hicks claimed he didn't know anything about it. Hicks said he wanted away from the whole deal. He sounded scared. Wanted to cancel the patent arbitration and walk. But his attorney was dragging his feet."

"Who's the attorney?"

"Dick Harper."

"And what did you say, Judge?"

"I told him I'd speak to Harper."

"Who was this shadowy group he sold control of his company to?"

"He said it was a Hong Kong conglomerate. His contact was over the internet. A Mr. Wang."

Kaminsky sighed. "This case just keeps spiraling in circles. But I know who's at the center. And I'm looking at him. Go now, Judge. But as soon as I have an autopsy, I'm going to want you back in my office. If this is a homicide, you're going to have a lot more explaining to do."

The Judge gave Kaminsky a mock salute, and retreated back up the gangway and to his car. He didn't need to be told to leave twice.

The Judge returned to his office, got his cell phone out and dialed the direct line he had for Dick Harper. Dick answered at once.

"Hi Dick. This is the Judge."

"Yes your honor. What's up?"

"It's something of an emergency, Dick. It concerns the patent arbitration and it concerns you. I thought we'd better meet as soon as possible."

There was silence on the other end as the Judge's words were digested. The Judge waited the silence out.

Dick exhaled a big breath he must have taken, and said, "Why don't we meet for brunch tomorrow at one p.m. at the Johns Club on the beach."

"That will be fine, Dick."

CHAPTER 35
1:00 PM Friday

The Johns Club was private club on the beach below the bluffs in Santa Monica. Sort of a family outreach facility for the membership in the stuffy Johns Club Downtown. The Judge pulled into its hedge-enclosed parking lot and waved the attendant away, preferring to park his own car. He opted for an end spot at the back of the lot. Leaving ample room between his car and the next car slot over. Hoping it wouldn't be filled with some huge SUV whose large swinging doors would nick his paint.

He signed in with the valet as Dick Harper's guest. Then proceeded down the long sidewalk bordering tennis courts where 30ish women were pounding balls back and forth, all kitted out in the latest tennis skirts, dresses and visors. Their kids were in school during the week, their husbands were downtown workaholics, and their fancy degrees and boundless energy had little outlet beyond tennis and charity work. This morning it was tennis.

The Judge marched up the stairs and through the center hallway of the club facility, all pale green and turquoise with rose color accents. Ignoring the obligatory black and white photos of old L.A. scattered here and there along the walls. He'd seen them all before. They hadn't changed in twenty years. He moved onto the outside dining deck overlooking the pool and the beach.

The Johns Club was a favorite for breakfast and lunch for the professionals who serviced business on the Los Angeles plain. Lawyers, accountants, bankers, real estate brokers, securities brokers, financial planners, computer consultants, insurance salesmen, they were all there like ducks on the rocks. Hunkered down on the deck at the tables, nodding at competitors and potential clients alike. Talking in guarded voices to partners, associates, or potential new clients. All very serious, secret and competitive. Only partially masked by broad smiles pasted on as acquaintances trooped by.

The Judge spotted Dick Harper sitting with his back to the ocean at a table shaded from the sun by a green striped umbrella.

Dick was wearing a blue striped dress shirt with cuffs rolled up, light tan chinos, and sockless loafers. His clothes read relaxed, but the deep wrinkles above the bridge of his nose read worried.

"How you doing, Judge? It's nice we're in this arbitration, more informal than the court room."

"We were, Dick. I think the arbitration is over."

"How so Judge?"

"We'll talk about that in a minute," said the Judge. "But there are other issues to discuss related to the arbitration."

Dick flashed his broad smile. "What's up?"

"You've heard about Frank Wolin, my law clerk?"

Dick's features immediately changed, taking on a mild funeral countenance. He seemed to have a face for every occasion.

"I heard about that. Took his own life. Young too. A whole career ahead of him. What a waste."

The Judge decided to lay it out for Dick even before the coffee arrived.

"Was Frank Wolin spying on me for you, Dick? Reporting back on everything I said in chambers about the case? Trying not so subtly to push me toward a favorable ruling for your client?"

Dick's mouth dropped open, but no sound came. He apparently had no face for this question. He looked like a gasping fish. Finally he stammered a "No... No... Of course not."

"Have you been secretly recording conversations between me and Frank in my office?"

Dick's face was turning pink. He was having trouble looking the Judge in the eye.

"Why would you say that, Judge?"

"That's evasive, Dick. It's a simple question. Is that your equipment in the adjacent office? The DVD recorder, motion detector, and antenna to the mini camera burrowed into the clock in my office?"

"I don't know what you're talking about, Judge."

Dick had recovered quickly and was trying a bluster. It was actually a pretty good bluster.

"I found the whole setup, Dick."

"I'm appalled, Judge. That someone would stoop to do that. But even more appalled that you'd think it was me."

"I took the DVD back to a geek friend of mine and he ran some recovery software to see what had been erased. There was a billing memo on it. Prepared on your law firm's letterhead. You shouldn't have been so cheap, Dick. You should have floated the two dollars and bought a brand new DVD to use."

Dick suddenly found great interest in studying his hands. He looked like he might be sick. The Judge was silent, waiting him out. Finally Dick looked up, heaving a sigh, his lips pursed into a solid line.

"My client made me do it," he said. "Threatened to go somewhere else if I couldn't keep up with the technology. Said everybody used stealth methods these days. Said I had to catch up with the times or quit practicing. Said it was only an arbitration. Not a court room trial. Gave me an ultimatum. It's been a lousy year for the law firm what with the recession and all. I needed the money."

"It was unethical. It was illegal. And if my decision in the arbitration case were to go for Randal Hicks and his public company, it would be invalidated. It was also stupid. You know you can be disbarred for this. Sued. Jailed."

"It was dumb I know, Judge. It wasn't even that helpful. It gave us some slant I suppose on how to make our arguments to you. That was all."

"Was my law clerk, Frank Wolin, involved?"

"Yes. My client asked me to approach Frank. Pay him on the side to be sort of a second advocate for us inside your chambers. Try and ease you into the right decision."

"The 'right' decision?"

"Okay, a favorable decision."

"How much did you pay Frankie?"

"10,000 up front, and another 40,000 if the outcome in the arbitration was beneficial."

"Frankie never got the second forty?"

"No."

"And you asked Frankie to do another job, didn't you, Dick?"

"Yes." Dick's voice was a whisper now.

"Tell me."

"From our surveillance it looked like you weren't going to allow the confidential report into discovery. I was asked to approach Frank again."

"To do what?"

"Make a copy of the report for us." Dick hung his head now.

"So you hired Frankie to steal the report?"

"Yes. But just to make a copy Judge. Then put it right back."

"How much were you to pay Frankie for the copy?"

"20,000 up front, 180,000 more after we validated the copy."

"Did Frankie have any second thoughts?"

"How'd you know? He tried to back out the Wednesday before your swim. Called and said he couldn't do it. He was scared."

"What time did he call, Dick?"

"About 8 p.m."

"What'd you say?"

"Told him he'd cashed the check. Taken the money. It was too late for either of us to go back. Told him these folks I worked for played rough. He'd best just go through with it. Told him he could get hurt if he didn't hold up his end after accepting the money."

"What'd he say?"

"He got angry. Asked if that was why I was having him followed. Said maybe it would be better if he met with Mr. Hicks directly, so both sides were at risk if anything ever came out."

"I told him that wasn't possible. He needed to damn well go through with his end just as we agreed. There was no turning back."

"How'd he respond?"

"He said okay."

"When were you to meet to get the copy of the report?"

"On Thursday, at 11 p.m., in Playa del Rey, in the Village."

"And did he show up? Give you the copy?"

"No, Judge. He never showed up. I waited an hour. Wolin never came."

"Why do you suppose, Dick?"

Dick looked at the Judge now, guilty eyes pleading for some sort of redemption.

"Cause he was dead. Cause he couldn't take the pressure. Cause he killed himself."

"Or he was murdered?"

"Murdered? Nobody's said anything about murder, Judge. There was no murder."

"I think there was, Dick. I think Frank Wolin was killed."

Dick's complexion turned from pink to white. It was good he hadn't had his lunch yet.

The Judge plowed on. "Your client was more interested in obtaining the confidential report than in winning the arbitration. True?"

"How'd you know that?"

"True?"

"Yes. My sailing instructions were to get the information on the 'new' technology at any cost."

"At the cost of bugging my chambers? At the cost of the corruption of my young law clerk? At the cost of your career? Perhaps at the cost of your freedom? At the cost of Frankie's life?"

"No. No, Judge. There was nothing about murder. I don't know anything about murder. I don't know who killed Carl Greene and I don't know how Frank Wolin died. I thought he killed himself."

"So here's the big question, Dick."

"Yes."

"Who was your client?"

"Why Randall Hicks of course."

"Dick, the time for bullshitting is over. I know Randall was set up as a schmuck with a pen. And so do you. Who were you working for?"

"I thought it was Randall. I...I..."

"Enough lies, Dick," the Judge interrupted. "Tell me about the Chinese conglomerate. Tell me about Mr. Wang."

Fear spread over Dick's face now. The Judge could see he was truly afraid.

"I can't talk about them, Judge. It'd be dangerous for me."

"You can talk to me about 'them', or you can talk to the police and then the DA and then the grand jury. And after that's all over, the State Bar. It's your choice."

Dick covered his face with his hands for a minute. Thinking. The Judge could imagine his sharp legal mind darting from one possible course of action to another, weighing risks and consequences, trying to figure a sanitized way out. Like a rat in a maze.

"Here's what I know, Judge. But you didn't hear this from me."

"Okay."

"The conglomerate is just a public shell, masking the activities of a group of very clever Chinese computer engineers who break into computers around the world and steal data. They are funded by the Chinese government. Practically a secret arm of the government. Commercial espionage is their mission. Jeffrey Wang is their Hong Kong lawyer. I took my directions from Jeffrey.

The law firm was failing. They were going to throw me out 'cause I didn't have any business. My entire book of business disappeared with this damn recession. I was desperate. Jeffrey offered a 500,000 dollar retainer which I took and brought into the law firm. It saved my partnership there. Gave me a year's breathing room. I agreed to represent Jeffrey Wang and his group."

"Did they tell you what you were going to do for the retainer?"

"Yes, Judge. I'm afraid they did. I introduced Randall Hicks and his public company, essentially a shell, to Jeffrey. Wang's group funded acquisition of control of Hicks' public company though a British Virgin Islands company I set up. Jeffrey funneled new money into Hicks' company. Assigned the existing technology to Randall's company. Arranged for Randall to assert that the technology was his own. Jeffery essentially manufactured the opportunity to bring a lawsuit against Carl Greene."

"And the goal was always to get Carl's new technology?"

"Yes."

"By hook or by crook?"

"Yes."

"Did Randall Hicks get in the way?"

"What do you mean?"

"Did Hicks go along with this program? The bribing of Frank. The effort to steal a copy of Greene's confidential report?"

"He didn't know about it. He took orders from Jeffery Wang like everyone else. But he wasn't included in our internal planning."

"Did he know how valuable the report was?"

"He no doubt guessed. He's no fool."

"Do you think Hicks might have obtained the copy of the report from Frankie in your stead?"

"I hadn't thought of that. Randall could have made some side deal with Frank I suppose. He didn't tell me about it if he did. I honestly don't know."

"Randall Hicks is dead."

The words just lay there, like stones dropped into a quiet pond between them. Concentric circles rippling out in all directions. Harper looked at the Judge, not comprehending at first. Realization and fear gradually spreading across his face. Into his eyes.

"How?" he finally muttered.

"Drowned. Hit his head, or someone hit it for him, and into the water he went."

"When?"

"Sometime early this morning."

"Shit."

"What were you doing at Frank's condo building on Tuesday, Dick? Were you there to see Frank?"

"No. I didn't know. No Judge, no way. Like I said, I was there to pick something up from one of our paralegals out sick. I didn't know it was Frank's building."

"Give me a break, Dick. Fancy partners like you don't trot out to pick up a paralegal's work. It's sent by email or fax, or a courier if you need an original document."

Dick looked up from his hands then, desperation in his face. Lowering his voice further he muttered, "Shit, Judge, do I have to spell it out? Sheila and I are having a bloody affair. I was there for our... you know."

"Christ, Dick. You're a mess. On top of conspiracy to steal documents, corruption of my law clerk, breaking bar rules and legal ethics, and violating the privacy laws, you're screwing one of your employees, setting your firm up for a sexual harassment suit. Do your partners know they have a ticking bomb for a law partner?"

There was panic in Dick's face now. "You're not going to tell them are you? Please. I know I've messed up. But it can all be fixed. Just don't tell my partners, or report me to the bar."

"I'll have to think about that, Dick." The Judge stood up, disgust on his face. "You're not helping the image of our profession with shenanigans like this. We're all tarred when this sort of conduct comes out. I don't know what I'm going to do."

The Judge turned and stalked out of the Johns' Club. He had no appetite for lunch.

CHAPTER 36
2:00 PM Friday

The Judge headed to *The Papillon* from the Johns' Club with the intent of kicking back for the rest of the afternoon. He was tired. It had been a hectic and emotional week. His arm was throbbing again. And he was still bummed about Frankie. Katie was off with her mother shopping. No doubt discussing plans for the big wedding reception. He would meet her later in Palos Verdes.

The boat would be his alone for a little bit. It was an opportunity to enjoy the old peace and quiet of a solidary existence aboard the yacht. The way he used to enjoy it before he'd become partnered up with Katy.

He climbed on to the swim step, up the ladder, across the aft deck, and unlocked the hatch. He slid into the main salon, tired, and glad to be in his own space. He slung his sport coat over the sofa and made his way down two steps into the galley. He could hear the small waves slapping softly against the hull as he pulled vanilla vodka and vermouth from beneath the small sink and poured a liberal amount of each into a silver martini shaker. He added a little ice, shook vigorously for a few seconds, and dumped the cold concoction into a martini glass, pulled from the upside-down rack above the sink.

He settled down into the sofa, kicking off his loafers, and drifted off to sleep. He was dreaming about Katy and the kid, a small monstrous male with evil eyes and a shrill voice, totally spoilt, who Katy wouldn't let him discipline or even touch. In the middle of his dream, or more nightmare really, his cell phone went off with a clatter. He sat up, stretched, retrieved his cell from his sport coat pocket and answered, expecting Katy.

The voice on the other end said "hello" with a male voice, but electronically distorted. It was a cold voice. Even menacing.

"Is this the Judge?"

"It is."

"Good. I've got a message for you from the powers that be."

"And who might those powers be?"

"That don't matter. You're one lucky son of a bitch, Judge. Damn near died twice, but still around."

"You're the one responsible?"

"That don't matter either. Here's the deal. The powers that be have decided you don't know what this is all about. Don't understand the significance of it all. Didn't really get a solid look at the new technology. Basically don't know jack shit."

"So?"

"So I'm calling to ask you politely to butt out of this. Drop your private investigation. Let the hack cops do their job. Let them run around like ants for a while before they move the whole thing to their cold case files."

"I assume there is a threat behind this somewhere. What's the 'or else'? Are they going to find me in a bathtub with my brains blown out?"

"You're pretty quick for a judge. They said you were stubborn and not likely to budge. Said you'd need a little demonstration. So here you go."

The Judge pressed the cell closer to his ear. Suddenly intent on each word as it dropped from the other end.

"Your sweet Katy is going to need special shoes if she's missing toes."

The line went dead. The disembodied voice had hung up.

The Judge, panicked, stabbed at his cell phone. The auto dial for Katy. Willing her to answer. The phone rang several times, then moved to voice mail.

"Urgent. Call Me," snapped the Judge. Then hit the redial.

He tried four times to reach her. On the fifth redial the phone was answered.

A voice came across the line. "Hello, this is Katy's cell phone." It was Florence Thorne, Katy's mother.

"It's the Judge. Where's Katy?" he barked.

She picked up the urgency immediately. Mirrored his anxiety intuitively.

"We're in a shoe store in The Beverly Center. Jimmy Choo's. Katy's been trying on shoes for the reception. Her purse and phone are here. She just walked around the corner to use the lady's room. She'll be right back, Judge."

"Who's in the store with you?"

"Just the shoe clerk."

"Katy may be in extreme danger. Go find her. Now. Move as you talk on the phone. Get her back in the store. Now. Under the lights. Keep me on the line. Move methodically, Florence. Don't panic. Pretend you're talking to an old friend right now and nothing's wrong as you move. But hurry. Get Katy. Take her back in the store, to the back. Try on a bunch more shoes. Stay in the store. Pretend you can't make up your mind. Don't leave until I get help there. Try to be calm. Look like you're enjoying your shopping trip. Smile now, Flo. Smile."

"I'm almost to the lady's restroom, Judge. But the store closes in 20 minutes."

"I'll have help there by then, Flo."

"Is Katy there, Flo?"

The line suddenly went dead.

"Shit," muttered the Judge.

Twenty agonizing seconds later the cell rang.

"Yes," said the Judge. Holding his breath.

"It's us, Judge." It was Florence. "No cell signal in the lady's room. I have Katy. She's okay. But we're both a little scared. We're walking back to Jimmy Choo's. Now we're inside. We'll try on some more shoes."

"Good. Go to the very back. Hang in there. Let me get some help."

The Judge called 911 and asked for help. He was routed to the LAPD. The desk officer said they'd have a black and white there inside 15 minutes.

He thought a minute, then called Steven Straw, his neighbor in Palos Verdes. Steve had a 17,000 square foot chateau above him on The Hill.

Steve was the landlord of The Beverly Center Mall. His dad had bought the land and developed retail space back in the day when most of the shopping was still downtown. He foresaw the enormous growth potential for the West side of L.A. long before anyone else. Steve had inherited the company and continued to build and manage, creating an even larger real estate empire.

Steve answered. Thank God he was available.

The Judge outlined the problem in 60 seconds and asked for help.

"I'm on it, Judge. I'll scramble the security at the mall. They'll be in that shoe store in under a minute." Steve hung up.

The Judge's phone rang again, 60 seconds later. It was Katy.

"Judge, what's going on? There's a security guard just came tearing in here. And now there's two more, lined up either side of the door. Now there's three, no four of them."

The Judge slumped back in his seat. Katy was safe. At least for now.

He explained briefly what had happened. The phone call. The threat. He didn't mention feet. Katy had gone quiet. She was processing.

"Why don't you go back to your mom's for now? Not home. Not the boat. The LAPD will be there shortly. Let them do their report. Then see if they'll give you an escort to your parents' house. Have the police call me when they arrive. I'm leaving here now. I'll see you at your parents' house in about thirty minutes."

Katy's parents lived in Brentwood, behind private gates. The drive from the Marina would give him time to consider his next move.

CHAPTER 37
4:00 PM Friday

Florence and Ralph Thorne lived in one of the most exclusive sub-communities in the City of Los Angeles. Brentwood climbed from the base of the Santa Monica Mountain range, squeezed between the 405 Freeway to the Valley on one side and Santa Monica on the other. Like a separate fiefdom all to itself. Its claims to fame included hosting part of the pentathlon in the 1932 Summer Olympics, a disastrous fire in 1961, and of course the site of the O. J. Simpson murder case in 1994.

The Thornes lived in a track of large estates protected by heavy gates and a security guard. They were expecting him at the gates and waved him through. Tall eucalyptus trees lined the road, providing a canopy overhead. Patterns of light splayed through the leaves onto the pavement and across his windshield. The Judge could smell the eucalyptus, mixed with the earthy scent of private stables and manicured lawns adjacent to the road.

Far off, glimpsed here and there through the trees and shrubs, was Los Angeles: row after row of small homes, deferred maintenance apartment buildings, strip commercial buildings, and at the horizon, downtown's skyscrapers. It was a view through the prism of distance, security, and most of all money. The people who lived here didn't have to live up close to the poor, the disadvantaged, and the blue collar workers who made the metropolis work.

The Thornes home was a stone manor house looking as though plucked from woods in the south of France. Two stories and an attic, grey purplish stone with pale blue trim, and three towering chimneys, as though fireplaces were still the primary source of heat in the 21st century.

The Judge pulled half way up the circular driveway and stopped behind Katy's Mustang, opposite steps leading to the massive front door. The door flew open as he got out and Katy came down the steps at a run, spilling into the Judge's arms. Frightened. Out of breath.

He held her there for a long minute, smelling the fragrance of her hair and feeling the wet splash of her tears of relief. Then they shared a long kiss.

She put her arm around his waist then and leaned into him, leading him up the steps and inside. Into the great hall where Florence stood waiting, wringing her hands with anxiety. Waiting for an explanation.

They sat down in the living room, a great room with a small wooden bar in one corner and a piano in the other. All fruitwood stained walls and high ceiling with beams crisscrossing overhead in darker hues. A picture window looked out over the circular drive and down the hill, providing a vista of the skyscrapers of

Downtown and Century City, and a peek-a-boo view of some of the Santa Monica Bay to the right.

Florence moved to the bar and mixed a brace of strong martinis, turning to hand them out with her eyes focused on the Judge. Waiting.

Katy discreetly passed, opting for a bottle of water.

"As you know, Florence, sometimes I get involved in criminal investigations," began the Judge.

"I know all that Judge. About the case on The Hill, and what happened over on The Island, in Avalon. Is this about that? Or the attack on you a week ago Thursday night?

"It's the week ago Thursday night altercation on the beach. I'm afraid this is another fine mess I've gotten us into."

"It's the arbitration, isn't it?" Katy chimed in.

"Yes. Not wholly my fault this time, but I... we," he reached for Katy's hand, "seem to be embroiled up to our eyebrows in something. I'm not quite sure what. But three people have died. And besides the attack me at on the beach, someone tried to stage an accident on the boat that almost killed us both."

"Oh my god. It's worse than I thought," Florence said in a small voice, taking an unladylike gulp of her martini and slumping back against the sofa, sitting very still. She looked pale now, her dry white skin faintly showing a network of fine veins. "Maybe I'd better call Ralph."

Florence got up and unsteadily walked out of the room, muttering her cell phone was in the kitchen. The Judge turned to Katy.

"We need to get you out of here, Katy. Right away. Somewhere safe where I don't have to worry. Can you take some time off? Perhaps you and your parents could visit Vegas. You said your folks have a condo?"

"I'm not going to leave you by yourself, Judge. That's a non-starter."

"But Katy, they threatened you. Not me. You! They're trying to use you against me. We have to take you off the field!"

"We come from a long line of frontier women, Judge. We're used to reloading rifles. And using them when we have to. We don't go scampering away at the first sign of trouble."

"This isn't the first sign. For God sakes. We could have died on the boat. We need to get you out of here."

"Nope, not going."

"What about our child?" the Judge whispered. "You're risking its life too."

"That's an underhanded argument, Judge, and you know it. You'd like to play on my emotions. But the fact is you need my help. We're a team now, you, me and our little half. We're sticking together. All in. Win or lose."

"But Katy…." The Judge had no other words. She'd deflected all his lawyer logic with a stubborn determination that was beyond rational. She was crazy. But he loved her for it.

"Tell you what, Judge. We'll…. you and me and the half… we'll stay here with my parents for a week. I'll reschedule my private consulting in Lunada Bay. Set everything out a week, and hang out here. You can do what you need to do during the day. Then come back here in the evenings. The guard gate will discourage anyone from following."

The Judge was doubtful. But Katy's chin was in the air. He knew there'd be no further concession. At least not tonight. Staying with his newly anointed in-laws for a week was not his idea of a vacation, or even a respite. And it was only marginally safer than staying at home. But it seemed the only deal in town. He took it.

Florence returned, cell phone to her ear, and then handed it to Katy. She was still upset.

Katy listened to her dad for a bit, answered his queries reassuringly, and announced she and the Judge were self-proclaimed house guests for the week. This seemed to satisfy Ralph. Katy smoothly brought the conversation to a close.

Florence perked up at the prospect of guests. She bustled off to deal with beds and bedding, relieved to have something mundane to worry about.

The Judge settled deeper into his martini and wondered how close-order drill with his in-laws was going to work out. He wasn't optimistic.

Florence reappeared briefly, the Judge suspected primarily to refill her martini glass, and then headed off to the kitchen to work up dinner for four. An hour later Ralph arrived home.

Dinner was served in a formal dining room at one end of a large mahogany dining table with candlelight from two large silver candelabras reflecting off antique tapestries hung on opposite walls. Florence was a very good cook. That likely explained why Katy wasn't. The talent seemed to skip generations, perhaps for a lack of need.

As dinner was winding down and everyone except Katy had had their fill of two bottles of an expensive cabernet procured from Ralph's wine cellar, a Floren Shafer Vineyards 2010, Florence turned to the Judge and said, "I've been thinking about what you said. About the homeless, Judge. You know we should have laws in Brentwood against sleeping in parks. If you do it, you should get arrested."

"You raise an interesting issue, Florence. The Great Recession has made the homeless more visible in communities because there are more of them. When homelessness become more visible, there's more pressure on community leaders to do something about it. The knee-jerk response is to address what is essentially a social issue with the criminal justice system."

"You mean you don't approve of such laws, Judge?"

"I mean it's easy for elected officials to adopt criminal penalties because the public costs are much harder to see than the costs of new shelters and services. Ultimately, though, Flo, it's much more

311

expensive to ticket the homeless in your park, generating subsequent court, prison and health costs, than to invest in more shelters and front end services. Besides, criminal citations just compound the problem, making it harder for the homeless to qualify for jobs and housing in the future. They have to check criminal boxes on application forms. They don't have an opportunity to explain they were arrested trying to simply survive on the streets. It's an automatic turndown of a job or a place to rent."

"But this is Brentwood, Judge. We've paid a pretty penny to live here. With our kind of people. Nothing against the homeless, but I choose not to mingle with them."

"Well, Florence, if the street and the park are privately owned by a private association that may work. But don't you think the homeless are entitled to be on the public streets and in the public parks in Brentwood?"

"No. We should have laws. We should criminalize it, just as you said Judge. These people need to be cited and hauled off. It's not right for them to come and just occupy the Brentwood parks."

"I think you're on shaky legal ground there Florence. Five members of the Supreme Court ruled some years ago that you cannot punish or criminalize truly involuntary or unavoidable conduct resulting from 'Status'. That's as contrasted to 'Voluntary Conduct'. To do so is a violation of the Eighth Amendment prohibiting cruel and unusual punishment. The City of Los Angeles, of which Brentwood is a part, got its ass

312

handed to it when it tried to enforce just such laws. Laws making it illegal for homeless people in Los Angeles to sit, lie or sleep in its parks and other public spaces."

"Well," said Florence. "Typical commie judges. We worked hard and we saved hard for our place in Brentwood. And we don't want it mucked up by a bunch of homeless hanging around our streets and parks."

"It's a sad problem, Florence," said the Judge. "Sad that one of the most prosperous countries in the world can't seem to take care of its own people. Over 44,000 people were counted as homeless in L.A. County in the 2014 census."

"Why are the numbers increasing, Judge?" asked Ralph.

"The Great Recession, Ralph. The high unemployment in L.A., despite the beginnings of a recovery. The gentrification of downtown and Venice, where cheap hotel rooms, motels and single-room apartments available to many of the poor have been eliminated. The high price of housing in the L.A. County. Rents keep going up and wages have stayed flat. Tonier neighborhoods resist all proposals for low income housing. Their battle cry is 'not in my backyard'. And the number of mentally ill homeless also began to surge before the turn of this last century as the Baby Boom generation began to display symptoms of depression, anxiety disorders, and other mental illness. Psychiatric hospitals and group homes now struggle to keep up with demand."

313

"Ok, Judge," Florence said, "I understand what you're saying, but I don't want them on my front lawn, or down the street in the park where my grandchildren will play some day. So what's the solution, Judge?"

"The most effective strategy, unfortunately implemented only spottily across the nation, has been to rapidly re-house newly homeless people and create permanent supportive housing, with mental health and addiction counseling. But securing significant money and the political backing to build supportive housing throughout L.A. County has been elusive. Ironically, a 2002 study which tracked 4,600 homeless people with mental illness in New York City over nine years, concluded that each person who remained on the street, shuffling in and out of jails and hospitals, cost the city and state $40,451 a year in services. While those placed in supportive housing cost only $17,277 per person, and even better, tended to stay off the street for good."

"My receptionist was once homeless," said Ralph.

All heads turned to hear more.

"For eight years, in her early fifties, Martha wandered the streets of Pasadena, sleeping in alleys, scouring dumpsters for scraps of food and smoking meth to fend off crushing depression. She told me her teeth were rotting, and sores broke out all over her body. She was sexually assaulted repeatedly and had her belongings stolen multiple times.

When things got truly bleak, Martha would check herself into the psych ward of a hospital, but she'd be discharged back on the streets within days.

314

Some of her homeless friends gave up and actually flung themselves off the Colorado Street Bridge in Pasadena. Locals call it the 'Suicide Bridge'. Martha said she considered using the bridge herself.

Fortunately, Martha hooked up with a worker from Housing Help, a Los Angeles homeless outreach center. He took an interest in her, escorted her to a processing center, and got ahold of counselors to diagnose her depression and post-traumatic stress disorder. He even found her an apartment and got a caseworker assigned to her."

"What happened to her after that, dad?"

"Today Martha's our receptionist downtown. She just turned 60. She lives in a one-bedroom apartment in Pasadena with her 8-year-old mixed-breed dog, Alfie. Takes the Metro into our office. She's confided in me that the paranoia and anxiety still creep in periodically, especially late at night, but the meds and a watchful caseworker help her through it. She works part time at our office in the middle of the day. Dresses very well and is very pleasant to everyone. The clients all love her and so do we."

"She was very lucky," said the Judge. "The system actually worked for her after a time."

Conversation went silent for a while then. The Judge considered how life might have been were his circumstances different.

Later after coffee and some aged brandy, Katy and the Judge, officially newlyweds as far as Florence and Ralph were concerned, toddled upstairs and down the corridor to Katy's old bedroom. It was a young

315

girl's room, all pink and white paint, coral drapes, an embroidered Japanese wedding kimono in shades of white and coral turned into a comforter for the bed. Small framed photos of Katy growing up, on trips, at a prom, and sailing with her dad, gave the room the slight feel of a shrine.

Fortunately, there was a large king bed. They stripped off their clothes and settled into the bed in a classic spoon. He slid his hand around and rested it lightly on her tummy, wondering what life would be like when this kid got lose.

CHAPTER 38
10:00 Saturday Morning

The Judge considered what to do over his coffee the next morning. Frankie had had a girlfriend. The Judge met her once at a networking function. He recalled she lived on the Canals. He searched information on his cell for a Cathy Logan in Venice. He called, identified himself, and explained he'd like to meet briefly, suggesting coffee. She readily agreed, asking if they could instead just meet at her house.

Cathy Logan lived with her parents in an old bungalow on one of the canal streets in Venice.

The Venice Canals, built in 1905, had originally been part of a real estate marketing plan. With their gaily painted arched bridges, dramatic lighting and romantic gondolas, they were a popular summer promenade in the teens and twenties of the last century. Much of the canals were filled in for roads in the thirties and the remaining canals faded in prominence as piers and amusement parks were developed.

But the canals were rediscovered and renovated in the early nineties. Houses alongside the canals had the advantages of water frontage and proximity to both the beach and the Venice shops and restaurants. The high paying Silicon Beach jobs further increased demand for the canal homes.

The Judge parked on Eastern Court and walked over a steeply arched Venetian bridge, its weathered floors protesting slightly at his weight. Its rails sported thick wooden Xs painted a white lacquer, rather than the florid colors of the twenties. The tide was out so there was little water in the canal, leaving assorted canoes and rowboats in bright reds, yellows and blues sitting awkwardly aground, still tied to posts beside the path. A faint smell of old water foliage wafted up, a sour smell that the inhabitants proudly claimed to be healthy. The Judge was not so sure. But despite the slight odor, it was all pleasant, with lavish gardens cascading out from the small lots, reflected here and there with the sky in the still surface of the water.

The Judge stopped at number 12, red carved numbers atop its mail box announcing Dr. Logan.

The house was a single story bungalow with a mansard roof tacked on top. All green stucco, antique windows of varied sizes, and weathered shingles of the false roof rising at a steep angle in an effort to create some presence. It was jammed between two double story remodels to either side. Its best feature was its small patio and garden in lieu of a front lawn, carefully tended and clearly loved.

She was sitting in a white rocking chair on the small concrete patio. Surrounded by a profusion of hydrangeas in purples and blues, and white agapanthus and cabbage roses which overwhelmed the small yard and spilled out above the path in a lunge for the canal.

The chair fit the house exactly, except on closer inspection it was made out of white resin, not painted wood. Very practical and too bad at the same time, mused the Judge.

318

She stood up and approached him as he entered through the small spoked gate, extending her hand to give a firm handshake. Looking the Judge in the eye. Her dad had taught her well. The Judge could see she'd been crying. Large puffy circles around both eyes, and a nose whose tip was quite red.

He felt sorry for her. He felt sorry for himself. He'd liked Frankie, despite the fact he'd apparently sold out. He'd been an engaging young man, full of life and bounce. The Judge found it difficult to reconcile the law clerk he'd liked and enjoyed working with, and the shadowy Frankie he'd watched stealing the report.

Cathy looked early twenties. Younger than Frankie. Five foot five, curvy, with one of those bodies that looked soft and promising now, but would turn stout later. She had bright hazel eyes, a round face with a small pug noise, not unattractive, set off by a pink complexion. Irish was in the mix somewhere. She wore distressed jeans, tight to pack things in, and a beige silk blouse that suggested class and money. She was a doctor's daughter. It fit.

"Why don't we sit out here, Judge? It's a little more private." Gesturing toward the lawn chair next to her rocker.

The Judge settled into the chair, wishing he'd brought a hat to shelter from the sun.

"We met once, Judge. You probably don't remember. It was an attorney's networking thing, Beverly Hills Barristers I think. It was my birthday. But you'd insisted Frankie join you at this mixer. So Frankie brought me with him and then took me out to a special dinner. *Valentino*'s. Funny how little bits and pieces of memories come floating back. Quirky little parts of our life together that'll never be again." She stifled a sob.

"I'm so sorry Cathy. So sorry," the Judge murmured. He remembered her, but it was a heavy duty networking gig and he'd only said hello and moved on. He'd not been there to babysit Frankie and Frankie's significant other but rather to find business. The practice of law was competitive. One had to be focused.

"He respected you, Judge. Said you were very smart, although a little needy."

The Judge maintained his sympathetic expression, hoping the flash of irritation he felt wasn't noticeable. *Needy indeed!*

"He didn't kill himself, Judge." Her eyes shot up to the Judge's, intense, willing him to believe. "He wouldn't have done that."

"They haven't done an autopsy yet, Cathy. But I don't believe he killed himself either. How long were you together?"

"Almost two years."

"Any plans for the future?"

"I've been pressing him to commit. You know how guys are these days. Skittish."

The Judge had heard. The millennials were moving back home in droves. Scarce jobs, low pay, and heavy student loan payments left them floundering in a sea of economic distress. Moving home meant rent payments could go instead to the loan payments. A mutual interest of the young person and their guarantor parents. Parents could dote a bit further on their kids living at home, give further instruction on life which would be mostly ignored, and insist on house rules that chafed. Kids could make their loan payments, enjoy home cooked meals for free, and spend what would have been their food money on concerts, trips and dating. It wasn't entirely satisfactory, this forced co-habitation of generations.

But there wasn't much choice as the Great Recession of the 21st Century lingered, continuing to unravel the economy and squeezing the middle class toward the bottom.

Cathy added, "Just this last week he'd said he had a large sum of money coming in. Said we could move in together. I was so happy. Told my parents, everybody."

Her eyes teared up some.

"Were there any problems he talked about?" the Judge asked.

"Only this patent case. He was very intent on it. Thought you were wrong in your approach, Judge. Something about discovery on a report. Wanted suggestions on how to sway you over to a different line of thinking. Never seen him so agitated over work before. I guess his first actual job in the law and stuff. He wanted it to be right."

The Judge knew why Frankie so badly wanted him to hand over the report to Carl Hicks and his lawyer, but held his tongue.

"Had Frank been behaving strange, a little odd, or out of character the last couple of weeks?"

"No...... He's been working really late, really odd hours. But then of course you know, he's been working with you."

"What do you call odd hours, Cathy?"

"Well. These late night cell calls. Sudden meetings you'd have late at night. Meetings at Starbucks and stuff. Kinda messed up our social life. I understand and all. Guess it's just the nature of the practice. But it plays havoc with trying to have a date."

There had been no late night meetings with Frankie. No late night calls. Frankie must have had other friends to meet. Dick Harper perhaps. Or even the mysterious Mr. Wang. He'd covered it by using the Judge's name.

"Was there another woman, perhaps?"

Cathy scowled now, shaking her head, turning a bit pinker. She didn't like the question.

The Judge quickly shifted to another subject.

"You said Frankie told you he was coming into some money? That he thought you could now live together?"

"Yes."

"Did he say where the money was coming from?"

"No."

"Did he say how much?"

"No. But it must have been a lot. He said he would pay off all his student loans in one swoop, and buy himself a used Mercedes."

"When did he expect it?"

"Any day now I think."

"When's the last time you talked to him?"

Cathy gave a small cry of pain.

"Last Thursday," she whispered.

"What time, Cathy? Was it late?"

"About 10 p.m."

"What did he say?"

"He was very upset. Said he thought he was being followed. Said he felt like someone was 'tracking' his every move. Knew where he was going to be before he arrived. Said he'd just returned to his apartment and someone had broken in. Something valuable was missing."

"Did he say what?"

"No. Said he outsmarted them though. Said he'd just delivered a copy, and still had a second copy."

"A copy of what?"

"I don't know. He was just muttering to me over the phone and walking around his apartment. Almost talking to himself. He was very agitated. I told him to call the police."

"What'd he say?"

"He said he was afraid."

"Did he say anything else?"

"I heard him mutter something else."

"What?"

"Something about being shortchanged. Only got a pittance down payment for the copy. Bullshit promises. Can't trust asshole corporate types. I don't know. Something like that. He was very upset."

"How'd the conversation end?"

"I calmed him down. I'm... was... good for him that way. We talked a little about the new apartment we were going to get. We agreed to meet for coffee on Saturday morning."

"Did he show up?"

"No." Cathy started to softly cry. "He never came. I waited an hour. Called him several times. No answer. I tried to reach him all weekend. I never talked to him again. Finally on Tuesday my dad called.

He'd heard the news on the six p.m. news. He told me."

Cathy broke down completely then, thrusting her face into a damp Kleenex she pulled out of her jeans.

The Judge stood up and patted her on the shoulder, saying again how sorry he was for her loss. Then walked slowly through the small garden and back out to the canal, deep in thought.

CHAPTER 39
10:00 AM Monday

As the Judge pulled into the parking garage Monday morning, his cell phone went off, buzzing away in his earpiece. It was Lieutenant Kaminsky, sounding all soft and buttery. Like a cat that had just inhaled a dish of cream.

The Judge knew what this meant. More trouble. Kaminisky wanted the Judge to drop by his office, sooner rather than later, for a little tete-a-tete. The Judge sighed, maneuvered the car back around, and pulled out of the garage, heading for the Santa Monica Police Station.

The great man came out to the counter himself to meet the Judge, escorting him back to the same mean little interrogation room he'd used before. The Judge sat down but Kaminsky continued to stand, his hands on his hips, towering over the Judge. Trying to be intimidating.

"So lots of things are developing Judge," Kaminsky said.

"Oh really, Lieutenant? Tell me. I don't do well with suspense."

"Well for one thing, Frank Wolen was murdered. You remember. That's your law clerk. And you just happened to be the one who forced entry into his apartment and found the body."

"The door was open. And the paramedics found the body. Not me."

"Yes, well forensics says he was hit over the head before he died. That the body was moved and positioned into that bathtub. It was a semi-professional job. Someone used a sap that didn't show marks so it wasn't obvious he'd been hit first. And the gun was fired with the victim's own hand while he was unconscious, so all the calibrations were right for a self-inflicted wound."

"I'm not surprised, Kaminisky. Frankie had shown no signs of wanting to commit suicide."

"Yes, you would know, wouldn't you Judge?"

"And there are more developments?" asked the Judge.

"Oh yes. Randall Hicks was murdered too. We think someone hit him with the same sap, rendered him unconscious, and then pushed him in the water. Hicks, the one you had the secret meeting with. The guy who died because he was pushed off your dock. In front of your yacht."

"We've been through this Kaminsky. I had nothing to do with that."

"So you say, Judge. So you say."

"Is that it, Kaminisky? You're just confirming things we've both suspected."

"There is one other small matter, Judge. I haven't had a chance to confirm it yet. So I thought I'd talk to you, first. Go to the horse's mouth, so to speak. Or is that the right end?"

Here it comes, thought the Judge. What possible additional fact could there be that could implicate him?

"Go on Kaminsky. Spit it out."

Kaminisky was standing over the Judge now, bouncing subtly on his toes. Obviously enjoying the suspense.

"There are rumors that Carl Greene's estate, with its new technology and all, may be worth a billion dollars."

The Judge sat up a little straighter. He hadn't heard a number like that floated before.

"So, Kaminisky? Lucky heirs, huh?"

"See that's just the thing, Judge. What I hear, and this is all off the record still, until a formal probate is opened. What I hear is it's all been bequeathed to one person in some sort of trust."

"Well, Kaminsky. Perhaps that's another motive to put old Carl out of his misery."

"That's exactly what I thought, Judge. We're on the same page finally."

"So who'd old Carl leave it to?"

"You, Judge. You."

The Judge was stunned. Without words. He just looked at Kaminsky uncomprehendingly, openly astonished.

Some part of him registered this was not the reaction Kaminsky had been hoping for. Disappointment was etched across Kaminsky's face.

"Is that all you have to say for yourself, Judge?" Kaminsky finally asked. Coming off the balls of his feet now, his enthusiasm flagging.

"I'm as totally surprised as you are, Kaminsky. I know nothing about it. I didn't know the man. Met him only three times and formally at that, inside arbitration. Why he would want to include me in some sort of trust in his estate boggles the mind. People don't just go around leaving a billion dollars to someone they don't know, even just as a trustee overseeing a trust. Where did you hear this? I'd like to get to the bottom of it as much as you."

"It was an off the record conversation with Greene's estate attorney, Judge. I expect he'll be contacting you in due course. I just wanted to be the first to give you the news."

Kaminsky was completely deflated now. The interview hadn't gone as he'd expected. Kaminsky marched to the door and opened it, indicating by his action it was time for the Judge to leave. He made no effort to shake the Judge's hand, and the Judge didn't offer.

The Judge walked out into the Santa Monica sun a bit dazed. What in the hell had Carl Greene done in his estate planning. And why had he named the Judge trustee?

CHAPTER 40
7:30 PM Monday

They sat down to dinner Monday evening in the pretend French chateau. The Judge, Katy, Flo and Ralph. The Judge had gotten to know Katy's folks better in this interval of hiding out at their Brentwood house. And they'd gotten to know him. Ralph had welcomed the Judge into the family with open arms. Appeared truly glad to have the Judge sharing his home. Flo was more reserved, but had softened considerably. Bowing to the inevitable. This tired old man was now her new son in law. She was stuck with the Judge now and seemed more or less resolved to make the best of it.

The Judge was peppered each night over dinner with questions about the case and what he'd learned that day. It was good grist for the mill. Everyone seemed to have an opinion of who had done what to whom. Unfortunately, he had three dinner companions, and therefore three entirely separate scenarios about who had killed Carl, Frankie and Randall Hicks, and why.

Flo was convinced Carl's gay lover had killed Carl in a fit of jealousy. In her view gays were over-sexed, over-emotional, and likely to turn on those who'd dumped them. She wasn't sure about the other murders, but posited that Randall Hicks had killed

Frankie to shut him up, and then was killed himself by a distraught investor who'd lost everything investing in Hicks' phony company.

Katy was of the view that Yana had killed Carl in a rage that Carl wouldn't share his new technology as part of the property settlement in their divorce. She had a dim opinion of Russian woman who came over to poach American men out from under American girls. She suggested Frankie found out what Yana had done somehow, and told Randall Hicks about it. Both Frankie and Hicks were then silenced by Allan Clark to protect Yana. And to protect what Clark thought would be his share in the new technology when he ran off with Yana. She believed Yana was using Clark like a cat's paw and would drop him like a rock once everything blew over.

Ralph put his money on Carl's mysterious silent partner as Carl's killer, positing a hot dispute between them. The partner wanting to sell out to Cindy Kwan and her group, collect his half of a big check and go home. Carl frustrated that result by stubbornly refusing to sell the rights to his new technology. Ralph was appalled by Dick Harper's lack of ethics, and liked him as the villain who killed first Frankie and then Randall Hicks, to hush them up about his illegal spying, videotaping, and bribes. Ralph posited it was a desperate attempt by Harper to save his lawyer's license and his career.

The Judge said it was too soon for him make a guess about the killer or killers, although he felt strongly it was the homeless gang that killed Carl in that ally. He just wasn't sure why.

The dinner conversation tonight had traveled over this ground and moved on to Ralph's new oil project planned for the Gulf of Mexico. Somewhere along the way the girls fell off that discussion and moved on to their plans for the big wedding reception at the California Club. The master guest list was growing by leaps and bounds. The Judge would be a considerably poorer after this butcher bill was paid.

Flo's excellent cooking and a special wine from Ralph's cellar had left everyone with a warm glow in their stomachs. Katy had declined any alcohol again at dinner, earning her a keen look from her dad who then smiled softy but held his tongue. The conversation shaded down into a relaxed lull over coffee and an upside down pineapple cake Flo had baked.

It was then Katy dropped her second bomb. Tapping her spoon on her water class to get their attention, she said, "I have an announcement."

Three heads snapped to attention, picking up on the excitement in Katy's voice. The Judge knew this could only be one thing. He cringed inside in anticipation. He supposed there was no easy way to do this.

Katy stood up and raised her water glass.

"The Judge and I didn't plan for this to happen. But it has. And we're both so very excited and happy. I'd like to announce to you two, dear parents, that I'm pregnant. You are going to be grandparents."

Florence's mouth dropped open, but no sound came out. There was silence. You could have heard a pin drop.

Then Ralph raised his glass high in a grand salute, saying "Congratulations you two, that's wonderful news. Wonderful, wonderful. Your mom and I are so excited."

The Judge stole a peek at Florence. She'd managed to crank her mouth closed, and now a small tear was sliding down one cheek. But it was a happy tear the Judge could see with considerable relief. Florence produced the largest smile he'd ever seen on her. And just like Katy, it was now traveling all the way up into her eyes. She turned from Katy to the Judge with new respect and a warmth in her face. The Judge could tell that as far as Florence was concerned he was in. In the Family, in the circle, in her affection, just in. He'd contributed to producing a grandchild. All other considerations paled against this blessed accomplishment.

It dawned on the Judge he'd gotten it wrong. He'd thought he'd been an old guy trapping Katy, taking her off the market when she truly belonged to someone half his age, knowing full well he was already on the way to being old and decrepit. But he was the one now trapped for life. He'd been spotted, stalked, bagged, and delivered by Katy into the world of marital commitment. His fate was sealed by his contribution to her production of their child. For better or worse they were tied together now forever. He'd hadn't a clue who the big game hunter really was. Now he understood.

CHAPTER 41
11:00 AM Tuesday

The Judge parked on Pacific Avenue and walked the short block down 18th to the Venice boardwalk. It wasn't nearly as busy during the week. He headed north in long strides, trying to get his cardio going, determined to extract exercise while he looked for Marty, the street kid he'd talked to before. There were homeless here and there along the boardwalk, and the adjacent lawns and benches, as always. But no Marty.

He turned and retraced his steps south, then kept going past his entry point, heading for Muscle Beach. He spotted Marty sitting beneath a palm tree, reading a tattered comic book. As he approached, Marty looked up, apprehensive, then showed a smile of yellow teeth as he recognized the Judge. A combination of friendliness and avarice showed in his eyes. He was remembering the fifty dollar bill.

"Hi, Marty, how about an ice cream?"

"How about a hamburger, Mr.?" said Marty.

"Done. I'm the Judge, Marty, remember?"

"I remember. You're the guy was ogling the boobs parade."

The Judge winced, but ignored the comment. His protest would only make it worst. They walked back along the boardwalk until they came to the *Sidewalk Cafe*. Marty ordered a cheeseburger, fries, a large shake and an apple pie turnover to go. The Judge ordered coffee.

They sat together on the bench across from the joint and watched the people go by for a time while Marty ate. He finished quickly. Meals were likely few and far between.

"So where do you live, Marty?"

Suspicion flashed across his face. Then he relaxed.

"I live with my mom."

"Do you live in an apartment?"

"No. In our car."

Marty's chin came up. Prepared to fight if the Judge wanted to make something of it.

"How's that like?" asked the Judge.

"It's okay, Judge."

"Isn't it a little crowded?"

"No. I'm smaller so I get the front seat. She gets the back. It's kind of a pain though 'cause we have to move it all the time. My mom has rules we follow, Judge. Just like everyone else."

"Like what?" asked the Judge.

"Like we rotate among several parking places so we don't get noticed. When we move around inside the car, we move slowly to avoid rocking. We keep the windows cracked open while we sleep, but not wide enough for someone to reach in. We have a porta potty I have to dump and keep clean. We try not to spend more time in the car than necessary. Mom says the more time we spend in our car, the more smells accumulate."

"Where do you park your car?"

"We hop around a four block area."

"Does your mom work?"

"She works a little, but she doesn't get paid much. She can't find a full time job. We live off of food stamps, gift cards for gas and food, and Mom gets Social Security disability. Mom does our laundry in the church annex. We take showers at the YMCA or on Venice Beach."

"That sounds pretty rough, Marty."

"Naw, we get by. It's kinda like Robin Hood. Sometimes people even come by looking for us so they can point and take pictures. Mom says we're a tourist attraction."

Marty looked up to see if the Judge would make fun of this.

"How come you're not in school, Marty?"

"I'm supposed to be. Mom thinks I am. But the guys in school don't understand about the car. They tease me. Some days I get tired of it. So I just don't go. It doesn't matter. School's pretty boring."

"Let me talk to a few friends I know… discreetly." The Judge quickly put up his hands to stem the immediate protest. "Perhaps I can get a little help for you. But that's not the reason I looked you up, Marty. I'm looking for those guys that tried to hurt me on the beach the other week. We talked about them before, remember? You were going to check around. See if you could find where they hung."

"I remember, Judge. There was going to be another fifty for me if I came up with something. Right?"

"I think that was our deal."

Marty lowered his voice now to a whisper.

"I hear they sometimes hang out during the day in Promenade Park. That's where they take on business I think. But you didn't hear it from me."

Marty pinned the Judge with his eyes, demanding anonymity.

"It's just between us."

"You'd best be careful pops. They aren't guys to mess with. They'd as soon kill you as look at you."

The Judge smiled. Age was all so… relative. He wondered if Katy thought of him as 'pops'.

He discretely got a fifty dollar bill out of his pocket, crumpled it up into a ball, palmed it, and then gave Marty the golden hand shake as he got up from the bench. He walked thirty yards, then looked back. Marty was still sitting on the bench, looking after him. Looking worried.

The Judge decided he would call a case worker he knew and see if some help and direction could be provided for Marty and his mom. Maybe a job and a shelter dwelling. Perhaps a different school where Marty could start fresh.

CHAPTER 42
Noon Tuesday

The Judge retrieved his car and headed for Palisades Park. The Park was a stretch of lawn and trees paralleling the edge of the bluff in downtown Santa Monica. It looked over the Pacific Coast Highway, the beach, and out across the Santa Monica bay to the Pacific. The jewel in the city's crown. At any time of day you could find joggers, lovers, bicyclists, picnicking tourists with make-shift lunches from the shops across the street on Ocean Avenue, and of course the homeless, scattered here and there, sharing the green space.

Locals and tourists alike ignored the homeless. As if they weren't supposed to exist in this people's park for the affluent. They focused on the sea view, the gardens and each other. At one point the homeless had become so numerous the city fathers shut Palisades Park down. Cordoning it off to everyone. There was an uproar and city hall relented, opening the park again.

But they'd first meanly spiked or ridged every surface, bench, concrete planter, and bus stop shelter they could. There was no clean surface above ground where one could stretch out and sleep. It had become a standup or sit down park. No longer a lay down park unless you brought your own plastic sheet, blanket or cardboard and stretched it out on the turf. Many did.

The Judge reached the Park and made his way casually through the light throng. He was just one more office worker from across the street, released from his drudgery for lunch. He looked to be meandering up the length of the Park, from its southern tip where Colorado Avenue led down over a bridge on to the Santa Monica Pier, northward parallel to Ocean Avenue for some thirteen city blocks, ending in Point Inspiration to the north. Paying attention to no one, lost in thought. Or so it seemed. But he was monitoring everyone, looking for someone who might resemble one of the gang members.

It took a good hour to walk up to the northern tip of the park and back twice. He saw no one of interest. He was about to give up when, two-thirds of the way back down the park on his second trip, opposite Wilshire Boulevard, he spotted a young man sitting on the ground with his back against a tree, motionless, smoking, staring out at the sea. He hadn't been there before. Early-twenties and white. His scruffy khakis, faded padded coat, shaggy matted hair and unshaven face, marked him as homeless.

But homeless, or only playing as such, he was the man that had attacked the Judge on the beach. It gave the Judge bitter satisfaction to note his swollen nose, a small piece of surgical tape holding things together across the bridge. The Judge unconsciously touched his own arm where a swath of bandage under his shirt sleeve kept stiches from unraveling. Marty had said this guy's name was Arty.

The Judge decided to watch a bit. He retreated to a large elm and pretended to be texting on his cell phone. He had an angled side view of the young man sixty feet away.

Nothing happened for about thirty minutes except for the appearance of a column of ants interested in scraps. Their conga line swerved around the Judge's feet, each insect hauling bits twice their size to some ant haven on the other side of the Judge's tree.

Arty suddenly turned his attention to his right, then raised his right hand slightly from his lap, making a reverse victory sign, his thumb tucked into his palm, his fingers pointed down.

Slowly walking along the path that fronted the bluff from the north came a young black man, also in homeless garb and markings, matted long hair, dirty face. Without appearing to, his head bobbed in an arc, carefully surveying a hundred and eighty degrees around him. He brought his hand down flat against his thigh as he passed, making a similar upside down victory sign, his thumb tucked into his palm.

Arty let the black guy pass, then casually got up and sauntered after him, keeping thirty feet behind, heading south along the bluff path. His head was on a swivel now too, surveying his surroundings. Stopping periodically to glance over his shoulder. Despite their markings they no longer looked homeless. There was too much purpose in their walk. What name had Marty used for the black guy? 'Juno'. This guy must be Juno.

The Judge left his tree and walked south across the grass parallel to them and the bluff path, moving around homeless here and there sprawled in the sun and small packets of tourists spreading out lunches on the grass. The Judge deliberately wobbled his path, stopping now and again to admire the views. Then speeded his step to catchup distance.

Juno cut away from the cliff path and across the lawn to the signal at Santa Monica Boulevard. He pushed the cross walk button as Arty caught up. Neither spoke or acknowledged the other.

When the walk signal flashed green they quickly crossed in single file. Still no acknowledgment of the other's presence. The Judge hustled and leaped off the curb as the signal turned to a flashing red hand, burying himself in the cluster of a Filipino family who also believed in ignoring lights. He must have stood out like a sore thumb, towering as he did above the small statured family. But neither of his quarry looked back now.

He fell back again after stepping on to the curb, while they picked up their pace, continuing up Santa Monica Boulevard alongside the corner office building, then right into the alley behind the building. He stopped at the edge of the alley and peered around in time to see them disappearing down the ramp to the underground parking beneath the building.

He waited a minute, moved down the alley to the parking ramp, and then cautiously down the ramp. The parking facility was dirty, bits of papers and debris scattered, and the light was bad, several ceiling bulbs burned out. He could smell the fumes of gas, rubber, and rotting food from dumpsters at the top of the ramp. The air was hot and sticky from the flow of air conditioning exhaust into the garage space. He could feel sweat trickling down the back of his neck. There was the low hum of coolers, and once a car pulled past as he slowly made his way down one layer of parking after another, trudging as though he'd forgotten where he'd parked.

He reached the bottom, five levels down from the ally and came up short against a blank wall. No young men. Only graffiti. He turned and began his way back up, looking more carefully between cars. Reaching the 4th floor down from the top, he heard an angry voice. Quickly extinguished. Moving in that direction he spotted a small door set into the side wall, opened a crack for air, on the fourth level. As he got closer he heard a murmur of voices inside. He supposed it was the stairwell to the building above.

He ducked behind a car on the opposite wall from the door and waited. Five minutes later a young man, looking to be homeless, Asian, mid-twenties, came out, looked around carefully without appearing to do so, then stepped back in behind the door.

The Judge reached into his sport coat and fished for a card he knew was there: Officer Saunders. Los Angeles Sheriff's Department. The cop that made so much fun of his claim it was a 'mixed' ethnic gang that attacked him. Well Officer Saunders could damn well see for himself.

He dialed the card's direct line and Saunders picked up. Apparently he was on duty. Good.

The Judge explained his situation. How he had spotted Arty, with his broken nose. How he was positive it was the guy who had attacked him. How he followed the two young men to this parking garage and at least three of them were here. Meeting. And they were indeed a mixed lot. He'd seen Arty, the white guy, Juno, the black guy, and now an Asian. He said nothing about Marty and the tip that led him here.

Saunders was attentive. He grasped the situation immediately.

"What level are you on, Judge?"

"Level four."

"Okay, don't move. Stay put. Get behind a parked car or something. I'll have three cruisers there inside fifteen minutes. And be careful. Don't let yourself be seen."

The Judge hunkered down behind a black Mercedes to wait.

A minute later Arty came out of the stairwell with another young man. A Latino. They stopped just outside the door and one of them pulled a pack of cigarettes. They both lit up. They spoke in a low murmur. The Judge couldn't make out their words. The Latino got a brief call on his cell phone, then quickly went back into the stairwell, motioning Arty to follow. A minute later the Latino came back out again, turned, and sauntered up the ramp to the beginning of the next level, three floors down from the ally. He leaned against the wall there. A lookout... or a guard? The Judge was now sealed in.

Arty, Juno and the Asian came out next, apparently having settled their business. The three walked out into the middle of the parking lane. Then Arty strolled out toward the Mercedes the Judge was sheltered behind. Christ, was he hiding behind Arty's car?

Juno headed in the opposite direction, and the Asian headed toward the back of the lot. Apparently they didn't even park their cars together.

The Judge slid silently out of his jacket, prepared to break Arty's nose for him again. But then there was a low squeal of tires. A private security patrol car slowly came down the ramp, making its rounds floor to floor, coming to inspect the fourth level next.

342

The Latino on the third level melted away. The three gang members on the Judge's floor moved briskly back to the shelter of the stairwell and closed the door, preferring not to be seen. Private security no doubt took a dim view of homeless sheltering in their garage.

The Judge moved too. He slipped out from behind the Mercedes and rapidly made his way up a level, to the third floor, nodding at the security patrol officer as the security car came down the ramp. One dumpy old man inside, driving slowly. Likely no weapon. But he'd have a radio. Still, the police were already called and on the way.

The Judge moved further, to the second level, where he squatted down behind a red Camaro.

Two minutes later, the Latino walked up to the second level, cautiously looked around, and then walk up to the first level. Exactly two minutes later Arty walked past the Judge's position and up to the first level. Where in the hell were Saunders and his cruisers?

Two minutes later, Juno walked past. And two minutes later the Asian walked past. Their staged departures were timed like a damn ballet. In the space of eight minutes the quarry had fled.

The Judge stood up, his knees stiff and achy from squatting. Complaining all the way as he moved to an elevator he spotted in the center of the floor. It whisked him up to the building lobby. The Judge sped through a service door which took him down a long corridor to a door with a window in it looking out on the loading dock on the back alley. He peeked out and watched the Asian emerge from the parking ramp into the alley.

The Asian lingered there, stopping to roll himself a cigarette, dumping in material from a small leather pouch he kept in his pocket.

As he lit up a disreputable looking SUV pulled into the alley. Dark green, like a telephone truck, it had multiple dings and dents, only partially covered by a layer of mud and dust that served as a second skin. The other three men were in the truck. It stopped so the Asian could climb in the back.

The Judge fumed at himself for not calling the police earlier. He could do nothing now. He was hardly up to making a citizen's arrest of four young men in prime condition, likely still with knives. The Judge winced at this thought, putting his hand to his arm, which was throbbing.

As the van pulled slowly away up the alley the Judge hopped out through the door and got its license plate.

The Judge was tired now. Adrenalin leaving him. He went back to the loading dock and sat down on its edge, choosing not to think what the seat of his pants would look like from the grease and dirt there. Five minutes later, three Santa Monica cruisers pulled into the alley in a hurry. Four officers jumped out.

The Judge waved them over to where he sat on his grease spot and told them his tale of woe. As he got up he wondered how he would explain this new pants travesty to Katy. His pants had been lost, ripped, and now greased. It wasn't a good month for pants. It felt like every time he turned around his ass was hanging out.

CHAPTER 43

4:30 PM Tuesday

The Judge picked up his cell and dialed Barbara. She answered on the first ring again.

"Hi Judgie. What's up?"

"Barbara, did Carl have a silent partner for his new technology? Perhaps a fellow inventor working on it with him, or a financier, or a mentor who originally came up with the idea?"

"Gosh, Judge, you're all business today. Can't we pretend just for a minute this is a social call?"

"Sorry, Barbara. But I really need your help here."

"I think there was a partner. I don't know who he was. But somewhere along the line he and Carl had a falling out."

"You said 'he'. Was it a guy?"

"I guess I don't know Judge."

"Might it have been one of Carl's other lovers?"

"Carl didn't have any other lovers once I came along, Judge. He had flirtations occasionally, but they didn't amount to anything. No one could satisfy Carl like I could. You remember about that, right Judge?" Barbara giggled.

"Yes, well, ah... did you know Carl had a gay lover?"

"You're good, Judge. How'd you find out about that?"

"I work at it Barbs. Carl told you about it?"

"Just a little, Judge. I was shocked at first. But Carl said it was only a flirtation. He had no real feelings for the guy. Just experimenting a little. I guess the poor man felt jilted pretty bad when Carl refused to return his calls. Went off the deep end, or so Carl said."

"Do you know who the guy was?"

"No. Carl never gave me a name."

"You think the guy was angry enough to attack Carl in that alley? To kill him?"

"Oh Judge." Barbara was going into a wail again. "I don't know. I don't know. Why would anyone want to do that to poor Carl?"

"Okay, Barbs. Take a deep breath. Now another. That's better. What did you think about Carl's gay lover when he told you? Did it make you feel awkward? Uncertain Carl was the person for you? Perhaps you thought you could reform him?"

Barbara blew her nose, forcing the Judge to yank his cell away from his ear.

"I was glad Carl told me. It showed trust on his part. I wanted him to be able to share anything with me. And then when he explained how it was just a flirtation, I decided 'live and let live'. We were having a wonderful time. Carl was going to marry me. I knew, the way a woman does, that I could keep him satisfied. He wouldn't be dabbling around anymore with gays or anyone else. He wouldn't have the energy. You know, Judge. You remember."

"Do you think Carl's gay lover might also have been his partner in his technology?"

"I don't know, Judge."

"Is there anyone else you can think of who might know who Carl's business partner is, or was?"

"Maybe his Ex."

"Alright, Barbara, thanks for the help."

"You don't get off that easily, Judge. You owe me a dinner now, and soon."

"You mean you want to come over and have dinner with me and Katy, Barbara?"

"Hell no. You know what I mean. You're going to get tired of this child, Judge. You'll see. Just remember my door's always open for you... and the rest of me too!"

The Judge smiled and said goodbye.

He dialed Yana, Carl's ex-wife, next, and asked if they could talk a bit more.

"Of course, Judge. In fact you're the very man I've been thinking about. Let's meet at The Penthouse at the Huntley Hotel in 45 minutes. As long as you're buying."

She sounded a lot warmer than last time they'd met. The Judge wondered what had changed. He busied himself with some client work, and twenty minutes later slid out to meet Yana.

The Penthouse, perched 18 stories above Santa Monica, provided stunning 360-degree views through a sweeping wall of windows from the Malibu beach and cliffs to the bright lights of Hollywood. The Judge lodged himself in an intimate corner table with the Pacific spread at his back, and ordered a martini, glad to be away from his office and almost through for the day.

Yana arrived five minutes later, creating a physical stir in the air with her entrance, tall, beautiful, feline, turning the heads of the three male patrons on bar

347

stools at the circular bar and the two male waiters work-ing the tables. The Judge stood as she approached. Perhaps to get a better look himself.

She was dressed all in white, offsetting her short dark hair and vivid ruby lipstick. She wore a sort of Marilyn Monroe dress whose top was two pieces slung around her neck, leaving a long décolletage and allow-ing her breasts to swing pendulum fashion as she moved. It was tight at her small waist, and short and pleated at the bottom, exposing long legs over spiked white heels. Simple, elegant, and WOW!

The Judge took the hand she offered and helped her into the chair beside him, careful not to crush the long slender fingers, made to play the piano, garnished with matching ruby nail polish.

"Thanks for coming, Yana. How are you do-ing? I'm sorry I upset you last time we met."

"Better, Judge. Thank you."

"I'm still trying to find out who did this to Carl. And a few more questions have come up. Are you still willing to help?"

"Of course, Judge. Whatever I can do."

"Are you and Allan Clark still an item?" asked the Judge.

"Allan and I… we take a break. There's no more Carl. So I look for someone new in my life. May-be a judge."

Yana's green eyes looked up, directly into the Judge's eyes, measuring the lift in her trial balloon.

The Judge ignored the innuendo, moving smoothly onto safer ground.

"Yana, did Carl have a silent business partner in his technology project?"

Yana's eyes narrowed. She considered her answer carefully. No doubt calculating how what she might say would impact any claim made to share in her ex-husband's new technology.

"I think maybe yes, but no more," she said.

"How long ago did Carl get the partner?"

"I think, maybe, two years. Right after I filed."

"Was he another inventor, Yana?"

"I don't know."

"When did he stop being a partner?" asked the Judge.

"Maybe three months ago. Not sure. Carl tried to give me as little information about his business as possible. But from the few things Carl said, there was big fight."

"Between Carl and the partner?"

"Yes. I think Carl's partner didn't want to go."

"So Carl forced him out?"

"I guess."

"Carl never said who he was?"

"No."

"Didn't your divorce attorney want to know about this ex-partner?"

"We try to get Carl's new technology ruled community property. If we succeed, then we would find out. That's what attorney says."

"Was there anyone else who helped Carl with money to fund development of his new technology?"

"I don't know."

"Carl never mentioned anyone who was giving him cash? Or a line of credit, or something?"

"No. Yes. One time he slipped. Called him Robbie."

"Was this money guy in L.A., Yana?"

"I think so. My impression was Carl used to meet him at Hollywood Park."

"The race track? Carl played the horses?" asked the Judge.

"No. Poker Club. Carl loved poker."

"So this might have been a poker playing friend of Carl's?"

"Yes. Yes. Maybe."

"And his name, or nickname, was Robbie?"

"Yes."

"Alright, Yana. Carl's lawyer said Carl had an earlier attorney. An old patent attorney Carl used to use. He helped Carl document information for a confidential report submitted into the arbitration. So confidential Carl's current lawyer was not allowed to look at it. Do you know who this earlier attorney might be, Yana?"

"Not sure. Maybe old Gerald Jenkins. Must be over 80. Carl's patent lawyer when we first marry."

"Know where I can find him?"

"Santa Monica. Top of the big office building. You can see water."

"Very good, Yana. You've been a big help."

"So now Yana has question for you, Judge."

"Yes?"

"My attorney tells me you're special lawyer. Super Lawyer."

"Well, I've had lots of experience, Yana, it's true."

"I want to hire you for my lawyer."

"Me?"

"Yes."

"For what?"

"I want to hire you on the site."

"The site?"

"Yes, quietly, for advice from time to time. Nobody knows."

"You want to hire me on the 'side'?"

"Yes, that's what I said."

"Okay, Yana. But I still don't understand. For what?"

"Are you expensive?"

"My fees are commensurate with my experience," the Judge said cautiously.

"Five hundred an hour," Yana said. "I'll pay double that, on the site, and we can have the fringe benefit. Like with my divorce attorney. I'll have the cash."

"But I still don't—"

"Once, twice a week," Yana interrupted. "You come to my place for the dinner. Gourmet Russian. The massage. We have relations. It is all good. You will live longer, Judge. In my country important lawyers all have these relations. Particularly if married. Men get tense during week. They need to relax. It's natural thing. They do better job. Live longer time. Are happier. Weekends for the family. Tuesday and Thursday for Yana."

She sat back in her chair then. She'd made her pitch. The Judge shook his head to clear the remnants of the vanilla martini.

"Yana, I don't need the... the... the fringe benefit. I'm happily married. But what is it you want me to do for you? What's the problem? Why do you need legal advice on the site... I mean on the side?"

"Oh. Well…. My divorce lawyer says we have a chance of a hot snowball in getting Carl's new technology made community property."

"You mean a snowball in hell."

"Yes. What I said."

"So I need help on that. Perhaps you can figure a way round. And then I need reasonable allowance from Carl's assets for alimony. I am not a cheap girl. I cannot live on cheap alimony."

Yana folded arms, indicating there could be no compromise here.

It certainly wouldn't be cheap to take care of Yana, the Judge thought to himself. Then cut that line of thought off quickly.

"Well, I suppose I could consult on the side a little," said the Judge, "providing there's no conflict of interest. The patent arbitration would have to be settled first."

"I cannot wait for that," said Yana. "I need you to write some checks now."

"Wait a minute, Yana. You're hiring me. You'll be writing checks to me for my legal advice."

"I understand, Judge. But I have no money. I have to get the money from you."

"Me?"

"Yes. You write me the big checks. I write you the legal checks!"

"Huh?" The word came out of the Judge's mouth before he could stop it.

"Don't be coy with Yana, Judge. You are Trustee of Carl's trust. You are going to control all his money. I need you to start writing checks now. Nice big fat ones. A girl has got to live and L.A. is an expen-

352

sive town. But think of all the fun we're going to have."

The Judge slumped back in his chair. He told Yana it sounded unlikely he could help her on the side because of conflicts, existing and potential. He'd be glad to refer three separate tough litigators whom he respected. He thanked her for taking time to meet him. He even reached across the table to formally shake her hand. Then threw a large bill onto the table and, not waiting for change, beat a hasty retreat for The Penthouse exit.

He could see two males shifting at the bar to get up, prepared to fill the space he'd vacated. He doubted Yana would be alone in her corner long.

CHAPTER 44
7:30 Tuesday Night

The Judge drove into the parking lot at Hollywood Park, maneuvering around potholes and rough
spots. This once famous racetrack was where the stars
would come to watch and bet on the great horses.
There was a time in its 75-year run when Hollywood
Park was the best thoroughbred racetrack in America.
The first ever Breeders' Cup was held here in 1984.
Some of America's most famous racing legends thun-
dered into the history books on this track. But no
more. The track had been closed, the grandstands
razed, and the 238 acre site was to become a 'new modern community' of homes, stores, entertainment, offices, a hotel, park space, and perhaps an 80,000-seat
football stadium for an NFL team.

The city fathers of Inglewood, the poor cousin
city surrounded by the octopus-like Los Angeles, announced this was progress. And no doubt it was. Progress for the moneyed interests that controlled the park
and would redouble their fortunes by its destruction.

But to the Judge it was sad. He doubted it
would improve the lot of the poor residents of Inglewood much. They wouldn't be able to afford the new
townhomes. The number of jobs gained probably just
equaled the jobs lost with the closure of the track. And
the community's loss of the open space, the fanfare, the
drama and the excitement of the magnificent 'Lakes
and Flowers Track', could never be replaced.

The card club casino was added to the complex in 1994, and curiously it would survive. Branded the Hollywood Park Casino, it was open 24 hours a day and sported 70,000 square feet of gaming space. Eighty table and poker games. It was to be remodeled. The lone remnant of a majestic place.

The Judge walked in, discreetly approached an attendant qua security guard, slipped him a fifty, and asked if Robbie, a friend of his and Carl Greene's, was playing tonight.

"You're in luck, sir," said the guard. "Robbie's just getting a drink at the bar." He pointed to a tall upright man with his back to the Judge. White hair, kitted out in designer blue jeans and a white and red checked long sleeve shirt. The man looked vaguely familiar.

The Judge walked up behind him and said, "Hi Robbie. How's the play going?"

The man turned, startled. It was George Roberts, Carl Greene's dentist, pale blue eyes now focused on the Judge with intensity.

Roberts recovered quickly, extending his hand.

"A surprise to see you here, Judge. Didn't know you were a poker player."

"I dabble occasionally, George," said the Judge.

"Great," said Roberts. "Shall we sit down? My feet hurt. That's what happens when you're standing over teeth all day."

They both purchased chips and then walked together to an empty table and slid into seats.

"I'm not really here to play, George. I was hoping to talk about Carl Greene and how you knew him."

The pale blue eyes turned cautious.

"Carl's dead," George said. Flat out, like it had always been.

"I know," said the Judge. "I'm trying to figure out who killed him. And why? You know any reason he might have been killed?"

"You said you play poker, Judge."

"Like I said, I've dabbled at it now and then."

"Let's play some poker, Judge, you and I. Maybe we'll learn a little about each other in the game."

"Perhaps you can teach me," said the Judge.

"Perhaps something. Poker isn't really a game of cards. It's more a game of psychological warfare."

"I was taught to play cautiously," said the Judge. "Bet when you have the right cards, play the odds, bluff occasionally to keep your opponents honest, check or dropout if you don't have a hand. Don't risk more than you can afford to lose."

"Sounds right, doesn't it? The way most people learn. It's the sort of players we like to have in the game. They fund our preoccupation with the sport."

"That's not how you play?"

"I start with a different mindset. It's not money I'm betting with. They're just chips. Chips to win or to lose. But I'm going to take them all away from you. I'll push you to your budget limit and beyond any chance I get. I get you sweating over how much money you might lose, I've got you. I'm going to own your budgeted money. All of it." This was said with a smile that didn't quite reach his eyes.

"And," he added, "bluffing isn't about bluffing now and then to keep your playmates guessing. Bluffing is about maneuvering your opponents to quit early, time and again. Small pots, big pots, I don't care. I'm here to win. They're just chips. You have some. I'll take as many of yours as I can. Kind of like life."

"What about luck?" asked the Judge.

"Some folks are luckier, others not so much. But everybody hits good streaks and bad. It's about maximizing your good runs. If the cards aren't there, you bluff your way 'round that. If the cards come back, you hang back and milk the pot. But you're not playing the cards. You're playing the other players. You read the players right, play the players right, you walk away from the table at the end of the game with your pockets full. There is no mercy in this game. You play to win, or you play to lose."

"Any other advice you want to give me, George? It sounds like I'm going to need help."

"I'll tell you this, Judge. The world is all about risk and reward. Mostly we humans make poor choices when confronted with risk decisions. We're almost hard wired to choose poorly. A very few of us learn to avoid this trap and to prosper. But the vast majority never escape."

"What're you saying?"

"Look at it this way, Judge. Assume someone offers you a game of 10,000 dollars on a free flip of a coin. A fifty-fifty proposition, right? Heads you're given 10,000. Tails and you aren't given anything. And since you're a poker player, or perhaps a stock market player, let's suppose this is a proposition you see over and over again. So the probabilities of this wager will work themselves out over a period of time.

"Okay."

"Suppose then, I offered you 3,000 dollars to walk away? Not take your coin flip?"

"Alright."

"What do you do, Judge?"

"What would you do, George?"

"You have a fifty-fifty chance of winning 10,000. You have P equals point five of getting 10,000 and P equals point five of getting zero. Or you can choose not to play the game and get 3,000."

"Right."

"Rationally Judge, the number needed for you to walk away and not take your coin flip should be a dollar above 5,000. Statistically over a period of tosses you win half the time, lose half the time, and average 5,000 ahead. Anything above that number is a plus for you. But most people will walk away for less. Sometimes far less. Sometimes people will walk away for 500 or 1,000. After all, it's money they didn't have before."

"I suppose that's true."

"Anyone who accepts less than 5,000 to walk away is known as 'Risk-Averse'. This is called 'Risk Aversion'."

"I guess that would probably be me, George. A bird in hand."

"But here is where things get more interesting, Judge. Turn my little experiment on its head. Tell people they are committed to a position, in their hand or in the market, where they have a fifty-fifty chance of either 'losing' 10,000 or breaking even on their coin flip.

It's the same probability as before. Over a number of flips they'll average a 5,000 dollar loss, avoiding the loss half the time and sucking up the loss half the time.

Then tell them they can either take their chances with the fifty-fifty game or they could accept a certain 3,000 dollar loss and fork the cash over. They have a fifty-fifty chance of losing 10,000 dollars. They have P equals point five of losing 10,000 and P equals point five of losing zero. Or they can choose not to play the game and accept a certain $3,000 loss.

What would you do now, Judge?"

"I don't know. I wouldn't want to lose the money"

"Of course you wouldn't. Most people wouldn't. But rationally, if someone offered you the chance to accept a 4,999 dollar loss and not play the game, you should take it. That equates to a dollar less than your actual risk involved on average over a series of coin flips. An offer to walk away and pay a 3,000 dollar loss is a great offer. You should snap it up.

But faced with this choice, people will play the game, flip the coin, roll the dice, or draw to an inside straight. They'll pray to God. They'll consult their stock broker. They'll swing their lucky hat around or do a rain dance. But they won't take the 3,000 dollar loss offered. They'll take the bigger risk.

Every time. Every single damn time. Nobody wants to 'lock in' a certain loss. As long as there's a chance they could break even, they'll hope. But hope is not a strategy, Judge. It's only an emotion.

This is called 'Loss Aversion'.

Human beings are just not wired for risk. Both parts of our little experiment are stupid. The first part is known as 'taking profits too soon.' The second part is 'letting losses run'. Most people are guilty of both. If you understand the consequences of our experiment, Judge, and can adjust your actions accordingly, you understand half of behavioral finance in the stock market.

And you might have a chance to be a winning poker player."

"Do you apply this risk theory to other endeavors, George? Perhaps business?"

George's eyes narrowed again. The Judge felt himself being re-appraised.

"You're sharper than you look, Judge. Let's play some cards."

George starting dealing cards on to the table.

"Five card draw. No jokers in the deck."

Roberts dealt out five cards to each of them. The Judge peeked at his. Then looked up to see Roberts focused on him. Roberts hadn't bothered to look at his cards yet. He was more interested in watching the Judge look. The Judge was under a microscope.

"Your bet Judge."

The Judge had a pair of eights, both red. A king of clubs, a three of clubs, and a nine of clubs. Not a bad hand in a game of only two players. He bet a five dollar chip.

"Come on Judge. This is a minimum 20 dollar table. Open your old lady purse and let those moths fly."

Roberts flashed a soft smile to ease the sting of his words.

The Judge could feel himself blushing. He retrieved his chip and reluctantly slid a twenty dollar chip into the pot. Why did it feel like he was throwing the money away?

Roberts' smile widened. He picked up his hand and had a look. Then he looked thoughtfully at the Judge across the top of his cards. He slid a 20 dollar chip in to pot, and two more, raising the bet by $40.

The Judge picked up his cards again and had another look. His hand hadn't changed. Instinct told the Judge to get out now. But Roberts looked so damn smug.

"I'll see you and raise you 20," said the Judge, putting three additional twenty dollar chips into the center of the table.

Roberts focused on how the Judge had taken the chips from his stack. The Judge supposed his fingers had been a little sticky releasing them to the pot.

Roberts slid another chip into the pot, matching the Judge, and then another six chips. An additional hundred and twenty dollars. The pot now sat at $280. It would be at $400 if the Judge matched Roberts' bet. Did the Judge want to risk another $120 on the chance to recoup his $80 already lost to the pot, and perhaps win $200 from Roberts? Not on a pair of eights.

The Judge folded.

Roberts smiled warmly at the Judge as he swept the cash and chips from the table and buried his hand in the deck.

"You an honest man, Judge. I like that."

"Then perhaps you'll tell me about you and Carl?"

The pale blue eyes regarded him again. Always assessing.

"Carl and I were old friends. We grew up together. He was mostly a nice guy."

"Until he wasn't?" asked the Judge.

"Carl was a clever engineer. A clever inventor. A lousy poker player, like you, Judge." Another smile.

What was Carl's new technology about, George?"

"Don't know much about it. Carl claimed it'd change the landscape of the oil industry."

"Was this technology a spinoff of the technology to convert excess flare off gas at the well head into usable crude for transportation? The one Carl had patents on. The one embroiled in my arbitration?"

"Don't know, Judge. Carl was very secretive."

"Why didn't Carl apply for a patent on his new technology?"

"He told me he wasn't quite ready, but close."

"Did Carl have a silent partner in the technology?"

"I've heard rumors, Judge, like you. But Carl never talked about it. I honestly don't know."

"I understand a lot of people want to buy Carl's technology, even though there is no patent yet?"

"Yes, Judge. Everyone wanted to buy the technology. The highest bidder was some outfit called DFERR."

"What's that?"

"The International Association for the Development and Funding of Environmentally Responsible Refineries. They wanted worldwide exclusive rights, or so Carl said. I guess they have deep pockets."

"Could DFERR be behind Carl's death, George?"

"I doubt it. I think they had a handshake with Carl to buy it. But in any event they're businessmen. They don't kill people. They've got more money than God. Why would they bother chasing a chicken-shit little technology like Carl's? I think they could have bought it. And paid handsomely. But I don't think they much cared if the deal didn't go through. There's always another technology around the corner these days."

"No one seems to have the schematics or the technical information for this new technology. I've been to Carl's shop. To his condo. No plans, no specs, no description of his technology, no nothing about it. It's all disappeared. Do you know where it might be?"

"No."

"Could you sketch out the science behind Carl's new technology, George?"

"Me? No. I'm just a dentist." George smiled. "And a poker player. I'm not technical at all. Carl never shared information like that with me, and I'd never have understood it in any event. Sorry, Judge. I can't reproduce the technology for you. I understood you were given a report that laid it all out in detail. Working drawings, protocols, menus, studies, calculations, lab results and initial trials data. Carl told me it was all in a report he was delivering to you."

"Yes, well the report's gone missing. I never got a serious look at it. You wouldn't know who might have a copy of that report, would you?"

"No."

"Are you sure George? Perhaps it's in the documentation for your loans?"

George looked at his hands for telltale seconds, but controlled every feature in his face. Finally he responded softly. He might have been talking about the weather.

"What loans, Judge? I made no loans."

"Oh but you did, George. You made substantial loans to Carl Greene to fund the development of his new technology."

"No loans, Judge."

"Let's not be coy, George. I haven't the time right now. I know about your loans. I have documentation. This is no bluff."

George stared at the Judge, all effort to hide his discomfort dropped. He'd forgotten the Judge had asked about the loans before, in his dental office. He looked... trapped. He took a deep breath and let it out.

"Alright, Judge. You've got me. I did loan a considerable amount of money to Carl so he could develop his technology. We weren't partners or anything. Too risky for me. I was merely the bank."

"How was Carl going to pay you back, George?"

"Well, that's where we had our falling out. I had to mortgage my dental practice to the hilt to come up with the development money to loan Carl. It wasn't a forever loan. Carl was supposed to license or sell his damn technology and promptly pay me back."

"And?"

"Carl kept horsing around with all these buyers but never making a deal. So he had no money to pay me."

"That would be a problem."

"It shouldn't have been. Carl had agreed to apply all revenues from his earlier patented device, the one for capturing gas flare off at the well head, to repayment of my loan. If he'd done as he'd promised we'd still be friends."

"But he didn't, George?"

"No. He kept stealing that money to do more work on the new technology. He hung me out to dry. We'd been friends for a long time. But avarice hides at the bottom of us all to some degree, Judge. I'd misjudged the extent of that greed in my old friend. He was screwing me into the ground while I had to make my loan payments to protect my dental practice loan. Just so he could build out his stupid new tech. It wasn't the deal we'd made."

"You must have been angry?"

"Disappointed is a better word, Judge. I'm a gambler. The loan to Carl was a gamble. But the technology worked. There were serious bidders for it, willing to pay far more than the amount of my loan and its accrued interest. This wasn't a situation of cutting my losses. I was going to come out okay in the end. It was just the damn timing. I needed my capital back soon. And Carl kept futzing around, not making a deal. Not coming up with new money to pay me out."

"So what did you do, George? Did you kill him?"

"God no, Judge. How would that help? His death has seriously complicated things for me. I need to get my money back. To save my dental practice. Now that Carl's dead, I'm just another creditor of Carl's Estate. I haven't a chance in hell of getting my loan paid anytime soon. Carl's death has been a disaster for me."

George folded his hands in front of him, emphasizing his position.

"I can see that, George, unless of course….."

"What?"

George leaned forward now.

"Well, just suppose you actually were Carl's partner, George. Suppose Carl double crossed you. Squeezed you out of your ownership interest in the new technology and dumped you into a lender position after it became clear the technology worked and would be extraordinarily valuable.

You might have been so angry you decided to kill Carl, steal all the plans and specs. Sell them to this DFERR for a big number. The technology wasn't patented. Who would know?"

George stared at the Judge, his faded blue eyes blazing.

"You're a real piss-ant, Judge. You know that."

George got up then. Turned and stalked away without a word.

CHAPTER 45
10:00 AM Wednesday

The Judge pulled his car up the ramp to the 405 freeway after descending the Palos Verdes Hill and traversed the flats in a frenzy of traffic that never seemed to abate. Going north. At least in theory. The 405 wasn't going anywhere. The Judge screeched to a stop at the top of the ramp, joining a parade of frustrated motorists idling fuel and belching fumes. Life in the LA fast lane wasn't fast this morning.

The Judge used the time to play with his cell phone, a Nokia Lumia practically the size of a small TV. The original round black and white TV tubes of the early days hadn't been much bigger. This cell phone was flat of course, perhaps a quarter inch thick, and was really a computer. The Judge put up with its size and the difficulty of fitting the damn thing in his pocket because he could mostly read it without his reading glasses, particularly if he spread his fingers just a little to make the images bigger. The trouble was, month by month, to read the damn thing he seemed to need an ever bigger finger spread. Just like his paunch. He hated getting old.

He got on the internet, keeping his phone discreetly below the dash to avoid a getting a ticket. He fumbled around in an effort to hit the right letters with his too fat fingers and the too small keys and his too short eyes, splitting his attention with the too stop and go traffic. Finally entering Gerald Jenkins, attorney, Santa Monica, and then the google search button. Next time he'd spend the damn two dollars and call information.

The law firm came up, Jenkins, Jenkins and Halsey, and he hit the make a call symbol, still keeping his phone below the dash. A young-sounding girl with a tweedy voice answered. He asked to speak to the senior Jenkins and was immediately passed through to the great man himself without further screening. Apparently the senior partner at this law firm had lots of time, little to do and no staff.

"Hello, Jenkins here," said a crackly voice, the kind that matures over many years of smoking, drinking, and fighting the good fight in court. He spoke a bit louder than normal, suggesting a hearing impairment. That would be him next, mused the Judge. First eyes, then ears, then the dick. And last thing to go would be his mind. Ooh Rah!

The Judge explained he was the arbitrator in Carl Greene's patent case, and understood Mr. Jenkins was Greene's long time lawyer. He wanted to talk about the current status of the arbitration.

"Are you in the area? Come on over," grated Jenkins.

"I'll be there as soon as the 405 lets me."

"Good luck with that, son," Jenkins snorted. "Get off and come overland. Like we used to do back in the day."

The Judge maneuvered his car back to the right lane, leaving a path of disgruntled drivers in his wake, and pulled off at the Manchester ramp. He cut over Manchester to Lincoln and rode it into downtown Santa Monica. Twenty minutes later he pulled into an office building on Wilshire Boulevard, a stone's throw from the Third Street Mall. It was a small office building, only four floors, with open air balconies. But the massive bronze letters pasted above its entrance proclaimed who owned it: JENKINS, JENKINS & HALSEY. The Judge rode the elevator up to the fourth floor, the penthouse suite.

The elevator doors opened to dump him into the middle of a large lobby. Apparently the law firm had the entire penthouse floor. The offices were all done with tongue and groove wood floors, stained a driftwood white fashionable at the turn of the century. Matching interior walls were an off white. Framed black and white photos of Santa Monica in the 40s and 50s were interspersed with large plants, manicured and cared for, anchored in bleached out pots. The firm had a daily plant service.

Opposite the elevators was a large conference room defined in glass. The view through the conference room looked out the exterior windows and over a long balcony, to the rugged Santa Monica Mountains. A peaceful view.

The Judge checked in with a teeny bopper receptionist. All scraggly bleached hair and gaudy tattoos running down one arm, dressed in a pale pink blouse and tight white pants that looked uncomfortable. She sat behind a large wooden table desk, also stained white. There was no modesty panel, so pants appeared the only option. She seemed to be the only one around. There was none of the hustle bustle in the lobby the Judge expected to see in a thriving law office.

The receptionist bopper seemed quite chipper and efficient, buzzing the elder Jenkins at once and directing the Judge to a white cotton sofa after inquiring if he wanted coffee or water. He'd barely settled in and picked up the Wall Street Journal when a brown spotted hand was shoved under his nose from above.

"Howdy, young man. Nice to meet you. I'm Gerald Jenkins."

Jenkins was tall, thin, and gangly. Definitely old. He had dark bruises under his watery blue eyes. His paper thin skin showed light veins and sunspots, offset by bright blush cheeks. His bristly white eyebrows needed a trim. He'd combed a few wisps of fine white hair over his bald pate in an attempt to subdue its shine, and plastered overly long curly strands flat against the side of his head with gel.

He wore an uncomfortable looking starched white shirt over his bony body, set off by a red plaid bow tie that drooped a bit at the edges, suggesting long use. Grey slacks surrounded the middle of his lean frame, suspended by plaid suspenders.

Jenkins partially walked, partially hobbled, showing the Judge back to his office. It turned out to be a modest affair next to the big corner office that likely belonged to his son, now the powerhouse partner in the firm. A mini balcony connected the two offices along the exterior of the building.

Many larger law firms still had mandatory retirement after age 65. A policy designed to make room for the younger up and coming partners. Senior partners were sent out to pasture with a strict non-compete agreement and a generous pension. Perhaps with a small office at the firm and a minimal staff commitment so the senior could dabble in non-profit matters if he chose.

But no practicing law for hire. Clients were carefully repositioned with younger lawyers, usually over a period of months or even years before the plug was pulled, to assure clients didn't wander off when the old partner retired. Elder lawyers didn't breach their non-competes for fear of losing their pensions. It was all very civilized. Very corporate. And absolutely sucked. Particularly if you enjoyed practicing law, were in good health and had nothing else you knew how to do.

Ironic. You took the people with the most experience and likely the best skills and declared them magically obsolete at the stroke of midnight on the beginning of their 66th year. Like Cinderella's coachmen they suddenly turned into field mice. Swept under the carpet and forgotten.

The Judge wondered if that's what had happened to Gerald Jenkins. Jenkins' small office carried more of the white wood theme. Off white walls, white stained desk and bookcases, and one potted plant that dominated the space. The bookcase was loaded with plaques, framed certificates and awards, some dating back to the early 60s when John Coltrane and Ray Charles were going strong.

Jenkins limped in behind his desk to his chair, gesturing the Judge to a matching black winged-back chair in front, the only non-white pieces in the office.

"I don't get many clients anymore," said Jenkins. You're my first visitor of the week and likely my last. You may be my last visitor ever. It'd be better if I were gone. Anyway, choose your questions well, young man. You won't get a second chance."

The Judge gave the old man a rueful look. He wasn't use to being called "young man". He supposed it sounded okay. It was all relative.

"As I explained, I'm the arbitrator in Carl Greene's arbitration. As you've likely heard, Carl's now deceased. His estate, however, is carrying on the litigation. Carl's attorney had given me a sealed envelope in response to a discovery request from the Defendant, a Randall Hicks. Carl was claiming the material it contained was privileged as confidential trade secrets and not relevant to the current arbitration. I was to review it and make a ruling whether the material was discoverable."

"And what did you decide?" asked Jenkins, snapping into the seasoned lawyer he was. Questions direct, right to the point.

"That's the problem. Unfortunately the material was stolen before I had a chance to look at it."

"You didn't lock it up in a safe or a safety deposit box, young man?" Jenkins shook his head. "In my day that would be malpractice."

The Judge could feel his collar getting tight as a light blush spread upward from his neck. This old guy didn't mince words. And unfortunately for the Judge, Jenkins was probably right.

"It's my understanding you're familiar with what was in the report, Mr. Jenkins. In fact I'm told you helped prepare it."

"And you want me to provide you with another copy," said Jenkins, beating the Judge to his request.

"Exactly," said the Judge.

The old lawyer just stared at the Judge for a while, not moving. Then he leaned across his desk and using his deepest crackly voice, asked:

"You got some identification on you?"

"My wallet was stolen a week and a half ago. I have a temporary driver's license I can show you."

"No picture ID?"

"No."

"No State Bar card with your picture on it?"

"No."

"You don't have your passport with you by chance?"

"I'm afraid not."

"So how the hell I know who you are? You could be anybody. I don't open my files or give out client information to any shmuck, wanders in with a story."

The Judge sighed. This was a difficulty he had-n't anticipated.

"Look Mr. Jenkins, why don't you look me up on Google. You'll find lots of information about me and many pictures that identify me."

"I'm not much for this online crap. Don't trust it. I'm an old fashioned lawyer. I like to see hard paper identification with your smiling face on it. Sides, even if you are who you say you are, I don't think I can provide you a replacement set of that report. I'd need specific instructions from the legally appointed executor for Carl Greene's estate, with concurrence of the estate's attorney. And maybe even a probate court order. I'd have to think about it."

"So you did represent Carl on this matter. And you do have a copy of the report."

"I didn't say that."

The color was creeping up the old man's face from his cheeks. The Judge could see he was getting riled. He didn't want him to keel over his desk.

"That's okay Mr. Jenkins. You're quite right of course. I'll talk to whoever's the attorney for the Carl Greene Estate. He can communicate with you. You two decide what documents and authorization you need to produce a second copy of the report."

"You mean 'if' I had a second copy. Yes, I think that's best," said Jenkins, sagging back in his chair. The effort of playing lawyer exhausting him. "Sorry to be difficult. You seem like an okay young man. But nothing ever changes, does it? No matter what I do. Always adversarial, always complications, always one more document or approval needed. And I used to be pretty good at it. I have all this experience. But no one cares whether I'm here or not anymore, whether I'm alive or dead. They even begrudge me my tiny office and phone. They'd like it for some firm associate moving up. I'm so damn old they consider me an embarrassment here. I think everyone would be better off if I just kicked off."

"I'm sure that's not the case Mr. Jenkins. You seem sharp as a tack to me."

"You're kind, son. Let me show you out."

Jenkins stood up, a little shaky but determined, escorting the Judge to his door and then along the hall toward the lobby.

Jenkins leaned in close to the Judge, putting a conspiratorial hand on the Judge's shoulder, and said in a low voice.

"Enjoy your time young man. Enjoy your practice. Don't ever take your health or your practice for granted. One day they'll turn on you."

Jenkins politely limped the Judge back through the lobby and out to the elevator, watching until the doors closed.

CHAPTER 46
10:30 AM Wednesday

The Judge exited the building onto Wilshire Boulevard and turned left toward Ocean Avenue where his car was parked. He vaguely heard a commotion behind him but ignored it as he pondered his next move. It was the paramedic's truck speeding around the corner, nearly flattening him in the cross walk, that got his attention. It screeched to a stop in front of the building he'd just left.

A crowd had gathered on the street in front of the Jenkins, Jenkins & Halsey office building. Bustling paramedics in yellow uniforms were lugging heavy medical boxes into the center of the crowd.

He turned and retraced his steps in a brisk walk. He pushed his way firmly though the crowd to its center, clothing himself with the judicial dignity that had worked so well in his courtroom when he was a judge.

The inside circle of pedestrians were all wide eyes and gaping mouths. The crowd had been backed out by the busy paramedics, now packing up their boxes. The police had arrived and were taking over.

The Judge looked up above his head at the face of the building. On a top floor balcony, four floors above, ashen faces peered over the rail.

The paramedics moved out, exposing the source of the crowd's interest. The small, thin, broken frame that had once been an old man. Now splattered with blood and other fluids, bone fragments sticking out here and there, he looked like a broken doll. He'd landed head first, still wearing the plaid bow tie, now askew, and the plaid suspenders. Gerald Jenkins. What in the hell was going on?

The Judge stood there for a moment, frozen in time. Had he somehow been a contributing cause to this old man's death?

The Judge jumped as a firm hand was put on his shoulder. He turned, ready to defend himself. Spooked.

"Well, Judge, fancy seeing you. And low and behold," Lieutenant Kaminsky made a flourish with his hand toward Jenkins, "another dead body. You seem to be a Typhoid Mary these days, Judge. Let's see now, how many bodies is it? First Carl Greene, then Frank Wolin, then Randall Hicks, and now this gentlemen, whoever he is. Please don't visit me unexpectedly, Judge. I don't want to be the next victim."

"It was only my pants at the site of Carl's murder," muttered the Judge, knowing he was quibbling.

"So you say, Judge. So you say. Why don't you come up with me and we'll investigate this one together."

It was more of a command than an invitation. Kaminsky and the Judge retraced the Judge's steps back up to the 4th floor. The law office lobby was filled with people now, mostly staff. The litigator attorneys were still away in court. The tiny bopper was huddled in the corner of the white cotton sofa, small tears occasionally sliding down one cheek. Her smeared mascara gave her raccoon eyes that somehow matched her tattooed arm. She looked even more Goth.

Secretaries and paralegals, mostly women, were milling about, some nervously chattering as though they couldn't stop. Others hunched with hands in their slacks pockets, or arms folded tightly across their chests, quiet and internal.

Kaminsky produced Jenkins' wallet and asked who he was. An elder woman, medium height but stout, iron grey hair clipped short, dressed a tad more expensively then the rest in soft summer yellows and green, came over, introducing herself as the office manager.

"Mr. Gerald Jenkins is our senior partner," she said. "He is... was... very old, but he still came in to work every day."

"Who was the last person to see him alive?" asked Kaminsky.

"He was," came a high pitched voice from the corner of the sofa. They all turned to the voice, the Judge finding himself the object of a finger pointed by the tiny bopper, suddenly come to life.

The Judge turned back to meet the assessing stare of Kaminsky, looking at him the way his mother-in-law looked at lobsters.

Kaminsky kept the Judge on the 4th floor for an hour, prowling around Jenkins' office, the adjacent balcony from which he fell, jumped or was pushed, the adjacent stairwell that led all the way down to the underground parking garage, all its doors unlocked, providing easy access in both directions. He insisted on a full account of why the Judge visited Jenkins, what was discussed, and how it was left. He zeroed in on the report.

"So this report you were asking Jenkins about. It was originally prepared by Jenkins?"

"Yes, Carl Greene and Jenkins."

"And Carl Greene obviously knew what was in it, and he's dead."

"Yes."

"And your law clerk, Frank Wolin, had it, and he's dead."

"Yes."

"And Randall Hicks may have obtained a copy, and he's dead."

"Yes."

"And Gerald Jenkins knew what was in it. Hell, he wrote it. And he's dead."

"Yes."

"And you looked at it in your office, so people may believe you know what's in it."

"Yes."

"So why aren't you dead, Judge? Is it because you're the one snuffing everybody else out?"

"Kaminsky, we've been through that. I didn't really read the report. Besides, I've had close scrapes three times now."

"Count them for me again Judge."

"I was attacked on the beach. The trap with the rabid dog. The carbon monoxide gas attack on my boat. Three times, Kaminisky. Three times. Where were you when they were trying to kill me?"

"Humph," was all Kaminsky could manage.

"Okay, I'm leaving, Kaminsky. You know where to reach me if you have questions or need more assistance."

The Judge turned and for a second time headed for the elevator. He could feel Kaminsky's malevolent stare at his back as he stepped in and the doors slid closed.

CHAPTER 47
11:30 AM Wednesday

The Judge returned to his office and carried on with his legal work, wondering if he'd still be practicing law when he was eighty. All he knew for sure was that a new kid, his kid, was on the way. USC tuition wasn't going to be any cheaper in 18 years. And he wasn't going to be retiring anytime soon.

About 11:30 his cell phone rang. The voice on the other end was older, female, and tired.

"Are you the Judge?"

"Yes."

"I'm Frank Wolin's mother." This was said in a small sad voice.

"Oh, Mrs. Wolin, I'm so sorry about Frank. He was a fine young man. On the way to becoming a fine lawyer. He will be sorely missed."

There was a pause on the other end of the line. Someone was taking deep breaths and trying to compose themselves.

"I need to see you Judge. Right away. It's important. It's private and about Frank. Can we meet this afternoon? Somewhere public but quiet?"

"Yes, of course. Where do you live?"

"I have a small apartment in Playa del Rey. But I don't want to meet here. I'm afraid someone might be watching."

"There's a little restaurant in Playa Vista not far from Frank's condo. It's on the corner across from Concert Park. It's called *Piknic*. Why don't I meet you there at 1:30? It'll be quiet. It has a small dining patio in front."

"I'll see you there, Judge. I'll be wearing a black dress and a black straw hat."

The Judge made some hurried calls to change the times for two scheduled conference calls, finished up a letter of intent for another client, and left his office an hour and a half later. He found himself scanning the underground parking lot before getting into his car, and watching the traffic behind carefully as he plied his way south to Playa Vista. He saw no one following him. But then of course that was the point wasn't it? He passed Frankie's condo building and drove deeper into the Playa Vista development. The Playa Vista Project buildings were all pretty much the same. Oh, there were different colors and trim used, and there was some variation in height and balconies. Even a few two-tory townhome projects were squeezed in. But it was the sameness that stood out.

They were all very much turn of the 21st century L.A. with their vaguely European shades of pastel. Squeezed together like the row houses of old London, only taller, with not much unique design. They would look old, tired and out of date in twenty years. Perhaps even a bit slumlike. There was nothing in their design to raise the human spirit. Homogenized dwellings thrown up on a budget. Reminiscent of tenement projects in New York and Chicago at the beginning of the 20th century, dolled up with pastel paint. Lip stick on the pig.

One of the few exceptions was the block-long park carved out in the middle of the projects. Lightly landscaped for minimum maintenance, laid out in levels, with a baseball field at its lower level, trails here and there above, and something of a running path defining its circumference, Concert Park was a treasure of green in the middle of Playa Vista. The Judge wondered if there were actually concerts here. Perhaps later in the summer. There were preschool children running amok in its small playground under the watchful eye of young moms and nannies, lounging on benches and using their words to share the morning's gossip. A couple of runners, a man and a woman, jogging around the park; and a teenage couple were having a picnic, sandwiches and salads spread out on the lawn. There were no homeless here. Apparently none allowed.

He drove down the western edge of the park and pulled in across the street from a small corner restaurant with an even smaller patio by its entrance door. The patio was filled with a handful of tables and chairs. This was *Piknic*.

He sat there for a minute and watched an ample older lady in a black dress, matching straw hat and large purse, slowly walk out of the restaurant carrying a latte and settle at one of the tables. There was a sadness about her that colored her movements. She looked apprehensively over her shoulder and around the restaurant, cautious of her surroundings. And she clung to the purse with a death grip. This was not going to be easy.

He walked to the patio and over to her table. He felt sad now too. He missed Frankie. Despite their disagreements about the patent case. Despite Frankie's betrayal of the Canons of Ethics, and his betrayal of the Judge. Frankie had screwed up big time. But the Judge still missed the engaging smile, the soft charm and humor, and the intellect. Frank Wolin wouldn't be easy to replace.

The Judge motioned the waiter to bring him a latte as well.

"Thank you for coming, Judge. My name's Jasmine," said Frankie's mother, offering her hand.

A brief scent of jasmine floated up from her hand.

"A pretty name," said the Judge.

"My mother loved the flower and the scent."

"I am so sorry about Frank."

"Yes, thank you. I'm still in shock. There's an unreality about it all. I keep thinking he'll call me later today. His once a week call."

Jasmine produced a tissue from her sleeve and dabbed at the corners of her eyes. Then willed herself back to the business at hand.

"Frank thought highly of you, Judge. He was so proud to be working with you."

"He was a bright young man, Jasmine."

"I want you to know he didn't kill himself, Judge. We're Catholic. Frank would never have taken his own life. Not under any circumstances."

"You're right, Jasmine. The police are looking for his killer and so am I. Did Frank have any enemies? Any money problems. Were there drugs or....?"

"No Judge. He didn't drink or smoke. I don't know anyone who'd want him dead."

"How were things financially?"

"The student loan payments are heavy. He had difficulty keeping up the payments on his condo. He said he was going to receive some money, Judge. Enough to pay off his student loans and buy a car. It was a side job, he said. Not through your law office."

"Did he say what it was about? Who hired him? Or what he had to do?"

"No."

"Do you think someone might have killed him over this money?"

"No, Judge. I think someone killed him over this."

She looked carefully around again. There was no one. Then she pulled a posted package out of her bag and slid it across the table to the Judge.

"This arrived yesterday, Judge."

The Judge opened the package and shook out a large sealed brown envelope. There was a note across its face, jotted in a hurry, in Frankie's hand.

"Don't open this envelope under any circumstances, Mom. If I suddenly disappear, take this envelope to the Judge. Go at once. Don't tell anyone you have it. And for God sakes don't open it. I love you Mom. Frankie."

"You take it Judge. Frank meant it for you. I don't want to know what's in it."

She stood up then, a big woman, perhaps five foot eight, early sixties, but shrunken now with a grief she'd carry to the end. She extended her hand for a final shake, another whiff of jasmine. Then she tottered out, leaving the Judge staring at the thick brown envelope sitting on the table in front of him.

It was his turn to look around. He felt exposed and vulnerable. No one was in sight except for a white coated waiter with a black bow tie who drifted on and off the patio, likely checking to be sure the Judge didn't skip on his bill. He called the waiter over and ordered a glass of water to go with the pain pill he needed. His arm was throbbing again.

He stared at the envelope a moment longer, wondering if he really wanted to open it. Its contents seemed to have the kiss of death.

He turned it over and quickly opened it with his fingers. Inside was another thick white envelope, also sealed, along with a single page of white paper, neatly typed, Frankie's scrawled signature at the bottom.

A note from the grave. The note was addressed to the Judge.

If you're reading this Judge, I'm in trouble. Let you down, bigtime. Call the police.

My crushing student loans, mom as cosigner. Missed payments on my car and condo. It all finally got to me. My generation are fucking indentured servants to these damn student loans. And mom co-signed. Even if I die she'll have to pay. They'll suck out her savings and everything she's got until she dies.

I know that's not an excuse. But perhaps an explanation of why. I took a chance to get out from under. I regret my mistake, but it's too late.

Randall Hicks, through his attorney, Dick Harper, offered me money to be their mole, report back your thinking on the case, try to sway your decision. I didn't want to do it. But I needed the money.

Then, when the motion for discovery of Greene's new technology was made, Dick Harper doubled the money if I could persuade you to grant their motion for discovery. Harper pressed hard.

When you decided to review Greene's disclosure report before making your decision, Harper was frantic. Demanded a copy of the report. Threatened to turn me into the State Bar. Said they didn't care about the case, only obtaining the report. I think they were going to copy the technology offshore. Harper said Hicks would pay me $500,000 for the copy. The cash was irresistible. It would pay off all my loans and give me a fresh start.

I took the report out of your locked drawer this evening. I made two copies. Delivered one copy to Randall Hicks a little while ago. Hicks is an asshole. He came up with a token cash payment and a song and dance about paying the balance later. I'll never see it.

I've just returned to my condo. Someone's broken in. The original report is gone. I've only this second copy. Can't return the original back to your office now. I'm screwed.

I'm mailing this second copy of the report to my mother. Hoping this will give me leverage. Maybe I can get the original report back now they have a copy. If something happens or I disappear I've asked my mother to get this to you.

I respect you Judge. You've been a patient teacher and a friend. You'll know what to do.

Frank'

The Judge took another check of his perimeter, then opened the sealed white envelope. He dumped its contents on the table. A complete copy of the original report and exhibits delivered to him by Bruce Williams on behalf of Carl Greene.

CHAPTER 48
3:00 PM Wednesday

The Judge sat back in his office chair, stretching his arms over his head, tired. He'd read the report, cover to cover, including every damn exhibit, many of which he didn't fully understand. He'd also made another copy of everything and sent it by Fed Ex to Bruce Williams, now the attorney for the Carl Greene Estate, and a lawyer he knew he could trust. His note had said the technology disclosed was the primary asset of the estate, that the enclosed report might be the only copy of the specs on the confidential technology, and that it should be locked up in a bank vault for safe keeping.

To say Carl Greene's new technology was disruptive would be an understatement.

The business of refining crude oil is a big and expensive business. The world is hungry for oil. But you can't just use it out of the ground. It has to be transported to a huge plant where crude is processed and refined into usable products: petroleum naphtha, gasoline, diesel fuel, asphalt base, heating oil, kerosene, liquefied petroleum gas, and other products.

A typical plant can have from 1000 to 1500 employees and contractors on site on any day. Perhaps 20 percent hold degrees, but over half are highly skilled process and equipment operators and skilled tradespeople. The plant's operation sends noxious material into the atmosphere, including benzene, mercury and other hazardous air pollutants. Some scientists contend the oil refining industry is one of the chief causes of greenhouse gas-induced climate change.

There are approximately twenty operating refineries of various sorts in California, with approximately half devoted to the production of gasoline. There are an estimated 140 operable petroleum refineries in the U.S., and another 18 projects on the drawing boards for locations across the Gulf Coast, the Midwest and the Rocky Mountain region. Plus international refineries, existing and planned, in Eastern Canada, Finland, Germany, the U.S. Virgin Islands, the Middle East, and Asia

A new refining plant can cost from five to fifteen billion millions dollars to build. Stakeholders who provide the necessary capital include sovereign governments, international banks, investment bankers, equipment vendors and, of course, the stock market.

Suppose you woke up one day and suddenly didn't need a refinery plant to process the crude oil? Suppose all the existing operating refineries were suddenly obsolete, the capital advanced by stakeholders to build and operate the plants lost, the new plant projects on the drawing boards abandoned? People would lose jobs, unions would lose membership, equipment vendors would lose orders, the capital stakeholders would lose a lot of money, the share price of oil companies with large refineries would drop though the floor.

But the air would be a lot cleaner.

That's what Carl Greene's new technology proposed to do.

Simple in design, it described the manufacture of a small and inexpensive unit for the wellhead, self-powered, to be placed on every well. The unit would do two things. First, it would convert the various grades of crude oil and gas coming from underground into their basic carbon components. Second, it would re-assemble those carbon components into specified finished products you dialed into the unit.

You put crude oil of all grades and gas from your well in one end. You got finished gasoline in any grade you wanted, aviation fuel, distillate fuel and residual fuel, out the other. The only byproduct of the unit was water vapor.

You practically eliminated the need for expensive refineries, with their enormous capital requirements to build and run. No more refineries polluting the ground and belching noxious fumes into the air. The effect on the refinery industry boggled the mind.

The concept was similar to the earlier technology Carl had patented. But the method was new, unique, and entirely different. Randall Hicks and his company had no right to drag Carl's new technology into the arbitration under the discovery rules. It was an entirely different sort of technology.

The report certainly brought clarity to why so many people were interested in Carl's technology. It explained why some people would be quite desperate to get their hands on it. The technology would be worth billions.

The Judge reviewed in his mind the events, step by step, from that night on the beach nine days ago.

Everywhere he turned, it seemed like someone was one step ahead. He'd gone to Carl's condo. It had been tossed. He'd gone to Carl's warehouse. Tossed and a trap had been set. He'd tried to hide out on the boat. Attacked with carbon monoxide. He'd met with Randall Hicks. Then Hicks was dead. He'd met with Gerald Jenkins. Then Jenkins was dead.

On a sudden hunch he got up and headed for the vacant office. The office where he knew a DVD recorder was still busily recording. The Judge entered the office, still unlocked, and opened the cabinet. The DVD player was there, lights winking at him, not recording now sound has stopped in his office.

He got down on his knees and stuck his head way back into the cabinet to take a closer look. On the ceiling of the cabinet in the back corner was a small lump stuck to its underside with veneer colored tape. It was hard to see. He pried at it with his fingers and it came off easily. It was a small black box, half the size of a cigarette pack, with a small antenna-like projection at one end and a very fine line running out the other.

The line ran in to the seams where the cabinet wood sides joined, down the back of the cabinet and under the DVD player. He pulled a small second piece of tape off the ceiling, revealing a winking light, this one blue. It looked like a transmitting device. The kind that might pick up the video signal recorded on the DVD player and transmit it over the air to someplace else. Perhaps another DVD player. Or a video monitor.

Damn. A spy spying on a spy.

The Judge carefully stuck the device back up on the ceiling where it had been and left.

CHAPTER 49
10:00 AM Thursday

The Judge returned to his Venice office the next morning and settled into his chair. The case had floated around in his subconscious all night while he slept.

There had been something out of place from the beginning. When he'd crawled up on the beach in the shadow of the great Ferris wheel. He still couldn't quite put his finger on it.

He glanced at the 3x5 cards stacked behind him on the bureau. He reached for them and began to mark them up. It was old fashioned. But it was so much easier to shuffle cards around on your desk than notes on a computer. Besides, he liked the textual feel of the cards in his hands. And the way he could lay them out, overlap them, point them in different directions, and slide them around on his desk. They were somehow more real.

First he listed the deaths, and attempts. He assumed they were all homicides. First there was a 3x5 card for Carl Greene's murder, in the alley in Santa Monica. Stabbed. Then there was the assault on him on the beach in Santa Monica. He counted it as an attempted homicide. Another card. Next was poor Frankie, shot in his bathtub behind a locked door in Playa Vista. Then poor Wheezy, the rapid dog, set up like a spring trap to nail the Judge.

Then the carbon monoxide attack on him and Katy in Marina Del Rey. Next was Randal Hicks, drowned on the Judge's dock, again in Marina Del Rey. Finally there was Gerald Jenkins, Carl's old attorney, airborne from an office balcony in Santa Monica. Fell, jumped or pushed? The Judge wasn't sure. He counted it a homicide.

The Judge now had a stack of seven cards.

He moved on to the people he'd talked to in the case, starting with a card for Carl Greene, even though they'd only met three times. He added one for Carl's attorney, Bruce Williams. One for Randal Hicks and a card for Dick Harper, Hicks' attorney. He made a card for himself, and one for Frankie. He made a card for Barbara, and for Carl's ex-wife, Yana Greene. One for Allan Clark, and another for Cindy Kwan. He added a card for Shadow, the Grotto Mistress Dominatrix. He made a card for George Roberts, the poker playing dentist who financed Carl's technology. He made cards for Frank's girlfriend, Cathy Logan, and Frank's mother, Jasmine Wolin. He added a card for the couple who were on the beach when he dragged himself ashore, Tony and Claire.

He made a single card for Arty and Juno and their two nameless pals in the Santa Monica gang. And one for Marty, the homeless kid who was no doubt still out there on the Boardwalk, shirking school. Who else had touched the case somehow? There was Kaminsky, the Santa Monica police detective. The L.A. Sheriff's officer who'd helped him on the beach, Officer Saunders. The pinched face nurse at the hospital. Ugh. And that damn reporter at the hospital, Lou Garo, the little asshole who'd had so much fun photographing him without his pants.

This gave him another stack of 21 cards, a total of 28.

He next considered the interests who wanted to buy the technology. There were the Russians, represented by Cindy Kwan, with assistance from Yana Greene and Allan Clark. He made a Russian Card. And there were the Chinese, represented by Jeffery Wang in Hong Kong, working through Dick Harper and Randall Hicks. He added a Chinese Card. And there was DFERR, the high bidder for the technology. He added a DFERR card.

The Judge made one last card, marking around its edges with a red marker, and labeled it "The Report". Now he had 32 cards.

He arranged the cards in various ways, letting his subconscious suggest how they might be connected. After a while, he decided to put card for the report in the middle and see who had touched it. He piled the cards around it:

Carl Greene, dead.

Carl's old attorney, Gerald Jenkins, dead.

The Judge himself. Two attacks on his life, three if you count Wheezy.

Frankie, dead.

Randall Hicks, dead.

Whoever looked at the report was dead. Except for the Judge.

Suddenly the relationships came into focus. The pattern was there. He even knew what he'd missed by pier that night on the beach. Foolish of him. Either

God does truly take care of fools or he'd been damn lucky.

He picked up his cell phone and dialed Cindy Kwan. She wasn't in but he left a message.

"This is the Judge, Cindy. I have a copy of the Greene Report sitting here on my desk in front of me. I'm willing to share it. But I'll need a 100,000 dollar payment to recoup for my time and legal fees in this matter. Call me soon if you're interested. There are other buyers."

He hung up.

Three minutes later his cell rang. It was Cindy Kwan. All business now.

"I'm glad you called me first, Judge. You did right. There'll be no quibbling about the price for your legal work. I'll have the cash tonight. Where shall we meet?"

"This needs to be a very quiet and discreet transaction, Cindy," the Judge said. Carefully enunciating his words. "Let's meet at midnight tonight, under the Ferris wheel on the Santa Monica Pier."

"Done, Judge. Don't be late." She hung up.

The Judge fished the business card out of his pocket for Officer Saunders and dialed his number. He was in luck. Saunders picked the phone up on the second ring. The Judge explained he had a copy of a missing report that he believed was the reason for the murders of Carl Greene, Frank Wolin, Randall Hicks, and maybe Gerald Jenkins. He was going to meet one of the principles who had been desperately trying to obtain the report. On the Santa Monica Pier at midnight tonight. The Judge believed the killer would be there. He needed backup ready to make the collar and close this case for good.

He could hear Saunders' intake of breath in anticipation.

"Good work, Judge. I knew you'd ferret this thing out. I'll be there with bells on, with four officers I trust. We'll wrap it up tight for you. Call me at once if anything changes."

The Judge stood up, stretched, than headed for the door. He stopped at the public phone in the building lobby and made one more phone call.

CHAPTER 50
11:35 PM Thursday

The Judge approached the Santa Monica Pier, walking down the Colorado Ramp from Ocean Avenue, proceeding carefully. There was an almost full moon spreading a soft light here and there over the dark and empty Pier. The big Ferris wheel, still now, hung like some giant bird at the outer end of the boardwalk, looming black against the sky. Its lights and sounds silenced. Its core still tacked to the same spot it'd been two weeks before, even though it'd made thousands of revolutions since the Judge washed up at its feet. The image of the great wheel and its sparkling lights reflecting in the surging surf would remain etched in his mind forever.

It had all started here. In sight of the Ferris wheel. It would end here tonight.

The Judge passed the Looff Hippodrome, now silent and closed, its operators gone. Built in 1916 by Charles I. D. Looff to hold a Looff Carousel, it was Santa Monica's first National Historic Landmark. Like the Sphinx it stood astride the beginnings of the pier, looking out over shifting sea and sands, echoing the laughter of many generations of children who'd ridden the wild horses under its colorful canopy.

He carefully picked his way out onto the pier proper, wondering if Arty and his friends would be out tonight, looking to spring out and finish their work. He knew he was a soft target. Exposed. His anxiety gave life to every shadow. He could almost feel eyes watching, biding their time. He caught brief movement to his right. Was it a glimpse of dirty khaki pants disappearing farther back into the dark, or just his imagination? He didn't know.

He reached the base of the Ferris wheel. No one was there. Would Cindy Kwan show? Or would this be just another game of tease and move the cheese. He supposed it was he who was the cheese. He shoved his hands into the pockets of his coat. Suddenly chilled.

Where was Cindy? He brought his wrist out of his pocket and looked at his watch. 11:55 pm. He was early. He'd try to think about something else.

Images of Katy came to mind. She was truly beautiful. And going for her first ultrasound in a couple of weeks. Perhaps a chance to see if the small peanut growing in her belly was a girl or a boy. He secretly hoped for a girl. He was officially neutral of course in discussing it with Katy. "Just so it has all its arms and legs", he would say. But he was fearful it might be a boy. His responsibility would be much greater. He doubted he'd be much of a father. He knew nothing about soccer and basketball. Or computer games. Or building model airplanes. Or surfing. Or even what little boys liked to do. Too old, too tired, too set in his ways.

A girl would be better. He could charm her like he did Katy. It'd be another soft soul in his life. He'd be surrounded by three females. Katy, the new little thing, and Annie the dog, but that'd be okay. And it would be Katy's job to school her in the ways of the world. Teach her about establishing a career so she was independent. Able to compete in the professional world with males, subtly using her sex as an advantage. Teach her the facts of life. About feminine wiles and how to attract and hold a male.

He'd have very little to contribute in the education of a girl. He would be the role model for what a suitable mate should look like, he supposed. Many girls ended up marrying their fathers, or so he was told. He'd be available for hugs and kisses, to write checks, provide wheels and chaperone duties. Until she grew to the age where it was no longer cool to have your dad around. God forbid she was athletic. He knew nothing about women's sports. He'd have to go to all her games of course and applaud loudly. Shriek until he was horse when there was goal made. Softly console when there was defeat.

He could do all that.

Suddenly there was movement on the other side of the Wheel.

Cindy Kwan stepped around in front of the Judge. She was dressed all in black leather. Jacket, pants, a jade green scarf wrapped around her neck. Bright red lipstick. Dark pools for eyes. He wondered if she'd come on a motorcycle. She looked the part.

"So you actually came, Judge." She smiled slightly. It wasn't a smile of relief. More like a smile of victory. "Did you bring the report?"

"Did you bring my cash, Cindy?"

"Let's see the report first," she said.

The Judge reached inside his jacket and brought out a large folded brown envelop, like the original one he'd found in Frankie's apartment so very long ago.

She reached into her leather jacket then. But what she pulled out wasn't an envelope of cash. It was a small revolver with a short nasty barrel, pointed at him. The Judge had forgotten how much bigger a barrel looks when you're staring down the muzzle.

"You occidentals are so trusting and so forthright," she said. "We're always amazed by your naiveté. Hand the report over slowly."

Her eyes had an intensity so stark the Judge thought of a shark and its desire to feed.

"Are you going to shoot me?" asked the Judge.

"Only if I have to, lover. You're hardly going to go to the police about how you delivered a copy of Greene's report to representatives of a foreign power. In this case Russia. Just hand the report over and we can both be on our way. No muss, no fuss."

"Perhaps it's not all here," said the Judge.

Stringing it out. Wondering where the hell Officer Saunders and his four trusty lads were.

"Is there something missing?" It was a hissed question, Cindy's gun hand wobbling a little with the tension.

The Judge spread his hands, almost dropping the envelope from his right hand. "Who knows?"

"You know. This isn't a game Judge. Tell me now and tell me true. Is it all there?"

"And if I don't know anymore?"

"You stand well on two legs, Judge. But a smashed knee cap can make a lifetime of difference."

The muzzle of the small revolver shifted lower, toward his right knee.

"If you know something, tell me now, and it better be good. If you don't know anything, then you shouldn't have opened your mouth. 'I don't know' doesn't cut it now.... Not unless you're still saying it after losing both knees."

Her eyes were alive now at the prospect of blood.

"I think it'll be quicker than that." The deep voice came from the shadows behind her.

She started to whirl, but froze mid turn at the unmistakable ratchet of a shotgun being cocked.

Two men were there. Vague shapes at the edge of the shadows. One stepped out into the soft moonlight. It was Officer Saunders, his service shotgun braced against his hip. Leveled at her mid-section.

"Just drop the gun, Ms. Kwan. Then put your hands up."

Cindy dropped the pistol.

"God, am I glad to see you, officer," whispered the Judge, hoarse now from the tension.

"She was going to shoot me."

"Yes, I see that. But it's a bit more complex, Judge," said Saunders. "I'm afraid I'm not here to rescue you. I represent my friend here. He has a different agenda."

The other man stepped out of the shadows. It was George Roberts.

"Hello, Judge. Looks like you're caught short in the middle again. You really shouldn't risk at poker. Or other games of chance."

The Judge tried to look stunned.

"You see, you were actually right, Judge. Carl and I were partners. I provided all the money. He provided the smarts. It was a 50-50 deal. But I'd written it up as a loan. Just in case the technology didn't work, Carl had to pay me back.

And the technology did work. Far better than anyone expected. But then Carl got greedy. Nothing was on paper about my 50 percent partnership interest. All the paperwork said 'loan'. So Carl decided he'd just treat me as a lender. Pay me back my money and some chicken shit interest. Screw me out of a half a billion dollars.

That was a big problem. You never want to cross a professional gambler. There was nothing I could do to get my half interest in the technology back. So I sold my information and services to another group willing to pay the same big bucks, but with a different agenda."

"DFERR" the Judge said, allowing the disgust he felt for organization and the murderous spree it'd funded to play across his face.

"Very good, Judge. Right on the first guess.

You think the powers that be were going let some amateur scientist with a tinker toy set destroy everything? Carl was stubborn and stupid. He wouldn't play ball. Wouldn't sell his technology so they could bury it, sit on it for 20 years, slowly introduce it as refineries paid out and were fully amortized. He wanted to make big waves. Be celebrated as the anti-warming hero of clean air.

DFERR's offer to me was simple. Kill the technology so it doesn't get out. Kill anyone who knows about it. Make sure the technology is buried forever, or at least for a very long time. At any cost. All traces of the tech had to disappear."

"And so you've been tracking everyone who saw the report or knew about how the technology worked," said the Judge.

"You've got it Judge. And we've been looking over your shoulder all the time. In fact everyone's shoulder. We have monitors watching recorders used by others, taps inside phones, video cameras strategically placed, and bugs inside computers. You didn't fart without us hearing. DFERR's been generous with their budget. First cabin all the way. And the things these techies' can do now are amazing."

"You make it sound like just another job, Roberts. But you've killed four people. Just snuffed them out like they were insects to step on. Like their lives were nothing," said the Judge.

"Actually there were only three, Judge. You kept slipping away.

And I killed no one. I just give the orders. The homie boys killed Carl."

Roberts gestured behind his shoulder with his hand. Arty and his three homeless friends stepped out of the shadows behind Roberts.

"I always like to have backup," said Roberts. "It's all about understanding the risks and playing the odds, Judge. Like I tried to explain."

"Did you kill my law clerk, Frank?" asked the Judge.

"Like I said, Judge. I just give orders. I'm on the administration side. Saunders here took care of your law clerk and Randall Hicks for me."

"Let's get this over with," said Saunders. "We don't need to be bragging about what got done, and by who."

"All for a few lousy bucks," the Judge said bitterly, ignoring Saunders, glaring at Roberts.

"Oh but it's not a few bucks, Judge. It's half a billion dollars I get paid. And it's fair.

There's billions of dollars in losses were this technology to be commercialized. It wouldn't only destroy the refinery operators. Huge losses would accrue to the bankers, the investors, the brokers, the land owners, the contractors and subs, the truckers and oil pipeline operators, the unions, and even governments who hold stakes in these refineries. It would make the subprime mortgage meltdown of a few years ago look like child's play. There would be a dislocation around the globe resulting in economic collapse and worldwide depression for everybody.

Looked at that way, I'm really saving the world."

Roberts smiled, satisfaction in his eyes.

Cindy was looking scared. No longer tough. A small tear trickled down one cheek. A minute ago she was going to cap the Judge's knees. Now she was staring at a potential shotgun blast to the midriff. The Ferris wheel had moved again. Her bravado had departed, replaced by fear.

The Judge looked at Saunders again. There was no adrenalin rush in his eyes. He looked at them as a farmer looked at his turnips. This was business. His was the face of a professional killer who'd long ago lost any feeling of identity with humanity.

The Judge looked to be stuck. He'd put his trust in the wrong man. Had badly miscalculated. He'd been let down and this wasn't looking good.

That's when the flood lights suddenly went on in a ring around them. Blinding everyone. Lieutenant

Kaminisky stepped out in front of one of the lights. His face red. His blue eyes cold.

He said in a low guttural voice that brooked no opposition, "Put the shotgun down Saunders. I've got eight officers with guns pointed at you from all angles. They'd like nothing better than for you to try a shot. But I don't think that's going to happen, is it?"

Saunders looked around wildly, then grew very still.

"No," he muttered.

He bent over and put the shotgun on the wooden deck of the pier. Then stood and raised his hands high. Two officers stepped forward, took Saunders' arms behind him, guided him to his knees, and cuffed him.

The gang members behind Saunders were similarly cuffed, then Roberts and Cindy Kwan. Roberts' face was contorted with rage. The consummate gambler had finally lost his cool. They were hustled down the pier toward cruisers that materialized from nowhere at its entrance.

"We got it all on video, Judge," said Kaminsky. "It was pretty much like you said. You can come down tomorrow and give a statement. I still don't like you Judge. But you've got balls, I'll give you that."

Kaminsky turned and scampered back down the pier to keep up with his catch.

The Judge stood there for a minute, watching a second police crew snap pictures of the scene, scoop up and tag the guns, and begin to dismount and retrieve the spotlights and battery.

He looked up at the Ferris wheel. In a few hours the wheel would come alive again, spinning, all lights, motion and noise. Around and Around. All risk and derring-do as it strove for the top. Surprise, fear, even panic as it suddenly tumbled over. Crashing down the back side. Always in circles. Pinned at the center to some destiny you couldn't escape. Never moving.

But the Judge's center was moving. Re-centered to a new place he couldn't quite make out. His life had suddenly expanded to two. Soon it would divide again into three. A change was in the air.

CHAPTER 51
10:00 AM Friday

They sat over breakfast on their patio in Malaga Cove, sipping hot coffee and enjoying omelets. Katy and the Judge. Annie the dog stretched out at the Judge's feet in case some morsel might be dropped. Hope sprang eternal in the heart of a Golden Retriever.

"So explain it to me, Judge. I am still a little muddled."

"Old Carl Greene found himself surrounded, like a stubborn old dog, by a pack of wolves. There were three groups." He held up one finger. "The Russians, who wanted to buy his new technology and were not above bringing emotional pressure to bear."

"That brat Cindy Kwan, and the ex-wife Yana, and her paramour who was his best friend, Allan Clark," said Katy.

"Right," said the Judge. "They used every trick in the book to persuade Carl to monetize the technology, earn Cindy a large broker's fee, and nail a half share of the money for Yana in the divorce proceeding."

Katy held up two fingers. "And then there was Dick Harper and the Chinese."

"Yes, Jeffery Wang." Said the Judge. "The Chinese wanted to steal the technology. They had no interest in paying for it. They just wanted their hands on that confidential report. It was the key to reproducing the technology in China. They ensnared Randall Hicks in their plot to create a trumped up patent suit so they could use the Federal Rules of Discovery to obtain access to the technology. The confidentiality agreement they were prepared to sign wouldn't have been worth the paper it was written on.

Then when it looked like I wasn't going to release the report to them in discovery, they bribed Frankie to steal the report. Which he did. The chance to pay off his student loans and set up his own place with his girlfriend was just too tempting. He made two copies and delivered one to Randal Hicks for a small down payment on the money he was promised. He was going to put the original back. But while he was delivering a copy to Hicks Thursday night, Saunders broke into his condo and got the original. Suddenly Frankie only had his second copy and no original to put back."

Katy held up three fingers. "And then there was DFERR."

"Yes. The International Association for the Development and Funding of Environmentally Responsible Refineries. They desperately needed to squash the technology. They systematically went about eliminating anybody who might have seen the technology and understood its principles. They wanted to make sure no one would be able to reproduce it."

"Because of the money they'd lose."

"Right. Billions and billions of dollars. Every oil refinery in the world would be obsolete overnight. The twenty plants on the drawing boards right now

409

would be canceled. The ten plants under construction abandoned. Practically every one of their members would have been broke within a short period of years."

"And they turned to George Roberts?"

"Yes. Carl's silent partner. Roberts had invested the development cash as a 50 50 partner with Carl, but had hedged his bets by documenting his investment as a loan. So if the technology failed to work, he could collect his money out of Carl's hide. Perhaps by foreclosing on Carl's other patented technology."

"But Carl double crossed him."

"Yes. When Carl realized how valuable his technology was, he unilaterally decided he'd rather pay Carl back his loan with interest, and keep the technology for himself. Roberts was incensed. But there was no way he could get his interest in the technology back. He'd been too clever and it came around to bite him.

So when Roberts was approached by DFERR to smother the technology so it never saw the light of day, and offered a huge check if he succeeded, he jumped at the opportunity. It suited him perfectly. It gave him a good reason to squash Carl, who'd cheated him. And it allowed him to maximize his rightful interest in the technology by selling out to the highest bidder. The one who had the most to lose and wanted the technology to go away."

"And Roberts hired Officer Saunders?"

"Yes. And Saunders hired the street gang."

"How'd you know Saunders was involved?"

"Something had been bothering me from that night on the sand when I came out of the water. I
410

couldn't quite put my finger on it. Then when I called Saunders to come snare the gang members, and they almost snared me, it became clear."

"What was it, Judge?"

"Saunders was a Los Angeles Sheriff's officer. Why was a Los Angeles Sheriff's officer on the beach in Santa Monica with his black and white, way outside his jurisdiction, the night I fished myself out of the sea? It should have been a Santa Monica Police officer there, but it wasn't. At least not at first.

And why was Saunders so insistent I come with him that night in his cruiser? Not take the ambulance which fortunately showed up quickly.

And then when I found Frankie. Why was the first cop to arrive a Los Angeles Sheriff's Officer, when Playa Vista is part of the City of Los Angeles? It should have been LAPD.

And of course in Marina del Rey, when we were almost gassed, it was L.A. County Sheriff's territory. But still, there was Saunders again. Mr. First on the scene.

It was all just too much of a coincidence."

"Was the street gang going to kill you on the beach that night, Judge?"

"I think there were going to knife me, tie me up, transport me to that alley with Carl, and try to make it look like a mutual knife fight. It was a stupid idea. Old men like me and Carl wouldn't fight with knives. In fact we wouldn't fight at all.

"When I got away from them on the beach, they called Saunders. That's why he hightailed it to

411

Santa Monica. Turned up at the pier and wanted to give me a ride to the hospital. A ride I doubt I'd have survived. You know I really wanted to ride in an ambulance for the thrill of it. I'd never done that before as a patient. Only with you when you got your nose smashed on The Hill."

"So the street gang killed Carl?"

"Yes. And they did such a botched job of it that Saunders took over after that."

"He killed Frankie?"

"Yes."

"And Randall Hicks?"

"Yes."

"But why Randall? I thought he was just a pawn. He never saw the report."

"So he said. But he wasn't quite truthful about that. When he talked to Frankie on the phone, Hicks accepted Frankie's offer. He met Frankie that night in Playa Vista. He didn't have a 500,000 dollar cashier's check. But he gave Frankie 20,000 in cash and a promise to pay the balance as soon as he verified the report. Frankie reluctantly took the offer."

"And that sealed Randall's fate?"

"I'm afraid it did."

"And it was Saunders who tried to gas us, Judge?"

"Yes."

"And tried to stop your investigation by threatening to kidnap me?"

"Yes."

"And he killed Gerald Jenkins, Carl's old patent lawyer who helped draft the report?"

"No. Roberts didn't know about Gerald Jenkins, and so neither did Saunders. That was a sad case. Jenkins was old, 85. He had stage four brain cancer. He was facing a miserable end. He was thinking about suicide when we spoke. If I'd listened more closely I'd of caught the hints. After I left he decided to step off his balcony."

"What about Carl's gay lover, Judge? Did you ever find out who it was?"

"Yes. That was quite a coincidence."

"Well go on then. Who was it?"

"Guess?"

"I don't know."

"He told me himself at the end. He was very angry Carl had been killed. He still had deep feelings he said. Anyway, he apologized. Said he'd let his emotions get ahead of him. Didn't act as professional as he should have."

"Who, Judge? Who?"

"Kaminsky."

Katy sat back in her chair. Shocked. Digesting it. Then she turned back to the Judge again.

"Okay, Judge. I've mostly got it. Except how did Saunders kill Frankie inside a locked bathroom?"

The Judge's eyes got distant. "Frankie was so far over his head, Katy. I wish he'd talked to me. He was a nice guy in a lot of ways. Just pressed against the wall economically, like so many in this miserable recession.

As to the bathroom, it's the classic case of death in a locked room, isn't it? Like a detective novel. There've been many solutions to that conundrum. Secret compartments, slow acting poison, darts through a heating vent, delayed killing, psychological pieces where the victim was tricked into pulling the trigger, either because he thought the gun wasn't loaded, or to save another life."

"How did it happen with Frank, Judge?" She asked softly now, reaching over to put her hand on his arm, sensing his pain.

"I'm afraid it was much less complicated for poor Frank. I checked the bathroom door. Self-locking from the inside, but an older door knob. When you close the door, the lock didn't automatically unlock."

"And?"

"Saunders hit Frankie on the side of the head. Dragged him into his bathroom and into the tub. Coldly shot Frankie in the head with Frankie's own gun. As though Frank were nothing more than a sack of potatoes. He set the stage to look like a self-inflicted wound. Saunders pushed the lock button on the inside of the bathroom door to lock it. Then stepped out of the bathroom and closed the door. The bathroom door remained locked."

"Of course. It makes sense. I'm so sorry about Frankie, Judge."

"It's one of those things I guess, Katy. Perhaps I should have been more perceptive about Frankie, tried to get close, become a real friend. Practicing law is so stressful. There's rarely time for comradery inside a law office during the work day. And of course outside the office I've been focused on you."

"And so you should, Judge. What's this rumor Carl left his estate to you? What was that all about?"

"Carl was surrounded as I said, and he knew it. There was his ex-wife, Yana, and his ex-friend, Allan Clark. There was Randal Hicks and his lawyer. And there was even his ex-partner, George Roberts. Carl had no surviving family. Once he was gone, he wanted and needed someone he could trust to carry out a special charge. But he didn't know who to turn to. Who he could trust. I'd only met Carl three times in the arbitration. But I guess he decided he could trust me."

"What was the special charge, Judge?"

"Carl had been homeless and on the street for a time. He'd had mental issues. He pulled himself back together with the help of Yana and his doctors. But he never forgot what it was like to be out there. On the streets. Alone. Broke. No shelter. No one to turn to. Destitute. He gave money every year to the Los Angeles Homeless Coalition. Helped where he could. He wanted his estate to go to help the homeless."

"And it's going to be a big estate, Judge? What with his new technology and all?"

"Yes. At least a billion dollars."

"Wow."

"So he created a Trust that would accumulate all this money with specific instructions on how to use the Estate funds to help the homeless."

"And how are you involved, Judge?"

"He made me the initial Trustee."

"Oh my God. You.... Of course. So is the Trust going to build a lot of housing and take the L.A. homeless off the streets?"

"Not directly, No.   Carl wanted a more permanent solution, and on a larger scale, nationwide. He understood that the homeless would always be left at the bottom of political priorities and budgets. They don't vote. They have no money to give to political campaigns. They will never be a political block that commands more than lip service from the politicians. They'll never have political clout like the gays and the Latinos and the Blacks."

"So?"

"So Carl's special charge is to use the Trust's money to form a Political Action Committee, or PAC. The PAC will campaign around the country on behalf of the homeless. Sponsor initiatives for more and better shelters and more and better services. Get in the face of the public. TV, radio, billboards, direct mail, and internet. Make John Q Public ashamed of the way these poor people have been abandoned to their plight in the midst of all the wealth in this country.

But the charge is uniquely specific in one particular way."

"Tell me, Judge."

"Jesse Unruh, the tall, rotund speaker of California's Assembly during the early 1960s, once said, 'Money is the mother's milk of politics.'

And so it is. The Trust is specifically directed to contribute money all over the U.S. to the political campaigns of those politicians who are willing to take a stand and promote solutions for the homeless.

Campaigning congressmen, senators, governors and mayors will find they can tap into big bucks from the Trust's PAC for their campaigns, if they have the right planks supporting aid for the homeless, and follow through once elected."

"And there's a billion dollars to give out, Judge?"

"Yes."

"My God, Judge. I can hear the sucking noise now as politicians line up to nurse at the nipples of your trust."

The Judge smiled, then reached over to put his hand on top of hers.

"Thank you for being so brave, Katy, so supportive. I'm sorry you got dragged into it."

"It was a wild ride, Judge. Ferris wheels and roller coasters are going to look pretty tame from here on. But then.... you've always been a wild ride for me. That's one of the reasons I love you so."

CHAPTER 52 – EPILOGUE
10:00 AM Monday, Ten Weeks Later.

The Judge stared at a smear of gel spread over Katy's belly. It almost wobbled like Jell-O with each breath. The nurse had gone a little overboard with the gel in the Judge's view.

Katy was nervous. She was breathing anxiously. Looking up at the monitor every few seconds, even though there was nothing to see.

Finally, after what seemed forever, Jim Blake came in. Jim had been a fraternity brother of the Judge's back so many years ago at USC. Pre-med.

Katy jumped as Jim put a plastic unit that looked like a TV remote on top of the jelly and began to slide it around her tummy. The monitor began to show indistinct images.

Jim pointed out the relevance of the shadowy shapes they were seeing. Katy was riveted on the screen now, her nervousness forgotten.

The Judge was secretly hoping for a girl. It would take the heat off coaching gigs. He wouldn't have another male competitor for Katy's attentions. And he'd heard that a special relationship existed between dads and daughters.

Katy had been convinced all along it would be a boy. "Our little Judge," as she'd been calling the baby.

"So that's pretty much the picture," said Jim. "Everything looks heathy and right where it's supposed to be. Did you want to know the sex?"

"Yes." The Judge and Katy answered in unison.

"Look here, guys" said Jim, pointing with his finger at a spot on the screen but turning to look at the Judge with a twinkle in his eyes. "Brass balls! Just like the Judge."

######

A Note from the Author

I hope you enjoyed your read. For my Mystery Lovers, here's a small test:

-*Who did the Latino gang member call that night on the beach as they huddled at the spot where the Judge went into the water?*
-*What was wrong with the Uniform Officer Saunders wore when he interviewed the Judge, fresh out of the water at the pier?*
-*Why did Kaminsky take the hunt for Carl Greene's murder so personally?*
-*In the parking garage the Latino gang member got a call from who?*
-*What did old Gerald Jenkins say to the Judge which might have tipped the Judge off the old man was going to step off his balcony? (See the questions in chapter 25)*
-*Why did the Judge make his one more phone call "from the lobby" in Chapter 49? Who did he call?*

I hope you enjoyed reading **Silicon Beach** as much as I enjoyed writing it, and perhaps here and there it made you smile a little.....

Davis MacDonald ☺

ACKNOWLEDGEMENTS

Thanks to those good friends that help me so much to write this book. Dr. Alexandra Davis, who was the first to see every word; my amazing Editor, Jason Myers, who did yeoman work on the edits and kept me on the straight and narrow; Justine Prado, the talented screen writer who helped me chart my way through the themes and chords of the tale and create clarity from confusion; Marc Hankin, the amazing Los Angeles Patent Lawyer who educated me on how the Patent Law works; Dane Low who helped me design the distinctive cover (www.ebooklaunch.com); my longtime friend, Garry Spain, who's introduce me to so many extraordinary experiences over the years; and last but not least, my old friend and poker playing dentist, Dr. Bruce Jones, who delivered an education on playing poker while I had to keep my mouth 'Open' in his chair.

Thank You All.

Davis MacDonald

Davis MacDonald

Silicon Beach is a work of fiction. Names, characters, businesses organizations, clubs, places, events and incidents depicted in this book are either products of the Author's imagination or are used fictitiously. Any resemblance or similarity to actual persons, living or dead, or events, locales, business organizations, clubs, or incidents, is unintended and entirely incidental. Names have been chosen at random and are not intended to suggest any particular person. The facts, plot, circumstances and characters in this book were created for dramatic effect, and bear no relationship to actual communities or their denizens.

About Davis MacDonald

Davis MacDonald grew up in Southern California and writes of places about which he has intimate knowledge.

Davis uses the Mystery Novel genre to write stories of Mystery, Suspense, Love, and Commitment, entwined with relevant Social issues and Moral Dilemmas facing 21st Century America.

A member of the National Association of Independent Writes and Editors (NATWE), his career has spanned Law Professor, Bar Association Chair, Investment Banker, and Lawyer. Many of the colorful characters in his novels are drawn in part from his personal experiences and relationships (although they are all entirely fictional characters.)

Davis began this series in 2013, with the publishing of THE HILL, in which he introduces his new character, "The Judge". THE HILL is a Murder Mystery and a love story, which in addition explores the sexual awakening of a young girl, how sexual manipulation can change lives forever, and the moral dilemmas love sometimes creates.

THE ISLAND, is a Murder Mystery and a love story, which also explores the dysfunctional attitudes of a small town forced to either drop old ways of thinking, or face extinction.

NEWPORT BAY, a Murder Mystery, will be published in the Fall of 2016. The first two Chapters of NEWPORT BAY are included at the end of this book.

All books are available on Amazon on Kindle and in paperback, at Barnes & Noble and other fine bookstores, and available at on-line shopping platforms. Watch for Audio Books to come out on each Novel.

HOW TO CONNECT WITH
Davis MacDonald

Email: Davis.MacDonald1@gmail.com

Website: http://davismacdonald-author.com/

Twitter: https://twitter.com/Davis_MacDonald

Facebook: Davis MacDonald, Author

Blog: http://davis-macdonald.tumblr.com/

Linkedin: Davis MacDonald

Amazon Author's Page: Davis Macdonald-Author

NEWPORT BAY

Look for **NEWPORT BAY** from **Davis MacDonald,** to be published in late 2016.

What follows are the first two Chapters from the Novel: **NEWPORT BAY:**

Davis MacDonald

Newport Bay

**A Mystery novel
set in Newport Beach and
the Orange County South Coast**

Davis MacDonald

CHAPTER 1

The Judge walked out onto the sand with a strong stride, trying to keep up with the golden retriever. She'd bounded ahead and disappeared into the mist when he unhooked her leash. It was October in Balboa, seven in the morning. An early rain storm was trying to start. Fog lay heavy on the beach, obscuring all but a few feet ahead. Dogs weren't supposed to be off their leash but the law was overlooked in the early mornings and at sundown out on Peninsula Point.

Annie the Dog was no doubt making life exciting for seagulls and sand pipers clustered at the tide's edge trying to snag an early breakfast. He could hear the faint squawking now over the thunder of the rollers and crack of the surf sliding up the beach like some serpent uncaged. The sand was soft under his feet, small particles clinging to his shoe tops. He could smell the moisture and the salt, mixed with the scent of drying seaweed. But no water in sight, the surf still lost somewhere ahead in the mist.

He turned to look back toward the small street and line of ocean-front houses to either side from where he'd come. But they'd disappeared now too. There was only the faint outline of sand dunes with scrubby ice plant and other succulents along their ridges. Was it a premonition? The sudden chill he felt for no accountable reason? Or only a drop in temperature in the soft breeze that stirred the mist into frothy shapes? Later he'd wonder. But that would be much later.

He turned again to look back, the lizard part of his brain sensing a change. That's when he saw them. Two black, bulky shapes slowly taking shape out of the mist. Two men. Heavy overcoats unbuttoned and open. Hands free, not in their pockets. White shirts and ties. They definitely didn't belong. They walked as if on a mission.

Their coats flapped open as they approached, exposing black leather straps at one shoulder each, the kind used to secure a gun holster. The Judge stopped and stood there watching them come, standing very still, his hands out in front of him to be easily seen.

"Are you the Judge?" shouted the older man, measured by a touch of grey in his hair and the beginnings of a small tummy the younger man lacked.

"Who wants to know?" the Judge shouted back.

"Just answer the question, buddy. We're kind of in a hurry here."

"They call me the Judge," replied the Judge, lowering his voice now they were almost upon him.

They reached into their coats together like Bobbsey-twins. The Judge considered his chances for a dash into the mist in the direction of the dog.

But the hands came out again holding leather card cases. They flipped them open as the senior said, "Agent Jackson and Agent Thomas, FBI."

"I know there's a law against having a dog with no leash on the beach," said the Judge. "But I didn't think it was a Federal offense."

An attempt to relieve the tension he felt. Tension in him. Tension in them.

"We need to talk. And we don't have much time. Your country needs a quick favor. And we need it now."

They came up on either side of him. Putting their credentials away. Huddling close. Nervous.

"Let me see your badges again," said the Judge. Their nervousness infecting him.

They dutifully dug them out and handed them over, one at a time, waiting impatiently while he took a careful look at each. Jackson handed him a card.

"Okay, gentleman. I guess you're who you say you are. And you obviously know who I am. What do you want?

"I guess you played golf yesterday afternoon at Big Canyon with Bob Mackey, the U.S. Attorney," said Jackson, handing the Judge his card.

"I did," said the Judge.

"I understand you're not a very good golfer."

"That's why he likes to play with me," said the Judge.

"He told us you'd say that." Jackson gave the Judge a tight smile. "And you're right. He likes to play with me too."

"So why track me down on the beach, gentlemen?"

"We're in a bit of a bind, Judge. We're looking for some help."

The Judge looked at them closely. It all felt too... pat.

"Mr. Jackson and Mr. Thompson, right?"

"Yes, Judge."

"If I call Bob Mackey right now, he'll know who you two are?"

431

"Yes."

The Judge got out his cell and dialed. He spoke briefly to his golfing buddy, nodding as he spoke, then hung up.

"Okay, Mr. Jackson, I'm listening."

We've got a religious group that's been generating dissent traffic. Here in Orange County. We're concerned. We've been watching and waiting. See if they're going to attempt an overt act."

"Okay," said the Judge, focused now.

"We have a trusted source inside that is highly thought of by the group. All the way to the top. He's extraordinarily important to our national surveillance effort."

"It's good you can count on people like that." Said the Judge. Non-committal, cautious.

"We can't afford to compromise his position under any circumstances, Judge. He's one of a very few primary sources we actually can trust for help."

"I'm glad to hear the FBI is doing its job, gentlemen"

"The handler in our agency has a meeting scheduled with... Mr. X, let's call him, this morning. In an hour. Some important information is to be passed. It's imperative we obtain that information.

"Okay." Said the Judge.

"It's also important we keep Mr. X calm...'relaxed'. Feeling secure. If he gets upset he might inadvertently blow his cover."

"So why are you telling me these state secrets?"

"We need your help this morning."

"Me? Why me?"

"Our handler has gone AWOL. He can't be found. We're worried. Mr. X is going to be very upset if his handler doesn't show.

"Any idea what's going on with the handler?"

"We're not sure. But even more troubling, we're beginning to suspect a leak inside our office."

"That could be a mess." Said the Judge.

"More than a mess, Judge. It'd be a national disaster. The Director has ordered that no one with connections to the FBI or the CIA is to go near Mr. X. No exceptions."

"I'm beginning to be nervous about the direction this conversation is going, Jackson," said the Judge.

Jackson pressed on, ignoring the Judge.

"We need someone unconnected with anyone in our agency or the CIA, or any Federal agency for that matter, to show up on Balboa Island in an hour, drive onto the ferry over to the Peninsula, and strike up a conversation with Mr. X as the ferry crosses the Bay.

"Just a conversation?" asked the Judge, tense.

"We need that person, 'you', to discreetly collect a jump drive from Mr. X. Then drive it up the Peninsula and over to Fashion Island where we've arranged a drop."

"You want me to replace your handler and collect your information?"

"Yes."

"There's several things wrong with your idea, Mr. Jackson. First, I'm not the handler for Mr. X, so he's still going to be upset. Second, he'll not have a clue who I am and won't trust me. Third, I'm not trained as a spy or a courier and I'm a miserable actor. Fourth, I'm running a networking meeting in an hour at the Balboa Bay Club so my schedule doesn't permit me to pinch hit for you. And finally it has the ring of dangerous work, perhaps even fatally dangerous."

"Look Judge, we've come to you because the U.S. Attorney says we can trust you. Says you can keep a cool head. And because you've never had an affiliation with the FBI or the CIA, or any other Federal agency."

"None of that makes me the right guy for your favor. There must be plenty of people you can tap."

"We've only just found out about this glitch with the handler. We've got an hour is all, Judge. We need you."

"How important is this information?"

"Very."

"What's the risk to me?"

"Nominal."

"I don't know, Mr. Jackson. It's not my type of gig. I'm just a hard working lawyer. I'd be all thumbs trying to look discrete."

"You're our only chance Judge. If you don't help, people could die, right here, in Orange County."

"How would he know who I am?"

"There's an emergency password to use."

"How would I know who to approach on the ferry?"

"There won't be anyone else on it coming that direction in an hour, back from Balboa Island to the Peninsula. And we have a picture of Mr. X for you."

"I don't know, Jackson."

"All we're asking you to do is drive onto damn ferry, get out of your car to look at the view on the crossing, and say good morning to a fellow passenger. That's it."

The Judge had reservations. Their story about how simple it would be sounded good. But the Judge sensed danger.

As he pondered their request a long blond shape lounged out of the mist, driving sandy paws into Jackson's stomach, almost knocking him over. All teeth, long moist tongue and smiling black gums. Annie the Dog had returned.

She lurched over to the Judge's other new friend, nudging Thompson's hand, demanding affection, wagging her tail furiously.

The distraction gave the Judge time to consider. They were the real McCoy. They were definitely in a jam. With few options and a dwindling time frame. It was his country too. It wasn't unreasonable of them to ask. He'd probably be okay if he was careful.

Katy, his new bride, eight and half months pregnant, would hit the roof if she knew he was playing spy. He wouldn't tell her. It was guy stuff. She didn't need to know.

The Judge looked up at Jackson, trying to catch his breath, and nodded his head. Jackson and Thompson let out sighs of relief together, tension lines lifting a little from their faces.

The Judge snared Annie with her leash and the four, three men and the quadruped, walked back toward the little interior beach house he and his wife had borrowed from her parents for a week. It was supposed to be a working vacation for the Judge. Apparently so it would be.

As they walked, Jackson filled the Judge in on the emergency password to use with Mr. X, showed the Judge a picture which he wasn't allowed to keep, explained the drill for dropping the information on Fashion Island, and went over the scheduled timing three times, emphasizing the Judge's timing had to be exact.

As the Judge's vacation cottage came into view, Jackson and Thompson melted away into the fog, as though they'd never been.

Perhaps it had just been a bad dream, thought the Judge. He stuck his hand into his pocket and pulled out the card he'd been given. It read: *Frank Jackson, Senior Supervisory Special Agent, Federal Bureau of Investigation.*

He thought about the last thing they'd said before they'd disappeared.

"What religious group is it? Is it the free-willed running water Baptists?" The Judge had asked.

"No." Jackson had replied.

"A Mormon splinter group from Utah?"

"No."

"Okay, what religious group, gentlemen?" The Judge figured he had a right to know.

Jackson had responded with a single word. A word that lay there between them, taking on a life of its own.

"Muslim."

CHAPTER 2

Forty-five minutes later the little ferry creaked as the Judge drove his XKE Jaguar down the sloping board ramp and onto its flat deck. It was a drive on-drive off ferry, both ends low to the water so vehicles could drive on at Balboa and drive off on Balboa Island. It had been a fixture in Balboa Harbor forever, dutifully plying back and forth across the bay all day and most of the night. He had fifteen minutes before he was to ride back in the other direction, back to the Balboa Peninsula from Balboa Island, and bump into Mr. X.

It was still early. He was the only passenger. An old captain with a grizzled beard watched him from the tiny wheel house, admiring the Jag. A young college student with acne was the deck hand, perhaps all of 19, sliding blocks under the Jag's wheels, then bringing the car gate down behind him.

The Jag was a convertible, racing green, vintage. The Judge was too tall and now too fat to look dignified in it. He stuck up above the windshield like a carrot top, his paunch pushing against the steering wheel. But he loved the car.

It had been tried and true since he bought it new in 1969. Except for the Lucas electrical system, which he overlooked, the way a proud parent overlooks a club foot. There had been a day when he'd felt swashbuckling in the car. He had been younger and thinner. Once. It was hard to remember those days now. Memories faded.

The Judge still felt he cut an imposing figure in his dark blue Blass jacket, tan slacks, soft blue shirt open at the collar. But only after getting out of the Jag. Damn near scraping the ground with his knees and throwing his enormous bulk skyward to free his frame from gravity and regain a standing posture from inches off the pavement in the Jag's low seat.

He walked to the stern of the ferry to watch the mist folding around the wake, making the shore line indistinct. The *Balboa Pavilion*, framed by the motionless Ferris wheel and the moored boats, big and small, lost color and then some form as the mist closed in.

This was the Balboa Peninsula, separating the blue Pacific from Newport Harbor, a long narrow strip of land lined with mostly vacation homes, terminating in *The Wedge*, a famous surf break shared reluctantly by surfers, boogie boarders and body surfers. Triangulated between the rock jetty leading out to sea at the mouth of the bay and the shore.

The Judge and his new wife, Katy, had borrowed the little house here for a week's working vacation. And the past four days had been great. The two had taken long walks along the beach at sunset, and sampled the fare of several famous Orange County restaurants in the evenings. Annie, their golden retriever, had come, racing around the beach in the early morning and as the last rays of the sun disappeared. Leash-less. Free. Chasing seagulls and daring the waves to get her wet.

He turned to look toward the ferry's bow. He'd be coming back across the bay to Balboa in ten minutes, hopefully engaged in a casual conversation on this same spot. Currently the stern, his position would change to be the ferry's bow when it reversed its course and headed back.

Balboa Island was rapidly approaching. Its color and form materializing out of the fog. A collection of roof tops, tied up boats, fuel dock and sand.

The ferry powered toward a point thirty feet up shore, compensating for a steep tide that would carry them diagonally into the ferry's dock. The water was an green grey, white whirls showing up at the bow as the blunt ferry forced its hull toward shore. The Judge had a networking meeting to lead at the Balboa Bay Club, just the other side of Balboa Island on the mainland. He'd have to be a little late this morning, his new charge preempting his schedule. He'd get this over quickly and be done with it.

The young dock hand suddenly jumped up from his perch on the side rail near the bow, waving his hands frantically in the air. Screeching at the captain to stop. The Captain slammed the boat into reverse, almost knocking the Judge over, stopping all forward progress. Then moved to neutral, idling the engine. The ferry sat there in the middle bay, drifting seaward with the outflowing tide, perhaps fifty feet from shore.

The young man leaned over the low ramp that was the bow, arms disappearing into the water, screaming again over his shoulder, this time for help.

The Judge arrived first, leaning over to see the young man with a death grip on a single arm and hand he had hauled partly out of the water. The balance of the person submerged. The Judge knelt down and helped, finding the opposite shoulder just beneath the surface, and together they hoisted the man up and on to the deck, soaking the Judge's suit in sea water in the process.

They stood there for seconds looking at their catch, the boat drifting to sea with the tide, the grizzled old captain rushing up to see.

"Son of a bitch," muttered the captain.

The young dock hand made a dash for the lee side of the ferry. Losing most of his breakfast.

It was the body of a man. Dressed in a dark suit. Leeching water in all directions on the deck. He wore soggy black shoes, heavily polished, a white shirt, and a red silk tie with a yellow emblem in the middle, still around his neck but loose, in danger of slipping off.

There was only one thing missing.

The man had no head!

######

Newport Bay will be available in the Fall of 2016.

Made in the USA
San Bernardino, CA
09 July 2016